CW01203409

Half-Life

Paddy Storrie

ISBN: 9781073329779

Typeset in Mongolian Baiti
Cover design: Callum Oriel

DEDICATION

For my wife Julie

Half-Life

2nd Lieutenant Ben Collins R.M. had much to prove - to himself, and to his superiors. Being cast into a dead end posting in the arse end of Scotland didn't seem to hold much prospect of proving anything. Until a routine convoy routing of nuclear warheads from the Atomic Weapons Establishment to the U.K.s nuclear deterrent force in Faslane goes badly wrong. One minute an amateur-hour act of sabotage by nuclear protesters, the next a full-on assault by a highly motivated and well-armed enemy, Collins is right on the edge. With only an elderly professor, a sarcastic Dutch exchange officer, and a troubled Afghanistan veteran to help him. And the enemy plans not to cause an explosion, nor to sell a warhead to the highest bidder: their far simpler plan stands to devastate the lives of thousands. Unless they can be stopped.

List of Characters

Lancaster, U.K.

Katie Foyle – radiotherapist, Royal Lancaster Infirmary
Shona Campbell - ditto
John Dawson, Ministry of Defence Police
Dr Abaya Shah, radiographer, Royal Lancaster Infirmary
Ali Shah – introduced to people as her brother, a garage mechanic, Bay City Motors, Lancaster
Emad Shah – her younger brother, N.V.Q. student, Lancaster College
Reem Shah – her younger sister
Duncan, Darren, and Steven – the Lancaster branch of "Nukespot"

40 Commando Group, Royal Marines

Lt.Col. Allen Scott, O.C.
Major Guy Waters, O.C. A Company
2nd Lieutenant Ben Collins, O.C. 1 Troop, A Company, callsign Nod Three Zero
Sergeant "Sean" Connery, platoon sergeant, 1 Troop
Corporal Ian Woolley, Section Commander, 1 Section, 1 Troop
2nd Lieutenant Maryam Maiwand, Intelligence Corps, attached 40 Commando

The Scientists

Dr. Ivan Timishenko
Professor Andy "Kiwi" Barton – Consultant, Defence C.B.R.N. Centre

43 Commando (Fleet Protection Group), Royal Marines

Major Steven Chandler – O.C., R Squadron
callsign Clyde 1 Alpha
Captain David Ledsham – his 2 i/c
2e Luitenant Joop de Jong, Exchange Officer,
Royal Netherlands Marine Corps,
callsign Clyde 44
Lt "Jimmy" Carter, O.C., Stand Off Escort Troop, R Squadron
callsign Clyde 14 Alpha
Lt. "Lyndon" Johnson, O.C., Recapture Tactics Troop, R Squadron

Commando Helicopter force

Lt. Lizzie Walker, Wildcat pilot,
847 Naval Air Squadron
callsign Junglie 11
Aircrewman Leading Rate Paul Field,
Door Gunner, Junglie 11

Special Escort Group, Ministry of Defence Police

Sergeant Adam Stackpole,
callsign Hotel 5 Alpha
P.C. Mark Dugdale, Motorcycle Outrider,
callsign Hotcl 6

Preface

Lop Nor

September

It wasn't the scream or the alarm which startled Chen from his daydream – it was the vivid electric-blue flash, as the air on the other side of the security glass ionised.

All the same, it was the shrieking North Korean technician visible below, rolling on the floor of the containment unit, which captured his full attention as the flash dissipated.

Pushing his chair roughly back from the supervisor desk, Chen leapt for the door leading to the wrought metal stairs leading down to the workspace where for the last seven hours, a team from the D.P.R.K. had been busily dissembling their warhead, nothing abnormal, nothing remarkable. Well it was remarkable now, and Chen was shitting himself that "remarkable" in his department was a state of affairs unlikely to end well for anyone.

Chen's dash for the door was interrupted as his deputy threw an outstretched arm into the older man's path.

"What the fuck are you doing?" he yelled above the blaring siren. "You know the procedures! When the radiation alarm goes, no-one leaves the control room without permission!"

Chen shoved the arm aside, irritated already by both his deputy's intrusion and the disabling noise.

"Have you no brain?" Chen snarled. "There is no risk. There is no contamination. Some stupid bastard has sent the warhead prompt critical and fried himself. We'll be fine. Until Xu gets down here. Then an irradiated Korean and a shit posting to Lop Nor is going to be the least of our problems."

Chen grabbed a portable dosimeter and threw the door open.

~~

As Chen and Li descended the stairs, their operating theatre clogs sounding softly down the 30 feet to the workspace, they had plenty of time to take in the train wreck they were going to have to avoid blame for.

The shrieking technician was rolling on the floor, attempting to tear off his white lab coat: his cap and facemask had already been discarded in panic. Chen was struck by the incongruous volume of the shouting and wailing he was hearing: he had rarely heard the North Korean team talking in more than a whisper in six weeks. Mind you, he reflected, if all the skin of his own face had been burned to a crisp by a tidal wave of gamma radiation, he too might raise his voice a little.

"Shut him up!" Chen shouted to Li. He ruminated that the Korean was already beyond help, and given neither of them could understand a language that sounded to them like guttural grunting at the best of times, they were going to get no sense from him.

Reaching the foot of the stairs, Chen looked instead at the warhead unit on its dismantling frame. To the uninitiated, including the uniformed guard force who had arrived and were peering through the control room window at them, it could easily have been a load of washing machine parts: there was certainly an absence of the pointy green cone you might have anticipated would be the identifying feature of a nuclear device. As Chen had observed through much of that week, much of the mechanism was already dismantled. The Uranium 238 which forms the "H-bomb" part of the device, also called the "secondary" had been removed. To set off the secondary, a nuclear warhead needs a triggering atom bomb explosion, which comes from forcing a ball or milled components of plutonium into a critical mass: where neutrons from the radioactive decay split neutrons from nearby plutonium atoms in an uncontrolled and violent chain reaction. This element, predictably, is called the "Primary" But there was no chance of that happening here, as Chen could see that the shaped explosives which drove the fissile primary into a critical ball had been made safe and removed.

All that the work schedule said should remain were the plutonium components of the "pit". These should, Chen knew well, need no more care in radiation terms than a set of juggling balls. He remembered well the opening lecture on nuclear metallurgy in his undergraduate degree. "Stays radioactive for ever; but decays so slowly it's not actually that radioactive. Will make a big bang, but only if you create a critical mass." Chen knew, however, that it would give you a hell of a surprise if you are dumb enough to create a mass below supercritical level. Even when Chen first studied the phenomena back in Beijing, "Prompt criticality excursion" seemed an altogether euphemistic label for the lethal flash that went with accidentally creating a "sub-critical mass": a mass of plutonium on the jagged margin where there are enough collisions at a sub atomic level to release a brief and lethal burst of radiation. He never thought he would get to witness one.

To his left, Li was manhandling the prostrate Korean, who was now on all fours shaking visibly and retching blood-stained vomit onto what had been sparkling white tiles on the floor of the disassembly lab. Chen could only guess at the technician's age given the way his features were scorched and swollen, but he looked like he had been at the younger end of the group of D.P.R.K. technicians. He certainly wouldn't live to be at the older end of the group. Chen pointed the sensor of the dosimeter towards the warhead assembly and heard only a reassuring soft crackle as the needle on the device barely flickered. He double checked the sensitivity range it was set to was on its usual, low-magnitude setting. No sense in being overconfident just because he wanted to show off to Li. On the floor below the assembly he now saw two shiny polished half spheres of metal, each not even the size of half a football. The business end of the warhead, the plutonium pit, its ultra-dense and highly reactive metal shrouded in shiny beryllium to stop it corroding and interacting.

"My guess is your friend there is the guilty party, though what his retarded mates were up to at the time heaven knows." Chen gestured to the three other North Koreans in the dismantling team. Working on the far side of the warhead, and having been blown to the floor by the heat pulse, their heads were now popping up into view like three unwise monkeys. Faces still hidden by the surgical masks which were the norm in the workspace, Chen and Li had even fewer clues as to how much of a dose the rest of the team had taken.

"Should we check them out? I can't do anything for this guy," Li asked.

"Not much point in wasting time on them either," Chen sighed. "If we think *we* are going to be in for trouble, can you imagine what Kim will have lined up for them? Let's wait for the cavalry to arrive. And get our story straight."

~~

Since first being summoned to the dismantling unit three hours before, Xu's mind had been racing. With three months to go of his posting to Lop Nor, he cursed his ill fortune. For two years he had feathered his credentials carefully as the go-to fixer for the complex's senior management. "Good enough to get promoted, not so good as to get stuck here" was his dictum. This had led Xu away from his original and relatively mundane responsibilities as a junior colonel in the main test programme, as China's military updated and refined its strategic forces. First to oversee the clean-up of contamination left by sub-critical tests done at the site long after the last sub-surface nuclear blast back in 1996; then to baby-sit the Koreans in the re-instated facilities at Beishan, southwest of the main base at Quinggir. The desired outcome – a posting of his choice back to the Far East, on the Pacific coast with his wife and young children. A command – maybe one of the newly commissioned strategic missile units working up to provide the party leadership with an asset to project power and dominate the Western Pacific. Maybe one of the new DF16 units threatening Taiwan.

"Well that isn't going to happen now," pondered Xu as he gazed out of his office window, taking in the featureless desert, the only interest a pair of Bactrian camels trudging nowhere in particular. When the shit hit the fan, everyone in the food chain gets bitten. The People's Liberation Army Rocket Forces was no more forgiving than any other part of the Chinese military. Xu reflected on what he had been told about the geography of Lop Nor when first posted there. High up near the Mongolian border, in a shithole populated by Uygur and sandwiched between the Taklamakan desert on one side and the Kumtang Desert on the other.

"It's a salt-lake," his appointments officer had told him. "Used to be a big body of water", he had continued, "The entire region drained into it – but nothing could ever flow out."

"Indeed," grunted Xu, as he searched for a way of getting out of the hole he was in.

~~

"Take this half-wit back to his cell," Xu commanded the guard commander who had brought Chen into the Director's office.

In front of him Chen was looking with resignation at his feet, his unruly mop of black hair falling over his wire frame glasses. Shorn of his lab coat, dressed only in the surgical style greens which were the normal attire for the Chinese lab teams, he looked slight and inconsequential. The effect was magnified by being between two stalwarts of the base guard force, specifically chosen by Xu earlier for their height and bearing. Both were armed and in full dress uniform, shiny peaks covering their eyes, steel-tough and intimidating.

None of this, of course, was for the benefit of Chen, who was broken and unable to register such niceties. It was for effect on the Director himself, a civilian. Xu thought it prescient to provide a bit of theatre to remind his Boss that Xu had his own assets, and wasn't necessarily to be easily scapegoated himself.

As the lab supervisor was taken by the upper arms and frog-marched out, the Director waited for the door to close before looking up from his desk at Xu.

"So, what was that all about? Remember, I may not be a scientist, but no bullshit. Did Chen screw up?"

"Chen is no more responsible than you or I, Director," Xu began. "Of course, we will have to throw him to the dogs for gross negligence," he shrugged. "But of course, you knew that before we spoke to him. As far as I can see, this wasn't really something one would expect."

"Go on."

"From the C.C.T.V. you can see the Korean get to the stage of removing the two plutonium shells which make up the "pit". These are the elements blasted together in a controlled implosion into a supercritical mass when the sphere of conventional explosive detonates." While Xu completely understood that the Director was a "party" man through and through, appointed for his reliability and connections, leading operations at Lop Nor required plenty of base understanding of weapons characteristics.

"That should be perfectly safe. If it wasn't, we wouldn't be doing it in such a low containment environment. Then Pow! The assembly goes prompt critical, big blue flash, heat wave, the Korean is on his back lit up like the Macau waterfront. My guess is he's managed to send it critical by getting his body too close to the components, while they were themselves also close enough to each other to be on the margin of critical."

"Is that possible?" The Director looked unconvinced.

"Indeed Director," broke in Ling, Lop Nor's Physics Head, who had been sat impassive, unsurprisingly not keen to pick sides between Xu and the Director.

"Any appropriate object placed next to a mass of plutonium will affect the neutron flux. Some things will moderate the flux; but a human body in close proximity will reflect neutrons back at the pit. It is unlikely but quite possible. But my guess is that the Korean…what's his name?.."

Each looked blankly at the others. No-one had bothered to find out.

"..has just become the fourth man in History to create a prompt supercrictical excursion."

"This has happened before then?" asked the Director.

Ling nodded and continued,

"The most recent case I can think of was in Saratov in 1997. It was a similar set up. A technician was working on a two-part assembly, with the lower part a potentially critical uranium core. He dropped a component next to the core. It reflected the neutrons and the core went critical. They estimated afterwards a release of 10 Gray of gamma radiation. Of course the two better known cases are from the early days. The first one was Harry Daghlian at Los Alamos in 1945. He was a technician, stacking tungsten carbide bricks around a plutonium core to progressively build a neutron reflector around it. By all accounts he was extremely careful, and used a neutron counter to monitor how close to going critical it was getting. It seems he realised at the last minute that the last block was going to be one too many, but then dropped it actually onto the core. He got a dose of 5 Sieverts." Ling noticed the confusion on the face of the Director, and decided to risk being accused of patronising him for the sake of clarity.

"I apologise Director. S.I. Jargon. I am afraid there are different terms in use depending on whether you are talking about a dose of radiation or its biological effect. "The Sievert is the unit for radiation dose. A chest X-ray is about 0.06 milli Sieverts. The biggest medical dose from something like a PET scan is still only milli Sieverts. Standing in the way of 5 whole Sieverts is not good."

"And what about "Gray". The Director decided if he was going to bullshit his superiors back in Beijing actually knowing the science was worth the loss of face to Ling.

"The Gray is a measure of *absorbed* radiation." Ling was happy to indulge. "For X rays and scans, you would receive a dose in milli Gray. But if you have radiotherapy for a tumour you might have 60-80 Gray."

"Then why is 10 Gray bad?" asked the Director.

"In radiotherapy the dose is spread over many treatments of 1 or 2 Gray at a time. And that radiation dose is sharply focused specifically to kill tissue. That's what the Gray measures. If the Russian received 10 Gray of absorbed radiation, across his whole body, that's double what it would take to kill him. In fact, if you expressed the amount of radiation into kinetic force rather than radiation energy, it is enough energy to shift a grown man 10 metres sideways. And all that energy is impacting body tissue," Ling said.

"You said there were three?" the Director asked.

"The last one was in 1946, and it was caused by the same core as killed Harry Daghlian. They started calling it the "Demon core". The next victim was called Slotin. The idiot was holding the two hemispheres of the core apart with a screwdriver." Ling rolled his eyes. "The screwdriver slipped. No-one knows what dose Slotin suffered as he wasn't wearing a dosimeter. To be fair to him, he apparently reacted quickly and used the point of the screwdriver to flip the top hemisphere onto the floor. That stopped the reaction and saved the rest of the technicians in the room. At least, for a while."

"And our Korean?", the Director asked. "What stopped the reaction this morning?". This time it was Xu who replied,

"You saw on the C.C.T.V. that when the pit went prompt critical the Korean fell backwards and dropped the assembly? With his neutron reflecting effect removed and the two shells apart from each other, there was no further reaction." Ling nodded in agreement.

The Director put his fingertips together, resting his elbows on the desk and looking from Xu to Ling for inspiration.

"Which still leaves the question of how the Koreans have ended up with a warhead so temperamental that such innocuous handling could cause such an event. Their technician was hardly in the territory of dropping tungsten bricks or wedging a core apart with a screwdriver." He let the question hang. It was Ling who bit.

"A best guess? Above all else the North Koreans wanted to be sure their warheads would detonate. We, of course take that for granted. But that's on the back of dozens of atmospheric tests here before the test ban. Unlimited resources..."

The Director snorted. Ling didn't know how hard he had to work to keep the show on the road.

"....computer simulation. We can ensure a very high and well-measured percentage of the plutonium in our warheads is Plutonium 239, with no contaminants, weapons grade. We can optimise the shaped charges and their simultaneous detonation for the implosion. So, at rest state we are using no more than 3kg of plutonium. Which is nowhere near a critical mass until the implosion forces it into one."

"I know all that."

"Yes but have you considered what it was like for the D.P.R.K. Their first test in 2006 was a laughingstock. Do you remember they told us to expect a 4 kiloton blast? Not quite Hiroshima level, but everyone starts somewhere. What did they get? A fizzle. 0.5 kilotons. I have farted more than that. We never worked out why it was so feeble; contamination so it had unacceptable amounts of Plutonium 240 instead of 239? Who knows? But if they then *expected* a given level of contamination, and then used a mass and design consistent with that deficit, they could have ended up with a core which at rest was closer to criticality then intended. One that took only a bit of mishandling by their technician to bring to fruition."

Each man sat contemplating Ling's diagnosis. At the end of the day it mattered little. For those responsible for a quietly unproblematic completion of the "Vientiane process" by which North Korea agreed to decommission its nuclear arsenal, knowing what had happened was not the issue as much as how to avoid the fallout.

"So where do we stand as of now?" the Director asked of Xu.

"Our Korean is in the medical centre. We could try to transfer him somewhere more top-of-the-line, but I doubt he would survive the flight. In any event, our people know more about radiation injury than most hospitals. The medical director is having the time of her life – apparently they have some new American meds which are meant to protect against the worst effects of radiation poisoning: Andostenediol, Entolimod, and something called Ex-Rad. They are trying them all."

"So, he might survive then?" the Director asked doubtfully.

"Not a chance, Director. The med centre are just pleased to have a live victim to be their guinea pig. He has the whole package of radiation effects. His bloods show his lymphocytes are all gone; his bone marrow has no red blood cells. The Doctor has estimated a 35 Gray dose, with a mixture of fast neutrons and gamma radiation. The Korean basically has 3-D burns across his whole body, inside and out. One of the D.P.R.K. security staff is keeping watch by his bed side. But the only place he is going is the morgue."

"And the rest of his team?"

"The D.P.R.K. Head of Security organised their discharge. I am told they are to be "treated" back in Pyongyang. My guess is that the treatment will be at the wrong end of a rifle range and involve an unhealthy amount of anti-aircraft guns."

"Then that's all the loose ends tied up", said Ling hopefully.

"Except us," murmured Xu.

Chapter 1

Beginnings

October

Katie Foyle sat perched on the edge of a tatty and threadbare patient chair in the waiting room of the radiotherapy unit at the Royal Lancaster Infirmary. While rain lashed the window, obscuring any prospect of a life-affirming view of the Lake District peaks which provided the backdrop to the city, her attention was focused only on her I-phone screen. Given an upbringing on the west coast of Scotland, which had left her with a soft but distinct accent, rain was par for the course. She tilted forward, forearms resting on her knees, as she navigated the necessary clicks and taps to sign up for yet another zero-interest credit card deal, which might help keep the wolf from the door for another 18 months. This had become the norm since her boyfriend had moved out - two months into a long lease on a flat she now couldn't afford in the nicer end of town. Not on a radiographer's salary anyway.

She brushed a rebellious strand of blonde hair from her cheek. The Meghan Markle messy ponytail was still holding on as the fashion look of the moment, helped by the fact that it had taken the best part of a year to become "a thing" in rural North West England. The look suited Katie –

or so people told her – and it was smart enough to look proper for work without being dumbly compliant. And she felt looking severe was not going to be a help to the patients she treated. Cancer diagnoses, and long regimes of chemotherapy and radiotherapy generally did little to make patients upbeat, bar the occasional saint who rose above it. A smear of pink lippie and a smile was all Katie could offer some patients, along with trying to be professional and accurate.

It was an instinct to care which had driven Katie into oncological radiotherapy in the first place. Through university and training in the same town and hospital, she had been struck by her set's general lack of compassion. In X-ray and imaging departments, the sick and palsied seemed to be shuffled in and out without a by-your-leave, the quality of the "film" being seen by some as the be all and end all. No names. No pack-drill. Scan 'em and send 'em. Which had led to the downfall of her long-standing student relationship, boyfriend unable to feel a need to do other than process patients through the department. In radiotherapy, at least you got to know patients, support them, see their outcome, good or bad. Now several months single, she was back on the market, but up to her eyes in debt, and staggering by on an N.H.S. salary, she was hard pushed to think of herself as a catch. At work the spartan and functional regulation blue trousers and blue piped blouse would hardly raise the pulse rate of colleagues, and would make a supermodel look like a sack of potatoes. Pretty, after a fashion, it amused her how cancer could make some patients keen to the point of recklessness in brazenly asking her out, but they were off limits if she wanted to keep her registration. Relatives and friends, on the other hand…

The afternoon appointments would be arriving soon. Katie set her phone to silent, tucked it into her bag, and headed back into the treatment area.

~~

The first sign of life each morning was the dogs. Always the bloody barking dogs. That and the same Afghan woman who daily poddled down the main drag of the village, to then squat and shit in the no-mans-land which separated the patrol base from the village. She was seemingly oblivious to the Marines in the sangar 50 metres away, who were able to see every stage of the process through their night vision optics. One of the troop joked that if she could monetize the secret of her regularity to the constipated readership of Cosmopolitan magazine back in the U.K., she could give up shitting in the street and retire to Topsham – the delightful and much gentrified village on the banks of the River Exe, just upstream from the Commando Training Centre. His mates doubted that her back story would tick the right boxes for the Cosmo editorial team.

2nd Lieutenant Ben Collins tuned the barking out, shook himself awake, and peered around his bed space. In the half-light everything was grey, but he had resigned himself weeks before to the prospect that this would not change, neither during each day nor any week soon. Just as years of civil war had drained the country of hope and aspiration, they seemed to have denuded the colour palette of the landscape. The designers of the British forces multi-cam kit might not have had Afghanistan in mind when they chose the pattern – "good enough for wherever you are, not "great for where you're not"" their mission statement said, but they had nailed a match for Kandahar. 6 months of wear in-country had added a patina of dust, grime, sweat, tea, and small arms cleaning oil to much of Collins' battledress. His kit had gone native.

Ben himself had not. On first posting out of training to 1 Troop, A Company, 40 Commando just as it was to embark on its first rotation on the new "Operation Lincoln" mission in Kandahar province, Collins good fortune cost him buying drinks all round for every member of his entry.

It was only after some consideration that his peers could see why Collins got the plum posting. There were others who had more charisma; many who were stronger; plenty who caught the eye more for their bearing. At 5 foot 9 and wiry in build, Collins was not one who stood out on parade, and from behind on exercise you could see only a giant Bergen with two legs sticking out underneath. His times on the bottom field and the endurance course in test week were unremarkable. But he was resilient, thoughtful, determined, and a sharp wit. He wouldn't shirk, and he wouldn't moan. The Directing Staff paid him about the highest compliment they would generally give a young officer: Collins "had his shit together".

On an October dawn in a patrol base in Kandahar province, getting you shit together for the new day involved one overwhelming priority- tea.

~~

As usual, the T.V. in the waiting room in the Radiotherapy unit was set to B.B.C. News 24. Katie paid it little attention as she pushed through the double doors, trying and failing to manage the challenge of getting through the door unscathed with a phone, bag, and her first take-out coffee of the shift.

"Shit," Katie muttered as she spilled the contents over her fingers. Fortunately, the flat white was typically underwhelming in temperature, and her uniform trousers provided an effective way of drying her hand. Wiping down her phone would take rather more care, and she sat to dig a tissue out of her bag to do the necessary.

Above her, a correspondent was being put through their paces by the studio anchor. Katie registered the familiar face of the B.B.C.'s long-time man in Washington, framed by the White House behind, as the breakfast host continued...

"So, John, take us through this surprise statement from the National security advisor."

"Natasha, what is striking is that the U.S. is making so little of the embarrassment of two of her global rivals. To have the evidence from their satellite reconnaissance of a radiation accident at Lop Nor test site so speedily confirmed by the Chinese government is unprecedented. But it clearly suits the administration to be able to evidence in some way, even through this apparent accident, that the North Korean warhead decommissioning agreed at the Vientiane summit is going ahead. For a President who continues to be under exceptional scrutiny, reminding people of one of his headline foreign achievements is more valuable than dwelling on any discomfort of the Chinese. Natasha."

Katie noted, not for the first time, the clunky habit of correspondents name-checking the anchor back in the U.K. to indicate they had finished.

"John, thank you." The host turned to a suited colleague across the desk. In contrast to Natasha, made up to within an inch of her life to survive the rigours of High Definition 4K T.V., the foreign affairs correspondent was drab. His suit was not quite grey, his shirt not quite white, and his tie managed to complement neither. He reminded Katie of her physics teacher. She surmised, given his lack of T.V. glamour, that he must be very good indeed at his job.

"Clive, what do you make of the Chinese disclosure?" the anchor pitched.

Katie finished wiping the last of the coffee from her screen and began looking for a bin.

"Natasha, I think someone in the Chinese government has recognised that they can turn this accident into a positive for everyone," he began. "To be candid about the incident appeases critics who wanted the U.N. to insist that the International Atomic Energy Authority supervise that North Korean decommissioning was really going ahead. Well, Kim was never going to agree that, and it helped everyone that China stepped forward as an honest broker. However much the Chinese and Koreans might have preferred this not to have come to light, it at least indicates to everyone that the agreed dismantling of their stockpile is happening. And the American administration can, of course, use the accident to bolster its claims that the North Korean arsenal's existence is a threat which must be removed."

Katie paused and listened only to await the weather forecast, which tended to come on screen as she came through the unit each morning. Though she wondered why, at this time of year, she even bothered to check. More rain.

Katie felt a brief flicker of satisfaction as she carefully lobbed the coffee stained hanky, watched it bounce off the back face of the battered metal bin below the T.V. screen and disappear from view, and headed off to start another day.

~~

An hour past dawn and with a weak sun showing just over the rim of the HESCO containers on the east side of the patrol base, Collins was on his third cup of tea. The mornings were getting chilly at this point in the year, and he valued not just the warmth, but also the reminder of normal routine back home.

Holding his black plastic mug with two hands, Collins looked back and forth between the annotated drone imagery on his lap, and the sand table model at his feet. A cluster of 1 Troop were taking a knee around his improvised diorama, amused by his attention to such a detail. Nowadays few patrols used such old school preparation, such was the immediacy and quality of overhead photos available for every inch of the battle space.

"Boss, I don't think much of your train set," said his Platoon Sergeant. Connery was grinning.

"No train track, Sir?" joined in a voice from behind him. Corporal Woolley, all 6 foot 2 of him, appeared at Collins' shoulder.

"It's the only model you are going to get your hands on, Corporal," Collins teased. After months on deployment Collins knew that the Troop were actually comforted by attention to detail, and as the fighting season got into full swing with the end of the baking heat of summer, stakes were getting higher.

"All here, Sir," Connery volunteered.

"Not quite Sarge." Collins scanned over the heads of the assembled patrol. "Mazz is coming".

~~

Katie's concentration on the screen was broken by the incessant ringing of the phone. It was Nasreen from the front desk.

"Alice is here with her Dad. I have told him that we cannot treat today." Katie could hear the exasperation in the receptionist's voice. "But he won't take it from me. Can you come down?" she implored.

Katie sighed. All morning the engineers had been in trying to fix the cyber knife. While sounding incredibly space age, it was actually now a rather dated mechanism, a stock in trade of therapeutic cancer work. By focusing radiation sharply at a 3D point, it had, at one time, revolutionised the way radiotherapy could be given, with much better precision and less collateral damage than Cobalt 60 source treatment. But it was showing its age, and this was the third breakdown of the month.

Setting aside planning the afternoon treatments on the department's other source, a more modern linear accelerator or "Linac", she stepped into the corridor and took the dozen paces needed to be back in the patient waiting room.

There, as expected, was the 8-year-old who had become a familiar face over the autumn. Freckled face, fair hair in an amateurish French plait, piercing blue eyes and slightly gappy grin, Alice Dawson gave Katie a cheery wave as she emerged. Her father was less cheery, and turned sharply towards her, clearly exasperated.

"Katie this in nonsense. This is the second time in a row..." His voice tailed off as if he had run out of the energy needed to be as aggressive as was required. He ran the fingers of one hand through his thinning brown hair, trying to keep a gentle hold on Alice as he did so, and to avoid his agitation reaching the shoulder he had in his grip.

"John, I am so sorry," Katie apologised, walking towards him palms open and fingers pointed to the floor in commiseration. "The machine is down again."

"For Christ' sake," the father muttered.

"Daddy!" scolded the little girl. "What would Mummy have said."

It made Katie smile to see the bulky middle-aged father look sheepish at the reprimand from an elfin child in blue and white stripy dungarees.

"They are working on it today, John. And we will re-book you as soon as it's fixed." She knelt so she was at eye level to the little girl.

"Alice, maybe Daddy can take you somewhere for lunch instead of having to spend an hour waiting for you here? Mightn't that be a much better Wednesday than you were expecting?" She raised the slightest of eyebrows at the father, and he took the hint - let's not scare the kiddie.

"OK, that sounds a plan. I don't have to be back in Barrow till 2. Let's get something in town. Just wait outside while me and Katie sort a new date."

The child obediently flashed a smile at both Katie, and Nasreen behind the desk, and turned on her heel to skip out, already planning how to arm twist her Dad into a "Happy Meal".

John paused, and took a pace closer to Katie, fixing her eyes with an imploring gaze. For all the formality and professionalism of his Ministry of Defence Police uniform, his furrowed brow and slumped shoulders made him seem a man at the end of his tether.

"Katie you know what Prof. Ingram said about the tumour." He was almost hissing in an effort to be quiet but forceful. "This has to work if she is to have any chance. It's not about convenience. Please. Call me later with news?" Needing to catch up with Alice, he didn't wait for a reply and was gone.

Katie was crestfallen. Shona Campbell, a new colleague just started, stepped up to her side.

"Lovely kid," Shona offered.

"She's dying," Katie replied.

~~

2nd Lieutenant Maryam Maiwand - Mazz - was the redeeming feature of the patrol base. Female company tended to be in short supply outside Kandahar. The occasional navy medic made her way up to the base at times, but the Commando generally had enough expertise organically to provide the cover needed for casualties. Female signallers could sometimes make an appearance, but were generally viewed by 1 Troop as too clever by half to merit any attention.

The same could be expected to be their view of Maryam, given she was from the Intelligence Corps. But there was her beauty. There are not many young women who you could send into an Afghan shit-hole and find them still looking as polished as Maryam did, day in day out. Slim, olive skin which somehow still turned rosy on her cheeks in the sun, bottomless brown eyes, and a bob of jet black hair, Maryam was stunning. Two further things added to her impossible allure. Firstly, Mazz was entirely natural, comfortable within herself, tomboyish, and happy to give the Marines as good as she got. To most of 1 Troop, much the same in age but not in intellect or background, she was more a scary big sister than object of misogynistic scrutiny. Sadly, of course, she was an officer, which placed her absolutely and irrevocably off limits. To everyone but Collins, who they ribbed mercilessly about his and 2nd Lieutenant Maiwand's entirely non-existent horizontal relationship. The unit might have expected to be lumbered with some nods from 30 Commando Information Exploitation Group, the Brigade's own experts in collating and utilising real time intelligence from the field. But Maryam was far preferable in being female, which could be a huge asset in information gathering and relationship building in counter insurgency; and she spoke Farsi, the result of her Iranian upbringing and heritage.

The Marines who were poised around Collins' sand model tried not to window-shop too obviously as Mazz came across the dusty compound to join the brief. Woolley's suggestive alert as she neared of, "Oy Oy Sir!" for once drew a glare from Collins, and a suggestion that "If you want to ever make Sergeant, Woolley, I would shut it.".

2nd Lieutenant Maiwand smiled at Collins and knelt. She resisted an urge to ask him where the train track was.

"All yours, Sean." Collins handed over to Sergeant Connery, known with inevitability throughout his marine career as "Sean", and the brief got underway.

~~

"She's got a stage 4 glioma. Its inoperable. Embedded in the brain stem." Katie anticipated Shona's question.

"Shite." Shona's broad Glaswegian accent made Katie's slight lilt sound insignificant in comparison.

"And as you might have heard, the "knife" is playing up."

"What does the Dad know?" Shona asked.

"Enough to know it's bad. He's a smart enough bloke. He used to be a police inspector but gave up to join the MOD lot at Vickers when his wife died of breast cancer years ago. He wanted a predictable job to bring up the kid. Now he may well lose her too."

The big Vickers shipyard at nearby Barrow was one of the biggest employers in the area, and within its workforce of thousands, required a big civilian security force to guard the sensitive nuclear technology. At one time that had been the four Vanguard class Trident submarines, built in the giant sheds at Barrow twenty years before. Now the last of the Astute class hunter/killer subs, at £1billion each, was about to be commissioned.

"And why is the cyber-knife down?" Shona asked. Part-time in the department, Shona treated only with the "Linac" – a machine where a linear accelerator, not a Cobalt 60 source, provided the radiation dose.

"It's like the rest of this place. Worn out. Badly maintained, underinvested. Apparently, they need a part on the way from Sweden."

The girls raided a half empty box of Roses chocolates from the Reception desk as they talked. Katie, as ever, struggled to remember what chocolate might lie inside each wrapping. But as lunches went, she had had worse than a caramel barrel and two orange cremes.

They sat in silence, not even interrupted by the T.V. As usual, Nasreen had muted the sound at the start of the clinic, so patients spent their waiting time watching the ticker along the bottom of the screen, and the sometimes joyfully inept subtitling as the captioner for the deaf tried to keep up with the news presenters in real time.

Shona broke into Katie's despondency.

"Have you seen this?"

"What? The football transfer?" Katie was looking at the rolling graphic ticker, not the interview underway on screen. Looking more closely, the leader of the Labour Party was, as far as one could tell from the captioning, committing that the national executive was going to vote on abandoning as party policy the maintenance of the U.K.'s independent nuclear deterrent.

Shona stood on a chair to mash the volume on the underside of the T.V. The remote control had long since gone missing.

"This was on earlier," said Shona. "Listen".

The mute button reversed, the Labour leader was talking. "...which is why I am convinced this is the time for a major change in national direction. The recent radiation accident in China should be a major reality check for us all. The nuclear stockpiles of the major powers are a standing hazard to the human race."

As ever, talking in broad brush and devoid of scrutiny, the party's front man could be very persuasive. The presenter seemed happy to let him go on.

"We have 160 warheads like the North Korean one in our arsenal right now. No one has been able to explain to me what these could ever be used for. With the North abandoning its nuclear programme, one of the few remaining reasons why the U.K. might need its own nuclear force has evaporated. And at what cost do we sustain and refine these weapons of genocide? The bill for this governments planned Trident replacement starts at £30 billion. All the while patients sit untreated for hours in A and E and the elderly die on trolleys in corridors."

Katie sniffed. "Well that will go down like a lead balloon at Vickers," she suggested.

"I suppose you are going to tell me that this is the way we magically get the money to resource this place and the rest of the N.H.S.?" Katie lacked much of a political backbone, and bar Brexit, had yet to vote.

Shona shrugged.

"No. It's a start. But do you trust that guy to do it? Whatever him and his cronies agree, half of the Labour Party would never abandon nukes. Something much worse than an accident in a desert in China needs to happen for things to really change."

Katie looked curiously at her colleague, then headed back to programme the Linac.

~~

Since U.K. forces had returned to Afghanistan that year on "Operation Lincoln", they had kept a low and even successful profile. "Operation Herrick", the ill-fated foray in Helmand province, was now not an experience anyone wanted to revisit. Few involved at the outset of Herrick could believe it had extended to twenty "sequels": service personnel tended to talk to each other in terms of which iteration of the six-monthly troop rotations they had served on, from Herrick 1 to an unbelievable Herrick 20. "Too shit for one sequel, let alone another eighteen," was the prevailing view, and few thought the 3000 killed and wounded it cost the U.K. was worth it. It was embarrassing to think that even after the amazing operation to transport a giant new turbine to the Kajaki dam under the noses of the Taliban, the machinery had never been subsequently installed.

Operation Lincoln was criticised in the media, and by the opposition, as another pointless entanglement. But it felt different at every level. For the troops, they were away from Helmand, it's "green zone" along the river, and hand to mouth support from an over stretched supply line: Collins and the rest of the Commando brigade piggy-backed the regional United States effort, worked within its chain of command, and thus benefitted from the whole panoply of resources. If you needed air support you would call up the F-15E Strike Eagle high above on patrol from Al Udeid in Qatar, or one of a flock of A-10 close air support planes from Kandahar. You would not be waiting on some R.A.F. loner, in a jet designed for another role entirely, with a small and makeshift weapons load; or worse still, some French or Dutch pilot with half the capability to help of the Americans. This was no longer a N.A.T.O. effort.

And the Taliban were no longer the main opponent. Since covert peace talks began with them in Kabul, brokered to no-one's pleasure or surprise by Pakistan's I.S.I., the Taliban had gone quiet. The possibility that they might be somehow brought into government in the style of the Ulster peace process was probably laughable, but endless war against them seemed less likely too. The U.S./U.K. war effort was careful not to alienate them, just as the Taliban was diplomatic to reduce its I.E.D. campaign. Afghanistan had once been a "pomegranate economy", growing some of the finest fruits in the region, until Russian bombing in the 1979 war trashed the irrigation needed to reap a decent harvest. The British Department for International Development had finally seen sense and was now no longer trying to crush poppy cultivation and turn the clock back. Instead, and exploiting a long-standing global shortage of reliable medical morphine and related opiates, the U.K. was happy to both see poppy cultivation, and to buy the whole crop for a good price. While below what the drug lords would offer, working to supply the British avoided the likelihood that one day their troops would rock up to seize your heroin and burn your fields to the ground.

The surprising catalyst for all this was the encroac of the Daesh - the so-called Islamic state - into sc Taliban heartlands. I.S.'s nihilistic ideology, and largely Arab or European personnel, were as alien to Taliban sensibilities as N.A.T.O. or the Russians in 1979, or the British in the 1800s had been. And they had the added insulting dimension of presenting themselves as the true voice of the Prophet, wishing to bracket Afghanistan into a greater Islamic empire. The Taliban took loyalty to tribe, clan, and their land as above any such thing. If freezing I.S. out meant accepting some limited western presence in the country, and letting the west do some of the heavy lifting, all well and good.

Hence, the strategy behind Operation Lincoln. Cultivate the Taliban. Encourage economic development, while soft pedalling contentious change. Prevent I.S. domination or intimidation of the populace or subversion of levers of power such as the police and interior ministry; secure the major population centres such as Kabul and Kandahar and Herat; but, and it is an important but, do not push so hard as to eliminate them. Engage I.S. visibly, forcefully, and to good effect; but keep them in play so the Taliban stay sweet.

As 2nd Lieutenant Collins and his patrol headed out to generate intelligence from a Taliban source, to follow up drone intelligence of an I.S. presence in the nearby village of Katdelay, it was heartening to think that there was, unusually, some point to it all.

Chapter 2

Ambush

Shamsul Khan was a simple man who counted himself lucky to have avoided much of the conflict that had come and gone through his district through the forty-five years of his life. As a young boy he got to tell a BMP troop carrier from a T-72 tank, a Hind gunship from a Hip troop transport helicopter, at the same age as he learned the routines of a farm which grew almonds and opium poppy in equal measure. As was his duty, he joined the mujahideen as a teenager, and the limp and scar which resulted from a firefight against equally terrified Russian conscripts was a lasting reminder of his honour.

Through the Taliban era, Khan had dropped opium cultivation for fear of the dire consequences of defying the regime of Mullah Omar. If you fell foul of the religious police, coming away with one limb short of a full deck was the most you could hope for. Production restarted in the new millennium, as N.A.T.O. could not seem to make up its mind whether its mission was counter-narcotic, or whether the counter-narcotic work was getting in the way of fighting the Taliban.

Well, at least that issue was cleared now. The British, who had reappeared in the district in the Spring, now wanted to buy his crop, not burn it. And the Taliban, still ever present but no longer ruling the roost, seemed to be willing to tolerate both the opium and the British. Which left only the Daesh, the outsiders, as a thing to be feared. And they were few and far between. Scratching his greying scraggly beard he had every reason to be proud of his past, comfortable with his present, and hopeful for his future.

Squinting against the low morning sun, Khan looked back at his compound, and saw his son Khalid skipping towards him. Normally this would be the time when the seven-year-old brought a pitcher of water out to him, to relieve the thirst of his mornings work. But Khan could see no pitcher, instead hearing Khalid calling to him.

"Father, please come. Ameera says there are armed men coming along the path beside the spring."

Ameera was Khalid's nine-year-old sister.

"The English soldiers?" he asked.

"She didn't say."

Khan sighed. He had better go see what they wanted.

~~

For 2nd Lieutenant Collins, the patrol had gone smoothly for the first two hours.

His unit was an ad hoc combination of Woolley's 2 Section, with a gun team from 3 Section attached to give more organic fire power. With Collins and 2nd Lieutenant Maiwand was Marine Drake, Collins' radio op, callsign Nod Zero One. His main function was to keep live comms with the patrol base, where support was available from the rest of 1 troop, a detachment of 81mm mortars from support company, and a quick reaction force of Afghan National Army, all under the command of "Sean" Connery. Collins worried that "quick reaction" for the Afghan National Army tended to involve activity of the headless chicken variety, but he knew he could rely on Sergeant Connery.

They had managed to move three kilometres in three hours - lightning speed compared to what used to be achievable in Helmand, but the Vallon mine detector could now be used in a thorough but not painstaking way in this benign environment. At only one point had a halt been called, while Woolley investigated a suspicious return from the Vallon, which turned out to be a piece of Russian era debris. Of course, mines from the Russian conflict could still kill and maim, as a paratrooper patrol had found to its cost a decade before. While waiting for the all clear, Collins crouched and shared some ration pack gum with Mazz, who grinned at him encouragingly, brown eyes twinkling from beneath the rim of her helmet.

"Ok, Mazz?"

She was leaning on her combat shotgun, a weapon which befitted a role where she was not expected to have to engage anyone at distance.

"Could do without the body armour." In spite of the cool weather and her relatively light load, beads of sweat were rolling down her temple, stripping streaks of cam cream from her face as they went.

Collins knew what she meant. When you took body armour off you felt like Neil Armstrong until your body re-adjusted. He tasked Marine Drake to send a sit rep back to Connery at the patrol base. It took a while - the Bowman radio continued to perform poorly twenty years into its life, but after several attempts Drake reported all O.K.

A signal from Corporal Woolley indicated it was O.K. to restart. Beyond a few scorched almond trees, the compound of one Shamsul Khan could be seen 300 metres to their north. It was the next checkpoint, and a spot where Mazz might pick up some intel on the local I.S. presence.

~~

The bodies were not long enough dead to smell.

Below a strand of thin rope, on which a threadbare rug had seen its last beating for a while, a young girl's body lay motionless. Only her body. Her head, torn from her neck with a rough blade, lay next to it, eyes open and staring.

Beyond her a couple of paces lay the corpse of a young boy, aged six or seven, in the same condition. Two metres nearer to the doorway to an adobe single story dwelling lay the body of a grey bearded man. Collins would have guessed him to be 55 to 60 years old from his wrinkled and weather-beaten face, but you could never tell in Afghan. He had been shot multiple times in the chest.

"What the fuck?" Corporal Woolley was appalled by the sight, but was professional enough to dispatch his section to take up fire positions, four covering arcs into the surrounding fields, three hard-targeting the doorway into the dwelling. The 3 Section fire team held position at the gate into the compound, General Purpose Machine Gun covering the way they had come in.

"What sick bastard did this?" Collins murmured. "And why do that to the kids and shoot the man?" He could feel himself welling up.

"I think they killed the kids first in front of him, and wanted him to see," said Mazz looking down at the sad remains at their feet. "Once he was dead, there was no audience, so they killed him with gunfire".

Collins concurred. "Woolley, check inside. Carefully."

By the time Marine Drake had called in a sitrep to the Patrol Base, Woolley was back, looking dismal.

"Same thing inside, Boss," hc reported. "One adult woman, beheaded."

"Fuck. Mazz what do you think?"

"Well unless the Taliban has gone back to being all medieval about opium production, it's got I.S. written all over it. Beheading isn't Taliban style. Targeting kids quite this cynically isn't Taliban style either. And then there's that..." Maiwand pointed at some black Arabic writing spray painted on the compound wall.

"I presume that's Arabic for "Islamic state was here"?" Collins asked.

"Nearly right, Ben. But someone has barely got started writing……and it stops mid-sentence..."

~~

Collins rapidly agreed with Sergeant Connery that the patrol should move out immediately. No short-cut back to base. The coordinates of their waypoints back were already fixed, along with pre-registered co-ordinates for mortar fire missions, or indeed, tube artillery from the base in Kandahar. While seeing the brutalised bodies left no one keen to hang around, it was safest and best to stick to the plan briefed on the "train set".

If they had been alert on the way down to the compound, the patrol was absolutely wired on the next dog-leg of their route. On Collins' model he had detailed moving from the checkpoint through an open field, which formed a rough oblong 200 metres wide by 300 long. Normally, he might not have wanted to expose the patrol in such an open space, but as Sergeant Connery had covered at the brief, there was always a calculation to be made between the lack of cover in the open, versus the risk of a mine strike on a path. While recent Taliban activity had been low, going in single file along an established track on the right of the field was a higher I.E.D. risk. Ditto following an obvious feature like the left boundary of the field, where a row of withered trees marked a low berm and ditch. As briefed, Corporal Woolley at the point of the patrol called on the personal radio net for "arrowhead" formation, stretching his arms behind him to reinforce the signal, a considerable feat given he was grasping a Minimi light machine gun in his right hand. While this formation necessitated each marine walking across terrain unswept by the Vallon, Collins assessed that the chances of hitting a random I.E.D. planted in the middle of a field were slim to none.

As always, Collins' mind was only half in the moment. There would no doubt be a reaction force to brief, probably flown out from Kandahar, to go back to the compound and try to maximise the intelligence take. While Collins' own patrol had been too lightly armed and lacking the scenes of crime kit to hang around and do the job, a proper evaluation would be required.

~~

As they reached the midpoint of the field, Corporal Woolley sensed movement to his left front in the treeline. But as he turned his right shoulder and burly torso to scan the flank, he no longer needed to wonder if he was imagining trouble.

With a "whoosh", a rocket propelled grenade fizzed past his head, rapidly accompanied by three others from the treeline in a ragged, and fortunately completely ineffective salvo. An old hand from Operation Herrick, Woolley was alarmed but unsurprised. R.P.G.s may be a cool weapon to carry at only 7kg, and great fun to fire. But generally fitted with a point-contact anti-tank warhead, they are little good for anything more than scaring the inexperienced: with the patrol throwing themselves into the dirt, there was nothing to strike and set off the warhead until the grenades impacted a hundred metres or more to their right. Moreover, the clouds of blue grey smoke which appeared at four points on the left made very clear where the firing positions were, and the marines down the left echelon of the arrowhead were enthusiastically blasting away at the treeline. Woolley heard the reassuring chatter of the section G.P.M.G., at the far-left end of the arrow, and he could see its tracer ripping into the berm and base of the trees, sending fist-sized lumps of bone-dry timber flying. While he could see no immediate effect, the gunfire was clearly not intimidating the natives, a number of firing points for automatic weapons opening up between the points where the R.P.G.s had been fired. Again, Woolley was heartened that almost all the fire was going over their heads. The Kalashnikov, like all fully automatic weapons, was hard to keep on target, especially in hands more used to hacking heads off or shooting unarmed civilians, than pulling off an ambush against a heavily armed enemy.

Woolley toggled the switch on his personal radio.

"Fucking amateurs."

~~

Hugging the parched earth in the central void between the two echelons of the arrowhead, Collins would be inclined to agree. But there were quite a lot of fucking amateurs. And the R.P.G. fire was already becoming more effective, one grenade striking the dirt and detonating between the two echelon lines, sending shrapnel showering past the prone figures of the marines on the right flank. And he had no idea what else they had in store.

Collins rapidly worked out his alternatives. Scanning the treeline to his left through the 3x magnification sight of his SA80 rifle, he could now make out several figures prone in the treeline. Unusually they had forsaken their usual black garb and were clad in egregiously inappropriate disruptive pattern camouflage, which was suggestive of being sourced from what Donald Trump might call "some shithole African country." In a sinister but almost comedic counterpoint to their dubious camouflage, Collins could make out each gunman still had the classic black balaclava: including one man crumpled in a heap the other side of a tree trunk which had been mangled by G.P.M.G. fire. "Cover from view may not be cover from fire," was a mantra Collins remembered from his Lympstone days.

The closest cover for the Marine patrol lay away from the gunfire, the other side of the slightly elevated footpath to the right. It looked a damn sight better than being in a shooting gallery in the middle of a parched field. But moving right would require breaking contact under fire, and the process of pepper-potting in pairs across into cover would mean that at any one time, half the firepower of the unit would not be engaging the I.S. ambush. While it would be ideal to find cover and then watch as an Apache helicopter obliterated the treeline, the patrol would be less exposed taking the initiative. Within 15 seconds of contact, Collins was giving his orders.

Giving orders by both personal radio and hand signal, Collins moved the 3 Section G.P.M.G. team, Nod Zero One Charlie, from the right flank to the head of the arrow. From there they could pour fire into the shorter leg of the inverted L-shaped ambush at the far end of the field. The rest of the right echelon were ordered to left flank, running as best they could to the end of the left echelon under the withering covering fire of the rest of the patrol. Collins gasped as he saw Marine Leach crash to the ground, only to watch him haul himself to his feet and stagger onwards again, struggling with the weight of his body armour, web kit, Minimi, and 400 rounds of 5.56mm ammunition. Thank fuck for that. From the right flank Collins moved Marine Wilkinson, carrying the heavy N.L.A.W. anti-tank weapon to support Zero One Charlie. That morning Wilko had been understandably unenthusiastic about having to hump the 14kg N.L.A.W. rocket in addition to his SA80, with, as he put it with unconscious but effective alliteration, "Fat chance of firing the fucker." Well he might now get the chance to send £25,000 of guided weapon down range. In the mean-time Collins set about getting some help from a local friendly Mortar Platoon.

"Hello Nod Three, this is Nod Zero One Alpha, fire mission, over."

~~

As soon as the contact report came in from Collins, Sergeant "Sean" Connery was up and running. The first action was to "stand-to" everyone in the patrol base, the A.N.A. reaction force moving with frenetic and unexpected speed.

By the time Connery got to the mortar pits, the Platoon from Command Company were Jonny-on-the-spot.

Within seconds they had fed the pre-registered co-ordinates of the treeline into the sighting settings, and as Collins had directed, they then set an off-set of 100 metres beyond the target: this would prove what fine adjustment was needed, and avoided the risk of the first round undershooting and landing on the patrol. As a further safeguard, Collins requested the first shot be a single smoke round, not High Explosive, so that he could observe "fall of shot" at low risk. The kill radius of an H.E. 81mm round was 35 metres, and the dumb rounds would land where you sent them regardless of who was underneath.

Sergeant Connery watched the loader rip off three of the four booster charges, the fat C-shaped wedges which surrounded the body of the round between its warhead and fins: with the target close to the patrol base, little extra propellant was needed beyond what was within the round itself. With the all clear from the Corporal leading the gun team, the round was dropped down the muzzle, the loader ducked and covered his ears, and with a hollow "Boof," Connery sensed rather than saw the first round on its way. Game on.

~~

As soon as she got over the shock of the first seconds of contact, Mazz had her combat shotgun in her shoulder and was firing at muzzle flashes in the treeline. At 100 metres range this was largely for the reassurance of doing something than in any hope of effect. Mazz had started the patrol with a full load of 7 rounds of buckshot, which was a good choice for likely close combat, but the ammunition had a maximum range of only 40 metres or so. Once all the rounds were expended, she could reload with solid shot: each a lump of lead 18mm in diameter. That would not only have the range to reach the tree line - a hit from solid shot would really sting in the morning.

~~

To Collins' professional satisfaction the mortar round impacted exactly where it should, detonating with a pop and showering a curtain of white phosphorous across the field beyond the tree line, white smoke billowing in the still air.

"Nod Three, this is Nod Zero Alpha, drop 100, fire for effect."

Instantaneously all three tubes of the Mortar Platoon were in action, the first rounds from each mortar still in the air, as the second round was being dropped down the barrel. With an overlapping series of colossal "Crumps", round after round impacted in and around the treeline to the left, the pre-registered target from where the bulk of the fire had been coming. A steady stream of fire was still coming from one single firing point to the front, but Collins had a plan to that too. He directed Marine Wilkinson at the point of the patrol to get the N.L.A.W. into action, confirming his fire indication with a series of rapid-fire rounds at the base of the tree where a heavy-calibe R.P.D. or similar machine gun seemed to be sited. With his SA80 loaded with 1 in 4 tracer rounds for just this purpose, in moments Wilkinson too could identify the firing point. Having only one shot, the potential embarrassment of missing vexed him at least as much as lying prone in a dusty field in Afghanistan while Islamic State's finest were trying to kill him, and the weapons designers seemed to have spent most of their time designing the N.L.A.W. *not* to fire. Getting it ready to launch required removing two different safety locks, while actually firing required two different buttons to be activated simultaneously. This no doubt prevented negligent discharges, but was not seen by the Commandos as very "Nod friendly": when under fire, having kit which is easy to unleash at the enemy speedily becomes rather important. On the plus side, the N.L.A.W. was designed to enable a direct hit on moving targets at much longer ranges, and had a fabulous sight system, so that once the flip up front and rear sights were fixed on target, the missiles would follow that point of aim.

As ordered, Wilkinson waited for Collins' direct order to fire, because the boss had other fish to fry. Firstly, he ordered Marine Leach's fire team, poised on the extreme end of the formation, to use the cover of the continuing mortar fire to pepper pot 50 yards to their left. As he ran, Leach was heartened to see two or three shredded I.S. militants who had clearly had inadequate cover from the barrage. More importantly, he could now pour grazing fire along the whole left tree line with only a sweep of 20 degrees or arc: you might miss a nearby target, but strike instead someone else down the way.

Leach got his Minimi up and firing, and Collins could hear it blasting away. Tick. He then called Nod Zero Three, and requested three more rounds per tube, with the last round of all to be another white phosphorous round to indicate no more were coming. Tick. Finally, he ordered all the left echelon to prepare to assault the treeline to kill anyone left - it seemed a bit too melodramatic to actually tell the Marines to "Fix bayonets!" and they seldom needed much encouragement. Wilkinson's N.L.A.W., all cued up, was to prevent the R.P.D. to the front cutting down the assault as it charged the treeline.

Only 90 seconds after the ambush had been sprung all was ready.

"Left echelon ready. On Wilko, Wilko..."

Collins lifted onto his elbows to get a better view of the smoke round when it fell, and to be ready to lever himself to his feet to join the assault. Hearing the different noise of the W.P. round and seeing bright eye-piercing chunks of phosphorous fly, Collins gave his final word of command....

"Fire."

Shadowing his C.O., Drake was in awe of seeing Collins on top of his game. There was a distinctive "Crack" at the head of the arrow as the initiating charge pushed the 2-foot-long missile out of its disposable tube, then a loud whoosh as the main rocket fired, speeding the N.L.A.W. missile to its target less than 100 metres away. The R.P.D. position and the machine gun crew serving it were obliterated in a massive boom. Freed from the hail of bullets coming from their front right, the Marines in the left echelon moved in, one running, his partner giving covering fire, ripping into what was now more a line of pollarded timber than anything resembling a tree. Collins lurched after the assault in a heavily laden jog-trot.

There was little left to shoot. Entering the treeline Collins was met by the sight of an I.S. militiaman who could only be described as having been "cored": there was a massive hole through his chest and abdomen, so that the main thing that connected his shoulders to his waist was not his body, but essentially the straps of his webbing. Looking to his left, he saw Leach run a prone body through with a bayonet stroke, while out of the corner of his eye to the right, Woolley ripped apart the last visible enemy in the treeline with a burst of Minimi fire. With the G.P.M.G. group having checked fire, and the patrol in cover, Collins felt suddenly utterly weary, the adrenalin burst of the contact spent. But he was also thrilled, and glowing from having performed well in his first contact.

All that changed in an instant. Looking back across to the middle of the field he could see a single figure, prone but moving, clearly suffering and wounded.

"Fuck."

~~

It was Mazz.

Having blasted off her seven-round load of buckshot, she had reloaded on her back, jamming the shells awkwardly into the housing in the stock. Pumping the weapon to put a round in the breach, she raised herself on one knee, pulled the butt into her shoulder, aimed and fired. Mazz wasn't sure if she alarmed the enemy but she certainly alarmed herself. Typically for the U.K. armed forces, budgets were such that she had never fired solid shot even on the range, let alone in anger: range staff were not keen to have their stock of N.A.T.O. Figure 11 targets shredded, and a solid slug hitting quarter-inch plywood was not going to go well for the charging infantryman graphic. Her first round sailed into the few upper branches of a tree that remained, but she pulled the butt tighter into her shoulder, and fired again at a camouflaged figure which briefly popped up to fire a burst from his Kalashnikov- and saw him thrown backwards in a cloud of expanding pink mist, as the solid shot struck centre mass.

Mazz was fixated and unaware of being targeted by gunfire from the head of the field until she found herself thrown violently to the floor, as if smacked in the right side with a baseball bat.

With no immediate pain for the first second, Maryam had a chance to form an incongruous thought that "This is what being shot feels like," but then came a fierce burning pain in her right armpit and chest, followed by a wet feeling down her right breast. In reflex she tried to take a deep breath, only to find she could not take her fill of air. Then came a feeling of panic, heightened by a cough which added a scarlet frothy stain to the floor in front of her, rapidly followed by another and another. Lying on her back and reaching into her armpit she could feel an entry wound the size of a conker, where the round had come under her raised right elbow and upper arm as she aimed her shotgun. Looking down at her chest she could see no exit wound in her body armour. But as her chest heaved, she could feel air being sucked into a hole somewhere on her right front.

In a battle-scarred field, 500 miles from her ancestors' home in Iran, 2nd Lieutenant Maryam Maiwand, Intelligence Corps, toggled her PRR and wheezed, "Its Mazz. I'm hit."

~~

Both Collins and Woolley were horrified to see Mazz down and exposed back where they had started in the middle of the field. They were even more horrified, as first one and then another round kicked up the soil next to her.

Scanning the end of the field through their S.U.S.A.T. gun sights, they could make out two sporadic muzzle flashes from the ditch before the poppy stalks that marked the beginning of the next farmer's land. They were just away along from where the R.P.D. position smouldered, whacked by Wilkinson's N.L.A.W. moments before. Like footage Collins had seen at school of U.S. marines fighting in Hue during the Tet offensive of 1968, the I.S. militia were using the "spray and pray" mindset, keeping head and shoulders in cover while holding their weapon up and firing un-aimed shots. Their goal was clearly to kill, without mercy, the wounded British soldier to their front.

The troop reloaded, and a barrage of 5.56mm and 7.62mm semi-automatic and automatic gunfire now tore up the soil on both sides of the I.S. ditch. Collins watched as Pat Tolua, a Lance Corporal born in Fiji, slammed his G.P.M.G. into position on its bipod and began blasting away, forsaking the norm of firing short bursts, for a stream of lead that would burn out the barrel in no time. Everyone loved Mazz.

The fire had no effect. With no more N.L.A.W. rockets to use, those like Collins who had a U.G.L. - a grenade launcher underslung the barrel of their SA80, switched to lobbing 40mm fragmentation grenades at the firing points in the ditch, Collins pausing between pushing each of the squat rounds into the breach to look 90 degrees right to where Mazz was still moving slightly, prone and now facing away from the enemy. Collins saw Mazz draw her Glock 17 pistol from its holster, hold it arm outstretched behind her, and commence firing.

~~

The burning pain was worse. The wet patch felt bigger, but most importantly of all, breathing was getting tougher with every breath. Mazz knew that she was sucking air into the cavity between her right lung and the pleura lining her rib cage.

With every heave of her diaphragm downwards towards her viscera, the vacuum effect which should have been pulling air down through her airway was also pulling air into the chest cavity, building pressure to stop the lung fully inflating. At the same time the lung, pleura, and cardiac cavity were filling with blood, most of which was filling internal space, not contributing to the spreading blood stain under her body armour. If Mazz had known more anatomy, she would know that the right lung is, in humans, the "good" side, with three lobes of lung compared to two. She would also know that her head was spinning because in addition to blood loss and anoxic desaturation, the air pressure inside her right chest was starting to push the mediastinum, the column of trachea, oesophagus, and heart, over to one side, kinking the cardiac arteries and reducing efficient flow of life-giving blood.

At the same time as wheezing and hacking, Mazz was conscious of the crack of supersonic bullets passing her, each one followed almost instantaneously by the sound of the thump of the same round leaving the barrel. Mazz summoned up all her will-power, and winced and cried out as she rolled onto her right side. Lying on the wound hurt like hell, but it might at least compress it, and stop some blood loss and air leakage. Importantly, it would ensure less blood from her right chest would get across and into her left side, preserving gas exchange in the two good lobes she still had to rely on.

"Come on, Mazz," she told herself. "You can do this."

Drawing her Glock 17 pistol, she cocked the weapon before extending her arm and blasting away methodically, one round at a time. She was damned if she was going to let them just pick her off.

~~

Woolley and Collins would have given anything for the new American 40mm rounds, which would proximity fuse above a concealed defilade target. For the moment the hail of fire at the two gunmen was having zero effect, and the I.S. shooters continued to hold their Kalashnikovs above the edge of the ditch to try to finish the job of killing Maiwand.

Collins next move took only a few moments. Calling the mortar Platoon again, he directed them to drop 50m and go right 100m, with another spotting smoke round to check this had achieved the goal of moving the impact point to the far end of the field. As soon as the shot impacted on target, he ordered “Fire for effect,” adding the warning that the patrol were now "Danger Close".

At the same time, Drake, Collins' radio op, was onto Connery using the company frequency, giving details of the contact and imparting the zap code of the one known casualty. Each soldiers zap code, a combination of the first two letters of their surname and last four numbers of their army number, allowed information on wounds and fatalities to be securely transmitted, so that medics and then the chain of command would get the essential info speedily. But Drake was very clear in his mind that this signal was not just about conveying information professionally, and Collins heard him shouting over the barrage of Marine gunfire.

"Guys, we have one casualty, priority one, will need urgent casevac. It's zap code MA2435. I say again code MA2435. Get Nod Zero Three to pour it on! Pour it on!"

~~

Even Command Company knew Mazz and were fond of her, and however fast their rate of fire during the initial contact, they upped it 25%. It was a noble effort by committed and professional men. They were relentless and determined not to let her down. Had they not been firing at such a tempo, they might have been quicker to notice the 18kg baseplate, designed to firmly root each tube to the floor, start to shift under the first of the mortars. And the soil under it start to shift, pulverised by the continuous recoil. And the sighting bubbles in the two indicators in the sight mechanism drifting just a little off.

Of course, it is easy to be wise after the event.

~~

After 30 seconds of the fire mission, and the constant automatic fire from the marines in the treeline, the I.S. gunfire was still not suppressed. The inevitable happened. Collins didn't see the bullet strike, but heard Mazz on the PRR.

"Ben, I am hit again."

It felt to Mazz like she had been kicked in the left buttock as hard as someone possibly could achieve.

She gave up firing the Glock. There was no way on earth that she was going to be able to reload it, and shooting without looking was not going to achieve anything given the patrol's aimed fire and the impacting mortars had done no good. Her left hand still holding the weapon, she reached down and instantly felt a bloody hole with her fingertips, while her leg now seemed to flop pointlessly.

With breathing harder still, Mazz felt truly frightened for the first time. Her pulse raced, but her oxygen sats were so low now that she was pumping useless volume, and pumping it less and less efficiently. A strange but single clear thought firmed in her mind.

"Is that it?"

She thought she could hear Woolley's voice but had no breath to speak. And he sounded so far away. She toggled the pressel switch on her PRR to show she was still alive.

Then all went grey. Then black.

~~

Collins reaction when Mazz was wounded again was immediate. He got up into a crouch, shed his pack and began to unclip his webbing.

Woolley mirrored him.

"Sir, where the fuck are you going?" the big Corporal shouted above the roar of battle.

"She is dying Woolley, I am going to get her!" Collins didn't pause.

"Sir, with respect you couldn't lift and carry shit. Leave it to the cannon fodder."

Collins knew he was right. At 6 foot 2 Woolley was a head taller and 30kg better built than the wiry Lieutenant.

"Keep the covering fire going Sir," Woolley gave a grin. "I will be back in a jiffy."

Woolley opened the cover of his Minimi, pulled out a nearly expended ammunition belt, and fed in a fresh one from one of the pouches now in the dirt at his feet. He re-cocked the weapon, then toggled his PRR

"Mazz..... stay still.....I am coming."

~~

Collins would come to replay the events of the next 20 seconds in his mind more than was good for him.

Freed from the weight of much of his kit, Woolley was up and running. Minimi in two hands at waist level, he blasted away on full automatic as he ran. While totally inaccurate Woolley wasn't going to outsource covering fire to anyone.

Return fire came from the firing points at the end of the field. Collins couldn't work out, in retrospect, how the Daesh realised the rescue effort was underway - he guessed that they sensed Woolley's burst of Minimi was coming at them from a different angle. Collins had continued to fire at the far ditch himself, while watching out of the corner of his eye the bullets snapping all around the section commander as he ran. The mortars continued to bracket the end of the field, throwing clods of baked soil and poppy stalks skyward. Then Woolley was crashing next to Mazz on the floor, throwing his Minimi to one side as he did so, and calling out on the PRR

"Boss, she is unconscious. Shot is the ass and maybe the chest too. Not hanging round. Coming back now." He was panting hard now as he spoke.

Collins bellowed for covering fire.

Woolley had no time to do more than take in Mazz's face, paler than he had ever seen before, blood coming from her mouth and nostrils. He got up to one knee, and by sheer brute force pulled the dead weight of the young officer and her kit and body armour up to his right shoulder.

"Come on Ma'am," he said in a voice gentle and respectful. It was not a tone his section would have thought he had in him. "Let's get you home shall we? Just like the bottom field at Lympstone..." he added softly.

Woolley's reference was to one of the final requirements of test week at the Commando Training Centre, a fireman's carry against the clock to simulate just this scenario - getting a wounded mate off the battlefield. The thought reassured him.

Hauling himself to his feet, Woolley ignored a bullet cracking past his head, jumped in the air an inch to settle the officer better on his shoulder, and began running in a crooked stagger back towards Collins.

Woolley had no siblings. He would have made a great big brother.

~~

Another set of three mortar rounds impacted, two on target and one a little way into the field. Collins thought of telling Connery to check fire, but no sooner had he formed the thought than he saw more gun fire from the end of the field, and this time, a yell as Woolley was hit. It seemed to be his left arm, which had been outstretched to help him balance as he carried Mazz over his right shoulder.

Woolley didn't break stride and kept going, still jogging towards them. Then he was felled, and, briefly motionless, dropping Mazz like a sack of potatoes.

"Woolley!!" Collins bellowed.

An answer came on the PRR.

"It's OK Sir, took a round in the chest plate, just winded. Coming now."

Quite how Woolley got Mazz up on his shoulder again with one arm useless no one could say. Many of them tried it on each other later and got nowhere. And they were not being shot at. Woolley was. And Collins saw the two balaclava-clad I.S. fighters were now more willing to take more risks to do whatever it took to avoid the Marines making their escape. As the fighter on the left popped up to fire a proper aimed burst, a hit to the head from small arms fire put him conclusively out of action.

"One left.. come on Woolley!" Collins thought.

Others were shouting encouragement above the din, firing all the time at the lone muzzle flash in the ditch, increasingly hard to see in the cloud of dust and debris thrown up by battle.

Woolley staggered towards Collins, his fireman's carry increasingly bent double, Mazz's body flopping limply over his back. Collins could make out the big Corporal grimacing with effort or pain, eyes scrunched so tight it was difficult to imagine how he was seeing his footing.

There were 20 yards to go when the next group of mortar rounds fell, the first, finally, impacting where it needed to. At the end of the field Collins saw the final I.S. militiaman blown into the air away from them, arcing like a rag doll into the blasted poppy stalks.

Then without warning, full in the face, came the devastating crash of a mortar round landing closer, much closer, too close.

Collins felt himself thrown sideways, ears ringing, face peppered with fragments. Next to him Lance Corporal Tolua was rolling, holding his neck, blood pouring from between the fingers of both hands as he kicked his legs in pain, desperate to see his wound but terrified of what would happen if he let go.

Woolley! As if awakening Collins remembered the two out in the open, devoid of any cover from the round which had fallen short. He barely dared look. As he blurred vision refocused, all he could see were two prone forms, motionless, barely 10 yards from cover. Between him and them, the roughly hewn, smoking, impact crater.

Collins looked for Marine Drake, and seeing him unhurt a few yards away, screamed at him to get the mortar Platoon to check fire. Leach, Wilkinson, and Collins, lurched drunkenly to their feet and staggered out towards the bodies of Woolley and Maiwand.

~~

By the time the "Dust-Off" MH-60 Blackhawk landed in the middle of the field, which had now been carefully prepped for it with the Vallon, all was ready for them.

Collins, free of other tasks with a reaction force now on site, watched as first Tolua made his way through the fierce downdraft to the chopper doorway, still unwilling to release his hold on his neck, but with the wound now covered with a field dressing which filled the void between his jawbone and his Osprey body armour.

Next came Mazz, ported on a collapsible stretcher by two American pararescuemen, looking ashen, still unconscious. Once in cover the patrol medic had been quick to assess her sucking right chest wound, and speedily locating the key spot between her ribs, had driven a wide bore needle into the pleural space. A sharp and sustained hiss signalled the release of the pressure which was collapsing her lung, and Mazz's pulse normalised. Once an air tight dressing had been applied to her wound, and with a chest drain substituted for the needle, she was breathing with more normal effect. The less life-threatening buttock wound was dressed, but left for someone else to resolve.

Finally came Corporal Ian Woolley.

Most of his kit and webbing he had removed himself before his dash into the open; his body armour had been ripped off him in the first moments after he was dragged into cover, as Collins and the others desperately searched for injuries. The Osprey vest was almost in bits, clearly having taken one heavy calibre round, but also smoking from numerous mortar fragments embedded in it. Woolley's helmet was in similar shocking state, a gouge taken out of it near the crown. But neither item could save him from the sliver of mortar case which, blasted at supersonic speed, had struck him below the chin, severing his spinal cord; and killing him instantly.

"I count eleven dead, Sir." It was Marine Wilkinson.

"Only one that counts for anything," murmured Collins, eyes tearing up. He zipped up the body bag, and got back to work.

Chapter 3

Aftermath

November

As Collins stepped out of the shower and into his hotel room, he caught sight of himself in the mirror.

The post-tour decompression in Cyprus had done little to erase the artefacts of his tour in Kandahar. His frame still looked out of proportion - neck and shoulders bulked up from hefting his pack and body armour, abdomen lean in comparison, showing the after-effects of the diarrhoea that was a frequent companion on tour. Collins forearms were expanded from hefting one firearm or another solidly for 6 months, while even the Mediterranean sunshine had done little to resolve his "Afghan tan": forearms and neck and face bronzed, with the rest of him pasty in comparison.

Collins could still not quite get over the feeling of pile carpet between his toes, as he stood and dried himself briskly, resolving to do something about hair which had now taken the form of an unruly brown mop. Sergeant Connery would surely not approve.

He glanced nervously at his No.1 dress uniform laid out on the tired bedspread. A haircut would postpone the moment he would have to put it on.

~~

Katie and Shona sat in the staff canteen, looking an odd couple to those queuing up to buy a panini or sandwich for a hurried lunch before rushing back to their ward or department.

On one chair perched the pony-tailed one-time grammar school girl, slightly shambolic and harassed, searching her bag and the hip pocket of her tunic for her phone before spotting it bold as brass on the laminate table in front of her.

Opposite her the angry obtuse forty-something Scot, pierced eyebrow, hair that trod a line between aubergine and indigo in the colour palette of Snips' hairdresser down in Lancaster town centre. Her posture was so poor that she almost seemed to be spilling over the chair rather than sitting on it.

While Katie provided the thoughtful and considered side of their incipient friendship, she was starting to appreciate Shona for being what she could not be: angry, strident, outspoken, opinionated. But if Shona came across as her own person, in fact she was nothing of the sort. Brought up in the Women's Peace Camp which was squeezed between a main road and the boundary barbed wire of the Royal Navy Submarine Base at Faslane, Shona's childhood memories were of intense fireside conversations about sexual politics and nuclear atrocity. This provided little common ground with a 21st century teenager brought up on a diet of Balamory, Blue Peter, Facebook, and Snapchat. But now shorn of boyfriend and immediate prospects of a settled life, Katie found more in common with the woman twice her age.

"So, what was she like?" asked Katie.

"Who?" Shona replied.

"Your mother. She must have been very principled to bring you up in a tent by the side of the road for ten years?"

"Yurt," said Shona.

"Say what?" asked Katie.

"The shelters we lived in. They were called yurts. Or benders. Which would also describe most of the people who lived in them."

"Including your Mum?" asked Katie.

"Eventually, yes. By osmosis. I guess it was pretty hard to stay straight when everyone around you was queer as a bottle of crisps." Shona smiled.

"It must have been a weird childhood?" Katie ventured.

"To be honest at the time I didn't know any different. It was me, and my Mum, and a whole load of kids to play with. The only men we came across often were the uniformed police minding us. In the end my Mum decided I needed an education so we moved into a council house when I was ten. By then the world had moved on and it was only the hard-core left." Shona took a bite out of what the packaging had billed as a "deluxe mozzarella and sun blush tomato pizza wrap". It was rapidly proving a disappointment.

"What do you mean the world had moved on?"

"And there's me thinking I was the one with no education," Shona sighed. "'89 the Wall comes down, and us and the Russians are suddenly best friends. China and North Korea weren't on the radar, and the only weapons of mass destruction anyone was talking about were Saddam Hussein's. Which, of course, proved not to exist, dodgy dossier and all that. No one was interested in Britain's nuclear stockpile. The Blair government made a big show of how our missiles no longer held actual target co-ordinates. And having Polaris, then one Trident submarine, then eventually four of them, became part of the national landscape. The C.N.D. disappeared up its own arse..."

"C.N.D.?" interrupted Katie.

"Campaign for Nuclear Disarmament. So, a gang of lesbians and kids in a makeshift camp beside a roundabout in Faslane became just a self-licking lollipop. It served nothing except itself."

"So, it was all bullshit then?"

"No, I didn't say that. We are now pissing up the wall vast sums of money on a new set of missiles and submarines. £40 billion minimum. And where will they be based?"

Katie shrugged her shoulders.

"Faslane. The other side of the same fence I was camped beside for a decade. And the U.K. Parliament seem to think they can plonk them there regardless of no-one in Scotland wanting them. Put the things in Portsmouth by all means. As ever the fucking Westminster government seems to forget that they cannot just call all the shots now."

Katie ground her teeth as Shona went into what Nasreen called "Sturgeon mode". Shona's periodic tendency to rant from the Scottish Nationalist compendium of victimhood had earned her the nickname "Nicola" from one or two colleagues who had lost patience. "Like Sturgeon before the make-over," had been another comment about Shona from those less than sympathetic, given that unlike the rest of the U.K., Scottish people still benefitted from free prescriptions and free University education. "Yeah but the downside is, you do have to fucking live there," had been mentioned as a balancing factor regarding the advantages of life north of the border.

"Time to go, I think." Katie made a show of checking the upside-down fob watch on her left breast, which sat next to a tin shield badge showing she was an alumnus of Lancaster University Medical School.

Shona cast half her "Deluxe Wrap" into the bin - a lesson learned; and the two of them pushed through the double swing doors into the corridor back to the unit. Katie decided to change the subject.

"Have you met Abaya yet?"

"Doctor Shah? The new radiologist? No. Any good?"

"I think she's going to be a godsend. Because of her background she has had to cope with all the old school kit, back of a fag packet calculations, that sort of thing. She is a whizz on the old Cobalt-60 machine."

"Her background?"

"She comes from the Middle East somewhere. Not the nice bit. I think she's happy to be out of it."

"Good for her," Shona replied.

As they came to the unit, Katie pointed above the door. "Did you see this?"

Above the standard "Nuclear Medicine" department sign, white type on green acrylic, someone had added a sparkly purple banner which read "We Radiate Excellence!"

"Oh, for fuck's sake," said Shona.

Katie rather liked it.

~~

For Lt. Col. Allen Scott R.M., the return home from Op. Lincoln, or Op. Lincoln 1 as it would now become, had been only empty. Making sure his Commando did not disgrace itself in Cyprus had focused the mind, but fending off bullshit from back in the U.K. had taken up any spare attention. It was bad enough that so late in the tour A Company had suddenly found themselves in such a vicious contact, and lost Woolley in the process; worse was having to work with the Colonel Commandant to defend the professional reputation of the Corps, and fight off the blowback from those who wanted to spin the incident as some kind of Iraq style cock up. There were some who wanted Op. Lincoln 1 to be devoid of sequels.

Things had not been helped by the newspapers. The fire fight had been the first major contact of the tour, and the death of Corporal Woolley along with ten I.S. militia had happened in a slow news week. Of course, the media was far more interested a week later when, with Woolley's funeral not even completed, the MOD announced the probability that friendly fire had killed him.

Now deskbound once more, and back in barracks in Taunton, item one for Scott was to establish with his team WTFN – "What The Fuck Now."

"Boss," sighed Major Guy Waters, looking over a steaming mug of scalding black coffee, "this isn't a time for playing "Witchfinder General"."

He continued.

"There wasn't a single person at the debrief who thinks this was anything other than an isolated tragedy. Sergeant Connery insists they were well briefed. The patrol was well suited to their planned mission. When they found the corpses at the farmstead Collins made good choices. For God's sake when I.S. decided to take them on head to head in a hasty ambush, they whacked hell out of them. It was a ballsy call to assault the ambush instead of trying to withdraw and go firm, but Leach and Drake and the rest of the patrol all back Collins. They say he was spot on."

"And what about those who say he was too aggressive?" Scott asked. The Colonel was too deadpan for Major Waters to tell if he was just playing devil's advocate.

"What with calling mortar fire?"

Lt. Colonel Scott nodded.

"Well what's the Mortar Platoon there for? The patrol was under heavy fire with no cover to speak of and no other asset immediately to hand. Fair play to Collins for having his targets pre-registered as he did. With no expected threat, his thoroughness paid dividends in spades. And anyway, which of us haven't dropped mortar rounds somewhere where we didn't want mortar rounds to land?" One might have assumed Waters would defend his own men - his demeanour was heartfelt.

"Yet we have a brave N.C.O., known and well regarded by marines across the Commando, killed by mortar fire brought in by his own Troop commander."

".... a point which the MOD saw fit to release to all and sundry when they should have kept their gobs shut," Major Waters added.

"Agreed. But maybe you don't remember the Pat Tillman story?" Colonel Scott asked.

"The name rings a bell. Wasn't he an N.F.L. player?" Waters' mind went back a decade to the years post 9/11.

"St. Louis Cardinals. He dumped a $4m dollar contract to join the Army Rangers, and became the pin up boy for the military. I'd forgotten too, but someone in Whitehall clearly did not. When Tillman was killed in action, at first he was presented as having been killed in by the Taliban. But before his body had even arrived back in the US, they knew he had been shot by his own side. His sub-unit were misidentified as enemy when their Platoon got split up, and he got shot in the head by his own side." Major Waters winced.

Colonel Scott continued.

"But that's only where the scandal started. Fellow Rangers on the spot burned his uniform and body armour to conceal the evidence. They burned his notebook as well: there were too many odds and sods in it that were critical of the chain of command. Then soldiers in his unit were not just told to conceal the truth, those going to the funeral were actively told to lie to Tillman's family. Three years later it was still being investigated and raked over. So, however unpleasant the effects, I think the MOD were right to bite the bullet."

"Fair enough, but Katdelay is old news quickly Boss," said Major Waters, taking a tentative sip of his coffee.

"Hmmmmmm. Unfortunately there's the fall out within the Commando too. You can imagine what some of the old hands are saying in the Sergeants' Mess Guy? Gung-ho officer gets their fellow N.C.O. killed?"

"Then, with respect Colonel, they should shut the fuck up!"

Scott said nothing. Rising from his desk he walked to the window and gazed across the empty parade ground. The rest of the Commando were still on post operations leave.

"Woolley is being put in for the Conspicuous Gallantry Cross you know?" he said.

"Collins should get one too," the Company Commander pressed

Colonel Scott was silent. He continued, without looking around.

"Guy, we both know that's not how these things work. And I don't think it would be good for the boy to have to deal with bullshit from the few know-alls in the Mess who weren't there and who think they know better. We don't need a unit set against itself. When they are back from leave we will have hacks from The Sun and the Mirror tapping up Nods in the pubs trying to get them to dish dirt on what happened. If anyone suggests Collins was at fault, and he is still in the Commando, then the whole saga drags on."

"Then what about our debt to Collins' father?". Ben's deceased father, had served with 45 Commando in the Falklands straight out of training, before going on to become its R.S.M. a quarter century later, and was a well-known alumnus of the Corps.

"He would understand."

Major Waters was silent but winced inside. He could sense what was coming.

"I think it would best for Collins' career development to have some time away from the Commando...." Colonel Scott's voice carried little conviction, and he continued to gaze out of the office window.

"After all, he has had a good year, worked up to what one could view as a highly successful tour...bar this situation of course..." Scott tailed off. "Maybe something a bit more niche than this. A bit of career progression?" Scott was doing a poor job of trying to sound pragmatic and hopeful.

Waters angered.

"Sir, honestly, I see no need or justice in doing that. Collins deserves better of us. Mess politics is no good reason for selling out my most promising troop commander," Waters said, barely able to control his tone of voice. The Major knew that Colonel Scott was generally fair and proper. Had he been got at? The MOD? Someone seemed to want Collins kicked into the long grass. The news cycle was moving on, with the Irish Guards in Kandahar now taking the fight to I.S. elements, helped by decent albeit patchy intelligence from Taliban sources.

"Sir, if we transfer him now, it will look like we are blaming him for Woolley's death too. How about we wait 6 months? Confront any bullshit head on. If there is nonsense about Woolley's death out in the Commando as a whole, let's do a full formal wash up. There are plenty of lessons to be learned: mostly of what Collins did right." From the lack of reaction he got from Colonel Scott, Waters sensed that he was wasting his breath.

Scott turned back from the window and re-took his seat. For the first time in their conversation, he looked Major Waters in the eye properly.

"I don't think so Guy. Collins is, unfortunately, damaged goods. At least until the dust settles. See to it please."

Major Waters placed his unfinished cup of coffee on the edge of Scott's desk, donned his green beret carefully, and saluted with a slowness that communicated just a hint of attitude. Then he turned on his heel to do the MOD's dirty work.

~~

Collins knew a little of the city of Exeter from his time in training. The county town of Devon, it provided the closest thing to nightlife Marines in camp ten miles downriver at Lympstone were able to get on their brief weekend passes. The clubs on the city Quay closed at 2am, and the female population had come to know that small groups of shaven headed young men were Commandos in training, and were best given a wide berth. The male population came to know to give them an even wider berth, dodging punchy Commandos trying to pick fights in pubs alongside the banks of the River Exe. But the city was still the best nightlife a Marine in training could get anywhere near. So, when Corporal Woolley had told him in idle chat that he came from the city suburb of Whipton, Collins had at least heard the name before.

He didn't know what to imagine as he drove up the inner-by-pass that morning, heading away from the city centre. Dinner the evening before had been a cursory affair, with Collins mind wandering back to that day in Kandahar as he tried to think of the right form of words to sum up what had happened. They didn't come. Nor did they come as he had sat that morning in the barber's chair at Vic's in Fore Street, getting a speedy "grade 2 on the top, zero high on the back and sides," having assured himself that he was in good time.

Passing St. James's Park football ground on his left, the bustle of a shopping area gave way to a busy street of red brick Victorian villa houses, which somehow didn't seem to fit as a likely home for the dead Corporal.

With one eye and ear on Sat Nav, Collins drove on in silence up Old Tiverton Road, finding his way into Whipton itself. Shared houses for University students, some of whom dotted the streets on their way to and from the nearby campus, gave way into more homely suburban streets. Clearly having their origins in the 30s or 50s, the hire car passed row on row of neat semi-detached white pebble-dashed houses. While now varied with a satellite dish here, a neat hedge there, new double glazing on one trumped by a basketball hoop on another, their homogenous style suggested these had once been Council Housing until the great Thatcher sell-off. Exeter was ringed with such estates, the city building out rather than up in its post-war expansion. While the streets had once been sparse in traffic, the money to buy a private vehicle being unusual in such an area, the estate now teemed with cars parked haphazardly in cul-de-sacs and narrow drives never designed for them.

Collins spotted the street sign he was looking for, a thin strip of slightly rusting white tin affixed to the side wall of the house on the end of the road. Turning right, he was alerted before he could react by the Sat Nav that he had reached his destination, but with no parking space he carried on, and passed a battered green acrylic shelter, which held a mixture of elderly locals awaiting a bus down to the town centre and shabbily dressed "Neets" waiting for the pub to open. Like many English towns, travelling just 400 metres could take you from a neighbourhood of smart flat conversions and detached family homes, into another neighbourhood far less affluent.

Twenty yards further on, he found his space in the car park of a Harvester Inn which had seen better days. Getting out, he used the side window of the Mazda to check his Sam Browne belt wasn't askew and his peaked No1 cap was straight. With his sharp trim and dress blues he could have come right from a recruiting billboard.

Puffing his chest out and taking a deep breath, Collins walked briskly back towards the front door of Number 16, drawing stares from the civvies in the bus shelter. A Marine in full parade gear stepping out from the Royal Oak car park was not the norm in Whipton, and generally would have attracted the wrong kind of vocal attention from the Neets - persons "not in education, employment or training". But Woolley's photo had been on the front page of the Exeter Express and Echo a month before, and locals had got used to seeing a police presence outside the home of the dead corporal's parents: initially to keep the media at arms-length when news of his death was announced, then again ten days later when the MOD announced he had been killed by “friendly fire”.

Of those present only Collins knew he was the "friend" who called the "fire". And from the newspaper coverage he had seen, he feared the reception he might be about to get at the Woolley home.

~~

Two figures tramped up the frozen rutted track to a wind-swept cliff top, leaving the shore and the jetty far behind them. The Arctic Sea from here to Murmansk in the East, and Norway 100 miles to the West didn't freeze even in November thanks to the warming effect of the Gulf Stream still making itself felt. They had long passed the site of the recent work to make Andreev Bay safe once and for all, a shambolic array of bright yellow diggers and cranes standing out against the snowy landscape. Most of the bevy of scientists and E.U. officials and journalists were content to busy themselves there; for the suits, this was where their budget was being spent. For the hacks, photos of rusting submarines, now sand coloured, free of identification, and stripped of their propellers and tail array, were much more attractive than capturing images of a lot of middle-aged men in hard hats standing in a building site. And to most of the Scientists, Chernobyl was the start of recorded history for nuclear accidents, and what had happened on the Kola Peninsula nearly 40 years before was beyond their youthful frame of reference.

The younger man took the lead, bent over slightly against both the incline and the gusting breeze, providing a windbreak to the colleague behind him. Dr. Ivan Timishenko had done this walk many times over the last twenty years, and knew that even in early winter a full fox fur hat and mountain grade anorak were the order of the day. His elderly guest had no such experience, nor would he have been inclined to pay deference to the elements had Ivan patronised him with local advice.

If there was such a thing as a "household name" in the field of nuclear contamination study, Professor Andy Barton would have been it. Except, of course, no-one called him by his christened name. With a New Zealand accent that had lost none of its edge after 40 years of travelling the globe, he introduced himself as "Baaaaahton", but everyone he worked with, knew, or even had family ties with, had come to call him simply "Kiwi".

Kiwi was not a man to be intimidated by weather. He ignored the icy flecks which dotted the lenses of his cheap black-frame glasses, and as for keeping warm, a haystack of greying hair that fell over his ears and down to his collar would have to do. A trim of the worst patches of grey hair could probably have taken a decade off his apparent age, but he has long resigned himself to "looking like a faaahking badger". His summer-weight blue windproof was unzipped, but was so thin it would not have done much even fully closed. Beneath it Kiwi was wrapped in a thick brown fleck Icelandic sweater, but not to keep out the cold; he was just as likely to wear it to the beach; or to a wedding. It had been a snap purchase in Thule twenty years before, and would be worn until it was lost or it fell apart. Worn by a hipster in a juice bar in Brick Lane it would have been ironic upcycled chic. On Kiwi Barton, it just looked like an old bloke's tatty pullover.

Kiwi's 1980s pattern army lightweight trousers had also seen better days. But most days are, of course, better than a day spent rummaging around an off-grid highly contaminated Northern Fleet nuclear waste repository.

Unless, of course you are Kiwi Barton. In which case such days are what you live for.

~~

Collins shut the car door, and white gloved hands shaking, gripped the steering wheel and rested his forehead upon it.

On the doorstep he had braced himself against the anger he expected from Woolley's parents, putting on a professional countenance, his "game face", much as he had done each morning in Kandahar.

Which left him totally unprepared for how things panned out. Met with a firm and formal handshake by a tall middle-aged man whose frame filled the narrow hallway beyond the front door, Collins had been taken into a smart lounge which looked like it had been cleaned to within an inch of its life specially for the occasion. Woolley's father looked an unlikely participant in such an enterprise, blue collar, kind in demeanour but sparse in interaction, inviting the young Lieutenant to sit in the armchair which had pride of place view of the big T.V. which dominated one corner. His host sat too, joining Woolley's mother on the sofa, but she had instantly bolted to her feet to organise tea, leaving Collins to take the surroundings in, as the two men sat in awkward silence.

Collins had done his homework and knew Woolley was an only child, and this was born out by the photos on display, which told of a church wedding with a crowd of happy guests; a babe in arms cradled by proud parents; a shabby looking young lad in a green sweatshirt school uniform; and then, just as Collins had in his own quarters, the passing out photo, full dress blues, proud as punch.

Woolley had joined the Marines straight from school, and the image showed a fresh-faced version of the 25-year old veteran that Collins had come to tease and rely on in equal measure. Collins momentarily felt a pang of envy for the dead Corporal, struck by the pride and respect he could see that Woolley's parents clearly had for their son. His own such photo was a different affair, his younger brother still in University his only companion with Mum and Dad some time gone. As Collins took in the pictures above the mantelpiece, he saw for the first time that Woolley's dad was turning over his son's green beret between his fingers, as if seeking still a physical connection with the boy in the photos.

Ben tried to break the ice, and shake himself from his own self-pity. "I hear they are naming the fireman's carry in the Commando tests "Woolley's run"," he ventured.

"So we were told." The father's face creased into the slightest of smiles. "He would have liked that. Did you know he failed the fireman's carry in test week and had to re-take it?" Ben shook his head. "I guess he passed it when it mattered...."

Once Mrs Woolley returned to the room the next half hour had passed as if on auto-pilot. Collins could now recite the events of that day, every moment, every decision, every fire order, without missing a beat. But it was very different giving the account to Woolley's parents. They prompted him often for more, or asked him to go back over part of the account, but always with exaggerated courtesy. They would not dream of calling him Ben. It was "Mr Collins" or "Sir", throughout, as if by some sort of family osmosis the parents had adopted the norms of address that their son had used. It had occurred to Collins that Woolley would be taking the piss something rotten if he had been there, seeing the exaggerated regard “his” Lieutenant was being shown by his Mum and Dad.

Woolley's mother winced as he told of the wound her son had taken to his arm; then both parents lent forward and held each other's hand as the story came to its end. Collins was pleased to be able to assure them that the Corporal's death came quickly. He was congratulating himself for getting to the end with voice steady and clear when Mrs Woolley quietly asked, "And how about you Mr Collins? Are YOU alright?" That was the point where Collins broke up into heaving sobs, which soon spread to all those present.

Now leaning back in the driver's seat, Collins was about to start the car when he found his thoughts drifting back to a long-forgotten poem studied years before.

"Three hours ago, he stumbled up the trench;
Now he will never walk that road again:
He must be carried back, – not carefully now,
Because he lies beyond the need of care,
and has no wound to hurt him, being dead.
He was a young man with a meagre wife
And two pale children in a Midland town,
His mates considered him a useful chap
Who did his work and hadn't much to say,
And always laughed at other people's jokes
Because he hadn't any of his own.
That night, when he was busy at his job
Of piling bags along the parapet,
He thought how slow time went, stamping his feet
And blowing on his fingers, pinched with cold.
He thought of getting back by half-past twelve,
And tot of rum to send him warm to sleep
In draughty dug-out stuffy with the fumes
Of coke, and full of snoring weary men.
He pushed another bag along the top,
Craning his body outward; then a flare

Gave one white glimpse of earth and what he knew;
And as he dropped his head, the instant split
His startled life with lead, and all went out.
That's how a lad goes west when at the front,
Snapped in a moment's merciful escape;
While the dark yea goes lagging on its course,
With widows grieving down the streets in black,
And faded mothers dreaming of bright sons
That grew to men, and 'listed for the war,
And left a photograph to keep their place."

Collins' phone "dinged" with the sound of an incoming WattsApp message.

"How did it go?"

His heart skipped. It was Mazz.

~~

Ivan Timishenko stayed a pace or two ahead of Kiwi up the hill, but tried to chat as they made their way single file to the crest. "So, Kiwi, what about the Lop Nor accident? You got a look in yet?"

Kiwi Barton was puffing and panting behind him, but Ivan put this down to the scientist's considerable age disadvantage. "You have got to be faaking kidding me, right?", he replied in between gasping for breath. "It's taken me the best part of thirty years to get a look at this place!" "Not my doing I assure you." Timoshenko was not in prime physical shape either. Too little blood in the vodka stream, a balance he had been tweaking on the way up through judicious dosing from an opaque bottle in his pocket. "I know that," Kiwi shouted above the howling wind. "And to be fair it wasn't anyone this side. The Yanks told me for years that if I came this side of the fence I wouldn't be working for them again."

"So, what changed?" Timoshenko asked.

"Let's just say future employment prospects in the U.S. are no longer a factor I need to worry about," Kiwi said. Kiwi had managed to catch up a little and the two men walked side by side towards the structure he had come to see. A windowless, sheet metal warehouse, atop a cliff in the Russian arctic: to Kiwi, it was a nuclear accident location right out of central casting, but to the Russian fleet in the cash-strapped 1960's it was, sinister appearances aside, an entirely logical place to store highly radioactive nuclear waste from refuelling submarine reactors. Something of what happened there had leaked out to the west - if leaked isn't an unkind pun for three quarters of a million tonnes of radioactive waste pouring into the Arctic Ocean. But for Kiwi, to see this place close up was a long-held ambition. Timoshenko had something of the proud father about him as he pulled open a heavy steel door, which was set into the side of what Kiwi might have called a shed on the basis of its build quality, had it not been for its colossal scale: 100 metres long or more, necessary to house the two pools which its Soviet designers envisaged as the optimum short term storage for spent fuel rods. At the time of the Cuban Missile Crisis, no one on either side was really thinking about "long term storage." Entering the cavernous space, it took a moment for Kiwi's eyesight to adjust to the half-light. There was no power up here anymore, and the weak winter sunshine that found its way in through missing roof panels left him blinking to focus.

"Mind your step Kiwi," Timoshenko urged.

"Always."

Stretching before them was the outline of the two repository pools, each 300 feet long by 10 feet wide, both covered by a heavy steel and concrete cap which was sagging in some places, and actually missing in others. Timoshenko took Kiwi by the elbow. "Don't step on it Kiwi. There's a 20-foot void below the cover most of the way along. Bar, of course, the point where there are still 25 drums down there, snuggling in a pile of boron, warm and toasty." He laughed.

Now he was accustomed to the murk, Kiwi could make out the crane half -way down the structure, running on rails which would allow it to access all points of each pool. Back in the day, it was meant to carefully lower waste into position so that each 350kg drum would be suspended mid-depth with sufficient water separation from its fellows to avoid unwelcome interaction.

Except, of course, that's not how it turned out. Operator error and mechanical failures over the years had resulted in a pile of dropped drums in the base of the pool, thermal reaction between them splitting casings and spilling all manner of fission products into the water. Which was bad enough of itself: but the welds of the tank had been done to a specification that assumed the pool temperature would be kept at a steady level by controlled decay of elements within the drums. In the freezing Arctic, the heating and cooling the metal casing was subjected to from the volatile pool water proved too much, and 20 years in, about the time one Ivan Timoshenko was being brought into the world, the welds started failing.

Looking through one of the gaps in the cover panels, Kiwi peered down into the gloom. "I hope you are going to tell me the story of the flour bags is a myth?" Timoshenko laughed.

"Soviet crisis management at its best! When the leak started it wasn't too bad, but the pool water was way too "hot" with radioactivity to send someone in to find it. So, some genius decided to pour 20 sacks of flour down the side of the pool where they thought the containment was failing. Oh, for the good old days of dough-based weld repair!"

Kiwi grinned. "And then the fun really starts."

"Indeed. Within months one tank was running dry and the other was leaking. So, they started trying to haul the leaking drums out to go into safer dry storage. Then it got a bit Keystone Cops: one of the workers thought he could rely on the steel cover to hold his weight." Timoshenko pointed vaguely to the right. "I don't know if he was the most stupid one on site that day or the guy who dived in after him. They came out covered head to foot in beta decay products, God knows how they survived."

"And where did the waste end up?" Kiwi asked.

"Well apart from the 20,000 reasonably intact drums still here in the dry storage pits, the rest went for "safe disposal" at Mayak."

Timoshenko smirked and raised an eyebrow pleased at his in-joke. The Mayak storage facility had been the site of the Soviets first foray into catastrophic failures in nuclear storage. Poor cooling of a not dissimilar tank to this one had led to it running dry, leading to a massive chemical explosion which blew a 160-ton concrete shield off the top of the tank and showered reaction products into the skies over the Urals. The sorry souls living in that neck of the communist paradise could from then enjoy the day to day company of a distinctly unhealthy amount of strontium-90 and caesium 137, to go with the radioactive soup that they could swim in at the local lake, into which 6 reactors had dumped untreated waste for many years.

"Ah yes. How is the "East Ural Nature Reserve" coming along?"

Having belatedly decided to evacuate 10,000 people from the area two years after the 1957 explosion, the Soviets had turned the area off limits.

"Well, you have to admit the "rebrand" sounds better than the "East Ural radioactive trace" or better still than the "Zone of Death""

"And when do they reckon it will be safe? It's been 60 years."

Timoshenko shrugged. "Probably not this century. Drink?" The Russian pulled the bottle from his parka, and held it out to Kiwi.

"Thanks, but no." Kiwi raised a hand.

"Have you got all fussy about your vodka Kiwi?" Timoshenko took a swig himself.

"I am afraid I need something a little stronger," Kiwi said. He rummaged into the inside pocket of his anorak, and pulled out a small brown bottle.

"Oromorph nowadays I am afraid." He took a swig and winced.

"Shit Kiwi, I had no idea, I am sorry."

"Me too," said Kiwi.

Chapter 4

First impressions

Late November

After a month in post, Dr. Abaya Shah had become a favourite amongst the radiographers in Katie's unit. Calm and confident, she had adjusted quickly to a set-up which was not dissimilar to her training in Damascus a few years before, but light years from her recent experience in the war-ravaged city. While President Assad's beautiful wife could still count on the best of modern treatment for her breast cancer, Abaya had spent much of the last two years at a much more rudimentary level, interpreting X-rays and providing acute care to those gassed and wounded by the Syrian Army and I.S. forces. To see her in the unit in her spotless white coat, petite and smartly made up, it was hard to imagine her fielding the broken bodies of women and children brought in by the infamous "White Helmets" of the civil response teams. The team warmed to her: unlike some of the radiological registrars, she communicated no sense of superior status. While to the general public “radiographer” and “radiologist” might seem synonymous, the trained doctors who filled the latter posts, applying their clinical training to diagnose and determine treatment for the former to execute, were often prickly and defensive of their standing. "I prefer "radiation oncologist"," was a pet phrase of one of the less popular Lancaster doctors, keen to establish clear blue water from the likes of Katie and Shona. With Dr. Shah it was, instead, "Call me Abaya," to the point where she actually stopped and corrected those who addressed her formally.

As Katie came into the unit office, Abaya was peering at a M.R.I. image, face close to the computer screen and brow furrowed. Katie would have left other clinicians to it, but Abaya was always happy to chat and Katie keen to learn. More importantly, even from four feet away, Katie could recognise the scan features before she could read the patient name.

"Alice?"

"Uh huh." Abaya didn't take her eyes off the screen, and the frown didn't shift from her forehead.

"Not good?"

"No. You did her treatment sequence didn't you?"

"Yes, we finished two months ago, she had 5 treatments with the cyber knife. I didn't expect it to buy her much time. But at least maybe get her to Christmas. Is she relapsing?"

"See for yourself." Katie pulled a swivel chair across from the opposite desk and sat next to Abaya. She took her glasses out of her hip pocket. While she needed them more than she liked to admit, Katie had been the plain girl at school, and didn't think even her new frames flattered her.

Dr. Shah took the mouse and used the cursor to draw attention to the key features of the scan. "OK so you know Katie has a brain stem glioma?" Katie nodded. It was a grim condition with a jaw droppingly poor prognosis. "Well as you can see here, Alice is in worse category than most." Abaya moved the cursor to show Katie the faint outline on the screen. "Obviously in the brain stem surgery is a non-starter. It's too risky to even go in there and biopsy it. Which is where you came in. And because it's diffuse there is no way of removing all the abnormal tissue, so killing the fast-growing cells is the best we can do. But if it's recurring after cyber knife treatment I am not sure where we go next. If anywhere. It might be time to call it a day?" Abaya wrinkled her nose.

"Have you met Alice yet?" Katie asked.

"I am seeing her tomorrow in clinic," Abaya answered.

"See if you still want to call it a day once you have met her and her Dad."

~~

Collins had lost track of all the places where he had slept rough. Woodbury Common to start, the pebble-bed soil in Devon which was the start point of every Royal Marine's career. Then Dartmoor, the peat hags between the Tors soggy but soft, bar the occasional chunk of granite digging into your ribs. For variety the snows of North Norway on mountain and arctic warfare training, and then a thin Karrimat in his basha in Kandahar. But as he came to, his senses told him this was none of those. That is, those senses which were fully functioning, as his head appeared to have been hit by a large rock at some point the night before. His cheek was pressed against a cheap red carpet of dubious age, and a skirting board and magnolia painted wall progressively came into clear view. He seemed to have been drooling. Collins could sense he was in his "green slug" issue sleeping bag, and an aching hip told him he had slept rather too long on one side. Rolling over he saw above him the bed, wardrobe, and sink of a single officer's quarters, then a chest of drawers against which a black Leki ski pole was leaning - the sort used by elderly dentists looking to Nordic walk their way to fitness without actually breaking sweat.

Finally, facing away from him, a pair of slender long tanned female legs, topped by what would have been a butt to die for had it not been for the fresh dimpled scar just below the pant line of the left cheek. Maryam.

She was facing away from him applying mascara as she scrutinised herself in a mirror affixed precariously to the wall above her chest of drawers, but evidently sensed movement on the floor behind her.

"Aha! Back from the dead!" Mazz looked down at him with a cheeky smile and twinkle in her eye.

"What happened?" Collins groaned.

"Do you mean before or after you were downing two shots to each of mine so that you were "drinking Woolley's share"?"

"Both." Collins could see Mazz was well into her routine for the day, khaki T-shirt concealing the scar left by the wound that cost her the lower lobe of a lung. Finished with her make-up and embarrassed to be undressed in front of Ben, Maryam pulled on her combat trousers and fixed her stable belt, a horizontal stripe of grey nylon topped and bottomed by stripes of Cypress green, matching the distinctive green berets which gave the Intelligence Corps their nickname - the "Green Slime".

Mazz gestured to an empty brandy bottle on a coffee table. "You seemed to forget that this was my Dad's favourite tipple when I was growing up. He said if it was good enough for Winston Churchill it was good enough for him. He had me and my sister drinking it neat before we were out of boarding school."

Ben's fuddled memory started to register them necking toasts to Woolley, and to their own survival, into the early hours of the morning. He blushed with embarrassment. "I hope I didn't disgrace myself?" he said.

"Ben you were the perfect gentleman. As ever. Insisted on getting your sleeping bag out of the car and bedding down on the floor." Collins wondered if he was imagining a hint of regret in Maryam's voice. He put it down to wishful thinking.

Collins watched as Mazz put both hands behind her head and with the practice of years, rapidly fixed her glossy black hair into a tight French plait, before donning around her neck a souvenir of Katdelay: she had looped a leather lace through a hole drilled in the flattened Kalashnikov round recovered from the inside of her body armour, and now wore it around her neck: as if the pain and impediment of her hip wound and breathlessness on every flight of stairs were not enough reminder of how lucky she had been. Collins blushed again as he thought he saw Maryam catch him in the mirror gazing at the unadorned beauty of the back of her neck. But if she did, she didn't say anything.

"Ben don't you think you had better get up? School today remember?"

Ben had, indeed, forgotten. Time to get going.

~~

Kiwi surveyed the cheap packing boxes which seemed to fill every bit of floor space in his tawdry office in an anodyne block in the South of England. It was no longer the homely space it once had been, the souvenirs of forty years in his field now heaped haphazardly prior to removal to his loft in nearby Andover.

It would have taken someone with considerable knowledge of the field to identify his bits and bobs. Kiwi's keep-sake of Australia was a bomb initiator assembly, not your standard digeridoo or boomerang. There were signed photos of his time working with the U.N. on anti-proliferation in Libya and Iraq, and some signage from a decommissioned Russian Strategic Missile base dating from the 1990s. Of course, there was nothing whatsoever to tell of his time with "Lincoln Gold", the scientific support team which was on call to the US Delta Force to go whenever, wherever, to disarm or disable stolen or improvised nukes in the hands of the bad guys. Kiwi kept his own counsel as to who could most be considered the "bad guys" at any moment in time - but working with Delta on what they coded as their "0400" mission - anti nuclear proliferation and counter-W.M.D. - was certainly where the big bucks and smart minds had been for a few years. And for all his lack of attention to his personal wardrobe, Kiwi loved shiny new kit.

He sighed. There was still so much to pack. So much to do. So little time.

He flicked the light switch, and pulled the door locked.

~~

Mazz checked her phone while Collins showered and rushed to get dressed. It felt odd to him lacing up his boots: like the rest of his combat kit, it had lain unworn since his return. Dress blues for seeing the Woolley's, and for the funeral, No. 2 kit for his meeting with a Major Waters, then leave, he noticed the tips of his fingers colouring with Afghan dust as he knotted. No matter how hard you tried, the traces of Kandahar would not dissipate easily.

They headed down the stairs together to the hallway of the single officer quarters block. Framed sepia photos on the wall told of the building's heritage as the Officers' Mess of R.A.F. Upavon, originally site of the central flying school and therefore the self-declared "Home of the R.A.F." The base was now designated "Trenchard Lines", and the home of, amongst other things, the 1st Intelligence, Security and Reconnaissance Brigade. Collins had to remind himself that Mazz would not be bounding down the stairs alongside him for a while, still on much-restricted duty while rehabilitating. He slowed his step deliberately but still had to pause a moment at the foot of the stairs for her to catch up.

"So Mazz," he read deadpan from the Brigade Statement of Purpose, printed big and bold for all to see as they entered the hallway. "How does it feel to be "providing a conduit into the Single Intelligence Enterprise to ensure that information is shared with Joint, Interagency, intergovernmental and multinational capabilities"?"

She smiled. "I don't know yet. I'll let you know when you tell me what it's like standing all day, every day, beside a Scottish loch baby-sitting a submarine."

"Touché."

Collins laughed but did a poor job of masking how despondent he still felt. While expecting to be moved from his troop command at the end of Op. Lincoln, to be told by Major Waters that he was being posted out of the Commando, as much a home as any he had now, was devastating. For a fleeting moment, he hoped he might get a switch to 45 Commando, which was just starting its work up process for deployment as the lead force in Op. Lincoln 3. To be told he was going, not to Four-Two or Four-Five Commando, but Four-Three, the Fleet Protection Group, was the last straw.

Once a small force named "Commachio Company" after a battle in Northern Italy at the fag-end of World War 2, the unit responsible for last ditch safeguarding of the UK nuclear deterrent had been stood up as a full Commando five years before. But this effort to give it equal status didn't prevent it being the ugly sister of the Commando Brigade. While providing niche capability in maritime boarding teams and sniper capability on ships afloat, the be all and end all of 43 Commando was last-ditch security of the Trident force at Faslane. Clearly important work. But to get as far as being shot by a 43 Commando Nod, someone would have to get past the normal armed MOD guard force, then the MOD police tactical support group, who toted more firepower than a N.Y.P.D. S.W.A.T. team. This meant a posting to Faslane was about as welcome as a hole in the head. 43 Commando was typically split into penny packets, never deployed as a unit, and had none of the recent operational experience of Herrick, let alone Lincoln.

"Do you know what you are going to be doing yet?" Mazz asked, as they walked together into the car park.

"It's better than it could be," Collins admitted. "R Squadron. "Dynamic weapons security"."

"So, does that mean you jog up and down the jetty while you watch the submarine?"

"Ha. The warheads have to be shifted back and forth from a place called Coulport on the Clyde to Burghfield in Berkshire for a make-over every now and then. That's 400 odd miles over public roads. I guess that is going to be quite an enterprise. Time for me to get a "Little Chef" loyalty card I think!"

Collins fished his keys out of his pocket and dumped his hold-all from his shoulder onto the tarmac. The door lock of his Triumph Spitfire was as temperamental and unreliable as the rest of the vehicle, but he soon succeeded, and reached underneath the hood to the two levers at the top of the windscreen which allowed the driver to lower the tonneau.

Mazz raised an eyebrow. "Ben are you mad? It's freezing?"

He had to admit she was right. A frosty Salisbury Plain winter morning, but with a crisp clear blue sky.

"I know. But I had enough heat in Kandahar last summer to last me a long while. And anyway, this view is something else." He was right. Although Trenchard Lines itself is a typical unsightly complex of 1950s' shit-build concrete, Nissan huts, and large green hangars from the R.A.F. era, the view from its hilltop site across the rolling Plain is stunning. A cold winter day showed it at its best.

"How long before you have to go up North?" Mazz asked. She was leaning on her ski pole a little, left hip still not quite trusted.

"I am at Winterborne Gunner till Christmas." Collins wondered how she would respond.

Mazz took his left shoulder by the very tips of her fingers and planted a peck on his right cheek. "Be good at school."

~~

To describe first impressions of the Defence C.B.R.N. centre as only "underwhelming" would be to exaggerate the site's charisma.

In fact, a lost and inept Russian G.R.U. officer down from nearby Salisbury might surmise that village kids had twisted the red and white sign advertising its presence to misdirect the unwary through a decrepit estate. Social housing on the left of a narrow driveway, probably at one time service accommodation for the base, faced shabby bungalows on the right which had seen better days. Once past the housing the road dipped under a railway arch, before rising again to a dead end, the only way out of which was the guarded gate into the base. If you get invited to the U.S. Army C.B.R.N. centre at Fort Leonard Wood, Missouri, expect to drive up to a modern building with an expansive frontage redolent of a big corporate headquarters – carefully manicured lawn dotted with ramrod straight flagpoles, and a smart junior soldier doing jive style salutes as he checks those entering. In Winterborne Gunner you get instead a sorry looking gaggle of single-story buildings and a freezing cold MOD policeman called Keith in a little glass booth next to a flimsy metal barrier.

Satisfying Keith with his Marine I.D., Collins pulled up as directed in a car park in the back end of the site, and began the fiddly process of battening down the cover of the Spitfire, conscious he was barely going to make his 9 am reporting time. The car park was hardly a quarter full. But if he expected his vintage blue S registration Triumph to be the most distinctive vehicle there, he was about to be disappointed.

First heralding itself with a dull and distant bass beat of a subwoofer with as much power as the vehicle itself, then the throaty roar of an over revved high-performance engine, a bright red Subaru Impreza swept in through what should have been the car park exit and pulled to a halt facing away from the Spit'. The driver, unseen behind over tinted windows which would have suited the chosen transportation of a Baltimore pimp, chose to gun the engine hard twice before shutting it down, and was rewarded as he got a most satisfactory flash and boom from the double calibre exhaust as over-rich fuel/air mixture cooked off. Only then did he step out, donning a pair of mirrored aviator shades in a practiced movement as he did so. While the engine was now quieted, some banging trance music mix continued to blare until quieted by the chirp of the key fob.

Collins was not sure rural Wiltshire was ready for the tall blond uniformed figure who stepped forward, looking rather like Goose from "Top Gun", but with even less reserve and diffidence than a US Navy fighter pilot. The black and yellow number plate identified the new arrival as Dutch, his camouflage pattern not radically different to that Collins was wearing himself but with slightly bigger blocks of colour, more brown, more green, less sand, and a generally darker effect. A "Cloggie".

"Hey! I am Joop!" he called rather more loudly than was needed as he approached Collins, hand outstretched.

"So I see," Collins grinned and took his hand. "I thought you lot were all meant to be environmentally friendly?"

"Of course! Look!" In the back window of the Subaru was a sticker from the 1980s Cruise and Pershing Missile Cold War era - a happy orange smiling sun with the slogan "Nuclear Power - Nein Danke!"

"An interesting choice for visiting the Defence C.B.R.N. Centre," Collins laughed.

"Well if you can't find laughs in atomic catastrophe, where can you find them?"

Collins decided this might not be as bad as he had expected.

~~

The formalities of being identified and badged by a bored receptionist took 15 minutes, during which Collins established Joop had not expected to end up at Winterborne Gunner either. The Royal Netherlands Marines regularly send exchange officers to the Royal Marines, but as Joop explained, the Dutch government had not yet established its attitude to Operation Lincoln.

"I was meant to be going to 45 Commando in Arbroath, but once they were slated to go to Kandahar, the pissy Dutch government decided my young life was too precious to be thrown away in your Boys' Own Adventure. So, they decided my year in England is going to be spent protecting your nuclear deterrent." Joop fiddled with the clip of his laminate photo ID, which confirmed him as Lt. Joop de Jong. Unlike Collins' photo, a mug shot which made him look like a dodgy Eastern European truck driver on a murder charge, Joop's showed him with a broad and cheesy grin.

"The Dutch don't put a black mark against all things nuclear?"

"To be honest I don't think the government knows what 43 Commando do. So long as there is no chance of me coming back from Afghanistan in a wooden overcoat draped in a Dutch flag I think their interest ends."

"I tell you, they did you a big favour," Collins suggested.

"How come? I would have loved getting some action."

"Oh, not Kandahar. They saved you from months in a shit climate surrounded by an incomprehensible populace with no civilisation or prospects of redemption."

"Arbroath?"

"You got it."

They were interrupted by someone buzzing through the door which led into the rest of the ground floor of the C.B.R.N. school. A sixty-something man, who consistent with the slightly tired surroundings of the reception area, was clad in a shabby brown jumper, and worn black shoes which had not seen polish since first purchased. He wore no I.D., and could easily have been someone on the site team. He was not. Eyeballing the two young men in uniform, one tall, blond and dashing, the other taught and measured, he moved towards them and nodded.

"I think you are mine," he said, and gestured to them to join him back the way he had come.

"And you are?" Collins fished.

"You can call me Kiwi."

He led the two Marines down the corridor, passing a number of offices and seminar rooms on each side, none seemingly occupied.

"Is this place always this quiet?" Collins asked to break the silence.

Kiwi answered without breaking stride. "The next set of courses only start in January," he said. "The centre gets really busy when it's all in full swing. They do a big course for officers who are taking up C.B.R.N. posts in battle groups, training for medics to deal with C.B.R.N. casualties, that sort of thing. Most of it is training the trainers who do C.B.R.N. at unit level."

"And do you lead some of that?" Collins asked.

"Faak no", Kiwi answered. "Dull as ditchwater. Aside from the Russians playing silly buggers with novichok. My area is a bit more specialised."

"Nuclear weapons security?" Joop ventured.

Kiwi turned the door handle to the final seminar room on the left.

"Perhaps better to say "Nuclear weapons insecurity"". He grinned at them. "When good times go bad." He indicted them to sit at the conference table, and took his place at a lap-top set up at its head.

~~

Hurrying to pick up her bag and phone from the unit office at the end of the day, Katie waved an apologetic hand at Abaya who was on a phone call.

"No, not too long, maybe a half hour. You can sort something to eat for you and Emad yes?" Abaya rolled her eyes in impatience to Katie, as if she was on the phone to a culinary simpleton. Which she was. Apparently, the respondent was at least reluctantly cooperative in making dinner, as Abaya finished her call and tucked her mobile away.

She motioned at worn photos of two young men blue-tacked haphazardly to the top of her computer monitor. "My brothers. This one," she pointed at a Middle Eastern looking teenager in yellow swim shorts on a sun-lit harbour wall, sandy beach behind, "is Emad. That was on holiday in Beirut before the war, three years ago. He is seventeen now and in College."

"He looks just like you," Katie said.

"Ha!" Abaya laughed. "He wouldn't thank you for saying so. He has been tricky since we came up here to Lancaster. The other one", she pointed to an older young man sat at a table at some kind of family gathering. Dressed up in a cheap tan suit, the photo appeared to have been taken at a more formal setting - a wedding maybe. .."is Ali. He was always the smart one, but when the war came the University shut and he joined the white helmets. He will be an engineer one day. For now, he is a car mechanic."

"But he's no cook?" Katie asked.

"In Syria it's not a young man's work. Since Mum and Dad and my little sister were killed, he does what he can.

This town isn't the easiest place to find familiar things for him to cook."

"I am sorry."

"That's O.K." She smiled tentatively. "Grocery retail is a dynamic business," Abaya said deadpan.

"I meant your family," Katie said.

"I know. I am trying to learn the English doctor sense of humour," Abaya winked. "It's O.K. You will not find anyone from my generation in Damascus who has not lost someone. I was lucky that getting my job here meant I could get what was left of the family out."

"Shona thinks it's the West's fault how things have ended up in your country." The unit's professional Scot had continued to be not short of opinion on all things political.

"It might be best not to get me started on that," Abaya said. "If I don't finish this and get home, who knows what train wreck Ali will have concocted for dinner."

~~

Emad barely looked up from his Xbox FIFA game at the sound of Abaya fighting her way through the front door of their pokey flat, juggling house keys and shopping bags. She was pleased to smell something on the stove, exhausted from her days work, and with the prospect of another working day the same ten hours away.

Moving down the hall-way and into the kitchen, Abaya didn't pause to greet Emad, instead seeking out Ali who was stood awkwardly over the stove, tending a casserole of unknown origin and quality.

"I don't know what it's going to be like," he apologised.

"That's O.K." She dropped the bags at his feet, and took him in a close embrace, kissing him passionately as he cupped her backside and pulled her hips against him.

Chapter 5

Awakenings

Early December

Alice and her Dad were last on the out-patients list. Nasreen booked them in, and flipped the unit TV from BBC News24 to something more suitable for Alice. Her Dad, bedecked in his dark blue MOD police uniform, nodded in appreciation and sat with Alice watching.

He had learned it was never good to be called in to the unit "out of sequence". Their next scheduled check with Prof Ingram, Alice's consultant since she had first fell ill months before, was not until mid-January. Katie was in her normal routine, calling patients through for therapy, but John couldn't help but call her over when she came into the waiting area.

"Katie do you know why we are back? I was hoping for a break from treatment over Christmas?" His eyes implored her for good news. He saw from her face that she had none to give.

~~

For Ben and Joop, Monday had been an eye opener.

There are numerous dimensions to the world of military nuclear security. Much of Kiwis background had been in clean-up following nuclear testing, then in anti-proliferation by nation states. In passing he had consulted with the US in particular on prevention of inadvertent release, and this would bear on their work in 43 Commando: preventing someone within the forces accessing the code sets and mechanisms to allow unapproved access, and designing systems and protocols to safeguard the assets in state control. Ben remembered seeing Denzel Washington and Gene Hackman head to head in "Crimson Tide", and had battled out with Joop to remember which star of "Reservoir Dogs" began his Hollywood career overacting a gun toting missile post technician in "War Games".

Within 43 this kind of dockside security would be more the preserve of O Squadron. Joop and Ben would be rather more in the business of defending nuclear warhead convoys in transit from attack – what was usually called “SOE” or “Stand Off Escort”. Or failing that, recovering a warhead once stolen, but, as Kiwi said, "that's a soldiering task and if I wanted to know about that shit I would have signed up for Vietnam when I had the chance. You can do all that stuff with your unit at Faslane."

Kiwi was similarly clear that they were not going to be playing bomb disposal, or kicking the door in on wannabe bomb builders in Birmingham bed sits. "The RAF Regiment has 27 Squadron for counter CBRN warfare work, and there are a few secret squirrels you don't need to know about. If you two ever get to see the inside of a nuclear weapon things have gone very wrong indeed." Kiwi looked at Collins. "Would you trust Joop with a pair of pliers and a selection of wires to cut?"

Ben put his hands to his face in mock horror.

"There you go. And because you won't be dealing with a "dirty bomb" scenario, we can skip some of the science relating to the nastier isotopes like cobalt and strontium."

"Nastier than plutonium?" Joop was surprised.

"Oh, for sure," Kiwi said. "The "R" for Radiological is the forgotten sibling of C.B.R.N. But you can do an awful lot of damage with a radioactive isotope and a nasty imagination. You might have heard of a "cobalt bomb"? It used to be beloved of apocalyptic doomsayers, the route to the end of civilisation. Well, it's actually a hypothetical construct which we don't think has ever been built, but the physics is sound. The idea was to have a normal H bomb but salt it with Cobalt 59 in a component called the tamper. Cobalt 59 is stable, but the fission detonation turns it into Cobalt 60 which is shitty stuff. The effect would be to irradiate huge tracts of land and make them uninhabitable for years - Cobalt 60 has a half-life of five years, decays to Nickel, and in the process gives off a load of beta and gamma radiation. Even the Pentagon under Reagan thought a cobalt bomb wasn't cricket."

Joop looked vague at the mention of cricket. "I'll explain later," Ben assured him.

"Strontium 90 is even worse. That gets produced in a fission detonation but also in nuclear power plant accidents like Chernobyl. It has a much longer half-life than Cobalt so it hangs around longer. It's not so radioactive but it's a bone-seeker. Because it's in the same periodic table group as calcium, the body takes it up from the environment and tries to use ît the way it would use dietary calcium - for forming teeth, bones, and so on. It will stay in your body for a decade, give you bone cancer, leukacmia, lots of nasties."

Kiwi took off his glasses and cleaned the lenses absent-mindedly. "It's really not stuff you want anywhere near you."

He continued, "The C.B.R.N. Squadron have to consider all those kind of isotopes as the kind of thing terrorists might exploit, and the authorities keep a very close track on those who have to use them in industry for legitimate purposes. But you have other fish to fry".

"By far the most likely situation you will need to deal with isn't a gang of Russian Spetsnaz hanging out by the side of the A1, or a miserable naval rating looking to blow us all up because he has got a "Dear John" letter. Road accident, fire, vandalism is the enemy. I need you to know and understand what happens to nuclear hardware when you expose it to those insults."

Kiwi clicked on his laptop and the screen was filled with a Diesel Locomotive coming at full pelt towards the camera. It was not a variant of train that Collins recognised, light blue in colour apart from a blue roof, two large buffer pads the size of tea trays extending out in front of it. The engine showed no signs of streamlining - the days when British engineering was all brute force and little design. From the make and model of attendant police cars and fire engines in the foreground as the camera tracked, the footage was evidently from the UK, but looked badly dated - Collins guessed from the 1980s, so about as old as his cherished Spitfire.

A second camera shot showed a low-loader trailer from an articulated lorry, on which was sat a white metal cube, about the size of the passenger compartment of an old Land Rover, deeply grooved, and marked in places with the yellow and black industry-standard radiation hazard sign. There was no tractor unit, and the low-loader had been set up astride the railway lines at a level crossing point.

Kiwi paused the film. "So, this was one of the first public demonstrations of the absolute safety of nuclear material in transit. It appeared on national news in the 80s. At the time the U.K. Nuclear industry had a deservedly shitty reputation for safety, and the tree-huggers were making a big fuss over refuelling rods being taken to and fro to Sellafield for reprocessing. Of course, no one in government gave two shits about the tree-huggers. But they did give a shit about the potential share price of the soon to be privatised arms of the industry. Hence this piece of smoke and mirrors.."

He pressed play, and had the usual experience, beloved of users of Windows media across the world, of it taking three goes to get it to work. "Faaking thing..."

The film leapt into life once more, and now tracked the Locomotive at high speed from left to right, a gaggle of bystanders in the foreground watching it hurtle towards the low loader. Impact. The white metal flask and low loader disappeared in a violent storm of metal fragments, bit of train chassis, bogies, and a cloud of grey-brown smoke interspersed with licks of flame. The camera had to continue to pan quickly as the welter of debris flew off to the right with little of the momentum of the train dissipated.

"Those buffers weren't very effective," Joop said.

Kiwi glanced up at him. "I think you and I are going to get on just fine," Kiwi replied.

~~

It was a downcast little group that shuffled past the Hospital pharmacy and through the sliding doors into the December evening rain. It was still only 4.30pm but there was already little natural light, John and Alice's faint shadows joined by that of Alice's aunt, who had accompanied so that John could see Prof. Ingram and Dr. Shah alone. While Aunt Janet had heard nothing of the consultation, John had done a poor job of concealing his despair, and she had rapidly switched in to take the lead on keeping the mood light. Alice was excited about her school nativity, and as far as she was concerned, a month of no treatment and with some improvement to her headaches and sickness, there was no reason not to be excited about Christmas.

Even in the gloom John and his daughter cast a distinctive outline to Katie, emerging from the Royal Lancaster's edifice behind them. She knew what the team planned to share with the family - but also that what a parent is told and what they actually hear can be two very different things. Katie guessed that supportive aunt or not, he might appreciate some kindness, and called softly after him.

The burly policeman turned towards her, not releasing his grasp of Alice's hand. "Oh. Katie. I suppose you know the score."

"Only a little," she lied. "Do you want to talk about it? I have only got a ready-meal lasagne waiting for me at home."

John saw little point in any more discussion; but was reluctant to be rude and was keen, as always, to set the best of examples to his precious daughter.

"The League of Friends is still open," Katie said, pointing back at the brightly illuminated foyer. "I can treat you to a cup of tea?"

"To be honest, I could do without spending any more time than needed in hospitals," John said. "But if you don't mind Janet?" His sister speedily assented to head home with Alice. John bent down to give the little girl a bear hug, explained that Katie might have some advice to help them, and joined her, sharing a single umbrella as they made their way back up the hill."

~~

Dr. Shah was working late again, as had become her habit. She was pouring over a dog-eared and coffee-stained manual for the old Cobalt machine as Shona came into the unit office.

"Oh my goodness Abaya, I don't think anyone's looked at that for years," Shona said. "Swotting up?"

"It's quite like what we used back in Damascus but not so well maintained!" she answered. "But at least these are easier to fix than people."

"It's a scandal," Shona said. "Here we are in England using worse kit than you had in a war zone."

Abaya frowned. "Shona I think you are maybe a bit sharper than the others here, but the scandal is not here. In Syria I was treating kids blown apart by Assad's barrel bombs, and with burn wounds down to the bone from white phosphorous. We had to pack mud on top of the phosphorous wounds to stop the stuff burning. And then there were the chlorine victims, weeping and retching, being hosed down so they didn't contaminate those in the rest of the unit."

"I thought that was just propaganda to get the Americans to help," Shona said, sitting with her elbows on her knees.

"If only they had helped I wouldn't have had to bury my sister. All the bullshit about who was responsible for the gassing, Obama shrugging and leaving that bastard Assad to murder us," Shona was shocked to hear Abaya speaking this way. "That little girl Alice we saw last thing today? All the thought being put into her care when she is doomed already? It makes me wonder where was the help for Reem? Where was the help for my sister? You English don't know how lucky you are."

"English?" To Shona it was an insult not an error. "Don't you bundle me in with them. I am sick to death of the way my people are being shat on by London. I do my bit."

An awkward silence fell between them

"I am sorry Shona," Abaya said, eyes tearing up. "I did not mean to offend you. I know you understand.

"I am sorry about your sister," Shona added.

"You were not to know," said Abaya, standing on tip-toe to put the manual back on a shelf. She started to sort her things ready to go home. "Tell me Shona, Alice's father, he is some sort of police officer?"

"Not normal police," Shona replied. "MOD police. The Ministry of Defence. They guard army and navy bases. Like down on the coast where the nuclear submarines are built."

"Oh I see. It must be very hard doing such an important job with a sick child. He was very upset. I shall try to look after him." Abaya checked her phone, donned a thick coat, and headed off shift.

~~

John sat at a corner table in the League of Friends, scrolling backwards and forwards through his diary. With the prospect of more treatment for Alice through Christmas, things were going to get tricky. It had been hard enough already, trying to sort shifts around her Cyber knife treatment. Had he been honest with himself, he would have realised stressing over his schedule was a substitute for dealing with the real issue. This time next year he would be without Alice.

Katie approached, fair hair with a wet sheen from the rain. John wondered if the watery over milked teas she was marshalling in polystyrene cups on an overlarge tea tray were going to be much help.

As Katie sat, John looked at her disconsolate. "I thought it couldn't get worse," he said, squeezing his temples between fingers and thumb. "I guess I should have known. It can always get worse."

"Do they have a plan?" Katie wondered if they were at the point where all that could be offered was palliative care.

"Prof. Ingram said the only thing left which might buy us a year is proton beam therapy." Katie noticed that like many parents and patients, John had already made himself an expert in his child's condition, forced by circumstance into expertise he never needed or wanted. Proton beam therapy was being sold as the "next big thing" in radiotherapy. Strictly speaking, it wasn't really radiotherapy at all, using high energy protons fired from a linear accelerator. The advantage came from being able to use higher doses, as the beam could be sharply focused, the protons not staying energetic and causing damage as they exited he body.

"He said the evidence was still patchy as to whether increasing the dose would help Alice. But in any event, she may never get the chance to find out." Katie knew full well that there wasn't a proton beam set-up within 50 miles of Lancaster, and they had never referred anyone for the treatment.

John spoke wearily, "America has 30 proton beam units. Jesus, the Mayo Clinic has 8 treatment rooms all by itself. There are some up and running in Germany, Japan, Italy, China. If we were in Poland or the Czech Republic we would be better off. But in England? We are like the bloody third world. Oh, except we are not. We have money to build nuclear submarines at £1billion a go. But not to help my Alice.

"I thought they announced some beam units are being built?" Katie suggested, more optimistically than she felt..

"Three, apparently. The nearest one is in Northumberland, of all places. Dr. Shah is calling all of them to see about availability. But even then Prof. Ingram is going to have to make a special case bid to the Trust to get them to fund the treatment. All the three centres are being built with private money, and they charge the NHS case by case, £100,000 a go. The Prof said that he thought he could make a case based around my losing my wife already, and Alice being all I have." He gazed into his tea hopelessly.

"How is she in the meantime?" Katie asked.

"She is good." John brightened. "Full of beans. Looking forward to Santa and all that. We will try to make Christmas really special, obviously." He brightened, but only briefly. "Because the M.R.I. is looking grim."

~~

Abaya cleared the dirty plates away into the sink and sat down at the table, bringing a bottle of beer for Ali as she did so.

"So, how do we stand?" he asked Abaya.

"Getting the Cobalt source was always going to be the easy part," Abaya began. "For refuelling it has to be easily removable from the head of the machine, and it comes out in one piece. The Cobalt source itself is about 3cm by 10cm, and it sits in a shroud of tungsten and lead, so it's quite safe to remove. The whole unit is only the size of a couple of house bricks. I can easily get it out."

Ali was listening closely, beer in hand.

"But then our problems start. We have known all along that we will only have until start of shift the next day before the alarm is raised. So everything else has to be ready, and we have to be on a flight or ferry that night."

Ali nodded. "That's not a problem. We can be at an airport within an hour. Flights go to Turkey several times a day, even at this time of year."

"Indeed," Abaya said. "But getting home and out of reach is the easy part. You want this to be spectacular yes?". It was an entirely rhetorical question. All three of them had been clear from the outset on the purpose of their long odyssey from Syria. "So, the problem remains: how do we use the unshielded source to cause maximum panic? If we could get a Cobalt-60 source without anyone knowing there would be some good options: hide it maybe in a public space with a really big footfall. Maybe a shopping centre? Or a railway station. It sits doing its dirty work irradiating passers-by - then we inform the papers and the police in one hit. There would be mass panic. No one understands radiation - the fact that few people would have got much of a dose in neither here nor there. You would have photos of that Russian guy Litvinov.."

"Litvinenko," Ali corrected.

"Litvinenko then," Abaya continued, a little irritated. "Everyone thinks they are going to go bald and die. Let them experience the fear we had to live under of Assad's gas attacks, while they all sat back smug and let him do whatever he wanted. In the 1980s there was a big scandal in Brazil. Some scrap dealers stole a radiotherapy machine from an abandoned hospital site, and the first the authorities knew was when them and their family turned up with radiation burns. It killed a handful of people, and hundreds of thousands ended up being checked for contamination."

Ali was unpersuaded. "It's not enough Abaya. I didn't come to live like this", he waved his hand around them, "for a publicity stunt. Or to make a political point. I came here to avenge my friends. And your family. People have to pay. They have to suffer like my squad did. Like your sister Reem did. Let them feel the pain and helplessness. Let their ambulance crews have some of the despair we had of dealing with mass casualties - of not even knowing what is wrong with them. Who has even heard of Cobalt? The government will get the media to spin that it's all a false alarm, and without dead and injured to prove otherwise we will have achieved nothing."

"Ali, I understand," said Abaya. "But if you want something more lethal and dramatic there are some practical problems."

"Go on."

"The Cobalt source is a lump of metal. To pulverise it or vaporise it so that it carries far and wide, we would need high explosive. C4, Semtex, something like that. That is way out of our reach. Of course, making low explosive, anfo, or something similar, that is basic chemistry. But the security services here are all on the look-out for people buying the component ingredients: and even if we made it successfully, the effect when it goes off is like one of Assad's barrel bombs. It goes off with a "heave", not a supersonic blast front. So, you would get a big bang, and probably plenty of casualties from the explosion, and as soon as the police turn up they would do their checks and find that there is radioactivity at the scene. But all we would have done is throw the Cobalt core a hundred metres down the road for someone in a hazmat suit to pick up." Abaya got up and fetched herself a beer from the fridge, continuing to think aloud as she did so.

"The alternative is to prepare the Cobalt core into a form which is easier to spread, harder to clean up, one that would create a big decontamination problem."

"So how about if we milled it?" Ali asked. "We have a lathe at the garage. If we powdered it. Or cut it into ribbon or filaments? Then an explosion would be effective in hurling tiny pieces far and wide? And anyone caught in the blast would have not just their injuries to cope with, but radioactive fragments of Cobalt embedded in them. Set it off in the open air, choose a windy day so even after the blast the debris gets far downwind?"

Abaya looked sceptical. "You understand the problem with preparing the Cobalt source in that way?" she asked.

"Of course," Ali said. "It's highly radioactive. I expect they have to take all sorts of precautions when it's being manufactured. Don't worry. I have no desire to come to harm. We have a computer-controlled lathe at the garage that we use for bits and bobs. It's no different from the ones in the engineering faculty back at the University. I would be exposed briefly while setting the Cobalt in place, but then it can work automatically. I could set it to grind away or strip the cylinder of Cobalt into ribbon, whatever you want. I don't know how long it would take. How hard is Cobalt? I am guessing pretty hard. I know they sometimes put it in as a strengthening element in alloy steel."

"That sounds promising." Abaya was heartened. "Now you have the dimensions of the cylinder, do some tests at the garage, check programming the machine is as easy as you think. And start buying up peroxide. At a very slow tempo, never the same place."

"What about you?" Ali asked.

"Something has come up at work which might provide a different opportunity. I need to dig a little more."

They clinked the neck of their beer bottles together. Things were going well.

~~

Shona had got the first tweet from the Nukespot feed at tea time: "Convoy reported Northbound M40 Bicester, four units".

Ten years before that might mean nothing for anyone in the North to do until the next day: the convoys had used a range of way points on the way up country to laager overnight securely: mostly army or airbases like R.A.F. Wittering or MOD sites in Stafford or Preston. The Nukespot group would have a chance to get a sense of whether convoys were taking the western route up the increasingly congested M6, or one of the eastern routes up the M1 or A1M. But someone had clearly decided that having Defence Nuclear Material - the authorities' euphemism for H-bomb warheads - lying around overnight in a hard-to-secure facility was not ideal. In particular, having warheads on an active airbase was a very bad idea when the MOD's own modelling suggested the most problematic accident that could befall warheads in transit would be an aircraft crashing on top of them.

Now, therefore, the convoys operated "continuous running", even in the depths of winter. That meant no more than brief pauses at secure crew change locations, so that weary drivers could be changed and the security detail refreshed, before the convoy would restart its journey to distant Coulport. Twitter and social media had part-enabled Nukespot to respond to the challenge, getting loyal supporters in position to log movement to and fro, even where convoy commanders changed routing to dodge around traffic issues.

Shona had long since concluded that logging warhead movements was achieving about as much as her childhood years wasted camped by the fence in Faslane. Posting photos on a website? Burying the MOD in freedom of information requests? Getting friendly MSPs to ask questions in the Scottish parliament? These token actions had done nothing. The years passed. Instead of Polaris warheads being moved it was Chevalines; instead of Chevalines it was Trident. If nothing more eye-catching was done, nothing would change.

But for what she had in mind, understanding and predicting the routing of the convoys would still be essential. And that meant forsaking a planned night in the warm with "I am a Celebrity get me out of here", and joining the rag tag bunch which currently made up the Lancashire caucus of Nukespot to see what was on the road tonight.

Shona did not drive, and stepped gingerly down her poorly lit front path to the point where a dark Citroen Cactus was double parked, engine running. She smiled at Duncan, a longstanding local Geography lecturer, who had reached across and swung open the passenger door. But then yelped, alarmed at the apparition in the back of the vehicle. Two additional passengers, each hidden by the trademark Guy Fawkes mask of "Anonymous", the anti-government anti-secrecy counter-culture wannabees were sat there, deadpan. One was gazing ahead; the other could apparently see sufficiently well to be tapping away at what appeared to be Snapchat on his or her mobile phone.

"This is Darren and Steven from my "Global Zones of Conflict" class," Duncan said brightly, apparently seeing nothing amiss in their choice of attire.

"Oh for fuck's sake," Shona muttered. She feared it was more audible than she had intended.

~~

Shona's inner despair was not helped by Duncan getting lost on the way out of town, grumpily excusing himself that the new Sat Nav was "very hard to interpret." Shona resisted the urge to make jokes about a Geography lecturer not knowing his way around his own town, hoping only that they could get to the point on the overhead bridge above the M6 to see the convoy pass.

The site was, at least, one Duncan had used before, and he pulled the car into a farm field gateway just before the bridge. Shona hopped out as quickly as she could manage, and flipped the front seat so that the two youths in the rear could extricate themselves. This they did with difficulty, neither deeming it appropriate to take off their mask to expedite the process. Shona left them to it, and headed up the way along the wet tarmac of the highway to the point where a brief expanse of footway had been added, skirting a single track bridge overlooking the motorway. Given the delay caused by Duncan's fussing, she was unsurprised that no sooner was she in place than the blue strobe of an emergency vehicle illuminated the night sky down the carriageway of the northbound motorway. The tempo of the flashes changed as further, unseen, vehicles, added their own drum beat of blue light. It was eerie to have the night sky strobe-lit by multiple vehicles without any of the sirens which normally would accompany such an intimidating force.

Shona got her phone ready to video the vehicles as they passed. They had previously chosen this spot because the bridge overlooked a long straight, such that a single image would often capture the convoy in its entirety, and so it proved tonight.

Coming into view, it appeared to Shona the typical arrangement she had seen before. Heading the motorcade was a police outrider, with another in what the police would call "lane 2", making sure any overtaking vehicle gave the convoy wide berth. A conventional looking Police Range Rover came next, though Shona knew these would not be any conventional police - most likely a heavily armed team from the MOD police Special Escort Group. Only behind the escort came the first of four articulated lorries. In the artificial lighting it was impossible to tell what colour the vehicles were - from seeing them previously in daylight Shona knew them to be the same dark green used by any military vehicle. They were more distinctive in any event by their total lack of any company logo or branding, which was completely out of kilter with the other brightly decorated and internationally based lorries which were the norm on the inside lane of any motorway. There was no L.E.D. disco strip halo-ing the driver like an H.G.V. Jesus, no discarded coffee cups or crisp packets on the dash. Each 7-axle lorry had standard six digit MOD plates, and the spacing between vehicles was impeccable - no tailgating microns apart, in the style of some Latvian who had driven right across Europe on a diet of energy drinks and Internet pornography. Between each lorry and its companion was a Mercedes van, unremarkable bar its military colouring and emergency blue lights flashing on its roof, adapted suspension concealing that its panels hid Kevlar armour and further teams of armed police. Finally, some way behind, came a conventional and rather shiny fire engine, albeit from R.A.F. stock rather than the civilian fire service, followed by a large tow truck capable of recovering one of the articulated lorries should it break down.

Having framed the shot and pressed record, Shona was able to take in Duncan leaning on the railings beside her. And then beyond him Darren and Steven. They had their backs to the convoy passing below, and still wearing their "Guy Fawkes" masks, were taking a selfie with the convoy in the background.

"There has to be something better to do than this," thought Shona, despondent.

Chapter 6

Road trip

The Recaro passenger seat of Joop's Subaru was comfortable enough, which compensated for all other aspects of a journey which had been distinctly uncomfortable. Leaving Winterborne Gunner first thing, Joop determined to dodge the likely jams on the M4 and M25 and instead headed North to Oxford, only then ducking East to their destination. Collins had his suspicions that the choice of route had more to do with Joop's apparent aspiration to be the next Max Verstappen, slamming down two gears before blasting past slower traffic, immune to the muttering of Kiwi in the back seat. The Sat Nav suggested that Collins wasn't imagining the speed of their progress, as their destination E.T.A. came down from 1100 to 1058 to 1055. For musical accompaniment of their headlong passage to Suffolk, Joop had chosen one of his inumerable trance music playlists, promising, "Ben you will be converted by the time we get there." Collins was sceptical.

By mid-morning they were passing signs for the American airbases at Mildenhall and Lakenheath, but the distance to destination still showed a dozen miles to go. Kiwi had told them only on arrival that morning that they were "Going on a little field trip", and had given Joop a

Thetford postcode as their destination. He said that they were going to look at "some ancient history."

Thetford forest came and went, and Collins watched more open farmland passing in a blur. This corner of East Anglia was sparsely populated, and with farming in the area all arable, signs of life were few and far between. By-passing Thetford itself, and sparing its inhabitants the sound of what Joop assured Collins was a "Jorn van Deynhoven trance classic", their route moved onto narrow B roads, which Joop seemed to enjoy all the more, sustaining his breakneck pace.

"I don't know why the Dutch government were worried about you getting killed in Kandahar, Joop," Collins suggested. "You seem perfectly capable of killing yourself in peacetime, and us with you. I know you are a "Cloggie" but there is no reason to drive like you are actually wearing some."

"Collins you are just not used to any car with more than 4 gears," Joop fired back.

Notwithstanding the tinted windows on the Subaru, he was wearing not just sunglasses – but the "Arctic explorer" type, thin frame, reflective orange lenses, and with the leather side panels between the frame and temple to prevent snow blindness. Ben had pointed out the lack of ice floes in Suffolk, even in December. Joop had clearly seen the movie "Starter for Ten", claiming dead-pan that, like James McEvoy, he had "clearly been poorly advised." Kiwi expressed thanks that there was only three of them, so "at least there will still be room for Joop's "faaking huskies"."

Joop's response to teasing was to change down a gear and go even faster, but Kiwi, sat in the back, soon tapped him on the shoulder to indicate a straggly patch of trees the other side of the field which the road was skirting. "We are here."

Turning right at the next junction, Collins could see between the trees a metal gantry holding a flimsy and corroded watchtower - akin to those in a World War Two P.O.W. escape movie, but with none of the air of malign intent. It all looked rather sorry for itself, 1950s shabby. It overlooked an interlocking series of fences of no real purpose now, with gaps and breaks in many places: a fence which looked like it would have been rather token in its effect even when the place had been in its heyday long ago. Then beyond the tower and fences was a series of low buildings and earthen berms, some substantial single-story brick structures, others rather odd, almost like cubicles, little taller than a standing person and about as wide and deep. Collins thought they resembled a public toilet; or, if you wanted to continue the P.O.W. theme, some kind of isolation cell.

"This, gentlemen, is R.A.F. Barham."

"Never heard of it," Collins said.

"The Air Force would be very disappointed if you had. This, for ten years, was one the V-bomber force's atomic bomb storage sites."

~~

Prof Ingram was on the phone to Abaya first thing, delighted.

"The trust has approved proton beam for Alice! Can you get onto the centres and see if there is any movement on treatment slots for her? As close as you can get? If we are to have any effect, time is of the essence."

"Of course," Abaya replied, albeit annoyed that as ever, his tone with her treated her as his skivvy rather than his right hand.

The company which had a private unit in Northumberland had another one in Reading - then there was N.H.S. units at the Christie in Manchester, or U.C.L.H. in London. Abaya emailed them all.

~~

Kiwi, Joop, and Ben got out of the Subaru. Joop retained the dark glasses in spite of the light level in this corner of rural Suffolk being as grim as normal on a winter morning.

"Now Joop, are you sure you don't need a white stick and guide dog?" Collins asked.

Joop ignored him

As they walked Kiwi explained the set up. At the time when the V-bomber force was the single component of the U.K.'s nuclear arsenal, two sites provided storage for the nation's weapons of last resort. R.A.F. Barnham served the southern group of V-bomber bases, such as nearby R.A.F. Honington, and further away R.A.F. Wittering, Cottesmore, and Marham . Up in Lincolnshire a second depot at R.A.F. Fadlingworth provided the same facility for the Valiant, Victor, and eventually Vulcan bombers on northern bases.

"I don't get it," Collins said. "I thought the bombers were all armed and fuelled, and ready to go at a moment's notice?"

"Eventually yes," Kiwi answered. "But this was built in 1954, and at that time Sputnik hadn't even been launched. I.C.B.M.s were way in the future, and there was an expectation that we would have a decent warning of an attack. While the number of weapons on each side was small, there was an assumption that an alert force of bombers would set off on their first mission with the weapons on-base, and then still have a base to return to. Weapons would be shifted from here to the front-line airfields for a second set of attacks".

"Jesus". Born after the wall came down, Collins had not had to grow up with the horrific norms of thinking of the 1950s.

Kiwi continued, as they walked on into the derelict site. "By the early 1960s the weapons were smaller and safer. It was decided that having a depot like this storing weapons between their construction at Burghfield and the jet bases was not very secure".

"No shit," said Joop, unimpressed at the ramshackle set up. "It wouldn't take much to break in here."

"Indeed. But getting away with anything would be rather harder." Kiwi indicated the two largest structures, "This is where the aerodynamic bomb cases were kept. The first British A-Bomb was called the "Blue Danube": it was bigger than a Transit van. The second, "Red Beard", was not much smaller. You couldn't lift one in the back of your Land Rover and crash the gates. The risk was not so much of attack or of theft: it was the weapons themselves that were the hazard. Which is where the "hutches" come in."

Kiwi pointed to the cubicles Collins had noted earlier. Now they were deep into the site he could see they were grouped in clusters, each cluster with a dozen "hutches", each hutch 5 metres of so from its neighbours. Paved walkways connected each hutch to a central walkway, rather like the veins on a leaf. "Any guesses?" Kiwi asked.

"From what you said they are too small to be bomb stores," Joop said. "The spacing is odd. It doesn't make efficient use of all this space. It looks like it was important to keep some things separate from each other."

"Not bad Joop. We will make a nuclear soldier of you yet. These highly secure and state of the art facilities, gentlemen, are where the actual bomb cores were kept. In this cluster here, there was enough plutonium explosive power stored to take out all of the major cities of European

Russia. Or, mishandled, to flatten the whole of Eastern England."

They followed Kiwi down one of the narrow footways to the closest of the hutches. Collins noticed that the door wasn't even solid steel, merely a veneer of steel which was peeling away from a rotten wooden base. The roof was bitumen felt, only the brickwork of the cubicle itself showing any sign of permanence. Kiwi pulled the door towards him, revealing an interior which could, without much stretch of the imagination, have been a long-drop shitter in Tangiers: a bare concrete floor in the midst of which was a circular hole about 50cm wide and similar in depth.

"This," he said, "is where a single core was stored. The pit would have been lined with stainless steel back then, and this plaster and floor", he tapped the wall, "is grit free to reduce the risk of striking a spark. And of course a key essential is keeping each core separated from its friends to avoid them interacting, hence the 50-odd hutches. So whenever a weapon needed transferring to a squadron, they would pull the core out of the ground", he held his hands apart to indicate the rugby ball size dimensions of a single core, "put it on a trolley, and wheel it along the walkways to the assembly building. There, the core gets slotted into the physics package with all the fusing and other components, and that unit goes into the bomb casing. Bobs your uncle."

"It's all a bit "Heath Robinson"," Collins said.

Kiwi shrugged. "We do need to remember they were in uncharted territory. And this site, bless it, does show that they recognised from the outset one of the fundamentals of weapons safety. Notice gents that the assembly building is separate to the core hutches." There was, indeed, not just space between them, but also a large earthen berm. "The explosive lenses that blast the plutonium into a critical mass over some poor Russian city are allowed nowhere near the fissile material until the last possible minute. Today's take-away lesson, my boys, is that explosives and fissile material don't mix. We will see back at Winterborne what can happen if you get casual about that."

They began to wend their way back to the car. The atmosphere was not a little sombre. This was a monument to the doomsday mindset of the 1950s and 1960s.

"Pub lunch gents?" Kiwi suggested, looking to brighten mood.

"Sure. Orange Juice for you though Joop. You drive badly enough sober!", said Collins.

The Dutchman didn't reply - he was fiddling with his phone to find a new track.

"Looking for "Blue Danube"? I can't imagine it's in your repertoire," Collins asked.

"Something altogether more appropriate I think." Punching play and starting the engine, the music began with the all too familiar trance music 138 beats per minute baseline. Joop talked over the music. "This is "Cosmic Gate" - "So get up"".

A sampled voice spoke over the top of the bass beat and melody. An American male voice, speaking in the style of a 1950s Cold War public service announcement, first sombre but then demanding.

"The end of the earth is upon us....soon this will all turn to dust....so get up!..forget the past!...let's go outside and have a blast!.......have a blast..blast..blast..blast." The music came to a crescendo and a powerful bass drop.

"Not bad Joop," Ben said, grinning. "I think you may have found one that I like."

~~

Getting back in the Subaru, Collins expected to be headed back to Winterborne. But Kiwi had other plans.

"Joop, we have a stop off on the way. Can you put Maldon in the Sat Nav?"

The Dutchman complied, and found the on-screen route planner setting course for a point somewhere in the Essex backwoods, where the Blackwater River meets the North Sea. It was an hour away, and the two Marines tried to grill Kiwi on the way as to what they were going to see. The old A-10 bases at R.A.F. Bentwaters and Woodbridge were only a few miles away, as was Rendlesham forest, site of a notorious U.F.O. sighting in the 1980s, but neither could see much relevance to their supposed training to defend Nuclear Materials against theft or extortion.

But Kiwi's agenda was rather bigger. After pulling up beside a farm gate, the Prof. led them over it awkwardly, and they made their way down a muddy track towards the water, spindly poplar trees marking a thin island out across the narrow estuary.

"So, what's to see?" Ben asked.

"Now?" said Kiwi. "Nothing. Nothing at all. Especially with the tide in. But had you been here a thousand years ago, facing out to Thorney Island over there, you would have had at your back two dozen Anglo Saxon nobles and hundreds of fyrdmen, called into action to defend against some Vikings marauding up and down the coast. To your front would be the Vikings, stuck on Thorney Island over there, unable to come ashore because the causeway across at low tide would only take two warriors at a time. And they had no wish to come across two by two to be cut down by the English."

"So," said Joop, "A Mexican standoff. What happened?"

"The English leader was called Brithnoth, a nobleman from Northumbria. The Viking leader sent a messenger and asked if the English would let them come across in good order and form up on the dry land where we are standing, so that they could have a fair fight."

"I am guessing he did the noble thing?" suggested Ben.

"Of course. Old English honour demanded nothing else. And, pragmatically, if Brithnoth had said "No", then the Vikings would have sailed off somewhere where the English forces were not, and plundered and killed as suited them. So, he let them form up, and so began the Battle of Maldon, 991 A.D."

Kiwi rummaged in his cagoule pocket and pulled out a much thumbed and tatty sheaf of papers, folded and clumsily stapled together. "This is the story of the Battle. It's an epic poem, lost for two centuries. I like to bring young officers here to read it. And to think. Not about protocol and policy and risk. Or career, or advancement. But about status, and privilege, and obligation. And about duty, and loyalty, and resilience. Like many Old English or Old Norse stories it has no happy ending. Brithnoth freely and some would say stupidly gave up the best tactical position you could have wished for. And he ended up beleaguered, cut down and finally betrayed."

As a cold wind whipped across the water, each read in turn, the others scanning the scenery, or eyes downcast scrutinising their shoelaces and fragments of straw from that summer's harvest in turn. It had come to Ben's turn as the story reached the point where Brithnoth was slain by the Viking hordes, and having supported their lord even in his foolhardy decision, some of his Anglo Saxon supporters began to evaporate and flee the fight.

Collins took the photocopy and read, at first stiffly, but soon with growing feeling as he caught the metre and form.

"Then fled those from the fight that wished not to be there.
Then were Odda's sons first in the flight
Godric from the battle, and left his good lord
Who had often given him many a mare,

He sprang upon the horse that his lord had owned,
Upon the trappings where no right had he."

Ben stopped a moment. The shadow of his father had always cast a long shadow, and the words spoke to him more than felt comfortable.

He began again.

"And with him his brothers - they both galloped off,
Godrinc and Godwig, they loved not the battle,
They went from that war - and the wood they sought,
They fled to the fastness - and saved their own lives,

And men more than had any right
If they had all bethought them of the blessings
That he had done them for their good comfort.

Even thus to him Offa one day ere had said
In the meeting-place where he held his moot.
That with proud minds many did then speak
Who later at need would not endure."

He paused. Kiwi sighed.

"You see gents, in the end it's not about competency, or about skill. It's about knowing your place in the scheme of things, and holding true to that. Right to the end."

Kiwi never tired of the tragic denouement of the story, where the remainder of Brithnoths loyal thanes surrounded his fallen body and fought to the last man. But for the first time on a visit to the Blackwater, he found tears forming as Joop read the final speech of Brithnoth's aged fellow:

"Brythwold spoke, grasped his buckler,
He was an old comrade, urged the men,
He full boldly cheered his soldiers,

"Thought must be the harder, heart the greater, spirit the bolder,
As our might grows less.
There lies our chief on the ground,
Good man all cut down; whoever may he grieve
Who thinketh from this war play now to go.
I am old in years - hence I will not,
But by the side of mine own Lord,
By the chief so loved, I think to lie.""

He refolded the papers and pocketed them, thoughtful. For a minute, the wind rippling the water was the only sound.

Chapter 7

W88

Kiwi stepped carefully down the flight of stairs to what the staff at Winterborne Gunner called "The Vault". Really it was nothing of the sort: but it provided the secure storage needed for the various isotopes and radiation sources the complex used in its training courses. Reaching the foot of the stairs he would have been able straightforwardly to swipe he way through the door into the secure area – had he bothered to carry his I.D. card with him. Instead he resorted to banging on the toughened glass at the bored technician in a brown warehouseman's coat who managed the release of such materials, sat behind a counter on which was sat a 2-foot artificial Christmas tree. Kiwi was a very familiar face and was buzzed through, where he signed in triplicate for what he wanted.

The vault held a panoply of unpleasant substances: cobalt and strontium just for a start, but then tritium, radium, and radioactive isotopes of caesium, chlorine, and nickel. But Kiwi wanted "the usual", which was handed to him along with a robust metal case akin to those used by sports photographers, along with the two sets of rubber gloves he asked for. It was a bit like being reunited with an old friend, and he clutched the metal briefly between his bare palms before securing it to go upstairs.

~~

"Done your homework Collins?" Joop teased, as he sat down for the final days input, laying his green beret on the table beside him. "Or was it another night of Kalsarikannit?"

"You have got me on that one, Joop."

"It's a Finnish word - for having a night in and getting drunk on your own in your underpants." Joop cackled.

"No. I did too much of that last week."

Normally Ben would have been averse to an evening wading through pages of nuclear history: Collins joined the Marines in part because he was a doer, not a bookworm. But his room was spartan, Winterborne Gunner was in the middle of nowhere, and having already overdosed on Netflix box sets, he was not averse to having something to occupy him. He found himself missing Mazz.

In reading only the skeleton overview Kiwi had provided, what he now knew about the litany of nuclear weapons accidents had left him open mouthed, re-reading several passages such was his astonishment at how the superpowers had got away with so many near misses. Nuclear weapons had variously been burnt in fiery plane crashes, or had their plutonium or uranium cores blasted by accidents setting off their high explosive triggers. Planes had gone down carrying them; in one case, in Eastern England, a handful of nuclear bombs had been lying around minding their own business when an out of control jet bomber crashed on top of them. They had been accidentally dropped, smashing through the closed bomb bay doors of a strategic air command alert aircraft. They had been lost by B52s over Greenland and Spain, been scattered over the sea by collisions during air to air refuelling, and lost for good by planes that disappeared in bad weather. In Arkansas a catastrophic fire in the silo of a liquid-fuelled Titan missile, caused by a dropped spanner, ended with a devastating explosion which blew the entire warhead out into the compound. An A1 Skyhawk jet bearing a nuclear bomb had even been inadvertently pushed over the side of an aircraft carrier flight deck into the Pacific. And of course, these were only the West's screw ups. Heaven only knows what had been happening on the other side of the iron curtain.

Kiwi shuffled into view the other side of the glass partition separating the seminar room from the corridor. Dropping a few of his bundle of papers, he stooped slowly and awkwardly to rescue them. On entry he fussed briefly to put his things in some semblance of order, as was his wont. Collins thought he looked tired; while Kiwi had said he enjoyed doing 43 Commando orientations, and being back in the classroom for a while, it had been an intensive two weeks.

"So, gentlemen, your homework. What conclusions have you drawn from our experience of nuclear weapons in service?"

"We have been incredibly lucky," Collins volunteered. "People have no idea. At one point in the late 1950s they were setting nuclear weapons on fire, or crashing them, or losing them, at a rate of about one a month."

"You will have noticed, though, one event notable for its absence?"

"None of the accidents has ever actually set off the core," said Joop. "The nearest misses were still prevented by safety locks in the firing mechanism. Even when they burned or blew up the physics package back in the 1950s and 1960s, you didn't even get a fizzle."

A nuclear fizzle might still be a devastating event, even part-detonation of the A-bomb trigger of a multi-stage fusion weapon leaving a very big hole.

"Swot," Collins murmured under his breath. Kiwi grinned.

"It's striking isn't it? In probably the closest to disaster we came, three of the four elements of the firing process were triggered, including the drogue parachute to float the bomb down gently while its parent plane escaped: but because the pilot cockpit switch for the bomb was still set to "safe", it landed gently in some farmers field. And of course, modern design is safer still. It's actually really difficult to create a run-away fission process and then harder still to turn that into a fusion reaction. If any of the components are damaged, you have got fat chance of a Big Bang. But you have a very decent chance of making a very nasty radioactive mess. You will have noted that some of the mis-drops didn't even detonate the high explosive - or in some cases, it went off, but radioactivity didn't even get beyond the lip of the crater. The Yanks have left one uranium core where they dropped it, 50 feet down under some farm in the Deep South. But if you get the right conditions - or maybe I should say the wrong conditions - then it can be very grim indeed."

Kiwi was still glad for an old-school blackboard in this seminar room: in an era of interactive whiteboards and touch screens, he dug his heels in and insisted on it. He said the feeling of chalk dust between his fingers took him back to his first years of lecturing. Picking up a chalk fragment from the groove at the base of the board, he drew a big rectangle, with the vertical on the right extended upwards a little to form a little chimney shape. Bottom right he added a little square. The intricate process took all of 5 seconds. He turned and held out his arms to present his graphic achievement to Joop and Collins.

"Australia," he announced grandly. "This is called the "Barton Projection". Good enough 99% of the time". He paused with an afterthought. "Do you know what happens when a New Zealander decides to emigrate to Australia?". The two class-mates shook their heads. "It raises the average I.Q. of both countries..."

Kiwi waited for a laugh that didn't come. "Jesus you guys are a tough crowd. Anyway, a nuclear tour of Australia might start here..." He put a big cross to the top left of the rectangle, Collins surmising somewhere above Western Australia. "Montebello Island, site of the first British A-bomb test. Over here," he added another cross way out to the right-hand side of the board, "Christmas Island, site of the first U.K. H-bomb tests. But here," he added a final big cross and wrote a label in the bottom middle of the rectangle, "the big one, Muralinga, South Australia. This, gents, is where I spent my twenties, studying the clean up after the U.K. atmospheric tests of the 1960s. And it's the dirtiest place of them all. Let me show you why."

Kiwi cued up his lap-top again and the footage on the wall screen showed a long-shot of a tower in some expanse of desert. To describe the scene as featureless would have given it a grandeur it didn't deserve. Ben and Joop sat, expectant. Watching video of colossal nuclear blasts and subsequent mushroom clouds was now very old hat, and they could now both give a decent assessment of the yield of a blast if shown its effect on structures and vehicles and told how far the targets were from ground zero. As the countdown reached zero, they awaited the flash and blast wave, but got nothing of the sort.

Instead, a powerful but smaller scale blast tore apart the tower, throwing flaming lumps of debris into the air, some of the debris burning only briefly, but other pieces flaming brighter and brighter as they fell. Meanwhile the remnants of the structure had turned into an eye-piercing conflagration, jets of molten liquid shooting like volcanic magma up and across, reforming on a desert floor which was itself alight. The raging fire took hold across the whole concrete base of the pad on which the experimental tower had been standing, grainy black smoke pouring from the pyre, but then moving unlike any smoke Collins had seen before. In spite of the clearly intense heat, sending sparks and residue headlong into the sky, the black smoke roiled a few feet above the ground, as if held down by its own mass.

"That, gentlemen, is what happens when you manage to set fire to 22 kilos of plutonium. Those molten jets going hundreds of feet up - that's liquid plutonium. For a heavy metal, it has a really low melting point, only 650 degrees. The black smoke is burnt and pulverised plutonium, hence why it's struggling to get off the ground, heavy as hell. If you watch you will see the crosswind eventually gets hold of it and will carry it two dozen miles away."

"Wow, what happened?" Collins asked. "This was some kind of catastrophic failure?”

"On the contrary," Kiwi said. "This was a major success. It was part of a test series at Muralinga called "Vixen" - a safety test series. The Americans did much the same in what they called “Project 56”. One reason why none of those military accidents you studied led to full criticality is what they did here. They removed one or more elements of fusing or triggers to be pretty sure that the device wouldn't detonate, but then exposed the plutonium physics packages they had designed to massive conventional explosions or raging jet fuel fires. They were not bothered about how much chemical or radiation pollution was spread: only that there wasn't any kind of nuclear explosion, not even a little fizzle. The weapons which went into service had to pass that process. I guess you can work out the downside for that corner of Australian soil?"

"It's radioactive for the next 25,000 years?"

"And that's the nub. There were 550 atmospheric nuclear blasts between 1945 and 1992, when the Chinese finally agreed to join the atmospheric test ban. That added up to the best part of 600 megatons of nuclear yield. But even though only about a quarter of the plutonium in a core actually gets consumed by the detonation, the contamination has been limited. In most cases all the fissile products were distributed far into the upper atmosphere, so the radioactive products, nasty as they were, were spread over a massive area - globally so to speak. No one worries about living in Hiroshima or Nagasaki now do they? Whatever radiation didn't fallout locally in the immediate aftermath got dispersed. But the safety tests in Operation Vixen spread huge amounts of particulate plutonium over just that local area. 120 square miles of South Australia is still uninhabitable even after the clean-up. It probably will never be acceptably safe."

He paused, and then theatrically flipped the two clasps on the shiny aluminium case which he had brought with him. This was the indulgent culmination of the D.N.M. induction, and he always enjoyed the reaction it evoked.

"Gentlemen there is no strict need for this, but given we have spent two weeks discussing this stuff, it would be a shame not to actually see and feel it. Gloves on please." It didn't occur to either Joop or Ben to ask why they were donning thick blue gauntlets when Kiwi himself did not. By now they trusted him to know what he was doing. "It's worth saying that were this to be pure Pu239 we would not be touching it this way. The pure element will react with the air and start to oxidise immediately. But if it is alloyed with about 3% gallium it makes it more machinable, and castable: this is the form it is in within a Trident warhead. We also couldn't treat it this way it was Pu240 or 242 – they spontaneously emit neutrons. And 238 wouldn't be very comfortable to touch: it gives off over 500 Watts of ambient heat per kilogram compared to only 2 for Pu239."

He passed to Ben a flattened anulus of dark grey metal about 2cm in depth and 4cm in diameter – essentially in the style of a chunky bracelet. Ben readied himself to hold it on the basis of an anticipated weight which hopelessly underestimated its actual mass – it sat in his hand with around ten times the weight he expected, unbelievably dense. He felt, at that moment, a sense of its sinister power. He passed it to Joop as Kiwi continued, "Of course it emits alpha, beta and gamma radiation, but its only when ingested or inhaled that it is a real threat. Good luck inhaling that lump! But get it burning and it's time to make yourself scarce. Do not, I cannot emphasise enough, do not try to deal with a plutonium fire. That footage from Muralinga? They just let that burn itself out, but there was one plutonium fire at the American labs at Rocky Flats in 1957 that they had to try to contain." Having secured the anulus back in its case, Kiwi relayed the story to them

"You have seen plutonium 239 burns like hell, but in a solid lump, like the one you just saw, it is like a log of firewood – lots of stored energy, but really hard to get started. The ratio of surface area to its mass is such that you won't possibly get it hot enough to ignite. But the same log if turned into wood shavings can then be lit with ease: lots of surface area, hardly any mass, each sliver surrounded by lots of air. If you take a lump of plutonium and turn it into shavings, it will spontaneously burn: there are some allotropes of plutonium 239 which will burn white hot even in a freezer. So, when it's being milled at Burghfield they generally do it in an atmosphere of pure argon gas because it's so volatile, and even then you have to get all the moisture out of the environment else the plutonium will react with that. In Rocky Flats in 1957, and again a decade later, they made the mistake of allowing a build-up of plutonium dust from milling to come into contact with a normal atmosphere. It caught light and took the whole block up in flames. And once plutonium is lit almost everything you do will only make it worse. If you add water it will strip the oxygen out of it to sustain the flames, and that leaves hydrogen gas which will add a nice explosion to the situation. Added to which, the water may act as a neutron absorber, slowing the neutrons down but making nuclear fission more likely in the process: if you surround plutonium with water it only takes 5kg in the right shape to form a critical mass. That's why the sample you just handled was shaped as a bracelet, not like a hockey puck: if it had been a single solid with no void, and one of you had cupped it in your hands, we could have been in a lot of trouble."

"What about CO_2? Or dry powder?" Joop asked.

"All useless," Kiwi replied. "Same with Carbon Tetrachloride. Whatever you chuck on it once its burning, it will strip the oxygen or chlorine off it and burn even more fiercely. The only think you can do is cut off its air supply: at Rocky Flats they turned off the ventilation fans, but not before a whole stack of plutonium smoke and soot had gone up the chimney and off towards Denver. They found out eventually that magnesium-based sand is the agent of choice. But good luck finding some of that by the side of a motorway when you have a warhead cooking off in front of a load of holidaymakers. If what you just saw at Muralinga were to happen to a shiny Trident warhead convoy on the M6 somewhere near Bromsgrove, you could seriously mess up property prices in the West Midlands. And if you were the officer in charge at the time, bye bye promotion."

"Don't worry Ben," Joop said, as he dug an elbow into Collins' side. "We all know your career is fucked anyway."

"Don't I know it," Collins shrugged.

~~

Kiwi's final input was to make sure his two charges could at least tell the wood from the trees in the one warhead assembly they would ever be likely to see – the W88, the standard Trident warhead, up to twelve of which sit on each D5 missile in the U.K. arsenal. Refined over 50 years, the latest incarnation could be seen as the Maclaren of nuclear destruction – over-engineered to within an inch of its life to be as small and efficient as a warhead can be, 475 kilotons of punch in a volume about the size of a kitchen peddle bin. On a bench to the side of the lecture room sat the nuclear equivalent of a Russian doll, a W88 warhead model correct in size and shape, albeit from burnished aluminium and steel and moulded plastic – for the sake of weight as much as anything, given an actual Trident warhead weighed the equivalent of Kiwi and Ben and Joop together.

Pulling apart the pointy cone of the warhead case, Kiwi explained that the void between case and the physics package would in service be filled by a wonder material called an aerogel. Known by its codename, "Fogbank", at first sight when the plans were leaked, observers guessed the gel cushioned the working parts of the warhead in operational service and post launch; but in fact, it went beyond that, turning into a plasma when the plutonium primary detonation occurred, which then helped to ignite the fusion process in the secondary. Visible then at the heart of the warhead lay what could be best called the "peanut": a single Uranium 238 capsule with a small upper chamber and a larger lower chamber. Taking that apart, Kiwi revealed in the upper chamber a hollow oval of plastic, simulating the high explosive lens. Deeper still, inside that, sat a flattened metal sphere that struck Ben as similar in shape to an Australian Rules Football but maybe half the size.

"You cannot imagine the effort which went into this shape," he explained. "Most warheads now use what is called a plutonium hollow-pit. For years it would be a perfect sphere, which would be compressed by shaped conventional explosives at the same time as tritium and deuterium gas is injected into the middle. You get a critical ball of plutonium, and a big boom. That's complicated enough. But it made warheads wide in the beam, which meant you couldn't fit as many on the missile and their range was lower. If you have enough supercomputer power, you can shape the plutonium in an oblate spheroid – like a mini rugby ball – sit it like this end-on, and time the trigger explosion so it compresses into the shape you need at the right time. The calculations needed to simulate it and model it are beyond belief, which is why some nuclear powers stick to something old skool. But obviously not the Yanks. When the rugby ball goes bang, the shower of neutrons then set off this box of tricks," Kiwi indicated a grapefruit sized ball of metal in the lower half of the peanut. "The Uranium 235 secondary. Even bigger boom."

"And they weigh?" Ben asked.

"In the W88 the plutonium rugby ball is only 3kg. They have really cracked getting a lot of bang for the buck. The uranium ball is quite a lot heavier but still portable."

"So, essentially, we are being tasked to protect – or maybe track down and recover – a lump of metal small enough and light enough to go in a handbag, let alone a rucksack?" Ben rested his thumbs under his chin, fingertips touched together in front of his nose.

"Am I getting the impression you now realise this isn't the pointless ball-ache most of the Royal Marines seem to see it as?" Kiwi grinned.

"I guess I do."

Chapter 8

A Syrian Christmas

Katie was already downing her second glass of wine when a knock at the door announced Shona's arrival. Abaya, cooking at the stove, dispatched Ali to the door, where he found the Scot looking uncertainly at him.

"Emad?" she ventured.

"Ali," he corrected, hugging Shona stiffly at arms-length. He was still getting to grips with social norms in his new country.

Shona handed him her coat, then a 2-litre bottle of Diamond White cider.

"Abaya said to bring something traditionally Scottish. This is the tipple of choice in bus shelters across Glasgow!" Ali looked at it dubiously.

"I have not tried this before. It is made of apples?"

"Normally yes," said Shona. "But Diamond White would probably view any trace of apple as an unwanted contaminant of the raw alcohol."

Ali laughed.

"Mind your feet," Ali said, indicating a pair of shoes of the hall floor filled with hay. "It's our Christmas tradition," he said. "Back home I guess Reem would have been the one to do it. You leave hay out for the wise men's camels. The smallest camel is the one who brings the presents."

Shona stepped carefully over them, and she and her host joined the others in the kitchen. "Katie! Hi!" She nodded to her friend, and kissed Abaya on both cheeks, the radiologist holding both hands in the air to avoid getting gunk on Shona's shoulders.

"Pardon me while I finish the dinner."

"Of course! It was so lovely of you to invite us. I am so looking forward to Syrian Christmas!"

"We are so glad you could come. It's our first one in England and it feels a bit strange celebrating three weeks before everyone else. And of course, everyone assumes we must be Muslim and tip-toes around us. I hope we can make you feel at home."

Abaya gestured to the kitchen table, where pride of place had been given to a bottle of "Bucky" – Buckfastleigh Tonic Wine, 15% alcohol, the drink of choice for those north of the border who find Diamond White a bit too sophisticated for their palate.

Shona looked confused. "Cumbernauld rocket fuel! Abaya…is that some kind of joke?" she asked tentatively.

"Yes." Abaya, Emad, and Ali smiled.

Shona's face creased into a grin. "Not bad guys, not bad at all. I'll have a large one."

~~

The unofficial 43 Commando Defence Nuclear Materials Handling Induction Course Christmas Party was a small affair at a curry house in Salisbury, which had been largely chosen for being equidistant between Winterborne Gunner and Upavon.

Joop had expressed faux horror at the slim chance of getting a table in the week before Christmas at the Salisbury New Taj Mahal, but in fact knew as well as anyone that since the novachok nerve gas murders in the cathedral city, night life there had never really recovered.

While Collins booked under only his first name, any waiter worth his salt in any of the towns where forces were based could have clocked him for a young officer at 100 yards, given he had chosen an attire of Sandhurst standards: worn brown brogues, chinos, blue shirt unbuttoned at the collar with sleeves rolled up just below the elbow in that way that looks effortless but takes years to perfect in public school. To complement the look came a heavyweight Harris tweed two-button jacket. Joop was merciless. “Jesus, Ben, do they actually teach you to dress that way? You look like you are off to a Brexit conference.”

Collins was not fazed. “I would be careful, Joop. Orange Superdry T-shirt? Torn jeans? Loafers with no socks? In the middle of winter? I would think you were a local, if it wasn’t for you having too good a complexion to be resident round here.”

Mazz had joined them soon after they arrived. It was normally quite hard to shut Joop up, but Maryam's appearance in the doorway, where she paused to introduce herself to a waiter, nearly managed it. While limping slightly she had foregone the stick, and had on an elegant crimson silk cocktail dress, enough heel to suit without being tarty, hair down in its striking bob. Collins reflected that he had never seen her before out of uniform, so had no idea as to her style or taste. She was beautiful.

"Ben, if she was down and wounded anywhere near me, I would be stamping on you to get to her first." Joop made a big show of beating Ben to his feet to take Maryam's coat, and of pulling a chair out for her to join them.

"Joop, thank you," she said.

Joop was turning on the charm. "Lovely to meet you. How unusual for Ben to invite you to something other than a fire-fight!"

Ben blushed. To be honest he would have been delighted to have set an evening up without Dutch and New

Zealand involvement. But he was too scared that Mazz would turn him down.

"Well," Maryam defended Collins. "At least it was a memorable date. Which is more than can be said of some I have had."

Introductions were made to Kiwi, whose brown pullover was getting another airing, a choice which he excused by saying that "at least it won't show up when I spill my Balti."

To Ben the evening flew by. As ever Woolley and Katdelay came up often, and the other two friends were respectful about what had happened. But it was more a time for thinking about the future. Ben was heartened that he and Joop would be starting together at 43 soon after Christmas for training at Faslane.

"What's left to do?" Mazz asked.

"It's all the mission specific stuff really," Ben said. "There are an awful lot of convoy procedures and comms aspects to learn, a lot of "actions on" too." "Actions on" was the template to be followed should any given situation arise with the warheads in transit.

"And what about you Kiwi?" The normally gregarious New Zealander had been rather quiet, and had eaten sparingly.

"It's my last course Mazz," he said with half a sigh, nodding at the two young officers. "I've not been so well of late, a few old war wounds catching up with me. Those two were my last hurrah."

The concern on Maryam's face was mirrored in that of Joop and Ben. Kiwi gave them no chance to grill him.

"But we have one last thing together. Before you run your first convoy for real, we tend to finish the D.N.M. induction shadowing the current S.O.E. troop on one, to see how they do things. So, we will be together in the New Year for that. Until then, cheers!"

The three soldiers clinked beer glasses, but Kiwi proffered a silver hip flask to the ritual, taking a long swig from it. Mazz wondered what was in it.

~~

"Shona you need to listen to Ali. You must be mad." Even four drinks in, Katie had been shocked at hearing her colleague's plan. "You want to try to stage a road accident to run an articulated lorry off the road? In front of dozens of police officers? While it's going at 60 miles an hour."

Abaya and her family had shared little over the dinner table of their old life in Syria: in contrast Shona had been as willing as usual to "Sturgeon" the others, detailing how "nothing will change until we wake people up." Ali had been attentive and interested in her description of the warhead convoys.

"Shona I spend too much of my time recovering car accidents on the M6. Have you any idea what a loaded lorry can do to a small car? You cannot just give it a nudge. It may be 40 tons in weight, a family car isn't even half a ton. It could roll over you without even noticing. Does it have to be on the motorway?"

Half a bottle of Bucky wine made Shona more forthcoming than she might have been. "We need publicity Ali. Blocking a major motorway with a crashed nuclear warhead lorry gets it. Denting its bumper at a T junction doesn't cut it." Shona took a swig of the red syrup in her glass and sighed.

"You need a stinger," Ali said.

"A what?"

"A stinger. You have seen car chases on TV? It's what the police use. One of those extendable metal frames with spikes on it to puncture the cars tyres."

"You can buy those sorts of things?"

"Why not? I would rather use a stinger than try to pick a fight with a lorry at speed."

"Wouldn't you stick out like a sore thumb stood by the side of the M6 waiting for the convoy?" Katie asked.

Ali thought for a moment. "What's the one time you see people stood by the side of a motorway?"

"When they have broken down?" Shona suggested.

"So that's what you do. Stage a breakdown on the verge. You said the lorries come past with a very careful spacing?"

Shona nodded, "They are very careful not to get too close to the armoured vans between each lorry."

"That's good", said Ali. "So, there is plenty of space to throw the stinger into. If the lorries are in the inside lane, they will have no time to react."

"Won't that be very dangerous?" Abaya asked.

"For who? The person why throws the stinger will be fine. Even if the tyres burst or the lorry goes out of control it will be past the ambush spot in less than a second. You want to film this I guess? You will have a great vantage point of the lorry jack knifing or screeching to a halt."

"What about the driver?"

This time Shona answered. "Hey they must be highly trained?"

"Even if they are not," Ali said, "When a lorry gets a tyre blowout they can normally come to a pretty safe stop, and a stinger is designed to release the pressure quickly but in a controlled way. It might be best to pick the last lorry in the convoy. Then you won't have others running into it or taking avoiding action."

"And then you go to jail." Katie was perfectly willing to put a downer on the plan; but she was equally unsurprised by Shona's reaction.

"Look, what will they charge me with?" Shona shrugged. "Probably no-one will get hurt. Those lorries look top of the range. I reckon criminal damage at worst."

“You might lose your registration,” Katie warned. The Royal College of Radiographers could end a career without much cause.

“What over a matter of political principle? Good luck with that. You won’t have heard about the Burnley Two.”

The others round the table had to concede that they did not, and Shona was happy to elaborate. In early 2017, two members of the “Swords into Ploughshares” group had scaled the fence of the British Aerospace factory at Warton just down the road in Lancashire. Armed with a hammer and intending to damage Typhoon jets about to be shipped to Saudi Arabia for use in the war in Yemen, they had been acquitted of criminal damage by District Judge James Clark at Burnley Magistrates court – on the basis that any damage they committed was with the intent of achieving a greater moral good. Katie had to admit that maybe the demonstration was not as doomed to end badly as she might have feared.

Shona was pleased. At last she had some sense of progress.

“Ali, I wouldn’t know where to start with getting one of those stingers. Could you help?”

Ali shot a glance at Abaya, who tilted her head in the tiniest indication of approval.

“Of course,” Ali nodded.

~~

Mazz had been reluctant to take up Joop’s suggestion that she should let Ben drive her back to Upavon.

“It’s no problem Joop, if I get breathalysed I’ll say being short of a lobe of lung throws their measurements off.”

But the Dutchman insisted, and Ben was pleased when she handed him her keys for safe keeping, and threaded her arm through his on the way to the Spitfire. Safely tucked into the front seats, the engine fired reluctantly in the frosty air, and Collins headed into the night.

"Can you find the way Ben? Hey, can anyone find the way in this thing? No sat nav?"

"It was built about twenty years too soon. No trance music either. Joop has yet to convert me."

He headed the car North out of town, the road following the River Avon, which flowed unseen to their right.

"How's the leg, Mazz?"

"Better thanks. I am running now, not much slower than I ever used to."

"Chest?"

"Ben you can't go around asking a girl about her chest." Collins smiled at her pretended offence. "All wounds are healing fine thanks. What about yours?"

Mazz knew full well that Collins had not been injured at Katdelay. It's not what she meant, and he knew it. But he struggled to answer.

"I thought it would get easier once the funeral was over. And once I had seen his parents. I think of it every day. You know it should have been me that was out there in the field the day you got hit."

He focused on the left side hedge which was picked up by the headlights for many metres ahead in the pitch black, using it to place the car in the road.

"Ben it was me who he died saving. How do you think that feels? His body shielded mine from the blast. In the state I was in it would have killed me." She spoke softly and with care over every word, as if it was a mantra she had fixed in her head for weeks.

They drove on in silence. What was there to say? Or to do? What came next was the best gift Ben could possibly have received that winter.

"Ben it might have been Woolley who saved me. But it was you who saved us, all of us, the whole patrol. Don't let anyone tell you otherwise."

~~

Tidying up together on Saturday morning, Abaya and Ali reviewed what they had learned.

"What do you think?" Abaya said.

"Shona is a fool," Ali replied. "She calls herself an activist but what has she achieved? What has she done? I think it sums up these people and how they let us down. They do token actions, take no risks, do nothing which will have an actual impact. Assad knew that when he gassed and killed our people. So do IS when they murder us."

"But are they useful to us? What do you think of these convoys she is tracking?"

"It could not be a better opportunity to shame the British," Ali said.

He went on.

"They think they are untouchable. It looks like they have not taken at all seriously the threat to their weaponry. Compared to stealing cobalt from your hospital, this would be real news. I don't know how we could use a stolen warhead. I doubt we could make it explode. But the shock to the British? It would be worth it. I have got half the peroxide we planned and I can certainly work out how to strip a cobalt source into ribbon on the lathe, but plutonium? That would properly sow fear like nothing else. We should do all we can to encourage their plot. We can use it."

"How?", Abaya asked.

"Shona and her group could be a distraction for a real attack on a convoy. We should encourage them to vandalise and attack a truck. They will come across for what they are – a bunch of amateurs. The police will be sucked into dealing with them as a stupid protest, and they will lower their guard. Then we can strike."

"You mean taking on the police guards face to face? With what?"

"Abaya getting the three of us into the country was way harder than getting hold of guns. What Syrian nowadays hasn't handled a Kalashnikov? Emad probably knows a way round a gun better than he knows his way around a kitchen. Down in Shepherds Bush there are people who can get hold of anything."

"But with only the three of us?" Ali's enthusiasm was taking Abaya totally out of her depth.

"It would be enough," Ali said. "If the police are distracted by Shona and her idiot friends, they will be totally off their guard."

Abaya was thinking.

"But don't you feel bad selling out your friend?" Ali asked.

Abaya sneered. "Ali, I owe these people nothing. The bosses behave as if I am lucky to have a job in their unit, when I am more qualified than almost everyone there. I want vengeance for Reem. If we have to use them to achieve that, so be it. What next?"

"I will find out about the stinger. It will not be hard to find something. For heaven's sake she could have Googled it herself. But if we were to attack we need to be sure Shona will not lose her nerve. I think I will need to be there, at her side, to bolster her and push her on. I have an idea as to how I can excuse being there."

Abaya agreed but had a final concern. "What about the armed police she said always shadow the convoy. Shona seemed to think they would not open fire. But what if they were to immediately deal with the stinger as an attack, and shoot from the outset?".

Ali thought for a moment.

"It is not the English way. But I agree. How can we find out more? Didn't you say that the father of one of the patients is some kind of military policeman?".

“That’s right”, said Abaya. “He must work somewhere local because he is always in his uniform when he brings her to clinic. But he might know nothing. And if he does he might not say.”

“Can you try?”

“Of course.” She thought for a moment. “I think I have a way to do it.”

~~

Kiwi had been based on the Plain for some years, but somehow, like the Londoner who has never seen Buckingham Palace, had never visited the hill that bore his name.

During World War One, soldiers from New Zealand had been based at Bulford, just a few miles from Winterborne Gunner. The main A303 from the South West up to London runs one side of the ridge-line above the military camp that carries the villages name. Invisible to the traffic and the other side of the ridge, New Zealanders who had volunteered to go half-way across the globe to fight for Empire carved a giant Kiwi into the chalk, forever to mark their presence into the landscape of Southern England ahead of their likely demise on the Western Front. It is little known that soldiers from the antipodes suffered 50% killed and wounded in the trenches, five times the casualty rate of British troops. Soldiers from Auckland, Wellington and Dunedin were all volunteers, and served mostly as line infantry, while those from the UK itself might be more likely to fill slots as engineers or artillerymen; less likely to have their lives thrown away in mass attacks across no-mans-land.

Having got off the bus down in the camp, the hill and the Kiwi loomed above him, and Barton initially began to walk with confident stride up to the right of the icon: following the same route as a multitude of soldiers had over the last century, for whom a run up Kiwi Hill had become a routine part of morning PT. But it was not long before he felt the pain in his chest, and paused to take a swig of Oromorph. It was getting harder and harder to conceal his pain levels from those around him, and he was pleased, for once, not to have to do so.

At least, as he had said to his oncologist at the Royal Marsden, "I would have been pissed if I had spent all these years surrounded by radiation only to be hit by a bus."

Kiwi started to puff and pant half way up. The primary tumour in his lungs was now proving troublesome but what the hell. As it said in the "Shawshank Redemption", either you "get busy living or get busy dying".

Apparently, the view from the top was well worth seeing. As he reached the summit Kiwi noticed that the outline of the flightless bird, which had looked so sharp and well defined from afar, looked rather shabby and haphazard close up, the chalk stained and uneven.

For the first time in many years, Kiwi longed for home

~~

Abaya re-read the email from the Proton Centre in Reading. So long as Trust funding was agreed, the unit could start treatment for Alice with immediate effect.

She pondered for a moment. If Alice's care was transferred to the specialist centre in the South, her father would most likely go too, and with him any prospect of tapping him for information on the convoys. Abaya couldn't risk that yet. Glancing at the door and adjusting her screen slightly so that she could be sure to have time to minimise her message before anyone got close enough to read it, she typed rapidly.

"Dear Carl

That is excellent news; however, the parent has requested that treatment start only after Christmas. Can we look to book a start date a month from now, mid-January or so?

Thanks

Dr Abaya Shah"

She hit "send". And began thinking of who, and how, they could best exploit the window of opportunity she had created.

~~

"What progress on the stinger?", Abaya asked Ali that evening.

"I have found something that's just right," Ali replied. "I was worried about your friend Shona having the strength to throw it fully into the lorry's path. She is all bulk and no strength. And while she should be able to time throwing it, she might lose her nerve. This.." he maximised a tab on his laptop, "is just the thing."

It was a device designed, it seemed, to overcome the same kind of problems as Ali described when Stingers are in police usage. A series of injuries and complaints had led forces to demand a power extended, push-button version. Stored in a box the size of a satellite TV terminal, and powered by a simple compressor, the device is placed on the road and would fire the stinger frame predictably into a vehicle path, while the controller could stand back at a safe distance. There was even a variant designed to ensure the launch could not be disabled by resourceful criminals using jammer devices.

Ali clicked to another site. "This I think is the best one." The Superspike claimed that its 2.5 inch spikes would work every time, shredding tyres, even run flats, with "up to 400 choke proof spikes per unit" and consistent success in Home Office and U.K. police trials.

"It's expensive," Abaya observed. "Do you think Shona or her group have the money?"

"I think we need to persuade her. We will probably only get one chance to do this. At any time the authorities could discover I am not your brother and start the process to deport me."

"What if she starts to question why we are so keen on helping her?"

Abaya's medical career left her wont to try to anticipate problems even where there was little reason to be fearful.

"I think she is a naïve fool," Ali said. "But I have thought of that. She said that one of her group is a university lecturer. What if I make out that I am keen to help, and in return hope he will help me get a place at the University to restart my studies? Then I can keep a closer eye on their plans and preparations. And it will give me an excuse to be there on the day."

"Good. Print off the information about the stinger device. Hard copy. Make sure you cut off anything on the print out which might show the device which printed it and when it was done. I will take it to work and give it to Shona. And I will mention you doing engineering at the University and whether her friend would help."

~~

"John I am really sorry," Abaya said, standing at her desk in the department office. Someone had once told her that standing instead of sitting when making an important phone call places you more on your mettle.

The voice on the other end communicated desperation and resignation in equal measure.

"Dr. Shah is there nothing you can do? I hcard that the trust agreed the funding, and the Professor said it was vital that treatment start immediately."

Abaya was ready for him. "John it's not as easy as that. All of us are doing our very best for Alice, but proton beam is very hard to get. The proton beam units have all contacted us but at the moment the earliest start date is not till some way into the new year. Look, leave it with me. I have a friend down in Reading, where one of the private units is. Let me see if we can pull some strings, see if we can get them to fit Alice in sooner?"

"I could call them direct if it would help?", he offered.

Abaya winced, "No John, that would be the worst thing to do. My friend could get in a lot of trouble if we manage to get Alice moved up the list. And so could I. Leave it to me and I will call your mobile when I know more. It might be a few days".

The voice on the line seemed calmed by what she had said. "Of course Abaya, I understand. I owe you one." He hung up.

Chapter 9

Four-three

Early January

Even in Collins' brief experience, he had come to see that post-holders in the rank of Major, whether in the Marines or the Army, come in a set of subtypes unlike any other officer rank.

Amongst majors can be found "gun" officers tipped to lead one of the Brigade's Commando units, high achieving one-time troop commanders now leading a fighting company of over 100 men: the largest sub-unit likely to fight together in a modern counter-insurgent conflict. Such men stand out for their bearing, confidence, and competence. But a month later the same officer, still a Major, can find himself in a backwater as a staff officer in MOD, or sent on some god-foresaken wild goose chase as a liaison with a combined multinational force headquarters. This will just be a broadening assignment, ahead of future command, a place for the aggressive and ambitious to kick their heels in for a couple of years, learning patience and humility.

But there are two other sub types unique to the rank of Major. One is the "dead wood", promoted as far as they are ever likely to go, early promise unfulfilled, not wanted but not yet cut adrift: maybe found a harmless backwater as families officer or running the stores, counting the days before they are pensioned off. And finally the "lifer", the rare senior N.C.O. who is selected 15 years or so in to be commissioned and leave the Mess of those who "fucking work for a living" to join the officers whose bidding they had done for most of their working life.

It was one of the latter who sat in front of Ben and Joop as they stood nervously in an office at Faslane. The name plate on his desk introduced him – Major Steven Chandler R.M., and the artefacts that adorned the office disclosed his background without him needing to. An engraved pace stick, which was used by Warrant Officers to lead squads on the drill square, sat in the corner below a silver salver bearing an engraving from the Sergeants' Mess at 45 Commando. On the bookcase to the left was Chandler's passing out photo, dated and clearly showing a "Nod", not a junior officer candidate; and a series of photos which looked like they were taken on Op. Herrick, with a rather younger and unshaven version of Chandler toting sergeant stripes on the rank slide in the middle of his chest.

What remained to be seen was what version of the "late entry" type Major Chandler would prove to be. Some were exceptional, blending grass roots experience of soldiering at section and troop level, with wisdom and maturity: such men had managed to reinvent themselves, adding from their studies, once commissioned, a measure of insight and a managerial grasp of what their unit is trying to achieve. Others carried with them only their self-righteous prejudices and know-all confidence, using their new authority to harass and undermine, with rote learned management speak justifications for each new misdirection of the more able people below them.

Before Chandler had even opened his mouth, Joop and Ben had clearly sensed which of the two types was going to command them. While they had spent the best part of three weeks together, the telepathic understanding of twins was still some way beyond them. They did, nevertheless, form the same thought at the same time: "Who is this wanker?"

Major Chandler had sharp hawk like features and marked crows-feet framing his eyes, as if he had either been smiling a lot or screwing his eyes up against the sun too much. The former appeared unlikely given the way he fixed the two men with glaring eyes, eyes which might once have been blue but which seemed to have had the colour washed out of them. His sandy hair was shorn, only his eyebrows suggesting what colour it might be had it only been allowed to grow. Tattoos on his bare, lightly freckled arms suggested allegiance to Plymouth Argyle; enough alone to cast doubt on his judgement and taste. A bulky gold signet ring adorned one little finger – a wedding ring was conspicuous by its absence. Either someone lost patience with him or the global female population had all seen him coming in time.

While a Captain whose name tape read "Ledsham" stood to one side stony faced, the Major clearly struggled to set aside the demeanour he must have adopted 20 years before when he was no doubt beasting recruits around the Endurance Course.

"Welcome to Faslane, gentlemen," was the closest to warmth and fellowship that he managed to attain. "De Jong, can I suggest that you forego the fancy dress" – he gestured dismissively at Joop's Dutch-pattern uniform – "and present yourself in future as the Royal Marine you will be pretending to be for the next eleven months?" Joop nodded, bemused. This wasn't generally the way anyone spoke to anyone in the Royal Dutch Marine Corps.

"Lieutenant Collins, note that we don't have a Mortar Platoon here in R Squadron. And we try to avoid ambushes rather than take the whole shebang right into the middle of one."

Ben stayed impassive. Joop winced on his behalf.

"I didn't want either of you in my unit, but Brigade seems think they know better. I told them I consider you both a liability, and now I am quids in. If you fuck up, I can say I told them so. If you do well, I am the leadership development genius. I will not hesitate to fuck over your performance review if you prove to be the dead wood I am expecting. Captain Ledsham", he didn't deign to either look at or indicate what they could only guess was his 2 i/c, "will oversee your range qualification and the C.Q.B. refresher. He will assign someone to do your comms induction. By the end of the month, one of you should be taking over a troop, the other in Squadron H.Q. That gives us a month to see which of you is the least useless." He smiled at his own witticism. "I should imagine by the end of the month we will have a convoy for you to observe and shadow. Is Prof. Barton going to come up to mind you, or have they pensioned the useless old codger off?" He didn't wait for an answer. "Ledsham will give you the nod, and you had better be ready. When we have a run up here from Burghfield I will have quite enough on my plate to worry about nose-wiping you two. You will need a driver. You will need to be Jonny-on-the-fucking-spot. In short gentlemen, you will need to avoid undershooting my low expectations of you."

His eyes narrowed as he asked if they had any questions, making very clear that they would be taking their life in their hands as they did so. Then they were sent on their way. It had been what the military euphemistically call a "meeting without coffee".

"Well, that went well," Joop said, closing the door behind themIf Collins had been under any illusion that he could straightforwardly rebuild his career at 43 Commando, he now knew better.

"Come on Joop, let's get you some kit."

~~

January 10th was a difficult date for Abaya, as it had been every year since Reem had been killed. The youngest child in the Shah family would have been thirteen that winter morning had she lived. Brushing her hair, Abaya gazed at the photo wedged between her dresser mirror and its frame, but there was no resemblance between the little girl in the fading picture and the one who had been brought gasping and trembling into Abaya's own hospital.

For all the misery of civil war, they had felt safe from gas attacks, most of which took place in the far North around Aleppo and Idlib. After using Sarin in 2013, the regime had been careful to only use chemical weapons in outlying areas, or to use chlorine, the use of which was deniable – I.S. or the militias were perfectly capable of sourcing and releasing such a gas, and Assad gave his army a free pass to use it whenever, wherever. But in 2013 Ghouta, a pretty suburb of Damascus which was the home of the extended Shah family, was one of areas of the capital not in control of the government, and the Syrian army forces were progressing at snail's pace. Maybe the populace should have realised that in such a clash, Ghouta might merit a Sarin attack: slow progress was not generally enough for Assad, when a profound collapse was required.

The first cause for alarm had been the hollow report of artillery shells; an empty thump rather than a devastating crash. Instead of the wailing of the wounded and weeping of the heartbroken, there was an eerie silence, broken only by the sound of scuttling rats and barking strays. Abaya had read that the animal kingdom had a strange sensitivity to threat and so it proved. As the first desperate phone calls came in o the White Helmets' command point in the foyer of her hospital, Abaya realised what was in train, and alerted those waiting: masks, gowns, skin cover to be maximised, each patient to be assessed at the door. Those beyond hope to be left in the courtyard. Two fire hoses were deployed to soak casualties and recovery teams alike, in order to try to stop any chemical agent contaminating the emergency room and everyone in it. She had barely finished issuing her orders than the first battered ambulance pulled up.

Two young men opened the back door and leapt to the concrete, turning back to haul from the interior a stretcher of steel and canvas, the material stained and re-stained the colour of tea. Upon it, blood had pooled, leaked, dripped, spattered, oozed, each episode a relic of suffering and misery. But no misery quite like that of the poor wretch on the stretcher, an old woman dressed in tatty nightclothes, fitting and spasming, face grey and cheeks flecked with spittle and sputum. Stood in the door, Abaya instantly held up her hand and shook her head, indicating to the youths to leave woman and carriage on the floor, before grabbing the arm of one of those tasked with the firehose to soak both the woman's rescuers. Nerve agents had a nasty habit of killing not just those in the line of fire but those who inhale traces from the clothes of the injured, or whose palms absorb droplets from their sweat-soaked skin.

It was the same story with the next ambulance, and a taxi, and a private car, and before she knew it, Dr. Shah was presiding not over a medical facility; before her were simply a pile of wretched dead, piled like cordwood. She remembered that the Japanese army officers had referred to the live Chinese they subjected to vivisection in Mongolia in World War 2 as “timber”; and so it still was.

Unlike the western mother who never loses their fitful anxiety for their child, regardless of the overwhelming likelihood of their safety at school or Brownies, Abaya had long set aside the worry of leaving family members to go to work. For all the colossal casualties suffered by the community, it was still an oddity in Ghouta for a family to be bereaved; the joke was that there were zip codes in the U.S.A. where you were more likely to be killed by gunfire than in Ghouta. But Sarin made a mockery of that, wilfully indiscriminate, a weapon to terrorise and intimidate. The trickle of casualties turned into a river and then a torrent. Abaya passed the job of triage to a weary colleague, and went into the building to manage those whose symptoms were sufficiently limited to merit a treatment.

Except what she was doing wasn’t treatment. Atropine might have been of use, had the gutted and eviscerated hospital had any such medication; sedation to calm fitting and twitching might have been worthwhile, but only really to mask the horror of the poisoning the victims had endured. Resuscitation had no place; how can one even think of mouth to mouth, re-inflating the lungs of a patient whose nerve and muscle control has prevented normal breathing, when the mouth and trachea and lungs you are inflating are corrupted by deadly chemicals. Abaya and her team of White Helmets rapidly realised they were in the business of decontamination, not treatment.

Until the moment when out of the corner of her eye, Abaya caught the briefest glimpse of a floral pattern that didn’t belong. A pattern that only sat comfortably in a family bedroom at home, tucked with a favourite toy into cosy bedding, warm and secure: not in a wretched shell of an emergency room, with hacking coughs and desperate wheezes marking the last gasps of forlorn men and women for whom even an expert could do nothing. Abaya tore a tattered curtain to one side and there, on a trolley in a darkened corner, was Reem. Her hair matted into a lump, eyes hollow and staring, Abaya could not tell if her sister could even register her presence in her empty pupils. Ignoring the stench of the involuntary defecation which so often went with such a poisoning, she put her ear to try to detect breathing – there was no sign of Reem's breath rising in her tiny chest, pyjamas stained brown by the child's vomit. It was almost impossible to hear in the bedlam of the emergency room, but thinking she could detect a whisper of airflow, Abaya grabbed a nearby oxygen cylinder, but could only hold the mask near the broken child's face: they had no spare masks, and even for her own little sister Abaya could not assume the guilt of contaminating it and making it unusable for others. Even in prosperous Ghouta, there was no resuscitation bag to manually squeeze air into Reem's barely working lungs; no face shield which would have allowed Abaya to safely to mouth to mouth. While the yelling of medical staff and crying of relatives would normally have held Abaya's attention, she had eyes only for Reem, baby sister, bookworm, delicate features turning grey before her eyes.

Abaya could not pinpoint the exact moment when Reem's life ended. There was nothing peaceful, or uplifting, or spiritual. Just an empty misery, and a brutal loneliness.

One of the White Helmets spied Abaya sat motionless next to the child's corpse, and began to reach for her shoulder to pull her back towards the door where other cases were waiting. But there was something about her absolute, profound stillness, which made him guess there might be more to the sad little scene than he knew. He drew the fragile translucent cubicle curtain around the doctor and her lost sister, and went back to those still fighting for life.

~~

In the days following Reem's death, Abaya's grief had turned to anger at Assad, but then morphed into something else. Assad was Assad. For Abaya's family and people, hatred of him was a given, and almost an irrelevance. There was as much point to it as hating the summer heat. But resentment for those who could do something and di nothing was a different matter. Who cared? Who acted? The Russians blamed the Free Syrian Army. The Turks blamed al-Nusra. The U.N. blamed Assad; his brother; the Minster of Defence; the Head of Military Intelligence; and various senior army officers. Ban-Ki-Moon said that evidence of a war crime was "overwhelming and indisputable," but decided to blame no-one, and did nothing. Mandated to oversee the destruction of the Syrian chemical weapons, the UN mission ended in the autumn of 2014 – but the attacks went on. The American Congress approved air strikes against chemical weapons stockpiles. Secretary of State John Kerry indicated that the air strike could be averted if Syria destroyed or handed over all its weapons. Syria agreed. America and her allies backed down; the attacks went on.

Along with Al Jazeera, B.B.C. News 24 provided a window not just on what was happening in Syria – but on how the rest of the world was viewing what was happening in Syria. And as the weeks passed and Ghouta returned to normal wartime life, and the barrel bombings and chlorine attacks continued, Abaya became clearer and clearer. On British news sites a single terminally-ill child's court process in London took up ten times the attention of the dozens of Reem's butchered in Syria. Christians in the west spent their column inches beating themselves about the abusive behaviour of their clergy, doing nothing to help their kin in desperate straights in Aleppo or Damascus. On T.V. the British trialed their brand new aircraft carriers, but did nothing to stop the Russians bombing on Assad's behalf. They and the Americans kept whole brigades and divisions of airborne troops ready to drop anywhere in the world at 12 hours notice – yet the Yazidi people on Mount Sinjar, easily defendable from the I.S. onslaught, were left to fend for themselves.

Before Easter of that year had arrived, Abaya was committed. Defeating Assad, and getting vengeance for Reem, required getting those with power invested in their war. And that meant taking steps to either coerce the west into taking sides against Assad, with all the force at their disposal. Or punishing the west's complacent citizenry for standing by.

~~

Abaya had tried to prevail on Katie to sound out Alice's father for anything he knew about convoy procedures, but got nowhere. While the radiographer and dad were friendly, and while Katie feared for how the stinger plan could go, she said she saw no reason to disturb a profoundly upset man with bullshit about a nuclear demonstration. Abaya speculating on Shona's recklessness and the harm she could come to didn't sway the argument. The radiologist would have to be more direct.

Summoning Alice and her father in for a "check-up" had been easy to arrange, and Abaya was pleased to see father and daughter sat in the corner of the waiting area for her paediatric out-patients clinic. The little girl had her head down, attention focused on a game on John's i-pad, but nevertheless her progressing illness was apparent in the lack of lustre in her skin tone, and the way her form seemed folded in on itself, her very posture circling the wagons against the cancer that was killing her. John sat next to her, fiddling with the ends of her hair absent-mindedly. Had one not known that Alice was the patient, one might have guessed that John was the one being crushed by illness, lost and downcast – carrying the burden not just of Alice's misfortune, but the shame and desperation of not being able to help her.

It was a given for medics seeing patients in clinic that watching the patient walk the dozen yards from their seat to the consulting room door would tell you more than you found out once they were inside; and there was no good news to be found in watching Alice. The deliberate delay to the proton beam treatment which Abaya had engineered had been entirely predictable in outcome. While Alice's gait was unchanged, the headaches and sickness which the expanding tumour caused had left her exhausted and dispirited since the turn of New Year. The vibrant zest which had still been evident in the autumn was long gone; Christmas had been observed rather than celebrated; and the little girl's smile was an empty replica of its healthy predecessor.

If Abaya's conscience was still alive and kicking, it struggled to intrude into her feelings. That page had been turned. She was there to complete a process framed a year before and thousands of miles away in a very different hospital, one where she had witnessed the needless death of a child just as fragile. Abaya went through the motions, welcoming Alice at the door, and settling into a tatty vinyl-backed chair behind her desk. The desk was handy barrier which saved her from being in the same piece of space as the sick child and desperate father, and she was grateful for it. Abaya managed to tune out as John detailed the worsening symptoms his daughter now endured daily. She was still attending school; caring for her guinea pig; struggling through the winter dark to Brownies; saying her prayers. But it was all a lie.

Having reviewed Alice's situation, Abaya was grateful to be able to summon Nasreen from reception to take Alice away, and as the door clunked shut, confronted the task that had been the real purpose of their meeting.

As soon as the door was shut John was immediate in his onslaught, demanding news of the proton beam therapy, castigating the world for its injustice. Abaya let him run dry, then gave their discussion abrupt and bald direction.

"John, I have been talking to my contact in Reading. We can bump Alice to the top of the list and begin her proton beam therapy. Immediately. But in return I will need an answer to these questions."

She slipped across the desk a scruffy and written list, on a page clearly ripped from a jotter pad, the top margin a tangle of part-torn holes from a wiro binder.

John braced in his seat as he read; looked up and stared with curiosity at Abaya; then cast his eyes down and continued reading down the list.

"I don't understand," he said. "Why on earth do you need to know all this?"

Abaya fixed him with a steady glare.

"Firstly, because a friend of mine wants to know. They think what is happening with the convoys is wrong and they want to expose it. Secondly because, at the moment, me and my contact in Reading are going to go out on a limb. If anyone were to find out that we fixed a waiting list to get Alice to the top, I would be struck off. And I do not know you – I cannot trust you. If you get careless and let slip that I have cheated the system to help Alice, all the comeback is on me. If you, in the same way, share with me things which maybe you should not, and which also would cost you your job, then we are both at the same risk. You blow the whistle on me, even by accident…" She didn't need to finish her warning.

John matched her gaze briefly. At any normal point in time he might have questioned Abaya. But possibly not. This was a stressed registrar trying to save his dying child, and looking to insure herself against blow back. There was no choice to make.

"Some of this I know already," he said. "The rest I can find out without much trouble. Write your mobile number on the list. I will call you tomorrow."

He nodded to the radiologist and left.

~~

Summoned by text from John the day after their consultation, she joined John at a window seat in a KFC barely 100 metres from the Infirmary, and immediately placed her phone on the table in front of them.

"Do you have what I need to know?"

"Of course"

"You will understand that I need to record you? If I break the rules by getting Alice her treatment; you share what you know about the convoys. If you expose me.."

"I think we understand each other." John finished her sentence for her.

As Abaya started picking at what KFC hopefully called "Popcorn chicken", John started talking.

~~

Abaya tapped briskly on the keyboard and in short order had everything in place. She confirmed with Proton Inc. in Reading that the family were now ready and keen for Alice to start her treatment. Nasreen was primed to pass the treatment schedule to the family, and to organise for the trust to meet the contractors extortionate billing.

~~

Spooning steaming baked beans onto a couple of rounds of toast, and carrying plates and trays from the cooker to the sofa where Abaya waited, Ali fleetingly sighed at the frugal life they were leading. It had been agreed from the outset that they would rent somewhere cheap and cheerful, keep a low profile, and focus on building a kitty in U.S. dollars for whenever it was time to leave. Compared to the relative wealth of the Shah family in Damascus, a three bedroom flat above a shoe repairer on the edge of Lancaster was a come down; and it had raised a few eyebrows with Shona and Katie, struggling to see why even a locum radiologist would be living in a setting little better than a student house. But they had accepted that the family had yet to work out their long term plans – for Ali finding an engineering course, Emad just finishing college, and Abaya herself on only a temporary contract, it was easy to excuse a short term tenancy on the wrong side of town. Ali wondered what their Christmas guests would have said had they seen the $40,000 which was sat in a laundry bag in the bottom of the washing basket.

For the moment, though, getaway plans were a way in the future; the pressing need was to establish how to orchestrate the attack on the convoy. How to stop one of the warhead carriers; overcome the accompanying MOD police; seize some fissile material; and make a clean enough getaway to have time to improvise a catastrophic release of radiation.

"What did he say?"

Abaya sawed off a small corner of toast and talked as she chewed.

"He knew plenty – he said that sometimes MOD police from where he works in Barrow are bussed over to Preston, and provide manpower to guard vehicles in the convoy for the last bit of the journey up to Scotland. They are always armed – with carbines and pistols, but also with asps and tasers and the like. Apparently more than half of their training and briefing is about the demonstrators: people like Shona. Demonstrators have been a thorn in the side of the convoys for years, but normally in the first and last part of the journey when it is going slowly on minor roads. So that's down in Berkshire near Aldermaston and Burghfield, and the last bit in the narrow roads near Coulport."

"Coulport?" It was not a name Ali recognised.

"It's just along the coast from the nuclear submarine base at Falsane. Coulport is the place they store complete missiles and fit the warheads to them: the submarines go there to be reloaded." For someone only recently introduced to the English staple of beans on toast, Abaya was polishing her dinner off speedily.

"So, the motorcycle outriders and the police in the cars are particularly alert in that part of the journey. A couple of years ago one single man held the convoy up for five minutes just by lying down in front of it on some minor road in Scotland. But apart from a breakdown or two, there has never been trouble with protestors on the motorway, so he said the guard force relax a bit. He actually said that the police from Barrow like the chance to do it – it's much less dull than patrolling the shipyard, and they sometimes get paid overtime. It's a bit of a day out."

"So could someone tail the convoy and report on its progress? Or could he leak us the route in advance?"

"No and no. He said that if any vehicle seems to be keeping pace with the convoy, or taking a close interest, the motorbike outriders find some reason to pull it over – brake light supposedly not working, something like that. He would probably tell me the routing if he knew it, but whatever route they choose is liable to change if traffic is bad or there is some other problem. But he said that the routing this year is going to be more predictable than ever before. There are two bottlenecks here in the North, because they can only use the west route up the M6 or the East route up the A1M – but theA1M is being upgraded, it's got lane closures and a 50 mile an hour limit. He thinks there is no way they will run the east route. The only problem will be finding out when the convoy will set off."

"And what about the lorries themselves. Are they armoured? Hardened? Do they have special tyres?"

Ali had shown Abaya what he had found on line about the warhead transporters used for transit across the United States. The National Nuclear Safety Administration took a very different approach to the MOD. The N.N.S.A. has 40 individual lorries masquerading as standard civilian Peterbilt diesel truck; but they are in fact "Safeguard Transporters", designed and built by Sandia National Laboratories. Travelling incognito with three teams of armed guards in unmarked Chevvy suburbans, the transporters are armoured, have run-flat tyres and auto-sanders to get traction if an attacker spreads oil on the road. There are firing points for two federal agents to engage attackers without leaving the vehicle. And the trailer they pull is also highly engineered. The back doors are 12 inches thick, and the set-up includes a feature where the crew in the vehicle can flood the trailer interior with gas. There are a variety of automatic devices which will engage any attackers even if the crew are all dead – and if the trailer tips beyond a certain angle, an inclinometer detects it and fills the entire space with expanding quick setting foam.

"Nothing like that," said Abaya. "It's a joke. They just use normal lorries with Royal Air Force Drivers."

"So, what happens when there is a breakdown?" Given their intent of taking out the tyres of one of the H.G.V.s, it was a central point he had tasked Abaya to find out.

"He said things have changed this year. They used to keep the whole convoy together, with the whole guard force. If a guard vehicle broke down they would carry on and make do with a little less security. If a warhead carrier had problems, they would all stop at the roadside while the recovery vehicle came up from the rear and winched it up. Then they would go on to their destination or the next checkpoint and sort themselves out."

"But you said the policy had changed," Ali prompted.

"It seems there was a lot of embarrassment last year. In broad daylight the whole convoy ended up on the hard shoulder on a dual carriageway down in the South. Lots of photos made it onto social media – not just taken by the protestors who track the convoys, but holidaymakers, annoyed commuters, bored teenagers. So now they intend to do it differently: get the main body of the convoy to a safe haven, with its guard force accompanying it. And manage the broken down vehicle with a smaller force for the brief time it takes to get it on the recovery truck."

"So, if we can get a single warhead lorry disabled, and its guard force up to its neck in dealing with Shona and her demonstration…."

"Then the odds are in our favour, not theirs."

Chapter 10

Bay City

Early January

In the 1970s calling a Lancaster car repair business "Bay City Motors" was probably a pretty good pun – with Morecambe Bay just down the coast and the lettering picked out in tartan. The tartan was now long gone, and the music of the Bay City Rollers was ancient history to anyone under 50 years old, but that didn't stop the business being something of a household name in the area. Countless teenagers started their driving career in a second-hand banger from Bay City, often one that had been sold and resold again after going through years being maintained by its mechanics for a little old lady or growing family. It was a given that all Bay City vehicles had only one careful owner, regardless of whether this was true or not. Fortunately, Lancaster was neither affluent or gentrified – the biggest store in the centre is still a Primark – so plenty of vehicles stayed in use long enough to break; and mechanics like Ali had plenty of work fixing them. Added to the local trade was the gravy train which was the M6 motorway, with an endless stream of breakdowns and crashes happening a handful of miles away: a workstream which had lucrative spin off benefits in putting back into sale bent and broken insurance write offs fit only for scrap.

With the nearest other significant towns Kendal, a dozen miles to the North, or Preston a dozen to the South, the family owners had a captive market and were happy to run the business on a loose leash so long as the profits kept rolling in.

That suited Ali. In 6 months he had carefully cultivated a reputation as a skilled mechanic, who was a bit green on some of the fancier emission control nonsense or engine management chips, but who could do the hard yards of welding and engineering: and who didn't turn his nose up at the drudge work of recovery, home-starting dead batteries, or sorting punctures and exhausts. Already he had his "regulars", so when Shona appeared at the reception desk on a Saturday morning and asked for him by name to get some advice on a second-hand car, no one thought it odd. Mid-twenties, dashing, lean, and dark, Ali was already being teased as a lonely housewives' favourite, and the middle-aged Scottish radiographer was apparently cut from the same cloth.

Appearing as requested at the door linking a cluttered and paper strewn reception area to the pits and ramps where a number of vehicles were being attended to, Ali wiped his hands on blue paper roll from a wall dispenser, and nodded to Shona. Quickly shepherding her onto the forecourt, the two stepped over to far side where a number of supposed second-hand bargains were lined up, each proclaiming its credentials in gaudy yellow vinyl lettering peppering its windscreen. Keen to get right into role as a customer, Shona stopped at the first car in line, a black boy-racer Daihatsu hatchback, but Ali shuffled her along with an arm across the small of the back.

"Let's look at this one Shona – I think it's a bit more your thing!"

Indeed it was – a bright blue 2CV, which had lesbian chic in abundance.

"Just follow my lead," Ali encouraged. He began walking around the car slowly, seeming to any idle observer to be pointing out interesting features, before popping the bonnet and fixing the stay carefully to hold it upright. He tried not to smirk as he thought what effect Shona's considerable bulk would have on the primitive cantilever suspension if she was actually to buy and drive the French classic – it would probably go down the road about as wonky as one of Bay City's less satisfactory cut-and-shuts.

Bending down to look below the bonnet at what to her was an utterly incomprehensible lump of oily steel, Shona began.

"Abaya said you had some news. She gave me this." She unfolded the details of the Stinger.

"I do. The Stinger to stop the lorry is easy to get hold of. Its £500 though. Is that a problem?"

Shona shook her head.

"The main thing for me is to make sure it's not traced back to me. Or that it draws attention to you, at least ahead of your demonstration. But that is not too difficult. You should be able to set up a Paypal or Apple Pay account, and then get it delivered to one of the corner shops or grocers which acts as a parcel drop."

Shona was impressed – she had not expected Ali's assistance to be so comprehensive or thoughtful.

"So, all I do is push the button and it fires into the path of the lorry?"

While the technology of her workplace was familiar, Shona was a bit out of her depth with things mechanical.

"Sure. No need for timing or brute force. As you can see according to the specification you could actually be 100 metres away and set it off by remote control – but I think that might be hard to time. If you are on the hard shoulder, you just hit the button the moment the preceeding vehicle passes, and the warhead carrier hits the spikes."

"You don't think they will see something amiss?"

"Your University friend is happy to pretend to be broken down?" Shona nodded. "Then you are in business. You get out of direct view at the front of his car and set the Stinger box on the tarmac. Each vehicle will be fairly close to the one in front, and those big trailers mean a driver in a right-hand drive lorry can see only 100 metres or so down the hard shoulder because the next truck in front is in the way. I have one other thing we can do but it depends on what your lecturer friend can do for me."

"I have talked to him about your application. He is very happy to recommend you."

"For what I am willing to do I will want more than a recommendation". Ali looked Shona in the eye. "You want the breakdown to be realistic yes? Nothing to arouse suspicion? And to be well hidden until you spring the trap? Well, what better than to have a big recovery vehicle pulled up behind you, amber lights spinning? We do motorway recovery all the time. Once we know the convoy is on its way and if we know the route, we get you and your friends faking a breakdown, and I can park our truck behind you."

Ali pointed right across to the other side of the forecourt, where a 3 tonne recovery truck with "Bay City Motors – Let's Roll!" in big type on its bonnet was parked ready for call out: one of those with a separate benched passenger compartment just behind the cab, so that a car could be winched on the flat bed while the stranded occupants had somewhere to sit as they were ferried to their destination. Shona could see that its bulk would provide an excellent barrier from view – and it would also feel a damn sight safer on the hard shoulder waiting for the convoy with the protection of its flashing lights pulled up behind them.

Shona only took a moment to make up her mind. "I'll see what I can do."

~~

Kiwi buttoned his shirt back up, noticing as he did so how loosely it now sat on his frame. For a while now he had sensed his collar getting looser, his sleeves becoming easier to roll up as he dragged himself from his bed each morning. The Oromorph was keeping the pain at bay, but for the first time in his life he felt frail and all of his age.

"How long?" Some people never asked the question direct. Kiwi was not some people. His oncologist, sombre and serious, knew not to mince his words.

"You know it's hard to say. Things have gone off a cliff a bit as you probably know? You might be lucky and get a year, but the weight loss is a worry. Are you eating?"

"Would you be?"

"I guess not."

"What should I expect?"

"The chest pain from the primary will probably plateau, but the breathlessness will start to get worse. As you can see on the C.T., there is no sign of brain mets, but headache or dizziness or morning vomiting might arise if any develop. Of course, we could treat that as it arises....but you have said that's not for you. You know you can change your mind about that any time?" Kiwi thought the last comment was said hopefully. Doctors never seemed to tire of trying to wring the last bit of life out of every one of their charges.

"I'd rather not spend the last months of my life an invalid."

"How do your family feel about that?"

"Fortunately, I don't have to worry about such things." Kiwi wondered as he spoke if he was trying to persuade himself.

"What do you plan to do?"

“Whatever I can fit in,” Kiwi answered.

~~

50-odd miles from the Royal Marsden, Maryam was also thinking about dying. Sat at her desk in Upavon that evening she gently pulled open the drawer, revealing a red flannel cloth which she unfolded to reveal the other physical artefact she had retained of the ambush in Katdelay.

Glinting in the light of her angle-poise lamp was a pistol: the Glock 17 which she had used to blaze away at the enemy while the life was ebbing from her. Of course, holding an unauthorised firearm was an offence which would land you in Military Prison quicker than you could say “knife”, a consideration which preyed on her every time she held it.

But grasping the weapon in both hands, running her fingers over the cold black metal, had become an essential ritual every night. Mazz no longer re-lived lying in the dust in that parched field as often as she once had; nor the pain of being hauled by Woolley across his shoulders, each remembered stride towards safety piercing her side like a dagger. But she still felt consumed by the loneliness of that minute in the open, bullets spitting around her. In the Field Hospital in Kandahar, chest drain sucking bloody discharge from her side into a clear plastic bag on the bed side, she had sworn that she would never be without means to defend herself ever again. It had not proved difficult to secrete the Glock in her belt order – and in the aftermath of the ambush, no-one questioned either how she had “lost” her weapon, nor why it had not shown up in the course of the ambush site being secured and exploited. Repatriated via the Forces Medical Centre in Birmingham, Mazz and her kit evaded the usual processes of screening, and the pistol had become a fetish, a keepsake which connected her to her fear at the same time as taking the edge from it. She worked the action, hearing a satisfying clack and taking in the reassuring precision of the slider transiting back and forward. Her hip had healed; her chest wound no longer left her breathless and anxious in every run; and with the souvenir safely stowed back in her desk, Mazz was just composed enough to click off the light and try to sleep.

~~

Ali struggled to comprehend how Shona possibly tolerated spending more than 5 minutes with Duncan without strangling him. In the half hour since the two of them had picked him up from work in the Citroen, the lecturer had taken the wrong turn having confused left and right, had taken the second instead of third exit from a roundabout, and had not got over 60 miles an hour even now they were on the motorway. For the moment, however, he was a potentially useful idiot, and the Syrian settled for a fantasy of stitching bullets up his back when the ambush finally went down. There was only so much limp liberal vegetarian tosh he could take.

Biting his tongue, Ali directed him southbound past Lancaster services, a unique landmark with its hexagonal tower on the Northbound side. Originally conceived as a tourist viewpoint over the bay and the rising moors to the east, the Pennine Tower stands 20 metres tall, resembling nothing other than an air traffic control centre transplanted into rural Lancashire. Legend has it that the Beatles drove 70 miles to eat in the 120-seat American Diner which used to attract locals who came specially for a taste of the exotic – but now the whole thing was mothballed and unused.

"This is a decent landmark Duncan." Ali tapped the driver on the shoulder and made sure he had paid attention. "Once you pass here you go on past the turn to Blackpool, then get off at Junction 31 and then come up Northbound."

Duncan obliged and brought the Cactus around the dog-bone roundabout below the motorway after taking the off ramp. It was still twilight, and Ali mused that at least at the pedestrian speed Duncan was driving they should get a decent view of what they were looking for.

It was Emad who had spotted the site a week before, driving with Ali on a recce of the M6. Browsing along Google Maps and a road atlas had revealed no way off the motorway other than established junctions, and this had stood to put the end to any plan to seize nuclear material from a convoy. But half way between a junction and the services on a scouting trip, Emad had seen a break in the verge and the tarmac of the hard shoulder opening out, and there was the rat run they needed: "Works vehicles only" read the sign, and Ali deduced that rather than just a safe staging point it might provide a short-cut off the motorway. A short-cut potentially unconsidered and overlooked even by those who patrolled the route for a living. Scanning the satellite imagery and then equipped with an OS map from a tourist shop in town confirmed Ali's hopes – the works' access fed a narrow lane which led through a short tunnel below the main West Coast rail line which paralleled the motorway, linking to the village of Caterall. Within a couple of kilometres, a vehicle leaving at this point would hit the main A6, for decades the main north south trunk road, fast and straight. Once through the small town of Garstang, you could be on your way North and safely housed back in Lancaster in 15 minutes.

Ali leant forward between the two front seats and coached Duncan and Shona to continue North past Junction 32, then look for the only set of power pylons to cross the motorway in those parts; he figured even in the dark these should stand out against a clear or moonlit sky. Then one mile further on they were to look for where the motorway rose up on an embankment; in daylight, they would be able to check position by looking out of the passenger window for a cue. As expected, the village of Bilsborrow could be seen, with a posse of canal boats tied up at a Marina on the Lancaster canal just after the waterway crossed a small brook on a Victorian aqueduct. A kilometre further on, the Cactus passed beneath a flyover, and Ali warned Duncan that this would be the point where he would need to start to pull over with his supposed breakdown. When the tree-line on the left of the motorway stopped, and the accompanying railway began to rise above the road on its own embankment, there would be 400 metres to go.

"I see it," said Duncan, spotting the large marker sign for the Works Access. "It's bizarre," he said. "I have been driving this road for years. I guess you never notice these things because they just don't apply to you."

"See the C.C.T.V. tower?" Ali pointed to where it stood, maybe ten metres high, exactly at the point where the works exit left the road. "On the day I want you to pull up right at its base."

Duncan nodded as they flashed past, while Shona, who had been taking photos on her phone as they progressed along Northbound, took one last shot of the access road and then put the device away.

"That's gold dust," Shona said. "Once the lorry's tyres are spiked and it pulls up, that camera should capture everything. If something goes wrong and the lads' footage gets seized before we can upload it, the traffic cam should make sure that we make News at Ten."

"The lighting won't be very good if its night-time," Duncan ventured.

"Sure, but you have seen the convoys. All the flashing lights and floodlights of the vehicles. It will still be quite a show with a warhead lorry and police cars and the fire engine and the tow truck. Good enough for our purposes."

"But make sure you pull up right at the foot of the tower where you are in the blind spot," Ali insisted. "If that camera spots you pulled up on the hard shoulder with the convoy on route they might send a traffic officer or police to investigate. You get in place, get the bonnet up, hazards on, and call my mobile. If we get decent warning I will be in place in the truck down at Junction 22 and I can be with you in 10 minutes. We set the Stinger up and wait."

Even at Sunday driver speed they were already nearly back at Lancaster Services, the tower looming ahead out of the rapidly darkening sky.

"Duncan has Shona explained the help I need in return for this?"

"Ali it's not a problem. From what Shona has told me you are very well qualified from Syria? The University has a very high-profile inclusion policy, and helping to put a refugee and one time "White Helmet" back on his feet will be great PR. And in this country Engineering is an area where we struggle nowadays to get decent applicants. I had a word with the Head of the School of Engineering and we can get the wheels moving as soon as you like."

"What about tuition fees?"

"For someone like you there will be bursaries and scholarships. Can Abaya help support you?" Duncan caught Ali's eye in his rear-view mirror and the Syrian nodded.

"I am sure we can work something out. I have some savings from the garage too."

At one time, with studies in Damascus trashed by the war Ali would have jumped at such an opportunity; but he was already past the point of no return on a different path.

"It would be good to get it all fixed up now," Ali suggested. "With a bit of luck, when you pull your surprise, I will be able to pass myself off as a duped recovery mechanic who just ended up in the wrong place at the wrong time. Shona may have a link to Abaya but if all you do is force a truck to a halt I cannot see they will dig too far into anything other than your protest group and its members. But just in case let's get my place on a course nailed down. It will be hard for your friend to take a place at the University away once given, a lot easier to deny me one if my name is all over the papers for the wrong reasons."

Ali was quite proud of his performance. The dupes were in the front of the car, not the back.

~~

Guns. Sourcing the weaponry for the ambush had proved more of an issue than Ali and Abaya had anticipated. While it remained true that Syrian connections in London would undoubtedly be able to help, the flaws of such a supplier were soon apparent. On one hand, the chance of the security services or anti-terrorist branch having surveillance assets watching the Syrian community were high: they could end up in an M.I.5 sting, or being gunned down before they had even started. Beyond that, the risk of transporting a stash of firearms 400 miles seemed unnecessary. Particularly when there was a perfectly adequate sources of firearms 50 miles away – in Manchester.

One advantage of Ali's work was that he got to meet a lot of people, some of whom had numerous friends with entrepreneurial attitudes and a diverse product range. Which is how he and Emad ended up on a January evening parked up in a recovery van beside a tower block in Moss Side with a holdall full of dollar bills. It was only 7pm but the street was mostly deserted: too late for those few who had spent their day in legitimate employment, a little early for most of those peddling sex and drugs. They sat and watched the street for a couple of minutes, as a variety of pasty-faced and lank-haired locals came to and fro around the foyer of the flats, but nothing was moving on the opposite side of the street: a row of two-story social housing built a decade or so before, to provide dwellings better suited to human's than rabbits. A sign proclaimed this side of the street to be a joint project between the city council and a not-for-profit venture providing "key worker housing". Given they were here to meet a drug dealer come gun-runner, Manchester presumably had a different attitude to what constituted a "key worker" to other more advantaged parts of the U.K.

Re-assured that there was no obvious sign of threat, Ali directed Emad to stay in the van and lock the doors once he was inside the property. The seventeen-year-old looked sceptical. Thoroughly adept at the ins and outs of survival from rocket and air attack in Damascus, the atmospherics of a dodgy postcode in Manchester were well out of his comfort zone. He pulled his hood over his head, leaned against the cold of the passenger door window, checked and gripped his mobile phone, and pretended to be asleep. Emad had learned enough even in the relative tranquillity of Lancaster College to know that being accused of eye-balling a passer-by was a sure-fire route to trouble, and he trusted that a huddled figure in a worn-out recovery van parked in the shadow between two street lights would be low profile enough for ten minutes.

Ali looked both ways and stepped quickly across to the opposite kerb and rang the door-bell which chimed pleasantly: a stark contrast to the rest of the exterior of the house, battered door protected by a metal barred gate, wheelie bin overflowing with black bin bags that a rat or fox had got to before the council's increasingly intermittent collection. Ali was braced for the door to be opened by some kind of enforcer, especially when a shadow behind the spy hole suggested the occupant was pausing to carefully check him out; the middle aged bespectacled Mancunian who actually appeared came as a surprise. As did what Ali could see of the interior, shiny laminate wood flooring, dark hardwood hall table and tasteful mirror, kitchen at the end of the field of view with smart tiling and moody lighting.

"Marco?" Ali said doubtfully.

"Of course. Come in."

Marco motioned for Ali to enter past him, and directed him into the lounge to the left. It was understated; tasteful even. Marco seemed to sense Ali's surprise.

"You were expecting something a bit more "authentic"? A couple of sullen gang members? Token pimp? Carefully arranged crack whores?"

"I suppose so."

"I leave those trappings to the wannabes who like the attention and are happy with the convictions and jail time that go with it. I prefer to blend in. I believe you have a particular need? Handguns are easy but the sub machine gun and special ammunition came at a price. Especially the special ammunition – that was hard to come by."

Can you show me.

"This, I think will suit your requirement well."

Marco opened the wooden cabinet built into the alcove below his large T.V. set, revealing a steel gun case secured by two heavy padlocks. He kneeled and withdrew from it two short black carbines, stocks folded, hefting them easily onto the rug. They were less than half a metre in length, familiar in general design while not recognisable as anything Ali had seen before, either in Syria or on T.V.

"This is a Vitaz-SN. Latest thing in the Russian forces – oh, and the Namibian Marines, apparently! Lots of the parts are the same as an AK-74 so it has a really good track record. They take a 30-round magazine, fully automatic, and see this feature..." he pointed to the slotted muzzle brake at the end of the barrel, "reduces the tendency to put 2 rounds on target and the other 28 into the sky." Marco worked the action and unfolded the stock with dexterity before passing it to Ali. It wasn't even 3 or 4 kilos.

"You are looking to protect yourself at close range?" Marco was old-school, and candour about the possible end use of what he supplied felt somehow rude. Ali nodded. "Then this will do you fine. Anywhere over 50 metres though, and you are wasting your time with the ammunition that you need."

Marco pulled four cardboard boxes from the gun safe, each of a hundred 9mm rounds, along with 8 slim black curved magazines. He fitted an empty magazine to one of the carbines with a satisfying click to show Ali the finished look, then opened a box of ammunition to show him.

"This is an "overpressure bullet". They are very bad for the working parts in the long run, but I am assuming you don't expect to be using these weapons on a regular basis. It's coded in the Russian forces as a 7H31 round, and it has a smaller lighter steel penetrator with a much higher muzzle velocity than a normal 9mm: it carries a lot of energy, and up to 50 metres it will go through any normal body armour". He rubbed his chin thoughtfully. "Well, maybe not a chest plate on a full top-of-the-range military vest, but anything in normal use. And if you are shooting at a target without body armour, the bullet stays intact and makes a big wound channel. For a small calibre weapon it gives a very solid outcome."

"And pistols?"

"I thought something that fires the same round might be good: so that means Russian again. This is the MP443-Grach." He pulled three pistols from the gun case one after the other. This time Ali did recognise the weapon: the Grach had been standard Russian issue for years, and plenty of them were in play in the Syrian Civil War. Not as pretty as a Glock or a Sig-Sauer, the Grach was more of a Browning 9mm look-a-like, used the same design principle, and was absolutely reliable. These, like the two Vitaz carbines, were brand new and box fresh, Ali feeling the light sheen of gun oil between his fingertips.

"You are happy?" Marco asked.

"Very."

"The price is $10,000 for the two Vitaz, $1000 each for the pistols, and $5000 for the ammunition." Marco looked at Ali deadpan. It was a steep price point, but Ali was an unknown quantity, and that would cost him a premium. He awaited the client's likely but pointless efforts to negotiate the price down. None came.

"Put two more boxes of ammunition and two more magazines in and call it a round $30,000?"

"Done. I have the other things you asked for too – but I will throw them in with my complements."

Ali pulled out his mobile phone, and checked Marco was happy for him to use it. "The money will be here presently".

Chapter 11

Back South

Late January - Wednesday

Ben and Joop were unsurprised to be summoned to the C.O. first thing on Wednesday morning. Over the previous three weeks it had been something of a regular ritual.

Most recent had been a roasting for their supposed deficiencies in the C.Q.B. house: standards in the Squadron were high, especially in the "Recapture Tactics Troop", whose role, as the name suggests, was to train to hunt down lost Defence Nuclear Materials and those who held them. The accepted orthodoxy was that this was unlikely to require normal section and troop attack drills, with a repertoire of support weapons in play, and movement across an open landscape. Rather, they would be likely to need to close in on and breach a variety of buildings against a fully prepared and forewarned enemy, in close confined spaces and against lethal opposition. In that context shooting at 50 metres counted as long range, and firearms training went down to as low as 5 metres close combat. Like most of those new to 43 Commando, Collins found particularly hard evolutions moving between using his C8 carbine and Glock pistol. In C.Q.B. you might not have the moment it took to switch a magazine on your main weapon, and to switch and draw a sidearm smoothly and bring it to the aim was easier to describe than to do.

Of course, Joop had approached the challenge by feigning confusion, hamming up his accent, and asking a bemused Royal Marine Corporal if "you mean we might actually have to fire our gunsh….in the Dutsch Marines we have heard of thish, but I have never actually seen someone do it…".

Ironically the Dutchman had fired a DiMarco C8 before. The short-barrelled sub machine gun was standard in Holland but in the Marines was unique to 43 Commando: anticipating gunfights inside buildings or naval vessels, the unit needed a low velocity weapon which would suit confined spaces, firing frangible rounds which would put a target down but which wouldn't go through dry walls or bulkheads or ricochet back at the shooter. While the SA80 or a Heckler and Koch could fire such a round, trial and error showed that the stoppage rate for each was way worse than the C8, and that left Collins way behind the Dutchman in speed, accuracy, just about everything. Joop wasn't slow to point out to Ben that for once he had "vallen me je neus in de bolter" – fallen with his nose in the butter – his scores giving him a head start in beating Collins to the troop command slot. Not that Major Chandler was minded to give him any credit – "barely adequate for our needs" had been his choice of phrase.

Pushing through the double doors into the Squadron Admin building, a low and ugly prefab at the heart of the Faslane yard, Ben was surprised to find most of the H.Q. desks unoccupied. The only Marine present was Major Chandler's clerk / typist, a position which Ben mused must demand a hard heart and Teflon coating: the young soldier looked up from his lap top and directed them down the corridor to the briefing room at the rear. "Watch yourself Sir," he added kindly. "They've already started."

Ben knocked gingerly and stepped in.

"Ah, Little and Large, what kept you?" Major Chandler had evidently recharged his sarcasm ahead of the first convoy of the year, probably his final one as OC of the Squadron. Stood beside a large HD screen with laser pointer in hand, he had begun a brief for the long-suffering Captain Ledsham and a mixed bag of other officers and Senior N.C.O.s: the collective brains trust of the unit. Ben and Joop had come to know well the two most similar to them in age and seniority: Lieutenants Carter and Johnson, known inevitably as "Jimmy" and "Lyndon", respectively currently commanding the Stand Off Escort and Recapture Tactics Troops. You probably would have to be a Marine to see the logic and comedy value in posting “The Presidents” to serve in the same Squadron together, but both had the best part of a year in post, and carried themselves with the easy professionalism you would expect. The remainder of those present had a focus on signals, logistics, or operational planning, and Ben had to remind himself that even this team was only a small cog in an operation that would pull in dozens of other staff from agencies all across the U.K.

The Major waited for the two late-comers to be seated, Ben was sure for the small-minded satisfaction of embarrassing them rather than to ensure a focused brief. Carter pulled out a seat for Ben and rolled his eyes in sympathy. Joop joined them.

The brief restarted. Chandler detailed that this convoy, designated imaginatively Transport 24, would be a continuous running convoy of 5 vehicles carrying a total of 34 warheads from Burghfield to Coulport, running from noon to midnight two days hence, Friday the 30th. The warning order, which had come in the day before from the snappily titled “Director Nuclear Movements and Nuclear Accident Response Group”, detailed no unusual issues, and no abnormal security precautions were required. The full brief for Carter and those accompanying the convoy would be done on Friday in Burghfield, with the MOD police Special Escort Group and others riding shotgun in the warhead lorries. For the moment, Chandler detailed that as usual the 24 Marines of the Stand Off Escort Troop would be flown down to Burghfield the day before the convoy: a "Junglie" Merlin HC4 from the Commando Helicopter Force's 845 Naval Air Squadron would come up from Yeovilton in Somerset to collect them, flying on to Coulport to bring them back at the end of the task. SOE troop's armoured Mercedes vans would be awaiting them in the vehicle pound at Burghfield, having sat there unused since the last North to South convoy in November. R.T.T. would be picked up from Faslane by a second Merlin on Friday morning, but would be taken to R.A.F. Brize Norton in the first instance, before shadowing the convoy in a series of hops up the spine of England. Loitering at a variety of MOD sites as the convoy made its way up the M40 and M6, Lieutenant Johnson and his troop would never be more than 20 minutes flying time from the convoy, ready to pounce on anyone doing a smash and grab. The Major himself would follow proceedings from a smaller Wildcat helicopter, this time from 847 N.A.S., which would sadly allow him to stick his critical and caustic nose in anywhere, any time.

While the brief from the various key players was professional and on point, Ben got a clear sense of those present going through the motions. Major Chandler was fiddling with his phone for much of the comms and admin briefs. "Probably on Tinder," whispered Joop with a smirk. "Or Grinder maybe."

"Are you allowed to be gay in the Dutch Marines?" Ben asked.

"It's compulsory," Joop said, blowing a kiss.

Ben made particularly careful notes of the squadron radio net: their shadowing would involve listening to the interplay of the different units and elements as much as seeing them, especially without access to the friendly-vehicle tracking technology that the Mercedes vans were equipped with.

Closing the brief, the Major signposted their role on the trip.

"Gentlemen, 2nd Lieutenants Collins and de Jong will be shadowing with Prof. Barton, as I know many of you have done in the past. Call sign will be Clyde 44. Collins I don't want the net clogged with idle chit chat and dumb questions clear? Listening watch only. You are there to observe only, no firearms to be drawn, and you have no status on this tasking. You can hitch a lift down on the Merlin but after that you are on your own. There is no vehicle allocated down at Burghfield, and I know Barton doesn't drive. You will need to sort something."

"I have an Intelligence Corps driver lined up from Upavon, Sir. Will that suit?"

Major Chandler gave a dismissive wave. "I am sure that will be fine. Make sure the vehicle I.D. is logged with all parties at the brief down South. And stay out of the way."

~~

If you see the signs to Burghfield from the old A30 as it jinks through the Berkshire countryside between Reading and Thatcham, there is little to suggest what an odd place it is. If you follow the signs, you first come to Burghfield village – a picture postcard place which must be little changed from the 1950s, pretty 19th century brick cottages intermingled with wooden-beamed Tudor houses. There is a Victorian-era village school, a bowls club, thriving pub, Post Office, and everything else you might want to have included if you ordered an English village from central casting for a sleepy Sunday night detective show.

But pass through the village and you cannot miss the monumental scale of the Atomic Weapons Establishment, seemingly dumped on the hill top behind. For one of the U.K.'s most secret sites, it is hardly tucked away, nor could it be. Having started life in World War 2 filling shells and bombs with explosives, it had grown to the foot-print of a large regional airport, a tangled jumble of low two and three-story buildings, hangers, warehouses, offices, not one seemingly having any design consistency to its neighbour. The one consistent feature is the fencing and razor wire running for miles around the perimeter, befitting the site's role in designing, assembling, maintaining, refitting, and then ultimately decommissioning Trident nuclear warheads. Armed MOD police patrol the perimeter, with carte blanche to use lethal force when needed, and with a focus sharpened by an episode in 2013 where thirty of their number were removed from their posts on "Black Tuesday" – a whistle-blower flagged a culture of sloth and complacency in the guard force which the senior managers, who had overseen that culture, saw fit to resolve by firing their subordinates. This won no popularity context but had a salutary effect, as anyone breaking in would find to their cost.

For John Dawson, the severe rigor of the management was less important than having a steady and predictable shift pattern. Now Alice was safely attended to in Reading General Hospital, with periodic sessions at the Proton Inc unit in the nearby Science Park, Burghfield provided some respite from the treadmill of his child's cancer treatment. Those on the establishment of the MOD Police guard unit had been quietly forewarned that their new colleague had a sick child and needed to be given a bit of space, and they had been kind and supportive from day one. The feedback on Alice from her clinicians had been encouraging.

So as Dawson drove sedately up to the barrier at the East Gate of Burghfield that morning, passing the small coterie of peace protestors on the grass verge as he did so, his mood was upbeat. His Sergeant had flagged the day before that there was the chance of some overtime at the back end of the week, accompanying the next nuclear materials convoy. Even a fortnight before John would have given it a miss. Maybe it was worth a go.

~~

The gaggle of shabby campaigners beside the East Gate had got used to the familiar signs of an imminent convoy. Had Burghfield been built from scratch, no doubt effort would have been put in to keeping key operations beyond the view of the perimeter. But it hadn't, and they weren't. So, as Mercedes escort vehicles were pulled from storage and moved across the site for fuelling, eyes were watching. But it was the arrival that afternoon of a series of matt green unmarked R.A.F. articulated lorries, rolling through the gate at pace and obviously with the anticipation of the security staff, that was the dead giveaway. It was this signifier which led to Shona receiving a text that Thursday evening from a long-standing contact – one who she had known since they had shared the same upbringing in the drizzle in the Peace Camp in Faslane.

"Lots of fuss at Burghfield. Reckon convoy moving in next 48 hours."

~~

Emad wondered what his on-line mates playing Call of Duty would think if they knew he had set aside his sub machine gun in-game, only to pick up a real one from under his bed. But their likely excitement was not something he felt. Unclipping the magazine and stripping apart the blow-back mechanism, with what was already an easy familiarity, he felt only empty. While Abaya and Ali had fallen into life in England with a measure of comfort, respected to a degree for their skills and noble back story in Syria, Emad was just another face at West Cumbria

College. In small town Brexit voting Lancaster, there was never likely to be a warm welcome to a gangly Arab-looking sixteen-year-old, curly black hair, thick eyebrows, and bum-fluff moustache. Not qualified the study A-levels and goaded like his fellows on an N.V.Q. course as doing a course for the "Not very qualified", he had found it best to separate himself from his white UK peers and just keep a low profile.

Abaya and Ali's fight was not his fight. Emad had been away with his grandparents when Reem was killed. One day she was there, the next not, no difference there between his sister and the school friends who had slowly leeched from his class, killed or wounded or departed as refugees to Turkey. What had hurt more was losing the attention of his older sister. After the death of their parents Abaya had brought him up, but the appearance of Ali on the scene took even her attentive and loyal focus elsewhere. Having to maintain the fiction that Ali was a blood-relative, to get him into the U.K. on the back of Abaya's work visa, didn't help Emad's feelings of abandonment and isolation.

Cleaning the short barrel and the bolt with a rag, Emad was neither enthusiastic nor anxious about what lay ahead. He had seen enough of killing for it to mean little to him. He saw no future in England, no prospects, no acceptance. He had no anger or determination or wish for revenge: only a sense that until Abaya and Ali were satisfied that they had made the West pay for its timidity and cowardice, the dark and misery of Cumbria is where he would remain. Emad had got in the habit of periodically gazing at the stash of dollars in its hidey hole. Abaya had shown him photos of the countryside where they would settle once all was done. The family had holidayed in Lebanon when times were better; and while not home, its polyglot people and relatively orderly polity was unimaginably attractive compared to the debris and wreckage of Damascus.

There was one route to some kind of future. And if that meant using the weapon he had in his hands to kill, that is what he would do. Reassembling the weapon took moments. As you would expect of a weapon from the makers of the AK47, it went together quickly and easily. Emad worked the moving parts which clacked in a most satisfactory way, then put the stock to his shoulder and sighted down the barrel at the alarm clock that would rouse him for another day's grind in a few hours. He sighed, slipped the gun between his mattress and the bed-board, and pulled a ring file out of his college rucksack to make a token effort at some work.

~~

While Emad studied half-heartedly, Ali brought Abaya up to speed at the kitchen table.

"From what we know or can guess about the weight and size of the plutonium component, the lathe at work will do fine," he began, passing her a phone showing an image of the machine at Bay City.

"Ali, it just looks like a grey box to me," Abaya replied, gazing at something that might be the bastard child of a shiny microwave oven and a shabby industrial dishwasher.

"Ok but you understand what a lathe is? You mount a die of metal on spindles, which rev it at really high speed. Then you use either manual control or computer-coded instructions to machine it with a tungsten carbide or diamond cutter. You can re-bore cylinders, fabricate custom parts to replace what's corroded on a vintage car, whatever. In our case we have a much more limited goal – strip ribbon off a block of plutonium. We know that stripped thin and fine and it should start to combust by itself. And once it's lit, the whole lot will go up."

"You are sure?"

"No", said Ali. "But I have read that when they make a warhead and machine its shape, they have to do it in an inert gas atmosphere to stop it catching fire. However, we don't know if they have come up with some kind of alloy which might be less reactive. Which is where this will come in." Ali held out a disposable picnic barbecue, the self-lighting sort which burns to charcoal speedily, paraffin impregnated paper wrapper guaranteeing it lights first time, every time. "A place called "B and Q". I thought it would be hard to get one of these in mid-winter, but they had them on offer! When we set the lathe going, we light this in the bed below the cutting tool. If the ribbon doesn't burn by itself this will get it going. By the time the fire consumes the lathe, and the die of plutonium stops spinning, the whole thing will be ablaze, and it won't matter."

Abaya pondered what he had said. As a plan it lacked elegance, but made good use of reliable, basic, and familiar equipment. If they managed to seize parts of a warhead, it should be perfectly possible to start a plutonium fire.

"This lathe Ali, it's in the back of the workshop is that right?"

Ali nodded.

"So, who's to say that any of the smoke and dust and radioactivity will get even out onto the garage forecourt?"

Ali fiddled intently with his phone, swiped with his finger, and passed the device back to Abaya.

"This will do the job nicely."

The phone showed an image of an orange and black unit, the size of a camping power generator, with an air horn to suck fumes in at one end, and a long, snaking, concertina like tube for feeding them out to the outside air running away out of shot in the image.

"We use this when we are welding, or spray painting. It's for blowing toxic fumes out of the confined space for the wind to dissipate. Its portable, we can put it right next to the lathe and leave the cover open. Of course, once the plutonium is lit and the inlet is sucking in smoke and radioactivity nicely, what it blows out will be rather worse for the neighbourhood than low-toxic welding fumes."

"It still won't carry far from the workshop," Abaya ventured.

"Don't you believe it. Think about Chernobyl. The fallout from the fire and explosion went for miles. I think the accident was first detected in Sweden. People around here still talk about a nuclear reactor fire at a place near here 50 years ago, at somewhere called Windscale. People all over the North were seen as at risk. And remember, it doesn't have to carry far to paralyse everything for miles."

Abaya and Ali had talked about the small population of Lancaster, and the limited radiation casualties that might result from exposure to a plutonium fire. But a quirk of geography made this almost beside the point. The main west coast railway line from London to Glasgow ran right through town, with no other route West of the Pennines. And the M6, of course, passed a mile or so East of the town, with no other link to Scotland bar the M1 and A1M the other side of the country. If they managed to irradiate just this corner of Cumbria, no travel through the area would be safe for years – maybe not generations. As a statement and reminder to the West that the destruction and misery and toxicity that their leaders chose to ignore in Syria could equally befall the green fields of home, it would make the wreckage of the Twin Towers look a minor irritation.

Abaya looked up from the screen at Ali.

"And you have the guns and ammunition. Ali it's taken a long time, but I think we are ready."

Chapter 12

Mounting Up

As the Merlin helicopter settled on the pad at Faslane, Ben found himself suddenly back in Kandahar. The rotor noise was like a familiar friend, but it was the smell of burnt avgas and the lube oils which coated every working part of the helicopter which hit home more. It looked odd to see the gunner/observer, khaki flightsuit clad, head crowned with a visored helmet, leaning casually out of the door on his safety harness, looking to call the final inches to his pilot, rather than behind a minigun ready to let rip on an Afghan enemy. But in the safety of Faslane the only audience for the landing were the two "chalks" of Stand Off Escort Troop, lined up off the lad below the foot of the "H", ready to file on once the ramp was down.

While it was still only Thursday afternoon, and their assignment was a day away, the Marines already made an imposing sight. Unlike armed police there was none of the affectation of jet black boiler suits, Wehrmacht-style fibreglass helmets, Walter Mitty special kit hanging off body armour like a Mexican bandit. And no balaclavas more suited to Val D'Isere than a criminal take down, leaving only a letterbox of eyes and eyebrows and a ridge of nose to give away the identity of the supposed super-cop inside. 43 were Royal Marines and proud of it. They were serving as soldiers, there to shoot and if need be kill anyone minded to attack the U.K.s vital security: they were on the down low, not there to deter peaceniks messing with the convoy, but there to provide last resort lethal force. As such, they were kitted as they would be for combat: multi-cam, Osprey body armour, belt kit containing principally multiple magazines of live 5.56mm ammunition, standard helmet. And for each man his DiMarco C8, 4x Trilux sight, the weapon resting across a thigh as they kneeled on the cold tarmac, or with unfolded stock resting on the floor. Beside each man was an olive go-bag hold-all, presumably of necessaries for their overnight stay in a billet at Burghfield. Ben thought it gave the enterprise a slightly odd air of a highly militarised spa mini-break.

Observing only, and with none of the war fighting kit of the S.O.E. Troop, Ben and Joop stood back, each trying to stop their green beret being blown across the pad by the downwash. Fortunately it was only moments before the ramp was down, and the crewman at the tail gave the signal to load. The Marines skipped forward quickly, bent forward into the gale, disappearing into the interior.

"First on, last off," observed Joop, and in a few steps they were up the ramp, and able to settle into two web seats at the rear of the cabin. It was a two hour flight, and the Dutchman dug out his earphones immediately. "New Alex M.O.R.P.H. Podcast!" He shouted into Ben's ear, putting two thumbs up with exaggerated enthusiasm.

"Knock yourself out!" Ben returned the gesture. For him, two hours of deafening rotor noise would be far preferable. As the pilot pulled pitch and the din increased further, he shut his eyes and tried to picture Maryam. It was a nice way to travel.

~~

The first sight of the Atomic Weapons Establishment from the window of the Merlin was hardly inspiring, but Ben was pleased to be able to pick out deep in the complex the gaggle of articulated trucks in a vehicle park ready for the transport. With them could be seen their accompanying Mercedes escort vehicles, pulled out of storage and ready to be occupied variously by Stand-off Escort Troop of 43 Commando, or the Special Escort Group of the MOD police. As one would expect from them doing about as many miles a year as a Royal limousine, they glinted in the sun, showroom clean.

As the helicopter descended and banked, the pilot flaring the nose upwards to bleed off airspeed, the convoy vehicles slipped out of view behind one of the larger structures, containing who knows what in the gamut of activity at the nuclear site. The Marines lining the web seats along the walls of the Merlin began fussing their kit, removing earphones, packing away iPads and paperbacks much as businessmen at the end of any dull short haul flight. Ben was more keen to scan the area around the pad for Maryam, who had promised to pick them up. At first glance there was no sign, but as the helicopter lost height and pitched forward for a well-timed touchdown, a dark blue saloon appeared from a tarmac roadway, pulling up sharply two dozen metres from the pad. The figure which appeared from the driver's seat was welcome and distinctive. Maryam Maiwand, now free of her stick, was still pedestrian and awkward in her movements, shoving the driver's door open with an elbow but then using both feet to push the door wide enough to emerge, hauling herself stiffly to her feet with hands pulling hard on the top and side of the door frame. But she was here and she was smiling, holding on to her green slime beret with one hand while waving enthusiastically with the other. Ben smiled at her lack of reserve, and stepping down the ramp as it opened with hydraulic whirr, he was delighted to be greeted with a bear hug, Mazz wrapping both arms around him and squeezing tight. He was less happy when she repeated the process with Joop, and threw his go-bag over his shoulder and headed to the car, trying not to reveal his disappointment in his body language. And failing. But then he also failed to see Maryam's smile at his discomfort.

"What the fuck, Mazz?" Ben was mightily impressed by Maryam's vehicle, as, to be fair, anyone would be. A midnight blue late model Audi A5 four door, 3 litre Diesel engine, looking like it was fresh off the forecourt.

"Nice isn't it? The C.O. uses it now and again."

"Now I see why the defence budget is fucked."

"It's a police seizure from the Proceeds of Crime Act. Instead of taking drug dealers' cars and auctioning them for peanuts, they are bumping them sideways to the armed forces as staff cars."

"And we get to use this to shadow the convoy?"

"Uh huh."

"Well it beats the shit out of a Land Rover."

"Doesn't it just."

Ben hopped into a luxurious leather front seat while Joop settled in the back. They watched Maryam gingerly perch on the edge of the driver's seat, before swinging her legs into the footwell, and leaning back.

"Oops." Mazz grimaced and reached into the small of her back, pulling from her stable belt a black shape which was immediately identifiable as a Glock pistol.

"Forgot that was there," she muttered, placing the weapon in the pocket in the driver's door, before punching the start button, engaging drive, and putting her foot down.

Ben exchanged a curious glance in the wing mirror with Joop, sat immediately behind him. If Mazz noticed she didn't say, gunning the Audi towards the gate, and turning out on the main road. The Sat Nav was set for Upavon.

~~

Shona was not particularly up to speed with the tropes of martyrdom video. Fortunately, Duncan's two tame undergraduates were, and had explained the importance of an iconic flag as a backdrop to the video which would hopefully accompany the traffic cam CCTV footage of Nukespot's show-down with the evils of nuclear warhead transportation along the UKs highways and byways. Amazon dutifully supplied a 6 foot by 4-foot Scottish Saltire with 24-hour next day delivery through Amazon Prime, and now she found herself sat on the piano stool borrowed from Duncan's daughter, with a Hwaiwei phone filming her political testament. She wondered what Lenin would have made of the set up, but her train of thought was interrupted by Duncan, directorial wannabe, counting down on three fingers and pointing that she should start.

"My name is Shona Campbell. If you are watching this, you will know that I have been arrested by the authorities. I have no idea what they will have charged me with, no idea what they will have said about me. They will probably be presenting me as unbalanced, or naïve, or infantile, or exploited by others. I am none of these things. I work for the N.H.S. saving lives. Saving lives when I can, given the unit I work in has to cope with equipment which would put the developing world to shame. I look after people with cancer. They need me. But I cannot honestly sit to one side, and spend my working day that way, while all the time the threat of nuclear destruction for millions hangs over us. The success of the authorities in this country of keeping our weapons of mass destruction out of sight and out of mind is to their credit: they are intelligent men and women who no doubt think they are doing right for their country and the values which they live by. That does not make them right. The ease with which me and my small group have disrupted a nuclear convoy, halting its progress and disabling a vehicle carrying weapons which could destroy a score of cities, shows how reckless our leaders have been. And undemocratic. We, the people of Scotland, reject the maintenance of nuclear weapons on our territory. Events today show the risk they put our citizens to, quite apart from the unwarranted threat they comprise to peoples across the world. We demand their removal from our land. We demand a public enquiry into the movement of nuclear materials, and how it was possible for a group of determined civilians to penetrate what was meant to be the water-tight security of the nuclear convoys. I have no way of knowing what will happen to me, what I will be charged with, what consequence I will face. I will accept the judgement of my peers – but in the knowledge that I fully expect my peers to recognise the noble motives of our protest, rooted in the traditions of Gandhi and Mandela and Martin Luther King, and to acquit me. If not, I can at least sleep at night. Can you?". She stopped talking and stared into camera.

"Fuck". Darren pushed the red button to cease recording. "That was actually pretty fucking good. No notes either."

Steven nodded. Duncan grinned.

Shona shrugged. "Do we need to do it again?"

"No – that is perfect. Times at 60 seconds. Just right for T.V. news – they should be able to show the whole lot," Darren said.

"And how will you make sure it gets out to public view?"

"It's not a problem," Steven said. "Twitter, Youtube, we will DM it to B.B.C., Russia Today, FoxNews, and Reuters. We will post on the Nukespot website. Jesus we can send it to Al-Jazeera and Islamic State if you like. Once word and footage gets out that a convoy has been attacked and a vehicle stranded, it won't be hard to get our message out."

"Good", said Shona. "If I end up in jail it had better be for something."

~~

On the other side of town, Abaya and Ali were admiring Emad's handiwork. Given their antipathy towards Islamic extremism, they had decided against a traditional "speech to camera". This wasn't going to be a narcissist back-slapping video farewell, Daesh-style. Instead Emad had put together a simple powerpoint slide show, with audio commentary over images of the civil war; victims of nerve gas and chlorine and barrel bombs, and torture victims of Assad's secret police. Then followed a rogue's gallery of those who had the power to restrain or even stop Assad, from Putin through Obama through the U.N. Security Council to British P.M. David Cameron. Because for the three Syrians, their attack was not about the U.K. possessing weapons of such horrific power: it was that they built them, postured with them, hid behind them, but in the end did nothing to stop the killing. Stopping some unpalatable Islamic regime coming to power in Syria was seemingly the limit of the West's objectives; and if that meant not calling out Assad as the gangster her was, and not leveraging Russia to pull the plug on his regime, so be it. Abaya had written the script and she wrote with power, and the sinister and threatening content was heightened by the voice synthesiser software Emad had used to both anonymise the speech and add to its effect. It had taken a bit of work to move the voice from something inappropriately redolent of Stephen Hawking to a tone more like the villain in "Saw", but Abaya and Ali were pleased with the effect.

"What about the exit plan?" Abaya asked Ali.

"As we discussed. At first I was looking at Turkey, but the British will be checking who flies there at the moment for fear of people slipping across into Syria and Iraq to join I.S. I think the Red Sea resorts in Egypt are better – "winter sun", family holiday, all that. Flights from Manchester are really frequent whatever day we have to fly. Once we are in

Egypt it will not be hard to get a connection to Lebanon. And there we disappear."

"You know that's a fantasy. They will come for us."

"There is no extradition to the U.K. from Lebanon."

"Who said anything about extradition? You think we can irradiate thousands of people and they will treat us like criminals? It's in range of a carrier from the Mediterranean, or a sub in the Gulf, or a drone from Djibouti, or special forces from Jordan. Every step you take if we even make it to Lebanon is just a step closer to your last step."

"Then why are we even bothering? Why even try to leave the country?"

"Emad – this has never been his fight. I owe it to him to have a hope of a future."

"He doesn't need a fairy tale to fight. He has grown up more than you think. He will pull his weight when the time comes."

"Good," said Abaya. "Because the time has come."

~~

Mazz had booked a guest room in the Officers' Quarters at Trenchard Lines for both Ben and Joop, but after beers in the bar Ben had insisted on seeing her back to her room. He waited till they were out of earshot even of Joop, who was downing shots of Slivovice with a keen female colleague of Maryam's

"Maryam… what the fuck is with the Glock? Since when do Army Intelligence Officers carry a pistol on an airport pick up. And since when is down the back of the trousers a standard mode of concealment?"

"Ben, it's not strictly an official issue."

"What do you mean "not strictly"?"

Mazz looked behind them as they padded down the lush carpet of the long first floor hallway. "O.K. It's not at all an official issue. But that doesn't mean I don't need it."

"For what?"

"For getting out of bed in the morning. Ben, I know it's not been easy for you to put Woolley out of your mind; but you have had a new posting, bullshit C.O., whole new challenge to master." She pulled a door key from the trouser pocket of her combats and opened the door, Ben following her in.

"I've been stuck here through the winter in the middle of fucking nowhere, light duties, no prospect of deployment, tossing those minutes in the middle of that field over and over in my mind. And it got worse day by day. The panic I feel every morning now is way worse than anything I felt then. I am not sure I actually was scared at the time. In that field I had you, I had Woolley and Drake and Leach and the rest of the boys, and a way of fighting. But I am scared now. I could have chosen pills. I could have hit the bottle. I chose the gun instead. It goes where I go."

"Mazz that defence won't stop you ending up in chokey."

Maryam shrugged. "It's a for-the-moment thing. When I feel the gun in my waistband the panic subsides a bit. It reminds me I survived and I can survive again. It connects me to who I used to be, not who I am at the moment. Crocked, scared."

"It's not loaded though right?"

"I am not sure there is any point in an unloaded firearm."

"Where the fuck did you get the rounds from?"

"Ben you know how shaky range procedures are with officers. They trust that we self-declare that we have no live rounds leaving the range. I got forgetful one day and ended up with a box."

"Maryam you know I will want to talk more about this." He took her by both shoulders and stared hard into her eyes. "There are better ways of dealing with this."

Mazz broke free from his hold and his glare.

“Sure. But after this job.”

“Would you listen to Kiwi if he talks to you about it?”

Maryam shrugged.

“Then let’s do that tomorrow. We pick him up at Winterborne at 9. Get some sleep.”

Chapter 13

Transport 24

Friday

It took ten minutes of elbow grease to strip the hoar frost from the windows of the Audi with the Velcro on the cuff of his combat jacket, even with Mazz ticking over the engine and running the heated window and blower. But Ben enjoyed the feeling of the freezing air on his face and in his lungs. Compared to the heat and dust of four months before, winter dawn on the Plain was priceless, and when a golden sun appeared on the horizon bathing the world in yellow light, even Upavon Officers' Mess Car Park transcended its shabby tarmac functionality. Ben knocked on the driver's window once he had cleared it.

"Mazz, don't drug dealers bother to keep scrapers and de-icer?"

"Seems not. They don't have Green Flag either."

"Shit. We really are living on the edge." He pulled the door handle and got in the front seat. "At least with Joop strapped in the back we can keep him away from the music controls. It's going to be a dozen hours in this thing and I am not keen on recreating some kind of all-night-in-a-Utrecht-warehouse festival experience."

Joop grunted, annoyed that he had been required to fold his frame into the back seat for the first stint. Mazz reached a hand across and mashed the media button on the dash.

"Don't worry Ben, idle hands in the Intelligence Corps end up with lots of time to create playlists. Do you know this?"

The woofer on the Audi sound system was better than its de-icing mechanisms, and a seventies disco drum-beat kicked into life. As the guitar solo joined, the melody was unmistakeable.

"Ha. Atomic! Very good Mazz. Now tell me you haven't got another 12 hours of nuclear-themed retro hits?"

"Of course not. Only the first 60 minutes."

The journey turned out taking an hour, slowed by having to take a detour to the A303 to stock up at a petrol station for diesel and a day's worth of snacks. Contrary to the counter assistant's expectations, it was the dark-haired woman who took the armful of "Rib n Saucy" and "Hot n Spicy" Nik-Naks and cherry Lucozade, while the tall guy with the accent made do with a dodgy raisin and muesli bar and a triple pack of Dairylea Dunkers.

"Jesus Ben. Is this what passes for cheese around here?"

"Joop, the only dairy thing about that stuff is the name."

The Dutchman scooped a knob of sweet yellow gunk with the first of a paltry allocation of tubes, leading to 5 miles of debate on why the manufacturers skimp on the mission-critical element of the snack, and the merits of tubes against the competing but ultimately even less satisfactory breadstick version. "Don't even get me started on crackers", put an end to the debate. After putting Kraft's product range to rights, a game of "beat the intro" featuring "99 Red Balloons" and "Love Missile F1-11", got them to the gates of Winterborne Gunner, and their scheduled R.V. with Kiwi.

“There he is!” Joop pointed to the left at a lonely bus stop, where the road to the base met the main road, where a thin figure waited, shrouded in breath condensing in the still freezing January air.

“Bullshit, Joop, you need your eyes tested,” said Mazz, slowing for the turn.

“I tell you it’s Kiwi. Look, shitty blue cagoule. And how many other dodgy old blokes are going to be at a bus stop in the arse end of Wiltshire at 9 in the morning.”

“No way. That guy is nowhere near Kiwi’s size.”

But Kiwi it was. Looking a shadow of his normal self, clothes hanging off him noticeably, stepping gingerly a couple of paces closer to the approaching Audi, small nylon holdall in hand.

Joop slid awkwardly across to the other side of the back seat while Kiwi got in. He smiled a greeting at the Professor, but his face fell as he saw the grimace on Kiwi’s face as he settled into the seat.

“Hi everyone,” Kiwi said. “I’m glad you did so well with the car Maryam. I could do with a bit of comfort. Not doing so good since the New Year.”

The car sat idling while Kiwi did up his seat belt, fumbling with the catch, and the three soldiers shot glances at each other.

Mazz twisted in her seat.

“Kiwi what is it.”

“Cancer I am afraid. Lung cancer. A souvenir, it seems of my time in Muralinga. Or Bikini. Or Montebello. Or any of five places in Russia; or twice that number in America. When you play with fire and all that...” His voice tailed off.

“Are you in treatment?”

“I am sadly past the point where that will do much other than drain the coffers of the N.H.S. “Mets” in the brain will be the next step.” He tapped his temple. “I am expecting something like the Cold War: an arms race between the lung and the brain tumours to see who can get me first."

"How long have you got?"

"I don't know." Kiwi's face registered the slightest smile which flashed into a broad if desperate grin. "What time is it now?"

"Seriously Kiwi."

"9 months? A year? I wouldn't be getting any Christmas presents for me if I were you. And I am not sure for how much of that I will be fit to travel or work. This really will be my last trip to Faslane."

"Some people would see that as cause for celebration." If Kiwi was minded to be ballsy, Joop was glad to support him

"Very true. So, let's get it over with Maryam if you don't mind. Let's get to Burghfield. You are going to see the whole circus with all the acts. It's quite a show. Now if you have all finished the interrogation, can I have a packet of those Nik-Naks?"

~~

Ali hated clear skies. Most winter days in Aleppo you could put faith in overcast skies and at least a bit of drizzle - in the far North of Syria up near Turkey, most of the years rain fell in a few months, and for most of the Russian and Syrian jets this made well targeted attacks difficult.

But Assad had little interest in well targeted attacks. By 2016 barrel bombs had been in use for four years, and rolling a 500kg oil drum of explosive out of the back of a Mil-8 helicopter would do just fine for flattening apartment blocks in East Aleppo. With the government forces in the West of the city stalled, destroying the districts to the South East of the historic Citadel was a priority, and Ali had got used to scanning the skies carefully the moment the beat of rotor blades was heard. Assad's Air Force had got more wily, and had needed to as the Free Syrian Army and the

Islamist rebels found sources of heat-seeking anti-aircraft missiles. By the end of November barrel bombings were coming at a rate of two to three a day, and had recently been accompanied by an apparently equally random series of blasts from Russian Kalibr missiles fired across Iran from the Caspian Sea or by Russian vessels in the Mediterranean. Of course the Americans and Royal Air Force could track all this happening with their A.W.A.C.S. planes and "Wedgetail" sensor jets. But they seemed happy to watch the slaughter.

The net was closing, destruction mounting, and however desperate the efforts of rebel factions, the pocket of resistance was shrinking. What was there to do? Having given up his studies along with five young University friends to become a White Helmet, Ali could see nothing to do but see his duty to the end. Thoughtful and studious and sometimes cack-handed, his group prided themselves in matching the bravery and physical strength of any team, and they had come to be called the "Almuhusun" by their peers - the geeks. But they were geeks who could dig, and geeks who would rip into their rubble with crowbars, drills, picks, and their bare hands, to release trapped citizens stuck under piles of rubble. And through November and into Advent, they had lived a charmed life. And they knew it.

Ali never even heard the bomb that killed his friends. Having rushed to a block of flats which had seen its frontage blasted by a barrel bomb, the White Helmets were helping shocked and bleeding residents down rubble-strewn stairwells and through shattered ground floor windows to a jumble of vehicles. He had no way of hearing the Sukhoi 34 flying way above the cloud base, crew relaxed and alert after only a brief flight from Latakia airfield nearby. As he helped a frail elderly woman in a blue hijab tread one step at a time down from the first floor, he wasn't to know that 30,000 feet up, a business-like Captain from Kazan in

Russia was watching the rescue effort on infra-red. Sitting right-seat in the weapons operator station, Captain Yashkin could have easily made out "The geeks" hustling backwards and forwards to and from the building on his helmet mounted weapon system, and would have tried to time release while as many were in the building as possible. This would be the classic "double tap" - which every White Helmet unit knew to expect, but which they could only face with gritted teeth as an occupational hazard of their role. Ali knew as he came down the stairs that dozens of civil defenders had been deliberately targeted this way. But in this case knowledge isn't power. The power was in the hands of Yashkin, who toggled a button for weapons away, and gave a thumbs up to the pilot alongside him, who began to pull Gs to go around again.

A year before Ali and the other hundred or so civilians in the firing line might still have rated their chances. Their apartment had been built post World War One during the years of French occupation as a barrack for French soldiers, and had a level of resilience and reinforcement which had given heart to its fortunate occupants during months of fighting. But the Sukhoi 34 brought with it a new tool to demoralise and destroy the will of the people: and in this case, destroy any sense that they could expect to be plucked from danger by caring and determined helpers. The B.E.T.A.B. 500 bomb Yashkin selected had no more explosive power than a barrel bomb - but was designed to penetrate deep into a concrete command bunker before exploding. Which made it just perfect to puncture the roof of a civilian apartment block, cut through all the way to the basement, detonate, and literally flatten the building and everyone in it.

And that included Ali, who had just reached the foot of the stairs. Of course he knew none of this. And would know nothing of it for another fortnight. It was only when he came around in a hospital bed in Damascus, and a pretty and slightly built young doctor took him through his X-rays, that he learned he was the only one of "The geeks" left alive. And he wept.

~~

Still up in Faslane, Major Chandler strode to his seat at a large conference table and laid on its surface a Lever Arch file 5 inches thick, plastic sheathing peeling off it, cover stained, haphazard post-its marking points of interest or importance in its many hundred pages. Of course, all of the content could be read as a PDF on any device you could think of – but Major Chandler was old school, and the heft of the "playbook" in his hand, reminded him of his, and its, multiple journeys guarding the convoy. While at the "sharp end" of convoy protection issues were simple – guard the nuclear materials, get them from A to B, shoot anyone who takes them – above and alongside 43 Commando were a panoply of commands and vested interests that had come to be nicknamed "The Octopus". At the front of the volume came the bible of Nuclear Weapons Security – JSP471, "Defence Nuclear Emergency Response", which detailed the nomenclature to be used for the range of nasties which might conceivably happen, from an accident in transit with no more than a dented bumper, to an unplanned release of radiation within a shipyard. Those less charitably disposed to Steven Chandler, which included pretty much everyone including his mother and dog, might suggest that after 2 years commanding the Squadron, he pretty much should know JSP471 inside out. And its bastard twin, JSP483, the bible of nuclear convoy operating procedures. However even the long-suffering Captain Ledsham would tell you they have the most arcane elements. Lose or set fire to nuclear defence material and you would be dealing with the Defence Nuclear Safety Regulator but also the catchily titled "DBR-DefSy-NucSy&EP": "Don't even ask" was

Ledsham's comment when Collins made the mistake of doing so.

If "Lyndon" Johnson and "Jimmy" Carter were conscious of Chandler's size 9s kicking their arse, to be fair to Chandler he faced a potential arse-kicking from all sides and agencies. First in line would be the Defense Crisis Management Organisation, but also with kicking rights would be the MOD, Department for Communities, the Commander in Chief Land Forces, COBRA, the Impact Management Group, and Uncle Tom Cobley. Uncle Tom Cobley and all, in this case, would be the Scientific Government Advisory Group for Emergencies. Calling itself "Sage" set a high bar for the bag of bollocks that was likely to be generated by a group chaired by the MODs Chief Scientific Advisor, including all-stars from the Dept. of Health, D.E.F.R.A., the Environment Agency, the Food Standards Agency, the Dept. of Energy, and even the Met. Office. Clearly there were all manner of good reasons for all these hat-holders to be interested in a nuclear incident – but their unseen presence didn't make Major Chandler any less tetchy, as he looked at the wall in front of him.

Opposite him was a webcam surrounded by six screens, the main one of which showed the audience he would be talking to at the auditorium at Burghfield. To its right, on a smaller screen he could see settling into view the Gold Commander of Transport 24, who would be chairing the video conference and would be leading the convoy in the first Range Rover.

Major Chandler didn't rate Chief Inspector Rachel Wood, in spite of her highly professional reputation, a rising star within the MOD Police having previously served in the Royal Navy, commanding a Type 23 frigate. Chief Inspector Wood could at least take solace that it wasn't personal, nor even sexist. Major Chandler didn't rate anyone apart from Major Chandler. She did, however, take exception to the Squadron C.O.'s body language. Chandler was an easy read at the best of times, and seemed to care little about the way others might take his huffing and puffing face to face. Shorn of the actual physical presence of other humans, and given a measure of safe separation by the barrier of the screen, Major Chandler's eye rolling, sighs, arm folding, looking at his watch, checking his phone, and yawning, was just fucking rude. C.I. Wood was, herself, on a small stage at the front of the cavernous auditorium, small webcam in front of her, a bank of conference screens behind her for the audience, but also another bank set into the desk top news reader style so she could see key players herself. Giving support to Wood, as well as unspoken sympathy for her plight dealing with Major Chandler, was MOD Police headquarters on the other side of the country in Essex.

"Come on then," grunted Chandler. "Let's get this over with."

~~

As the briefing stretched into its second hour, Collins found his mind wandering. It was a long way from how he had imagined his future when he had passed out on the Lympstone parade ground, lashed with unseasonal squalls on a July Saturday. The Marines he had seen ahead of him at that point was the force that had shaped the life of his father, and the one he had briefly touched in action in Kandahar.

R.S.M. Collins had done the full gamut of operations and exercises through a 25-year career. First had come the Falklands, which for Ben's father, as for so many young men, proved a life changing three months. Thankfully able to leave protecting the beachhead at San Carlos to despondent colleagues from 40 Commando, 45 had to endure the 100-mile yomp across East Falkland, but at least got to see action at Two Sisters ridge, smashing their way through the ring of fortress Mounts between 3 Commando Brigade and Port Stanley.

Then came a decade freezing on exercise in snow holes in Northern Norway, dodging insects in bivvy bags in Belize, and wading chest deep through mangrove swamps in Brunei. Hong Kong had been an occasional treat in those days, but there were still operations for 45 Commando with regular cycles through 3 months long reinforcement tours of Northern Ireland - it was a blessed relief to the Marines to have the chance of a bit of riot control and "cordon and search" across the Province, without ever having to do the two year tours which line infantry and Royal Artillery units endured

By 1990 Ben's father, by then a Sergeant, was on the verge of leaving the Brigade, but then came Gulf War One, with 45 Commando assaulting the Al Faw Peninsular in Iraq as part of Schwartzkopf's 100 hour war.

Then during the Blair years, Chief of Defence Staff Sir Mike Jackson ensured that his beloved Paras were at the fore front of anything and everything, from taking down the West Side Boys in Sierra Leone, to capturing Pristina airfield in the liberation of Kosovo. Disillusioned with the shrinking chance of getting any action in a Commando unit, Collins senior passed selection for the S.B.S. at the ripe old age of 38, and was in prime position when 9/11 led to the allied invasion of Afghanistan. Having lost seniority on joining Special Forces, by 2001 Collins' father had regained ground, and had been promoted to R.S.M. just before his death in action, fighting 100-1 odds containing the escape of Taliban forces from their imprisonment at Mazar-i-Sharif.

And what, Ben thought, had he done in comparison? His one shot at command in action, possibly the only one he would get, had ended in him killing one of his own section commanders. Was he just climbing on a "borrowed ladder?" The words of the poem from beside the Blackwater came back to him again:

"He sprang upon the horse that his lord had owned,
Upon the trappings where no right had he."

Ahead lay two years of tedium of training and convoy protection. Beyond that? The Commando Brigade itself seemed under permanent threat of the chop, as the Trident Replacement programme and the two Royal Navy aircraft carriers sucked the budget into big ticket items. Meanwhile, even getting ammunition and fuel for routine exercises was getting harder and harder. With fellow members of his University course minting it in the City, the question of "what it was all for?" came to be a more significant question than it had ever been before.

A sharp elbow from Joop into his ribs brought Ben back in the moment.

"Wake up Collins. Time to go."

~~

"What a knob".

Fortunately, the Wildcat co-pilots observation of Major Chandler was only audible on the internal intercom. It was prompted by the Major striding across the Faslane pad, carbine in his left hand, lever-arch file tucked under his left arm, right arm bent at the elbow with a single circling finger indicating to start up.

"He thinks he is Colonel Kilgore," observed the pilot, and Chandler, did, indeed, seem under the delusion he was in "Apocalypse Now", not commanding just a one-day-only lash up of his personal Wildcat and a troop-carrying Merlin from the Commando Helicopter force. Admittedly there was one warlike feature of his chopper - the Wildcat would normally only port the crew chief's door mounted Browning M3 machine gun on active service or at the range. Here, flying over British soil, it was as ready for action as any of the men of Recapture Tactics Troop, boxes of 50-calibre ammunition visible at the feet of the gunner. Major Chandler liked that, and was looking forward to his day. No one else on the Wildcat was.

~~

Shona's phone buzzed at noon on the dot. "They are moving. 5 warhead carriers. Usual escort. Updates when I can."

And indeed, the "circus" was on the road. Forewarned by Gold Command, the uniformed plods at the gate moved into position where they could restrain and contain the handful of scruffy protestors keeping their lonely and chilly vigil at the gate. And no sooner had they shuffled into position than the first units of the escort sped into view, police outriders followed by Land Rover followed by the first Mercedes van of Stand Off Escort Troop Marines, for whom this would be a long day on the road. Ben and Joop watched from the Audi, Kiwi pointing out to them from the back seat the way every last detail was choreographed.

"You never want the lorries to be stationary, else you will have C.N.D. Fraggles climbing on, and chaining or gluing themselves to them. The MOD police have bolt cutters and all sorts to cut them free but it's a right pain. The glue especially. So, everyone gets rolling deep in the complex, the gate goes up, and they get through at no less than 20mph."

Ben had to admit it was impressive; the R.A.F drivers, invisible to the eye such was the polished sheen of their windscreens, kept exact pace and beautiful spacing, speeding past the protest cordon as the police outriders slewed their bikes across the main road, stopping traffic with enough flashing lights. If looking cold and sulky had the power to stop a nuclear convoy in its tracks the protestors were delivering in spades, but that was the limit of their response. In 30 seconds, the whole shebang of five warhead transporters and its every support element, even the fire engine and recovery lorry, was out of the base and flying down the main road towards Burghfield village. A congratulatory message came from Chief Inspector Wood as Gold Command on the main secure net to all stations, while on the 43 Commando radio net there was only silence. Nothing to say, so say nothing. If anyone was interested in speaking to callsign Clyde 44 they were resisting the temptation.

"Let's leapfrog ahead to up by the M4 and we can see how they cope in traffic."

~~

It was late afternoon when Shona got the tweet at work to confirm that the convoy was moving on the M6 North near Crewe. She didn't know whether to be relieved or scared. Having tracked the convoy to its brief crew change-over in Stafford, and heard of its departure from there an hour before, there had remained a slim chance of it switching to the Eastern Route. Now there was no doubt. Within 90 minutes it would be passing the point where the fake breakdown would be staged, and she would have to put her money where her mouth was. The last patient of the day on the linac machine seemed to take forever, but soon Shona was hurrying out into the fading winter light to the Cactus pulled up outside. Its occupants were upbeat and excited - well, they weren't the ones who would be firing the Stinger, nor the one whose face would be plastered on the T.V. news. Of course, none of this would happen unless Duncan could find his way to the right spot, so Shona paid no little attention to his route out of town. In the rear Steven and Darren were arguing about who would film the festivities, largely on the basis that whoever filmed and uploaded on 4G would have to use a hefty amount of monthly data allowance. The "Guy Fawkes" masks were clearly due to get another outing, but Shona managed to dissuade the two students from a plan to approach the lorry once it was disabled to spray peace symbols on it. "The police will fucking shoot you", were her exact words, and it was a reasonable supposition: patience might be shown to a grungy peacenick trying to climb on a truck at a road junction, but who knows how the guard force might react to a sudden incident out of the blue.

Conversation turned how best to get Shona in camera shot as the vehicle ground to a halt, and they realised that no one had checked how far a lorry might travel stopping from 60mph to standstill. An argument in the back seat, centred on who scored higher on the Driving Theory test, and therefore who knew best, produced eventually a guesstimate of 200 metres. Shona reflected that the last time she ran anything like that was in a primary school sports day 35 years before, and wondered whether having an out of breath overweight Scot bent double coughing her lungs up, in an otherwise impressive image of a paralysed nuclear warhead lorry, was the effect she was looking for.

Her train of thought was interrupted by her phone ringing, and she looked quizzically at the incoming number. Shona half assumed that it was the usual call asking her about "that road accident you had which wasn't your fault" but answered to find it was Ali - who previously had avoided any electronic contact with her. He was brief and to the point.

"I am at Bay City, ready to come help. Call me as soon as you are stationary."

Shona had barely got the word "O.K." out of her mouth before he rang off.

~~

Abaya had called in sick early that morning, not willing to risk being caught out by any change in convoy timing; Emad had no-showed for College, knowing that so long as they got money for him being on roll, none of the College management minded too much who attended; Ali, on the other hand, had got to work bright and early. His principal task - to persuade the scheduled recovery driver for the evening that Ali would take the shift in return for a swap later in the month. Ali didn't actually say so, but alluded to domestic beef, and a need to stay out of the way for a day until dust settled. This proved sufficiently persuasive, especially with a Nations League football match on TV that night. So, Ali had no trouble ending the day with the keys to the recovery van, and a call divert set from the emergency recovery number to his own phone. Of course any and all calls apart from one that evening would get short shrift.

Staring at the workshop space, last person at work, Ali tried to imagine the challenges ahead. He was confident the Stinger would stop the lorry, and that Shona and her group would totally distract the element of the guard force who stayed with it. While only three strong they had the firepower to overcome the MOD police. How easy would it be to break into the trailer and take the warhead pit? There had been more information in the public domain about the warhead than there had been about its mounting for transit - but he knew what he was looking for. While they would not normally feature in recovery work, he had loaded into the floor of the passenger space a powerful hydraulic jack normally used for H.G.V. recovery, an angle grinder, sledge-hammer, and set of bolt cutters. It seemed a decent assumption that engineers would want to make anything due to be blasted into space as light as possible; especially as they would have to compensate for the tremendous mass of the plutonium and uranium in each warhead. So the structure should be weak enough for a "brute force disassembly" to be do-able. The casings of the warheads, if they were in place at all, would be thin and hopefully weak: when warheads were mounted on a Trident at Coulport, the nose cone of the missile itself provided the necessary strength during launch, and on the way down to target they key to warhead "hardness" was aerodynamic design and shielding from electromagnetic pulse, rather than brute strength. Taking the warhead apart should also be safe. Even if the high explosive lenses were in place, Ali knew the warhead was designed to be safe in any road accident, which meant smacking its fabric with a sledgehammer should be just fine.

But that was just the start. How would the guard force react when they realised it was not just an over-the-top peace demo? Would they send units back from the rest of the convoy? Or did they have something else up their sleeve? The getaway route down the works access has been well scoped out and should help them shake off a pursuit, but would it shake it off long enough to get back to Bay City? The lathe was ready, the high-speed extractor was set up and the filters from it were now dumped to the side, and Ali pulled from a carrier bag the two disposable barbecue trays. For a moment he wondered if their plan wasn't as much of an amateur lash up as Shona's. Recent history was littered with terrorist actions which had looked hopelessly ill-advised in hindsight, from "underwear bombers" to 21/7. Ali could cope with pursuit, even to the mountains of Lebanon. He could not cope with shame. Or a failure to avenge his Syrian friends.

~~

John Dawson, as the new boy, found himself allocated not to one of the rather comfortable MOD Police Range Rovers dotting the convoy, but riding shotgun in a cab 8 feet off the ground. Almost literally riding shotgun, in that he was toting a Heckler and Koch MP4 clipped to a harness on his flak jacket. It had been pretty clear in the briefing at Burghfield that, for most of the allocated guard force, this was a jolly lads' day out, and friendship groups dictated the deployment of officers to vehicles. A day off-base, away from the oppressive supervision of Burghfield Management, and with overtime for extended hours: what's not to like?

So, John had instead the company first of an R.A.F. sergeant of similar age and no little experience, who had driven the route multiple times and seemed highly capable. Of course, family had come up, and the driver showed sympathy and concern for Alice, and John's plight in caring for her. A crew change at Preston though saw his replacement by a younger aircraftsman for whom uttering the phrase "I'm Dan," seemed to stretch the younger man's conversational range almost to breaking point. John had to turn to his own thoughts; of Alice mostly, tossing over and over in his head every nuance of every word the Prof. had shared with him in their last phone call. In constant dialogue with the team at the proton beam unit, their latest assessment had the headline message of "guardedly optimistic". John had not dared to ask what they were guardedly optimistic about. That she would recover? That she might live a little longer? That the treatment was working at all? In a treatment path that had seldom held any good news, he had decided to quit while he was ahead.

Trolling up the M6 he was pleased to see familiar landmarks coming into view, and smiled at how it had taken a ride in a nuclear convoy to get him close to home in Barrow. Staring up ahead at the now familiar sight of the three other warhead carriers, vans, police cars, and outriders, he wondered briefly about Dr. Shah and the curious bargain he had made to get Alice her treatment. But only briefly.

~~

It wasn't easy in the fading light for any of the occupants of the Cactus to pick out much of the scenery either side of the motorway, but the list of cues Ali had given them worked well, and as the digital clock on the dash ticked around towards 5pm, Duncan indicated carefully and brought the car to a halt on the hard shoulder. Above them the high pole supporting the Highways network traffic cam reached up into gathering gloom, and Shona was pleased to see that it's field of view was as they had previously observed - pointing North, towards the Service Station a couple of miles away. Of course, any imagery of their stunt which was captured on C.C.T.V. was a bonus, complementing whatever Darren could film and upload.

In spite of the dropping temperature and associated grumbling, the two students climbed out of the rear seats and did a dutiful impersonation of bereft travellers, stuck by the side of road, awaiting salvation. Meanwhile Duncan managed, after some fumbling, to raise the bonnet of his car, and Shona put the call in to Bay City. Ringing off, she then checked Twitter to see that the convoy was apparently still only just past the M62 interchange. Even at the speed of a recovery truck Ali should comfortably be there to help and support before time got tight. Before settling on the crash barrier by the verge with the others, Shona finally checked the Stinger in the boot of the Cactus. They had agreed to leave it there until Ali arrived. While the breakdown was out of view of the traffic camera, who knows if some highly unhelpful Highways Agency Patrol might come asking awkward questions. And questions about what they were doing on the hard shoulder with a hydraulic-powered Stinger device ready to be shot across lanes 1 and 2 might be particularly awkward.

~~

No one in Ben's Audi paid any attention to the Cactus on the hard shoulder as they sped past it. Just as they had paid no attention to any other routine parts of the roadside landscape on the way North. The trip had been uneventful, bar a small segment of the M6, where a traffic holdup led Chief Inspector Wood to issue one brief code word, which set in place a rolling roadblock behind the nuclear transports. As Ben and Joop saw, this allowed the convoy to slow but not stop, allowing the hold up to clear, and preventing the convoy ending up either in slow traffic or worse still, stuck and surrounded by who knows who in surrounding cars. Ben and Joop could hear Gold Command in conversation with Weathersfield to discuss a possible re-route using one of the contingency plans from their D.M.O. plan, but all passed smoothly.

After tailing for an hour after that, Kiwi suggested they overtake and head to Lancaster services: partly for "refuelling" of the increasingly weary passengers, but also because he promised that Lancaster could offer a unique view of the whole circus passing by. And, indeed, he was right. Food in hand, they followed him through a door marked "Staff only" to a corridor space cluttered with the debris of daily operations out front: skips on wheels overflowing with fast food waste, tray trolleys awaiting clearing and decanting, along with a couple of Eastern European cleaners on their mobile phones. Once the latter identified Kiwi and his group as something other than their shift supervisor, they seemed not minded to ask what the largely uniformed group was up to and went back to tapping at their devices.

Neither would have been in the job long enough to know that for Kiwi, sneaking his group up into the semi-derelict tower which made the station such a landmark was almost routine. When it had ultimately been taken out of use half a dozen years before, about the same time as it was given listed status, he had managed to cajole a key to the stairwell from a bored builder engaged in the final stripping out of fittings, since when he had informally visited the site most times a convoy took the Western M6 route. The two lifts up the column of the Pennine Tower were long broken, leaving many flights of stairs to negotiate: but following his shocking disclosure that morning, the others cut their tempo discretely to try not to test Kiwi's fitness too much. Nevertheless, the New Zealander still leant hard on the bannister, stopped twice briefly to catch his breath, and came to the final landing "faahking" and "shitting" in familiar style. As he sucked in the dusty and stale air of the restaurant space, the others saw immediately the benefit of making the effort. Both up and down the motorway the view was unbroken, a couple of miles each way in uninterrupted sight lines. More to the point their extra height meant that the sun, which would surely have been out of view to all those at car park level, still peeked over the horizon over the waves of the Irish Sea, visible past rolling farmland to the west.

Kiwi, now recovered, joined them.

"What is this place Kiwi," Maryam asked.

"I am told that long before you were even a twinkle, this was a service station like no other. Table service, smart uniformed waiters and waitresses, steaks, and roasts and grills, "After Eight" mints with your after-dinner coffee. People used to come here just for the food and the prestige of having been. And the view, of course."

It was hard to believe now, the stylish American diner tables stripped out, banquettes salvaged, about the only surviving fixture and fitting being two fluorescent strip lights which cast a wholly ineffective and flickering pallor across a grim octagonal space the size of a tennis court. Kiwi himself took in the scene, reflecting on what he saw in a way that had not previously occurred to him. "All good things come to an end," he muttered, quiet enough for none of the others to hear.

He took himself in hand, and stepped across a gritty concrete floor which crunched as he placed each foot.

"This is what we are here for," he said, pointing South at the stream of vehicles headed their way. "Gentlemen, if you want to get a real handle on what 43 Commando are tasked to do, here is where we can see. If they are on their mettle we should see the whole thing, textbook formation, safe as houses and long may it stay that way. When I am long gone, keeping this process safe is going to be your job."

"I think I can see it," Joop said, and sure enough towards the southern horizon you could start to make out the multiple flashing red and blue strobes of the warhead carriers and their supporting guard force. Between the tower and the imminent task force he spotted a different light, a couple of miles away, about at the limit of where a single vehicle could still be discerned. This one was a single amber light, strobing slowly, to the side of the headlights of the lines of cars headed towards the Scottish border, across all three lanes of the motorway.

"What's that I wonder?" Joop thought out loud. No-one knew.

~~

"For Fuck's sake Duncan." Cold, scared and nervous, Shona was starting to wish she could initiate the protest by throwing the gormless ginger lecturer under the wheels of the lorry instead of the Stinger. "Will you do as Ali says. Turn the engine on, leave the key in the ignition, and join me out front."

Nothing had yet gone wrong. Ali's recovery vehicle had arrived with time to spare, pulling up on the hard shoulder behind the Cactus at a slight angle, in a convincing mimicry of what seemed to be standard roadside practice nowadays. He had climbed down from the cab with barely a second glance at Darren and Steven, who were sat impatiently on the barrier, Guy Fawkes masks twiddling in their fingers. Instead he had immediately gone to Shona, established where the Stinger was, and had taken it to the front of their little piece of automotive theatre, setting it on the floor just by the front bumper of Duncan's car. Powering it up, a green light gave reassuring confidence that all was functioning. From that point, Ali's priority was to get Duncan out of the vehicle and down the road somewhere. They would need that car.

~~

If anyone in the convoy gave the flashing amber light of a recovery vehicle on the hard shoulder a moment’s thought, they didn't vocalise it on the radio net. As dusk fell, most minds had wandered to the final destination three or more hours away. Critics of "continuous running" would later make hay with the argument that crew fatigue and lack of vigilance was a bigger problem than they had previously faced, when convoys took three days to get from A to B, lying up overnight. Of course, that was easy to say afterwards. Certainly, the motorcycle outriders who flashed by the stranded Citroen gave no warning to the Range Rovers, who said nothing to the lorry drivers and their close protection, nor to stand off escort troop in the Mercedes vans. John Dawson was thinking of Alice. Gold command was thinking of her next promotion process. And Dan, in the cab with Dawson, was untroubled by any thought at all. One or two said later that they thought the recovery vehicle might be something to do with the "Works Access", given the giant sign on the verge beside the truck. This, of course, was to the good fortune of Shona and Ali, who, it proved, had happened upon one of the optimal moments to pull a surprise on the guard force.

Moreover, the later inquiry would find that it was the very professionalism and predictability of the convoy that was its undoing. Exactly as seen by Nukespot months before, and confirmed by John to Abaya before Christmas, the vehicles passed in procession, in perfect formation and sequence.

Ali crouched by the front of the Cactus, hidden in the shadow it cast from oncoming headlights, and he flinched progressively more as first police car, then Mercedes van, and then the speeding mass of the lorries, flashed by. He counted as four Warhead Carriers passed him, then a van, then a Range Rover, and then he pushed the button.

Chapter 14

Stinger

High up in the cab of the fifth "Truck Cargo Heavy Duty", Dan sensed rather than saw the frame of the Stinger flash in front of him, and stamped on the brake.

To be fair to Mercedes Benz, the Actros lorry responded brilliantly, anti-lock working as designed, but the driver sensed the loss of tyre pressure as the cab lurched forward. More evident still was the alarming "thwack" as each successive axle ran across the mat of tungsten spikes, the device finally wrapping itself around the rearmost two wheels like metal spaghetti. As Shona had been promised, whatever Dan's conversational limitations, his driving skill was spot on, and he kept the vehicle locked in a straight line as it came to a rapid halt. Darren and Steven's driving theory test guestimate proved wide of the mark, the rapidly deflating tyres combined with the heavy load pulling the T.C.H.D. up in a cloud of smoke from trashed rubber in only 80 metres. Dawson, thrown forward against his seat belt by the rapid deceleration, lurched back into the seat back, cursing.

Behind the lorry the escort struggled to react. Having been cruising steadily up a straight dry road, the MOD Police Range Rover immediately to the rear was suddenly faced with the lit brake lights on the trailer of the lorry. The S.E.G. Driver reacted as fast as he could, as the car continued headlong towards a wall of green tarpaulin, the back of the T.C.H.D. suddenly seeming to fill his windscreen. Slamming on the brakes himself, it was soon apparent that the Range Rover would overshoot the truck, and he wrenched the wheel to the right, the police car passing the smoking truck and coming to a halt in the middle lane, 50 yards further on. If the police driver was about to congratulate himself for his evading collision, he would do well not to expect a vote of thanks from the final police outrider, who, swerving to avoid the Range Rover, had no choice but to lay his bike on its side, both motorcycle and rider skidding across the cold tarmac at 60 mph. The Stand Off Escort troop driver in the final Mercedes van had more time to react and did rather better, coming to a safe halt between the trailer, and a Citroen and recovery lorry on the hard shoulder.

In the final Range Rover, the Sergeant in the front seat was on the radio to Chief Inspector Wood almost before the car came to a halt.

"Zero this is Hotel 5 Alpha. Tango 5 halted. Load and vehicle stationary, but intact investigating, out."

In her own vehicle at the head of the convoy C.I. Wood wondered if she had heard correctly, and directed Hotel 5 Alpha to "Say again." In the five seconds it took him to do so, message staccato as he unclipped from his seat belt and jumped from the vehicle, Gold Command and the rest of the convoy were already 200 metres more up the road from the incident.

Wood's first thought was to check what support the three MOD police in Hotel 5 Alpha had on site – the final unit of 43 Commando, Lieutenant Carter, Clyde 1 Alpha, was a team of heavily armed marines, and would be back there with the T.C.H.D. Along with the MOD police officer sitting in the cab of Tango 5 itself, there should be plenty of help on site. And the convoy recovery vehicle could be there within 5 minutes from its position 2 miles behind. The decision was a speedy but simple one. In seconds Wood had directed her comms team – get Major Chandler and Recapture Tactics Troop in the air as a precaution, and alert as a matter of routine the Nuclear Accident Response Organisation, largely for the moment as a back-covering exercise and because it's what the "book" required. And tell the rest of the convoy to keep rolling – you don't compound what might be a minor breakdown by stranding the whole convoy by the roadside.

~~

John Dawson in Tango 5 heard the interchange with Gold Command and was about to leap down himself to join the team exiting the Range Rover, but was immediately gestured to stay put by an MOD Sergeant racing back up the road from their vehicle. Because it was already clear to Sergeant Stackpole that this was not a mechanical defect – the Mercedes lorry was squatting awkwardly like an infant elephant trying to get to its feet. While the Stinger wrapped around the back axle was not visible, its effect was clear even in the falling light. The Sergeant struggled to remember the callsign of the 43 Commando team in the van further back, where following traffic was now pulling to a halt behind the stationary police and military vehicles, hazard lights flashing. But he could see the van decamp four of its Marines, while the Commando driver turned the vehicle to stand across the middle and outer lane, preventing any foolhardy vehicle trying to get past.

Gesturing his fellow officers left and right of him with a sharp movement of an open hand, Adam Stackpole brought his Heckler and Koch to his shoulder, and looked past the lorry in Lane 1 to the hard shoulder and verge. When he saw 4 people stood sheepishly next to the road he didn't know whether to laugh or cry. Or think of the shocking amount of paperwork that was about to come his way. For the moment, he settled for sharing what he had found.

"Zero this if Hotel 5 Alpha. Sitrep. Tango 5 disabled by a Stinger. Members of the public in plain view on hard shoulder filming – it's a likely anti-nuke protest. Suspects making no effort to escape. Dealing now. Will need additional Hotel assets to complete arrest and detention. Clyde units with me are securing the perimeter. For the moment policing action only needed."

CI Wood sighed. "Zero, send more details on the civilians, over."

"I am approaching now. I see a fat middle aged woman wrapped in a Scottish flag, being filmed by two others, probably male, but faces hidden by "Anonymous" Guy Fawkes masks. She is using Tango 5 as her backdrop. And there's a middle-aged man in yellow Hi-viz watching the show."

Stackpole took his finger off the pressel switch so that he could clip his carbine to his body armour, instead pulling his Taser from his webbing. In his peripheral vision he could see his fellow officers still with weapons drawn, hard-targeting the sorry little group on the hard shoulder. Well it didn't hurt to be careful. He pressed to talk again.

"Tango 5 will need recovery but looks intact in all other regards. Hotel 6 was off his bike but has remounted and is headed back up the road to marshal traffic. The Clyde unit is securing that end of the incident. No injuries at this time."

Rachel breathed a sigh of relief. It was unprecedented for protestors to take on the convoy at full speed, but not unmanageable. She kept Chandler and the recapture tactics troop on its way, and got her team to contact Weathersfield to get Lancashire Police support – H Division: motorways, armed response, air support, they would be just the job. If she managed to get the response right, this might just be a feather in her cap rather than a blot on her copybook.

~~

50 yards down the road from Ali and the fake breakdown, Shona had watched open-mouthed as the lumbering juggernaut came to a dead halt in no time. Darren, opting for slo-mo mode on his mobile phone, struggled to frame the shot with his vision obscured by his Guy Fawkes mask, but nailed the lorry grinding to a halt, and high-fived Steven before immediately uploading it. First to Nukespot's Twitter feed, then Instagram, before jogging 30 metres to line up Shona for an impromptu piece to camera. The Scot was almost as delighted that the anticipated 200 metre sprint would not be needed as with the success of the Stinger. She knew things were likely to get hostile very quickly, with a police motorcyclist dusting himself off and straining to right his bike, while other officers were rapidly decamping from a Range Rover which had overshot the lorry. With her political testament already pre-recorded, a quick shot of the stranded lorry, brought down by her protest would be ample – especially if the accompanying MOD police made the mistake of over-muscular arrests for what had essentially just been a bit of criminal damage. The Scottish Saltire might alienate a bit of possible English support – "bloody Jocks" and all that but at the end of the day, the Scottish Parliament as much as Westminster were the audience she needed to appeal to. Facing Darren and trying to ignore the sounds of the police squad coming up behind her, Shona began her live piece to camera.

~~

As the T.C.H.D. lorry lurched to a halt and its escort vehicles took evasive action, no-one was paying attention back up the road to the stranded Cactus, bonnet up, or the recovery truck pulled up behind it. This suited Ali just fine.

Keeping to the side of the vehicle next to the verge, he walked calmly back the few yards to the recovery truck. The near side door of the little passenger cab opened as he neared, and he saw first one then two pairs of lower legs appear below the door sill – Emad, then Abaya.

As he appeared round the door, Emad passed him one of their two Vitaz carbines and a slim green canvas shoulder bag of magazines. Emad hiked his own bag higher up his shoulder, freeing both hands to cock the weapon. Abaya appeared behind him, Grach pistol in hand.

"Well done," said Ali. "Now remember, timing is everything. Sometime in the next minute will come the moment when everyone is focused on Shona and her friends. That's when we have to strike. And we have to take down the whole guard force first time."

"What about if Shona and that lot get in the way?" Emad asked.

Abaya gave him the reassurance he needed. "Emad they are spineless and weak. They have been useful until now, but no longer. The police are our target, but if they get in the way, that's their problem."

Armed and ready, they moved cautiously to peek around the front of the Cactus at the developing incident. The black-clad police were approaching the protestors 80 yards away, while nearer to them a small group of men in camouflage garb were debussing from a Mercedes van pulled across the motorway. To their right, traffic had stopped, with two drivers already out of their vehicle to discuss a minor collision, the day-dreaming tailgater unable to stop in time as the S.U.V. in front braked sharply.

"Good," thought Abaya. The more civilians in sight the better for the moment, distracting further the guard force already struggling with plenty on its plate. They would shift out of the way soon enough when the shooting started.

~~

For the Merlin and Wildcat crews, hopping up the centre of England from Brize Norton via MOD Stafford had brought them uneventfully to their final stop, Fulwood Barracks in Preston.

Built to house troops to quell incipient aggro from the populace at the time of the Chartist Movement in the 1840s, it had now fallen out of substantial use, home only to a skeleton Infantry Brigade Headquarters and a Medical Battalion. It was, however, in the right place for a laager and refuelling halt, and the flight crews and men of Recapture Tactics Troop had been able to watch the convoy stage through the base, drivers changing with fresh R.A.F. drivers brought in by minibus. With both airframes shut down, a crew from the Marine's own specialist unit, 338 Commando Petroleum Troop, were still topping up their tanks with JP4 fuel when the first alert came from the convoy now thirty miles to the North.

The initial frenzy of the response was whipped to even higher intensity by the antics of Major Chandler, berating the fuel crew to decouple so "We can just go with what we have got." The Wildcat's pilot and co-pilot looked grimly at each other – all very well for him to say, he wasn't the one responsible for a multi-million pound helicopter and all in it. But they had got used to his antics, and found solace in the thought that, unlike Captain Ledsham, they only had to put up with him for a few more hours.

Starting an abbreviated procedure to spool up the two jet turbines, with Chandler nagging them to "Fucking get on with it!" the co-pilot flipped a switch to speak only to his colleague as he watched the dials.

"Do you know the last time I was here I was told an interesting story."

"Really?"

"Apparently this barracks was the site of the first ever recorded "fraggings". Right here on this parade ground."

He kept a wary eye on the R.P.M. gauge and the jet pipe temperature, and gave a thumbs up to the Marine stood in attendance with a fire extinguisher.

"A 19-year-old private was getting shit from his Captain, way back in the 1860s. He was given 14 days in the guardroom for no reason, so he got his revenge. Apparently, he got his musket and took aim at the dodgy Captain when he was crossing the parade ground with the C.O. Hit the Captain but only after the musket ball had gone right through the C.O. first. Two dead officers with one shot! The squaddie's ghost is meant to haunt the Officers Mess here."

"I wonder if he is available for a sequel?" the pilot replied, grinning.

"If so tell him we rather like our Captain – but if he would like to shoot Major Chandler, we would be very grateful."

With that the pilot wound on the power, lifted the collective stick, and pushed forward to gain translational lift. It's red anti-collision flashing, the lead component of Major Chandler's private air force was coming to the rescue. The co-pilot got on the U.H.F link to Gold Command and Weathersfield.

"Junglie One-One airborne. Junglie One-Two is in trail. E.T.A. at site in one-zero minutes".

~~

"Something's wrong."

It was Collins who first noticed a gap start to appear in the sequence of flashing blue lights, between the main caterpillar of T.C.H.D.s and guard force vehicles still coming towards them, and a group of two or three vehicles seemingly stationary. Worryingly, from their lofty vantage, it appeared they were static where the strobing yellow light from before was still turning. Their fears were soon confirmed when the convoy hove into view – all was in perfect order; except for the small matter of a missing lorry full of Trident warheads.

It was something of a cross cultural achievement that the Marine, the Dutchman, the New Zealander, and the Anglo-Iranian all managed to say "Fuck" at almost exactly the same moment.

"Let's go," implored Joop, relishing the prospect of some action at last. The others needed no persuading. Their efforts at getting back to the Audi in the style of a Le Mans sprint start would have been less comedic, had their little clan not included an elderly bloke with lung cancer and a young woman recently shot full of holes in Afghanistan. But at least the short head-start allowed Joop to get in the driver's seat while Ben got in behind him, reaching to where the secure radio had been left in the back seat.

As Mazz climbed into the front and Kiwi the rear, Ben was able to fill them in on what he had gleaned from radio traffic.

"It's not a simple breakdown, it's some kind of protest. They have managed to stop the warhead lorry, but we have one police unit and Jimmy Carter back there with his serial. It's contained, no damage to the lorry, and Johnson and the galloping Major are on their way."

"Which way?" Joop asked. The Sat Nav suggested an eye wateringly slow route up North, then doubling back way past the scene of the incident, before coming back up North. It would take forever.

"Well there's no traffic coming northbound Joop," said Mazz. "So I think heading Southbound down that carriageway at high speed will be just fine thanks."

"I hoped you would say that," said Joop, turning the Audi the wrong way out of the car park and accelerating flat out. "Should be 5 minutes max this way."

Chapter 15

Casualties

Shona's anti-nuclear Scottish nationalist diatribe came to a close, but with Darren indicating that the forces of law and order were about to do some reaping, she told him to keep filming. Turning to face the music, the Scot could see the imposing figure of Sergeant Stackpole coming towards her from the cab end of the lorry. Kevlar helmet, body armour with a black carbine clipped across it, the police officer had arms outstretched in front of him with a black and bright yellow device held in both hands, pistol style. And it was pointed at her.

Darren kept filming, and it was great footage. Shona now had the Scottish saltire held outstretched in both hands behind her back, Jesus style, so that all he could see of her was the blue and white flag and a couple of chunky legs ending in clumpy DMs. Beyond her were the stormtrooper-style balaclava-clad police officer and the nuclear lorry. Off to each side creeping into view, two other police with firearms pointing also at Shona.

Stackpole decided it was time to bring this nonsense, whatever it was, to a decisive close.

"Armed police! Show me your hands!"

Shona did nothing.

Stackpole went ten decibels louder. "Armed police! I want to see your hands now!!"

“Fuck off, fascist.”

“Don’t be fucking stupid. You have made your point. This is a nuclear lorry and you are pissing round way out of your depth. All of you! On the floor now, face down, hands out!”

Behind Shona, Duncan, in his fetching high-viz, and his two supplicant undergraduates, decided enough was enough. Darren stopped filming and lay down on the tarmac, phone still in hand, peeling his Guy Fawkes mask off as he did so. Steven and Duncan were quick to follow, Duncan a little disappointed that he was having to lie akimbo in cold verge-side grass on which frost was just starting to appear. The sergeant’s two colleagues stepped forward, training their MP4s on the prone figures.

Shona was made of sterner stuff.

“Fuck off copper! Go ahead and arrest me.”

Stackpole was starting to lose patience.

“Miss I am going to arrest you, but it’s up to you what it takes to do so. I am very happy to put you down with this Taser if that is what it takes. You have attacked a nuclear weapons convoy. So far as I am concerned you are still a threat to it. Now, what’s it to be? Taser? Or will you get on the fucking floor and show me your hands!”

As with much of the kit used for nuclear transports, no expense was spared even on new-model tasers, and the X2 in Stackpole’s hands had the new laser feature, allowing him to illuminate on Shona’s torso exactly where the two darts would fly if he fired. He lit her up with two dots right on the centre of her ample chest.

Shona sniffed at him. “You wouldn’t dare!”

~~

From the side of the Bay City Truck Abaya watched the arrest unfolding. But more problematically, so increasingly did the team of Royal Marines who had taken up position between the developing drama and the stationary traffic.

A police motorcyclist had removed his helmet and was starting to deal with the two drivers who had collided, and the soldiers were alert but uncertain. Abaya could count five of them, four kneeling in a cordon stretching across the carriageway from lane one through to the central barrier, a fifth upright walking back towards where Stackpole and Shona were in their Mexican standoff. While each soldier had seemingly taken an arc to cover, they were increasingly casting eyes back towards their officer and the protestors, three of whom were now lying face down. It certainly didn't help that the headlights of the queuing traffic were blazing full in the faces of the Marines, making it impossible for them to discern much of what was going on at the front of the gathering traffic jam. As you might expect, drivers and passengers were staring to emerge from their vehicles, phones in hand: something interesting was clearly going on.

Abaya made her decision. She whispered to Ali to take the four kneeling soldiers – Emad to take the three police officers. She would get the Commando officer, standing and only 25 metres or so away, the easiest target for her pistol fire. The two young men gave their Vitaz sub-machine guns a final check. Abaya took her Grach in both hands and released the safety. It was time.

~~

"Miss, I gave you fair warning."

Stackpole pulled the trigger and the barbed filaments of the Taser shot across the few yards between him and Shona, passing through the flimsy material of her hoodie and embedding in her chest. She went down like a stack of spuds, twitching.

Which meant no one was looking the right way as Abaya, Ali, and Emad stepped out of cover and opened fire.

Lieutenant Carter never even heard the shot that killed him. Even hitting a standing target at 25m with a pistol is a decent shot. Abaya got lucky. Aiming at the standing soldier's centre mass, the recoil of her first round lifted the barrel just enough to send the bullet through the back of his neck, exiting just under his left eye. Carter was dead before he even hit the ground.

To her left Emad raised his Vitaz to his shoulder and did just as he would have done on Call of Duty or Grand Theft Auto: place you sight picture just so, double-tap the trigger, and put the target down. Switch to the other black shape 5 degrees of arc to the right. Sight picture. Double-tap.

Stackpole's two fellow S.E.G. officers, focused solely on the protestors prone on the floor, did not even have a chance to turn to the sound of gunfire, let alone fire back. Struck twice in the left side, P.C. Mark Chester might have hoped his body armour would save him – and against a normal 9mm round fired at around 380 metres per second it would have done so. But the overpressure rounds sourced by Marco did exactly as advertised. If you double the mass of a bullet, you only double the impact effect; but adding to the velocity of a bullet increases its impact force by the square of that increased speed. The 7N31 rounds are lighter by a gram than normal 9mm, but are not just up at 610 metres per second but are highly refined in design – the tip of a slender steel penetrator core can be seen at the front of the round, separated by an invisibly thin sliver of polyethylene from a bi-metal sleeve which surrounds it. Hit a soft tissue target and the whole lot hits you – but striking Kevlar or a similar resistant material, the bi-metal stops but releases the steel core to pierce through to the target. Which is exactly what it did to Mark Chester, one round penetrating rib, lung, aorta, and oesophagus, before stopping when it hit the front of his body armour on the way out. The second round, penetrating his shoulder, proved an irrelevance. Downed and bleeding heavily from his wound and a gush of blood rushing from his open mouth, Chester died speedily.

P.C. David East was 10 yards further on, and lightweight overpressure bullets would have lost a lot of their velocity had he been even a little further away. But fired with such a high muzzle velocity, he still had little chance. Hit in the groin and stomach, his body armour didn't even come into play, and he was thrown to the floor by the 600 kilojoules of kinetic force each round brought with it. East's MP4 was thrown yards away, and he lay in a heap, gasping for breath, thumb trying to find his personal radio pressel switch to raise the alarm.

While Emad was measured and disciplined in his fire, Ali was anything but. Four heavily armed Marines would not be looking the wrong way for more than a moment, and Ali engaged them on full-automatic. Spraying bullets across the carriageway, the nearest three soldiers went down like skittles, the first hit in the legs by rounds fired low ricocheting off the tarmac. The second had time to bring his DiMarco carbine to his shoulder, before he was stitched across the chest by three bullets. His military-spec Osprey body armour did enough to stop even the steel penetrators getting through, but could do little to shield him from the blunt force trauma of the rounds impacting: what is known as the "backface signature". Deforming the back face of his chest plate with phenomenal force, it was akin to being hit three times with a sledgehammer, and it broke two ribs, their sharp ends penetrating lung and blood vessel and felling the marine like a tree. The Corporal was no more fortunate, hit in the face by one of the final rounds, dropping like a stone. The final few rounds of Ali's "spray and pray" disappeared high and wide past the opposite carriageway into the Lancashire countryside, missing the next Marine by a yard. Ali saw the soldier throw himself over the aluminium barrier at the central reservation, and ducked to change magazine. The Marine immediately raised his head to engage, thinking he might have a moment to catch his attacker in mid-reload. But both Abaya and Emad still had rounds to spare.

The soldier sighted his weapon at the front of the recovery truck, selected full automatic, and blazed away, 5.56mm rounds turning the windscreen into glass pulp, and smacking through the bonnet into the engine compartment. But the big diesel unit did a job of protecting the three Syrians, and while Abaya and Ali stayed down for a moment, Emad's confidence of youth meant that he did no such thing. Dodging five paces to the right where he could fire across the empty cargo space of the vehicle, he took careful aim at what he could see of the Marine hidden behind the barrier, and opened fire. His target stood no chance. At 10 metres the HN31 round will go through 8mm of steel. The flimsy crash barrier barely even slowed the bullets down, and when the Marine was bought to the floor by a wound through the knee, Emad could take careful aim at him below the level of the aluminium, and shoot him dead.

In ten seconds, all but Sergeant Stackpole were down and dead or wounded. Turning towards the gunfire, Stackpole had no time to detach his Heckler and Koch from his chest rig, but he threw the Taser handset to the floor and grabbed his Sig Sauer pistol from the holster on his right thigh, and dived to his left under the rear wheels of the lorry trailer. Showing as little as possible of his torso, he leant around the deflated tire at a young man he could see, kerbside of a recovery truck, throwing a curved magazine to one side and pulling another from a shoulder bag to replace it. He fired twice, and Ali felt the bullets whistle between him and Abaya to his side. He fumbled desperately to reload, unused to the Vitaz, while Abaya ducked to the verge and returned fire with her pistol. Stackpole followed the movement of the diving shape and fired again and again at where the armed figure had disappeared. But Ali was ready now, re-cocking his weapon and firing on full automatic again at the wheel arch and the policeman behind it. The thick rubber of the tyre and the metal of the trailer deflected some of the shots with a thwack, but the sheer law of averages was on Ali's side. As Stackpole leant out and aimed another double tap at the source of the gunfire, a shot to the right shoulder flung him from his place of cover and into proper view. Kneeling with his left hand gripping his wound, pistol still in hand but with no ability to bring it to bear, Stackpole for the first time got a proper view of two gunmen. Or actually, one gunman, a twenty something Arab-looking man, mechanic's overalls, short carbine in hand. And an Arab woman, jeans and Converses, shoulder bag, pistol drawn and pointed his way.

He could have probably given a really good description of the two shooters to any follow up investigation. Which is why they both raised their weapons and shot him to death.

~~

"Clean up!" is what Shona heard the woman shout to the other assailants. Duncan and the others had taken advantage of the final shootout with Stackpole to leg it away from the road and out of view, but shocked and breathless all Shona could think to do is stay where she was. Disorientated, having passed in seconds from fronting up Stackpole to witnessing his violent death, her brain struggled to compute that the voice she heard was familiar; that gait of the woman was one she had seen many times before at work; and that the man in mechanics overalls who cut down the policeman with gunfire was Ali, who only a minute earlier had helped her launch her protest. What were they doing? What was happening? Who were they if not a harmless refugee family?

Getting up and running was asking to be shot. Shaking with fear, Shona lost control of her bladder and peed herself. But she also gritted her teeth, braced herself, and managed to lie as still as a corpse as Ali and Abaya approached where she and P.C. East lay. Shona caught his gaze, and looked appalled as his eyes widened in fear. Abaya's sneakers came into view as she stepped past the Scot, moving right up close to the policeman, who looked up at her imploringly. It was to no avail. Abaya looked down at the wounded officer, took careful aim, and shot him in the head. Shona blinked as the ejected brass cartridge case plinked right in front of her face.

From some way away she heard three further bursts of gunshots: it was Emad, ruthlessly finishing off the two wounded marines in the cordon, and then spraying fire over the jam of traffic and the mass of drivers and passengers who were now running for their lives - and needed to be kept running. Their plan had no space for some have-a-go-hero to get in the way, and Shona next heard the "pop" of three smoke grenades which Emad pulled from his shoulder bag and threw on the carriageway, shielding the ambush from view of anyone coming from the South. He had three more to top up as needed.

Somewhere above her, Shona heard Abaya speak again.

"That's it. Let's see what we have got."

Chapter 16

Fighting back

Joop was accelerating past 50mph down the off-ramp to the service station in the Audi when he heard the alarm raised over the secure net.

"All stations this is Tango 5. Shots fired! Wait out!"

You could sense the panic in the callsign's voice. Ben wondered who it was. A moment later he was back again.

"Tango 5, confirming shots fired, callsign Hotel 5 under fire! Two men down. Hotel 5 Alpha is engaging two gunmen. Automatic weapons!"

The last comment was somewhat superfluous, as even over the sound of the engine hitting the rev limit, they could all hear the gunfire.

"Tango 5, this is Zero Alpha." They could hear the voice of C.I. Wood, now five miles up the road. "Clyde 14 in the escort van should be on scene with you."

"Tango 5, no sign of them. Shots fired behind this vehicle out of view. The only people standing at this time are two gunmen, young, Arab appearance."

In the front Joop and Maryam looked at each other alarmed.

"Zero Alpha can you keep them in view and report."

In the cab, Dawson could only watch in horror in the mirror as first the Sergeant by the rear wheel was cut down, and then a figure stepped forward to shoot the young P.C. on the floor.

"Tango 5. Negative, I don't think they are going to wait."

The Audi was still speeding south, but all were very much aware they risked arriving at a gunfight under dressed.

"What do you think?" Mazz said.

"Anyone got any other plans?" asked Kiwi. "You two have just spent weeks learning nuclear convoy protection. There seems to be a fucking nuclear convoy to protect."

"Time for some desperate glory then?" Ben offered. "R.T.T. won't be on site any time soon."

"Are we a little light on firearms for this?" said Joop.

"Not totally Joop," said Mazz, reaching behind herself and pulling out the Glock and working the slide.

"I guess that seals it," said Ben. "Zero Alpha, Tango 5, this is Clyde 44, heading south on the northbound carriageway from Lancaster Services, dark coloured Audi. E.T.A. on site five minutes."

In a Range Rover five miles to the North, C.I. Wood turned to her comms team, confused.

"Who the hell is Clyde 44??"

~~

John Dawson remembered the old saying that "Objects in the rear-view mirror may be closer than they appear." Well the armed figure silhouetted by the headlights of the vehicles behind looked pretty fucking close enough. In the driver's seat Dan appeared frozen to the spot, so Dawson elbowed him hard, glared at him, and directed him to get out as quietly as he could, and then run for it.

Shaken from his daze the R.A.F. driver did as he was bid, Dawson following him down, and unclipping his carbine as he did so. But there was no way Dawson was going to follow the disappearing airman. Flicking his safety to “fire”, he carefully edged around the front of the lorry, barrel pointed to the floor, trading better concealment for the extra half second it would take him to raise the weapon and fire.

It had been ten seconds now since he had seen his fellow officer murdered. Heart pounding, he took a deep breath, and took one last step.

In any normal drill, Dawson would have expected to aim centre mass and drop a figure 10 metres away in less than a second. But he froze. And he froze because the woman staring at him was the same one he had seen for weeks at the hospital. The kind, ever helpful, white-coated expert who he had trusted to save his daughter. Who seemingly stood half-facing him, pistol by her side. His astonishment trumped his training.

“Dr. Shah?” he said, eyes narrowing as if unable to believe what he was seeing.

Abaya was equally taken aback – first at the appearance from nowhere of another black clad police officer, almost in touching distance. But also, that somehow he had recognised her. Who was he? The balaclava and helmet made it impossible to see, and the voice was distorted by the fabric of the mask. He seemed paralysed, as if unable to make a next move without an answer.

He would never get one. Abaya’s right arm flashed up into a firing position, and while Dawson was jolted back into reality and tried to follow her move, he was way too slow. The Syrian jerked the trigger again and again, firing every round she had, continuing to shoot as her target fell, until the working parts stayed to the rear to show the Grach was empty.

To get the balaclava off the dead policeman necessitated removing his helmet first, and Abaya had much else to do, but she had to see. When she did, she shrugged, and went back to help Ali.

By the time Abaya reached the back of the trailer, Ali had lain his Vitaz on the tarmac and was hustling back from the recovery lorry, awkwardly carrying a set of bolt cutters and hydraulic jaws. It seemed a poor toolkit for breaking into a warhead trailer, but they had rightly deduced that surrounded by heavily armed guards, the truck itself would have limited physical security. So it proved. Two simple padlocks secured the container, and these delayed them only seconds.

Lifting the levers which held the doors closed, Ali swung them both open to reveal the contents. While car headlights gave some illumination, it still took the two of them a while to make sense of what they were seeing. A reinforced space-frame cradle stretched across the width of the trailer. Shoulder height, the cradle sat on a heavy-duty blue metal sled, complete with a series of slots presumably for a rig to load and unload. The sled was secured to grooves in the bed of the lorry trailer, with 6-inch bolts securing it to fastening points on each side, and within the space frame the secured contents were hidden by a rectangle of tightly stretched green plastic, pulled taught by load straps. The sled and cradle in immediate view seemed to be separated from another further towards the cab by a metre of open space – presumably to ensure the fissile material in one unit was kept well away from the one on the next sled. That's assuming that the contents hidden by the green polypropylene were, indeed, the warheads everyone expected.

There was no time to waste. Ali withdrew a Stanley knife from his overalls, slid forward the blade, and ran his fingers over the plastic to check nothing was immediately beneath where he was going to cut. It felt like there was air space the other side of the cover, so he punched the point of the blade into the top left of the side facing him, pulling the knife in a single steady movement to the top right corner.

Pushing his fingers through the slit at the top right end and holding on, he then quickly slashed downwards until he got to about the level of his right knee. Stepping a pace or two to the left, he repeated the process down the left-hand side of the dustcover, so that two thirds of the package within the metal exo-skeleton was revealed to view.

Ali puffed his cheeks and exhaled at what he could see inside. Sat in a moulded base of polystyrene which exactly fitted its dimensions was a pointed black cone lying sideways across the centre line of the vehicle. It was barely a metre and a half from base to tip, and at its base was only maybe half a metre in diameter. The most striking thing was the finish – a burnished matt black, akin to what someone with more cash than sense might choose as the finish for their luxury BMW. It was granular to the touch. The only blemish was a seam in the cone 10 cm up from the circular base, and another 10cm down from the point. Bright green arrows pointing up and down each side of the seams indicated where to insert an allen key to unlock the bond and allow the cone to be disassembled. With Abaya watching intently, Ali was quick to remove the tip, easing the cone up a centimetre or two out of its polystyrene base and shuffling the black metal out of the way, revealing the fusing mechanism. Harder to pull out of its travel packaging was the main body of the black cone, but he soon had it placed on the floor alongside the space frame, revealing the shiny metallic peanut, 30 cm across at its widest point, 45 cm from end to end. Made itself of Uranium 238, Ali knew the "peanut" contained both the Plutonium primary he was looking for, as well as the fusion uranium secondary which made this an "H-bomb" – and now was not the time to be trying to get at the latter. Bolt cutters quickly severed a metal pipe which came from the base of the cone, feeding through a seal on the side of the peanut. If Kiwi had been there, he could have explained that this was a booster feed for Tritium, topping up the gas in the middle of the plutonium pit inside the peanut. It didn't stand up to a bolt cutter very well, and nor did the various leads and wires from the fuse assembly.

Ali tried to lift the peanut from its housing but was surprised by its weight. While Abaya was yelling for him to hurry up, he thought it worth having one go to crack it open, and applied the hydraulic jaws to break in. It was a long shot – Uranium 238 is non fissile, there because following the detonation of the U235 fusion secondary, the nucleus of its atoms will split in the wave of high energy neutrons, massively magnifying the effect of the blast. Strictly speaking, this makes the W88 a "fission-fusion-fission" design. Whatever its lack of potential as the initiator of a nuclear device Uranium 238, "depleted uranium", hard and heavy, is also brittle: and it was especially so, because for the transit of the warheads to Coulport, they were without both the "Fogbank" plasma layer, and the shaped conventional explosive to set off the primary. Cranking the powerful jaws, the peanut first bent, deformed, and then broke, cracking loudly and revealing its hidden innards: in the top half a dirty grey metal oblate spheroid, a mini rugby ball, the size of a bag of sugar. In transit condition it was separated from the interior of the peanut by bubble wrap: bespoke deluxe bubble wrap, no doubt costing thousands, but bubble wrap none the less. It provided little resistance to the crushing force Ali was applying.

Within 120 seconds of climbing into the back of the T.C.H.D., Ali was stashing 3kg of highly fissile Plutonium 239 into his shoulder bag.

~~

P.C. Mark Dugdale could do nothing to save the Marines murdered where they lay by Emad Shah; as a motorbike outrider he carried no firearm, and could only watch in desperation as the gunman went from soldier to soldier. With purple and green smoke now billowing from the grenades thrown to the road surface, he could get only a sketchy sense of activity around the rear of Tango 5; and was waving animatedly at the few remaining vehicle occupants who had stayed rooted to the spot in spite of the gunfire. The gunman was variously scanning the halted traffic for threat, and looking back over his shoulder to the warhead lorry, clearly impatient to get away from the scene. Dugdale could, however, alert Gold Command to what he was seeing. Which was two silhouettes climbing down from the back of the T.C.H.D. trailer, and heading back towards a dark Citroen Cactus on the hard shoulder with its hazard lights flashing.

~~

"Clyde 44, this is Zero Alpha, location over"

In the back of the vehicle Ben was quick to confirm they were 2 miles south of Lancaster services, and could see the flashing emergency lights of the static police and Marine vehicles about a mile further on.

C.I. Wood tried to update them. "Zero Alpha, Hotel 6 is on site and reports three, I say again three armed suspects on site. Hotel 6 believes that Tango 5 has been compromised. Both Junglie call signs are on the way and 5 minutes out. Hold short of the incident and report."

Ben was unimpressed.

"Clyde 44, we heard Hotel 6 confirm persons have been in the back of Tango 5 and are now mobile. Over."

Rachel tried not to get let her tetchiness cloud her reply. "Zero, that is correct. But please await armed units. Do not, repeat, do not, look to challenge."

While Ben was on the Bowman radio, Joop was trying to make out a running shape coming towards them on the central reservation.

"Who is that?"

“Keep going Joop,” Mazz replied. “That’s one of ours.”

Joop had the Audi over 100 mph, but he could now see the headlights pick out the multicam battledress of the driver of Tango 5 legging it away from the ambush.

“Shall I stop?” Joop asked.

“Fuck no!” said Maryam. “Go faster”

In the back seat Ben took his cue. “Zero, this is Clyde 44, negative your last, persons about to flee the scene. Engaging, out.”

In her Range Rover C.I. Wood turned confused to her driver.

“Engaging? With what? I thought you said they were unarmed observers.”

~~

As Ali and Abaya hurried to the hard shoulder, plutonium pit safely stashed, the engine of the Cactus was just as Duncan had left it and as its designers would have hoped – gently ticking over. Ali gave the shoulder bag and his Vitaz sub machine gun to Abaya and headed to the driver’s side door, and Abaya shouted loudly to Emad to give up his place on the cordon and get in.

Emad turned to join them, and as he headed back to the car, he had a chance to take in the crime scene. In the dim light the pooled blood next to his victims looked black rather than red, and he took in the open rear doors of the T.C.H.D., the black-clad corpses of the police up beside it, and the ample form of Shona prostrate on the tarmac, apparently dead too. There was no sign of the rest of the Nukespot group. But there was a set of rapidly approaching headlights. Really rapidly approaching headlights, coming the wrong way up the motorway. Ignoring his sister’s command, Emad ran past the warhead lorry, reloading with a new magazine as he went.

“Emad! Come now!” Abaya screamed. He paid no attention, and brought the Vitaz to his shoulder.

~~

With the headlights of both the T.C.H.D. and the Cactus and the jam of vehicles all shining in their face, Joop had no idea he was being shot at until he saw the muzzle flash of Emad's Vitaz. It strobed again and again, Emad showing decent fire discipline to try to hit the speeding target with three or four round bursts. Opening fire at 200 yards range gave him precious little time to lock onto his target, but three of the occupants of the Audi flinched and then jumped as two rounds came through the radiator and smacked into the engine compartment.

The fourth occupant did not. While the others might have expected her to lean out of the window and open fire with her Glock left-handed, Mazz was going to do nothing of the sort.

She didn't take her eyes off the muzzle flash, but managed to yell to Joop a simple instruction – "Keep going!"

Joop braced himself and complied, even though his left ear was then struck by the deafening crack of Maryam firing her pistol right next to him. Not once, but again and again, the rounds punching hole after hole in the windscreen in front of her. At 100 metres to no effect; nor at fifty; but just as Kiwi shut his eyes on the assumption that they were either about to be shot, or about to mow down the gunman, one of Mazz's shots seemed to hit home.

The young man could be seen to lurch, bending down and over to his left, the barrel of his weapon pointing down and towards the floor. Joop now slammed on the brakes, conscious that beyond the gunman there was a jam of vehicles. They were all thrown against their seat belt, but Mazz continued to fire, a second round hitting Emad right in the gut. Like all abdominal wounds this would doubtless have proved agonising; had he not instantly been thrown headlong by Joop driving right into him, the Audi decelerating rapidly but still travelling at 40 mph or more. Emad's form flew up in the air and out of their view, while the saloon slewed to a halt level with the rear of the warhead lorry.

There was no time to gather their breath. To their right front, erratic automatic weapons fire blazed from the passenger side window of a small hatchback. But the fire was wild and high, and no sooner had the shooting started than the vehicle was moving. Heading not at them, but ducking off to their right, down a small off-ramp labelled "Works vehicles only."

Mazz leapt from the car and fired her remaining five rounds of 9mm at the tail lights, as it disappeared out of view.

Kiwi shouted for Maryam to get back in, but was caught short by Joop.

"No Kiwi, this car is fucked. Let's get another one."

Joop was right – the engine of the Audi was smoking and steaming. It may not have gone to meet its maker in the Manchester drug wars that one might have expected to be its destiny – but in just as terminal a shoot-out, beside a warhead convoy in rural Lancashire.

Joop jumped from the car and legged it towards the queue of stationary traffic 50 metres away. Mazz turned, reloading with a fresh magazine from her combat jacket, and headed back the way they had come, looking for the gunman she had hit. Kiwi opened his door and moved to the back of the T.C.H.D. And Ben? Ben was astonished to see a civilian lurching to her feet over towards the side of the carriageway. A Scottish flag lay at her feet, and two metal filaments glistened in car headlights, stretching from her chest towards a taser handset; which lay in the outstretched hand of a dead police Sergeant a few yards away.

She was lumbering and rather overweight, arms outstretched above her.

"Don't shoot!" she shouted, in regardless that all bar Mazz were entirely unarmed.

What in God's name was going on?

~~

"Zero, this in Clyde 44, on site, one gunman down. Vehicle leaving the scene down service road. Occupants armed, number unknown. One civilian on site, apparently unarmed. Wait out."

While Ben moved towards the terrified civilian, Mazz hustled at a crouch towards the shadow of the figure she had cut down with her fire through the windscreen, and she could see it crumpled and akimbo on the road. She assumed the target was down for good. Shot twice and run over by Joop, it seemed a safe bet. Emad's guts had been ripped open – the 9mm round might not be an overpressure bullet, fired at only 310 metres per second, but shooting it through the toughened glass had sent it spinning, expanding the cavity of the wound. Tumbling and yawing, the second hit struck heavily profused organs like the liver, and Emad from that point was doomed.

But stepping closer within ten metres of the shattered form, Maryam could see first the head and neck of her target lift off the tarmac, then a right arm reach down to a cargo pocket, withdrawing a pistol and moving jerkily to raise it. For a brief moment Maryam felt for the young man on the floor. She has been in a similar position in the heat and dust in a field in Afghanistan a few months before. But that day and the months of anxiety since had changed her. There was no way she was going to allow anyone to take her life. Dropping to one knee, she raised the Glock, and fired. Not once. But seven times in barely two seconds. She filled the shadowy form full of lead.

"Fuck you, you fuck."

It wasn't a use of language Mazz had as her normal turn of phrase. But she was a different beast to the one who had flown out to Operation Lincoln a year before. She ran the last few yards to the shattered form, kicked a pistol on the floor hard away from it. And shot him twice more.

~~

The stocky Scottish woman might have been tottering around like a drunk, but in the circumstances Collins was taking no chances. Grabbing her collar with his left hand, he took her left arm by the wrist and twisted it hard and behind her back, before frog marching her the few yards over to the Audi. Forcing her down onto the bonnet face-first might have caused an unsightly dent, had the vehicles resale value not already been curtailed by the bullets which had come and gone through its windscreen and radiator; and by the imprint left by Emad as he was mown down.

"Who the fuck are you?" Ben fired. "And what the fuck is going on?" A fierce shove against Shona's neck and wrist accompanied every hard consonant.

"My name is Shona. This was meant to be a protest. Stop the convoy, get some film of it stuck on the motorway. Then everyone started shooting."

"Everyone?"

"I fainted when that Sergeant shot me with a taser. When I came around the mechanic who helped me set up the stinger was shooting – and all these police were dead."

"A mechanic?"

"His name is Ali. Ali Shah. And his sister was with him. I saw her shoot that poor sod by the lorry. God knows where she came from – and there was another one with a gun too, the one you ran over. I couldn't see who it was. But I am guessing it was their brother. Now will you get off me."

"Was that them in the car?"

"Uh huh – the sister is a doctor at the hospital. Can you see my friends? I had three people with me, two young students and a bloke with a beard."

Ben cast his eyes around. The only bodies he could see on the tarmac were those of police officers – apart from the single dead gunman upaways, who Maryam had just killed.

Ben released the pressure on Shona, pulled her upright, and spun her round, patting her down quickly. He had decided she was an unlikely nuclear terrorist: just a belligerent Jock.

"There's no-one here. You said she was a doctor?"

"Yes, I work with her. She is called Abaya Shah." Ben was impatient to see into the rear of the cargo trailer, seeing Kiwi clumsily trying to climb up into the load compartment. Keeping Shona's left arm behind her back for the moment, he propelled her forward with the heel of his hand against the middle of her back. The Scot humphed in protest but moved as directed. Having followed and watched these lorries for a decade, she was as keen as anyone to see what on earth was inside – what was worth all this mayhem

"What do you know about her?"

"Not much. She is a locum. Came a few months ago. I know where she lives though, I have even been there once." Bens eyes widened. "She comes from Syria. Her brother, Ali, he was one of those rescue workers in the civil war."

"The "White helmets""

"That's right. The whole family came as refugees. Ali said he wanted to study at the University." To Shona the whole thing felt unreal. Describing her acquaintances as if to a stranger in a coffee shop, when they had just murdered four men in front of her.

"I am guessing they are all big on Islam."

Shona stopped in her tracks, and turned to look quizzically at Ben, as if she knew that the answer she was going to give didn't add up. Her brow furrowed into a frown.

"Christians..... they are Syrian Christians. I even saw them celebrating Christmas..." Her voice tailed off in puzzlement.

Before Ben could ask more, Kiwi reappeared. Short on agility and in pain from his chest again, the Prof slowly sat on the metal floor of the T.C.H.D. trailer, before shuffling forward on his backside to minimise the drop to the floor.

"Kiwi?"

"They've got a plutonium pit, Ben. The peanut is ripped open. The uranium secondary and the tamper are still there."

"Jesus. You!" he turned to Shona and pointed at Kiwi. "Stay with him!" Ben ran back to the trashed Audi, sprinting right past Maryam as she trotted up, wondering how on earth he could put into words what he had found in the last 60 seconds.

Chapter 17

The Octopus

In the States, as you might expect, there is a fondness for codenames for nuclear weapon events. “Broken Arrow” for any kind of accidental event with a nuclear weapon; “Faded Giant” for a reactor accident; “Dull sword” for a minor incident with a weapon; or “Empty Quiver” for a weapon stolen or lost.

The English, of course, take a different path. Collins felt that radioing in “Nuclear Transport Emergency – Weapon – Road – Release of Radioactive Material Confirmed,” hardly captured the drama of things, but having swotted to learn the bullshit associated with his new role he wasn’t going to deviate.

He was surprised to instantly get Gold Command ask him to repeat his message, but realised this was not due to his lack of clarity. C.I. Wood was struggling to believe that the one thing they drilled and planned to avoid was, in fact, happening. Her deputy in the back seat immediately got out the play book, silently giving thanks that at least they were still South of the border and he wouldn’t have to deal with both COBRA in London and some faceless and contrary gaggle of suits in the Scottish Government Resilience Room. Wood left him to it. The best way to limit the imminent shit storm would be to get the bloody thing back.

"Clyde 44 this is Zero Actual, what other units are on site, over."

"Clyde 44 wait out."

Ben was interrupted by Joop running up. He was breathless and panting, in great part because he was toting an armful of C8 carbines and two flak jackets unzipped and carried through the arm hole. Ignoring Kiwi and Shona and dumping the 30 kilos of assorted kit at Ben's feet with a clatter, he couldn't conceal his shock.

"Ben they are all dead. Carter and his whole team. All five of them. Most of their weapons still had the safety on – the poor sods didn't even get a round off. And it looks like some scumbag finished them off at close range. I don't know what sort of rounds they are using but I've not seen anything like it. Body armour did no good as far as I can see. But I got these for the ammo."

Collins turned back to the radio.

"Clyde 44, all callsigns and serials we can find on site are down. No survivors. Four times S.E.G. and five Marines K.I.A. Over."

In her command vehicle Wood was mouthing "Recovery Tactics Troop" to her deputy, who had been in touch with the Junglie call signs. He held up two fingers, Churchill style.

"Zero.." She paused trying to remember the call sign of Chandler and Johnson, but failed. "Romeo Tango Tango is two minutes from you. Wait and secure the site. Over."

Ben looked at Kiwi and Mazz. Kiwi shook his head and pointed animatedly down the off ramp to the works exit. Ben gave him a thumbs up.

"Clyde 44, negative. We are now fully armed with recovered weapons. We have a civilian who has given positive I.D. on two remaining gunmen, details to follow. Seen leaving down works access two minutes ago, in dark Citroen Cactus. We are in pursuit in…." Joop swept to a halt in a new vehicle. Ben raised an eyebrow. "… a White Audi S.U.V."

Not waiting for an answer, Ben took the Bowman radio and picked up a C8, while Maryam shoved her Glock into the small of her back and picked up the rest of their newly acquired arsenal.

Ben ran around the front of the car and jumped in.

"Another Audi Joop?"

"Brand loyalty mate."

With Shona and the rest of the team bundling into the back, and the doors still closing, Joop floored it and sped down the works access road.

~~

Abaya was shaking as the car sped through the dark.

Ali had sped through a gravel yard at the foot of the off ramp, zeroing in on a single-track tarmacked roadway which led under a narrow tunnel beneath the main west coast railway line. The lights on full beam lit the dripping brickwork walls of the Victorian-era arch, only a foot gap either side and no room for error as he accelerated past 50mph.

"Why didn't he come? He had time to get in." Abaya was shocked, trembling as she tried to release an empty magazine from her Vitaz to load another.

"They were soldiers." Ali said, not taking his eyes off the road as he changed down to take a right turn onto a main road at a T junction which he knew from his map recce to expect. Careful not to lose the back end as he turned, he squeezed every ounce of acceleration out of the piss poor engine of the Cactus, heading North on the A6. "Emad bought us time. With any luck they will lose contact. They have no idea who we are. They probably won't have the vehicle registration – and even if they do it will only lead them to that idiot Duncan."

"But he was my brother, Ali!" It was as if Abaya was only now processing that essential detail herself. In avenging her sister she had now lost the only other member of her family still living.

"And he was very brave," Ali said softly. "Which is what we need to be now."

He took his eyes off the road to peer up into the night sky through his driver's side window, looking back over his shoulder towards where the blinking of emergency lights still lit up the darkness the other side of the railway embankment. In the sky to the south, two flashing red anti-collision lights could be seen, closing fast and descending. Trouble was brewing.

~~

Major Chandler was in meltdown. "Zero Alpha, this is Clyde 1 Alpha, 90 seconds out, send sitrep on Landing Zone, over."

"Zero Alpha, wait." C.I. Wood was approaching saturation such was the load on her and her team. Having handed over command of the remaining convoy to her MOD police deputy, she was heading south on the opposite carriageway of the M6 back towards Lancaster, siren wailing. In the rear her comms group were in touch with Weathersfield and the MOD; the tentacles of the "Octopus" were starting to flex, and people who had left Whitchall were rushing back to their desks. The National Security Council and COBRA were being alerted that the biggest UK nuclear incident since the Windscale pile fire of 1957 was in full swing, though pedantic grey men in grey suits were arguing over whether this was strictly speaking a "Level 5" or "Level 6" on the seven-point I.N.E.S. scale. Fortunately, the supportive and encouraging culture of the Ministry of Defence kicked in. Of course, that isn't true. The words "support" and "encourage" disappeared from the Ministry in a defence review in the 1970s. Fairer to say the normal *wholesale* level of back-stabbing was about to move up to *industrial* levels. Rachel couldn't have been in more shit if she had sent a load of plain clothes officers to shoot someone who turned out to be an innocent Brazilian electrician.

"Zero Alpha, the L.Z. is insecure. No known friendlies or hostiles on site. Local police are holding 2 kilometres south at this time. Roger so far over."

"Clyde 1 Alpha, roger so far."

"Zero Alpha, your callsign Clyde 44 has left the scene in pursuit of a dark Citroen Cactus, hostiles and stolen material on board. I need you to secure the ambush site and Tango 5, over."

Major Chandler grunted agreement, but then flipped his comms switch to the intercom of Junglie 11.

"Pilot, let's get this shit heap on the ground. Get the Merlin to land behind us. As soon as I have got that half-wit Johnson and his troop safeguarding whatever is left of the cargo, we are going after them."

In the cockpit Lt. Lizzie Walker clicked her switch on the cyclic stick to reply.

"Major, you realise we have no Night Vision Goggles? We are going to be very limited in what we can do? At least, what we can do safely."

Chandler was seldom full of sweetness and light, but his response transcended even his low standards of civility.

"Let me do the strategy please. Just you fucking fly where I tell you."

Walker changed her grip on the cyclic stick, to enable her to extend a single middle finger upwards as she replied.

"Of course, sir. Landing in sixty seconds. Hold on…"

~~

By the time Joop had negotiated the tunnel and pulled to a halt at the T-junction with the A6, Ali and the stolen plutonium pit were long gone. But given the link to

Lancaster, there seemed only one sensible way to go. He hauled down on the steering wheel, and headed North.

Ben twisted awkwardly in the passenger seat to speak to Shona, who was sat shocked between Kiwi and Maryam.

"Shona!" He spoke abruptly and with exaggerated clarity. "Where will they go? What will they want?"

Shona pondered.

"I don't know." Her voice tailed off, shorn of all its previous hubris. "It was just meant to be a demo…"

If Ben could have reached her he might have slapped her. Good job he couldn't.

"Shona you say they are not Muslims. They are not extremists. Are you sure about that?"

"Absolutely." Shona shook herself out of her dazed state. "Dr Shah…"

"That's the woman?" Ben interrupted.

"Yes, the woman. She was a hospital doctor in Damascus, she used to have to treat all the victims of Assad and the Russian bombing. Barrel bombs, and gas attacks, all that sort of things. Her brother Ali went out to the places where there had been air strikes or artillery fire, rescuing the injured and bringing them in."

Joop listened in but kept his foot to the floor. The Sat Nav screen gave some idea as to likely twists and turns ahead, and he kept braking to the last minute and to a minimum, to the discomfort of Kiwi in the back.

Ben probed further.

"Could they be stealing it to sell?" Ben was starting to feel completely out of his depth. How the hell did one go about marketing and finding a buyer for 3kg of plutonium/gallium mix, in just the right handy format for a nuclear weapon primary. How would you possibly hope to evade the forces of law and order long enough to collect the proceeds? And if you were stealing for the massive pay-out you could realise, why would this look like some kind of amateur hour family venture – why not hire the firepower and muscle you need to vastly improve your chances?

Mazz felt Shona shrug next to her.

"All I can say is they were angry."

"Angry? With who? Assad? Russia?"

"With us. With the West. With America and Britain. Their little sister got killed in one of the nerve gas attacks – she actually got taken into the emergency room where Dr. Shah was working, I think. She was ten years old, maybe eleven. Dr. Shah said the little girl died in her arms. This was maybe five years ago, but she had a rage as she was telling me, a rage about the West and the United Nations. When she spoke about it, she was consumed by anger – I learned not to ask her again. She tried her best to help her patients; but when she talked about us as a people she held the whole lot of us in contempt."

As the Audi hurtled into a small village, Ben caught a flash of an L.E.D. speed sign: a "sad" red smiley and "Your Speed. 80mph" censured them as they blasted past the village store.

Mazz leaned forward to speak better to Kiwi.

"Kiwi. What do you think?"

Kiwi sat silent for a moment.

"They aren't Muslim, but they are angry; they hate the west for not helping when they needed help; they want revenge against someone, and that someone could be us. And the good doctor is a radiologist, so she will know exactly what she has got and what harm it can do."

Joop butted in. "But it's just a solid lump of plutonium isn't it? With none of the conventional explosive or fusing needed to set it off. And back at Winterborne we held a ring of plutonium in our hands. So how can they use it to threaten any…"

"They burn it," Ben interrupted.

"They burn it," Kiwi echoed. "And they poison the entire area with the fire. Just like Rocky Flats. Just like Project Vixen at Muralinga. But what do they have to do to get it to burn?" It was an odd place to be testing them on a lecture on a wet Wednesday weeks before in Dorset.

"Find some way to fragment it, or pulverise it, or shred it. More surface area to react, and up it will go."

"Dead right," said Kiwi. "And our gunman is really a mechanic?"

Shona nodded vigorously. "For sure, I have been to his garage. Bay City Motors, everyone knows where that is."

"Then that's where they can get what they need. Where else will they be?"

~~

"Five miles," Ali said.

Abaya leaned forward to look into the passenger-side wing mirror, looking for any sign of pursuit, but saw nothing. Nevertheless, the nearer to Lancaster they got the more nervous she became.

"Ali let's get off the main road and come in the back way by the river."

"This way is faster."

"Ali they must know we got from the motorway onto the A6, a roadblock could be just around the corner. They have armed police out and about at all times in this country."

Abaya didn't know how far off the mark she was. Seven years before there had been a scandal in the North West, when one Derek Bird, a disaffected joiner-cum-taxi-driver, had driven around Whitehaven in Cumbria, first targeting a handful of relatives and friends with whom he had a grudge, but ultimately killing multiple random locals in drive-by shootings. There had been a dearth of Armed Response Vehicles to stop him, so that his mass shooting, second only to Hungerford and Dunblane in recent history, ended with him taking his own life rather than being apprehended or stopped. As a result, the number of A.R.V.s had been rapidly expanded, and Weathersfield had multiple units from Cumbria already headed to Lancaster. Notably they were reinforced by units of the Civil Nuclear Constabulary from Sellafield. The bastard twin of the MOD Police, the Civil Nuclear Constabulary were tasked with defending nuclear power plants, and nuclear fuel in transit, though their remit and jurisdiction didn't normally extend more than 5km from whatever they were guarding. Armed with the same Heckler and Koch carbines and Glock 17 pistols as the MOD police, two C.N.C. units were speeding to the area in Ovik Crossway vehicles – a variation on the Warthog chassis used in Afghanistan, ballistic protected, and better suited than Cumbria A.R.V.s to the job in hand. Looking like a boxy grey Land Rover on steroids, the two Crossways with their strobing blue lights were scaring the shit out of sleepy locals in the Lake District as they sped South East.

Ali thought Abaya was probably right, and turned left off the main road onto the B5272 which paralleled the A6, running a few degrees west of North. He had done enough recovery work around Lancaster to know most of the nooks and crannies, and knew that the by-way from Garstang to Cockerham village was a relatively untravelled route and not one likely to be blocked. Adding 10 minutes to their transit to Bay City, it seemed worth the detour, and he even started to catch his breath for a moment. Until, over the engine sound of the Cactus, he heard the wop-wop-wop of a helicopter.

~~

Major Chandler had limited information. But that had never previously stopped him taking a definitive position on the next best action.

A dark Citroen Cactus had a stolen plutonium pit on board, along with unknown hostile persons. The breakdown lorry bore the imprint of Bay City Motors of Lancaster – and the latest view of Kiwi and Clyde 44 was that the garage was the likely destination of the thieves.

He had found the final approach to the ambush site thoroughly nauseating – which would have pleased Lizzie as that had been exactly her intent. She had thrown the Wildcat into a 180 degree turn which banked the helicopter past the vertical – a distinctly dubious practice, as turning the rotor that way subjected it to forces which could theoretically detach the blades from the rotor hub. Lizzie felt it was worth the minimal risk to get the bossy Major to throw up, but it had been the unfortunate Captain Ledsham who had ended up throwing his pack-up lunch onto the carriageway.

Major Chandler gave him a look of disdain and began directing Lt. Johnson and his R.T.T. marines, who had landed more conventionally 30 metres further down the roadway. Once they were in place, and Johnson was talking to a lone police motorcyclist who was on site looking dazed, he peeled a fire team of Commandos from the troop to re-embark on the Wildcat. Taking care to give a wide berth to the tail rotor as they hustled around the helicopter, they jumped up and into the cabin by the far door – the cabin door on the nearside was almost entirely filled with the 50-calibre Browning Machine gun, insect-likc visor concealing the face of the airman gunner behind it

Flying North-East at the Wildcat's D.N.E. speed – "do not exceed" - it seemed to take only moments to have the lights of Lancaster City in sight through the pilot window, while the A6 below was lit up like a dancing ribbon of light by the traffic on it and the streetlights beside it.

Chandler toggled his pressel switch to speak to the pilot and observer, giving them the ostensibly impossible task of finding a Cactus sized needle in a Lancashire sized haystack. But while the pilots lacked the NVG goggles to enable flight in the dark close to terrain, the sensor turret at the nose of the helicopter had outstanding optics for a ground search. Lizzie kept her eye on the artificial horizon and heading, but her co-pilot was glued to the one of four multi-function displays on the console, which had been dedicated to an Infra-Red feed from the optics.

Scanning traffic for an individual vehicle amidst dozens of others might have been a thankless task. But the Cactus they were chasing had one design feature which changed the game. Scanning from 1000 feet altitude, the targeting pod was easily able to reveal a hatchback vehicle with a tell-tale profile, its side elevation marked by the curious artefact of its trademark design: both side and rear doors were not simply sheet steel, but had distinctive contoured rubber panels, designed to protect against the shit-fest of scrapes and scratches associated with a Saturday afternoon trip to IKEA. You still might end up divorced by the end of the day, but your car would still be in good nick. On the I.R. scan, the metal and rubber of the side profile came out a radically different tone. There was no other car like it.

Of course, the Citroen Cactus is a popular model, especially with the liberal vegan left. However, heading North-North-West on a B road towards the Lune Estuary, there was, however, one other thing which raised their suspicion; as they looked at the target car on the cockpit monitor, odd snowflakes distorted the image. A legacy of the unshielded radiation from the plutonium pit in the shoulder bag on the back seat, messing with the sensor array in the turret. And there was one final tell-tale. As the helicopter closed on the vehicle, and presumably the occupants heard its approach, the target slowed and switched off its headlights.

Of course, having been alerted by the pilot, Major Chandler could have directed Clyde 44, or an A.R.V., or the

C.N.C., into a position to apprehend or kill. That was not his choice.

"Zero Alpha, this is Clyde 1 Alpha, believe target in sight, engaging, over."

~~

C.I. Wood turned to her colleagues. "Is he fucking mad?"

"Zero Alpha, can I remind you that you are in an uncontrolled public space, and your jurisdiction is only in support of the civil power on request. Over."

"Clyde One Alpha, can I remind *you* of the rules of engagement which not only permit, but require my force to protect national nuclear assets with all means at our disposal, including lethal force. Over."

C.I. Wood's mind was racing. Engaging a vehicle with a helicopter mounted 50-calibre machine-gun might be standard in Kandahar. But it wasn't in rural Lancashire. And the ways it could go wrong were too legion to mention.

Rachel checked in with her team.

"What else have we got on the way?"

A frazzled Inspector in the back seat looked glum.

"R.T.T. are on the ground and two fire teams have mounted up in the Mercedes armoured van that was abandoned on scene. But they couldn't follow the route the attackers took through the works access. The vehicle is too big to get through a tunnel under the west coast train line, so they are going a long way around."

"The local A.R.V.s?"

"The Chief Constable of Lancashire is shitting a chicken about committing them to an unknown terrorist situation. They are moving up to the ambush site to relieve R.T.T. Then we can get the Commandos back on the Merlin and fly them to the target. Maybe ten minutes."

"Civil Nuclear?"

"On their way down from Sellafield, ditto Cumbria Constabulary A.R.V.s. But like us, they won't be in the Lancaster area for 20 minutes at least."

"And Clyde 44?"

"The last we heard they were headed to a garage called "Bay City Motors" on the Quay in Lancaster. They believe that is where the Cactus is headed."

Rachel reflected that none of the exercises they had run on an attack on a nuclear transport had gone this way. Plus ca change. Everyone was on their way. No-one was here. Major Chandler was determined to take on the attackers on his own, from the air, using heavy weaponry in an area they had not recce'd and with unknown civilian presence. It was fraught with risk.

On the plus side if Chandler managed to disable the vehicle out there in the sticks, the follow up to kill or capture those inside would be much easier than if the car made it to Lancaster or beyond. And more importantly still, it was his decision, and his demand, to engage them. Not hers.

The best way to play it would be to let him crack on. If she tried to stop him and all went well, there would be no good outcome for Rachel, and all the glory for 43 Commando. If, instead, you get a minibus full of nuns or primary school kids hit by 50-calibre machine gun fire, well, it's all down to the Mad Major. Rachel was rather pleased with her solution.

"Ma'am, do you want to reply to Clyde One Alpha?" the Inspector asked.

"Not right now, I don't think. Not right now.."

~~

With no headlights Ali was loath to drive at pace, but at least the road itself was familiar. "Park Lane", as the B-road was known in those parts, had the advantage of being almost dead straight, and ambient light from a caravan park gave him some sense of depth. The downside was that there was almost no cover from view on this length of road: an odd pub, a farm, some kennels, but no forest, and open farmland either side. From experience with the Russians, and the double-tap airstrike which targeted his team, Ali was under no illusion as to the ability of an observer a mile up to see them. He had to hope it was part of the police search, or air ambulance, or whatever. Even if it were the former, they could track him but only vector other units to try to block them. Time was on their side.

~~

Interview any Vietnam-era helicopter door gunner and, having stared past you and murmured "You weren't there, man," they will tell you that if you are flying parallel to a moving target but at overtaking speed, you don't aim in front of the target. You aim behind it and "walk the rounds" into the target as you speed past it. And this is, indeed, what door gunners serving in the Commando Helicopter Force are taught. When they manage to get some range time. Which Aircrewman Paul Field had not seen hide nor hair of in 6 months on the Squadron. For the moment, he was more concerned at the battle of wills going on in the cabin behind him between his pilot, who he knew and respected, and a Marine Major who had managed to piss off the entire crew in half a day.

"Pilot, I am saying we have positive I.D. on a vehicle last seen ambushing the transport. That vehicle has to be stopped before it gets into a built-up area."

"Sir, it is reckless and actionable to open fire on what might just be a local with dodgy headlights. Or crooks who think we are police and want to shake us off. I am not going to jail for life for helping you shoot a bunch of muppets on a Friday night booze up."

"Pilot, I have informed the convoy commander we are engaging."

"Sir, I can drop you three miles ahead. Your fire team can stop them and engage then if they are who you say."

"Young lady..", Chandler almost spat the salutation, "That would give us no time to set up even a hasty ambush. And if they change direction and take a new route, we are in the arse end of nowhere while they get away."

Lt. Walker had to accept he had a point. She turned to look at her co-pilot who offered no more than a shrug. Lizzie spoke on the intercom to her gunner.

"Paul I am coming down to 200 metres, overtaking the target vehicle down its right hand side. Confirm you can see the vehicle, lights off, passing a pub….now now now."

Gazing from his position in the left hand door of the Wildcat, the eighteen year old had none of the fancy optics available to the co-pilot, but the illumination of the pub car park and fascia allowed him to pick up the dark shadow of a car shooting past.

"Target identified. Warning shots Sir?"

Major Chandler was having no half measures.

"Gunner, destroy the target, get it now."

Field set his sights 50 metres ahead, squinted slightly, took a deep breath, and with the palms of each hands against the spade grip of the heavy weapon, pulled the triggers.

He had not fired at night before and the effect was startling. A blazing muzzle flash two feet long lit up the entire side of the Wildcat and blinded him, so that he flinched and let go of the triggers with only five rounds down the barrel. Before Major Chandler could bollock him, he had regained his senses, and was sending multiple short bursts towards the target; but only to see the one-in-four red tracer rounds drift to the right of the target and splash into the road surface and field 100 yards ahead of the vehicle.

Ali equally nearly threw the vehicle off the road as he wrenched the steering wheel in reflex reaction. He saw the torrent of fireworks blazing from the sky to his right, to impact a second or two in front of the speeding car. His response was a triumph of judgement over instinct. Ali calculated that the gunner would realise their mistake, and would surely adjust now the fall of shot could be seen. That meant the only best course was not to slow, but to accelerate, hoping that the gunner would over correct. Ignoring a shriek from Abaya in the passenger seat, he flicked the lights on with his right hand, changed down two gears with his left, and stamped on the accelerator, willing the pathetic engine of the Cactus to accelerate. He was just fast enough. As the Wildcat overtook the car, Field adjusted 20 degrees of arc and fired again. Had Ali not accelerated, the Cactus would have found itself poked full of more holes than its succulent namesake could ever deliver. A 50-calibre bullet, the size of a thumb, would rip any person inside to bits. Instead, he could see sparks flying in his mirror; and had there been any day light, would have seen chunks of tarmac and of the verge and hedge thrown into the air.

"Shit," said Field under his breath. Major Chandler was less restrained.

"Pilot, will you get out in front and get low enough for this half-wit to hit something." He gestured to the pair of Marines from R.T.T. in the cabin to lock and load in case they too needed to engage the target through their own side of the cabin.

"Major, I will come around in front but we are not going lower. We have no N.V.G. remember, 200 metres is the lowest we go."

"Just get the fucking target will you."

Those in the cabin felt the Wildcat bank to the right, head off track ten degrees, and then bank the other way after a few seconds.

Lizzie was cross. Cross with Major Chandler, cross with having to endorse firing heavy weapons at a civilian vehicle, cross at Field for missing. And tired from 12 hours on duty and 6 hours of flying. She continued her check on the four screens of the functions of the helicopter, which showed the vital instruments of night flying: altimeter, airspeed, artificial horizon. Coming round to a westerly heading she looked across past her co-pilot to the target, which was now going full bore, lights blazing, right at them. With no deflection to allow for the relative movement of the car and the helicopter, it should be a much easier shot.

Looking back from the dark outside to the gloom of the cockpit she did a double take.

The artificial horizon said the helicopter was in straight and level. But she would swear to her dying day it was more like 20 degrees of right hand bank. Lizzie gently moved the cyclic stick to the left to make the aircraft feel level. But when the artificial horizon said they were banking to port, she still felt the significant bank to starboard was still in force.

Lizzie had "the leans". This phenomenon is well understood by aircrew. The vestibular canals of the inner ear are tricky organs, with a fluid called endolymph which moves within the canal, moving out of synch with the canal structure. The endolymph "lags" a little, the back wash stimulating tiny hairs, which translates to a feeling of movement. However, a slow and steady turn allows the endolymph fluid to "catch up", so that the hair cells aren't stimulated: the sense of relative acceleration passes, even while the turn continues. Of course, in daylight the other visual inputs are strong enough for the brain to adjust. But in the pitch dark over Lancashire countryside, there was no such help. And trusting the instruments is a challenge when a stack of aircraft crashes have been caused by dodgy software in so called "glass cockpits" like that in the Wildcat.

Field found the urge to put in a left control input overwhelming. To her co-pilot, and to the gunner in the rear, all they perceived was a steepening left bank, and Field assumed she was trying to give an angle to give an easy shot without tipping the barrel of the M3 down towards the skids. The artificial horizon told the truth – the Wildcat was banking left ever more steeply. But Lizzie was so convinced that it actually tilted to the right, and she had not yet hit straight and level, that she was leaning over to the left in her seat: leaning in the direction of her falsely imagined vertical – hence "the leans".

Paul was preparing to open fire again when he sensed the Wildcat slipping into a bank sufficiently steep that he risked shooting through the rotor disk. But he had not got as far as toggling his pressel switch to talk than a shout came first from the co-pilot.

"Lizzie!" The second-stick had glanced back across the cabin to see Lt. Walker leaning towards him, beyond the already steep bank angle, as if trying to will the helicopter further onto its side. At this point a shout of "I have control" and a seizure of command would have done everyone a favour. Instead Lizzie was jolted into action. But not the right action.

Instead of obeying the artificial horizon, which told the truth and demanded a right control input to recover, the shout led Lizzie to fix on the radar altimeter, which had slipped to 150 metres. In her inadvertent steep bank, not all of the draught from the rotors was providing lift, and the Wildcat had started to leak height. That too could be fixed. But given Lizzie thought the helicopter was flying level, when it was in fact now in a 45-degree bank, the reflex thing for her to do was to add power on the collective stick and pull to gain height, at the same time as pulling back on the cyclic with her right hand to pull up. If the Wildcat had been orientated as Lizzie's senses told her it was, the helicopter would have leapt in the sky. In fact, it was the worst possible thing to do.

In a bank, the extra power and lift went not into gaining height, but in tightening further the circle the Wildcat was carving across the sky. The force being generated by the rotor disk was going into pushing the helicopter into the turn, not keeping it in the air. After a day of faultless flying, Lizzie's every control input was now conspiring to kill them all. At the last second her co-pilot seized the controls, but they would have needed another 500 metres of altitude to correct and recover.

The rotor tips were the first component to strike the ploughed field to the West side of the road; but the cabin, aircrew, and embarked group of Marines hit milliseconds later, the whole exploding with a fiery crump which carried miles in the cold air.

It would definitely be Major Chandler's last convoy.

~~

"What the hell was that?"

It is not unheard of for New Zealanders to take some pleasure in kicking the establishment. On this occasion though, Kiwi felt almost ashamed to intrude on C.I. Wood's forlorn efforts to contact Junglie 11. But intrude he did.

"Zero Alpha this is Clyde 44, Prof. Barton speaking, over."

"Zero Alpha, send, over."

"Clyde 44, Can you confirm the last sighting of the target vehicle, over."

"Zero Alpha, Junglie 11 was engaging about 3 miles south of Lancaster, on the B5272 somewhere near Cockerham".

"Clyde 44 confirm you have lost touch with Junglie 11, over."

"Confirmed."

"Us too. There was just an explosion and fireball in that vicinity. I think Junglie 11 has crashed, over."

There was a long pause.

"Zero Alpha, roger."

Kiwi was sufficiently gracious not to plough right on, allowing a moment before continuing.

"Clyde 44, that position is consistent with the attackers heading to Lancaster. Our assumption is they are intending to combust the pit and contaminate the whole area. They are believed to be Ali and Abaya Shah. Syrian. One an engineer, the other a radiologist. The engineer is currently working out of Bay City Motors on the Quayside. Roger so far over."

"Zero Alpha."

"Clyde 44, what other armed units are close, over?"

"Zero Alpha, we are closest but still 15 minutes out." The convoy commanders Range Rover was at 90 mph in the fast lane of the M6 headed back South. "More Clyde assets are about to leave the ambush site in Junglie 12, also likely 15 minutes from Lancaster, over."

Kiwi leaned forward to speak to Joop, who had been flashing past slower traffic on the A6, the powerful engine of the Audi Q8 taking it flying by the Friday night traffic. "How long?", he asked. Joop held up all five digits of his left hand, then placed it back on the wheel, changed down on the paddle shift, and blazed past a double decker bus taking students from the University into town.

"Clyde 44. We will be at the garage in five minutes. What's happening with the Octopus? Over."

It wasn't a polite term to use for the mass of government agencies, advisors, and police and military stake holders in defence nuclear material transport. But he knew the Chief Inspector would get the shorthand.

"Zero Alpha COBRA is calling everyone in, as per the playbook. First conference is due at 2100 Zulu. Over." Kiwi checked his watch – over two hours away.

"Clyde 44, roger. You need to prioritise. If they get 3kg worth of plutonium lit and burning well, you are going to need some bits more than others. Take this down…"

~~

Ali and Abaya were barely over the helicopter unaccountably banking and crashing into the field beside the road when trouble struck again.

Ahead aways down the road appeared the hulking shadow of an old-fashioned cattle truck, the wooden slats and bars down the sides and rear containing a cargo of live sheep. Stationary and blocking their path, Ali briefly considered pulling out to pass it: but while the road here was wide enough for two cars to pass each other, the breadth of the truck was too wide for him to pass without putting the driver's side wheels in the ditch. The tail lights of the lorry were lit crimson, and he was just about to hammer the horn to get the driver to move when he saw why the lorry was stopped. Lit up in the lorry headlights was a slightly sorry looking police Transit Van, pulled up in a lay-by on right of the road, facing towards them.

"What do you think?" Abaya asked.

Ali looked over his shoulder and tried to visualise the route they would have to take to dog-leg around the obstruction to get to Bay City. Too far.

"If they have stopped a truck then maybe our description isn't out yet. Let's get closer." He sensed Abaya reaching down the side of the passenger seat, where her pistol was likely stashed. Slowing the car carefully, he reached across with his left hand and held her wrist. "Take it easy," he said gently.

Coming within 20 metres of the rear of the lorry, he could make out a gaggle of shadows stood beside the cab, pretty much filling the roadway between the vehicle and the right-hand verge. The Cactus' headlight picked out two yellow high viz waterproofs edged with the standard police checkerboard trim. The larger of the police officers probably would have been stocky even had his shape not been bulked out by his thick jacket, while the silhouette of his colleague appeared female in stature and form. It was the former who seemed to be taking the lead, notebook open as he seemed to be in conversation with an adult male clad in rather more sports leisurewear than would be conventional for the farming community of the local area. Further to the side was a youth not at all dressed for the weather or time of year in jeans and a T-shirt, his gaze darting left and right as if planning a next move.

However, the next move came instead from the female P.C., who left her colleague to it and walked slowly towards the Cactus. As the lights illuminated her rather better, Ali reassured Abaya. "It's OK, I know this one, local force. Make sure everything is out of view." Ali pressed the button on the door sill and the driver's side window glided down, letting in a rush of cold air and the noise of a dozen ewes bleating.

"Oh, Ali. It's you."

"Hello, Candy. Trouble?"

"If not nicking "Red Diesel" its fly-tipping, if not fly-tipping its sheep-rustling. You don't speak Romanian I suppose?"

"I'm afraid not. Will you take long?"

"I don't know. I will go see if Tom is getting anywhere." She turned and ambled away, muttering something about European integration which would be unlikely to please advocates of a multi-cultural Britain.

Abaya watched her impatiently. "We could force them to move?"

"Indeed. But this might be one that is quicker to talk our way through. Have you got your hospital I.D.?"

Abaya picked at a lanyard round her neck and pulled out her plastic photocard.

"Let's see if that helps."

They stepped out of the vehicle and walked together up the right side of the lorry. The male P.C. appeared to be struggling to work out how best to use sign language to communicate "sheep", "paperwork", and "H.G.V. license", while the shifty youth seemed to have taken on a role of interpreter between the policeman and his fellow suspect. Candy had her back to them, and she jumped startled at Ali tapping on her shoulder.

"Candy is there any way they could just move the lorry ten metres forward? Abaya has been called in to an emergency at the Royal Lancaster, and we have to get there fast."

Abaya took her cue and waved her badge at the P.C. "I'm Ali's sister. They need me in X-ray. There's been a serious accident of some sort."

Candy looked her up and down. "Blimey, Ali, you never told me you had brains in the family. Hang on here, I will see what we can do."

She walked over to the gaggle a few metres further on to speak to her colleague, and they saw Tom put his arm out, palm upward, as if trying to quiet the youth whose body language was suggesting ever more frenetic pleas of innocence. While they were out of ear shot, the signs looked positive. The male P.C. took three paces backwards himself, and gestured to the youth to stand out of the road beside the Transit. He then pointed up towards the cab of the lorry, and tapped the sportswear fanatic on the arm as if to endorse that he should get in and start up. But amidst the movements came one movement that made Ali freeze. Candy had turned away from the others and put her index finger up to her right ear, as if trying to lodge her ear piece better. She shot a glance back towards Ali, turned away and seemed to listen more, then spun her torso round, eyes widening in alarm.

They had been rumbled.

Ali went for the Grach pistol in the pocket of his overalls; only to fumble for the way into the pocket, not once but twice. The male P.C. caught Candy's sudden movement and turned to her quizzically, while Ali resorted to reaching his left hand across to the front right thigh of his overalls, pulling the trouser taught so he could get into the pocket.

His finger-tips finally found the cold metal, but before he could pull the pistol up to firing position he heard a single crack of a gun shot from behind him. Abaya had beaten him to it, and at such close range her aim was spot on. The bullet caught Candy full in the face, and she dropped like a sack of potatoes, the contents of her skull spattering the roadway. Tom was transfixed. His hand hovered over the Taser and asp on his belt, but his mind was focused only on his dead colleague. Then another gunshot and the zip of a bullet coming past his face snapped him into action.

Two more bullets cracking past him, the middle-aged copper covered the remaining yards to his Transit van faster than his front row forward colleagues in the police rugby team would have thought possible, and he threw open the driver's side door. Leaping into his seat, he started up, slammed into reverse, and floored the accelerator, hurling the Transit away from the shooter whose muzzle flash was still strobing again and again to his front. He heard a double clank of two rounds hitting somewhere on the front of the van, the second of them coming through and hitting the passenger seat, dusting powdered fabric padding into the air.

He was conscious of the ditch either side of the road, but that was not why he slammed on the brakes once 30 metres away, tyres skidding as the Transit came to a halt.

That was down to the fury he felt at what had been done to his friend. Selecting first gear, he blipped the throttle once, then stamped on it. In a vehicle with better response than a late model diesel engine Transit with 80,000 miles on the clock, the van's headlong rush would have been more impressive still. But it nevertheless caught the Syrians unawares, with Abaya in mid-reload clumsily trying to slip a new magazine in and to re-cock the weapon.

Ali, on the other hand, still had several rounds left, and had good time to line up a shot at the driver's side windscreen. He drilled a double tap of two rounds which would have been bang on target had Tom not had enough street sense to take cover, bending his whole top half to the left across the gear stick to lean over the passenger seat, the rounds showering him with glass but doing no other harm.

He kept his foot down and the Transit kept accelerating, and Ali kept shooting. Suddenly Ali caught movement in the corner of his eye, a flash of track suit top, and found himself thrown sideways by a furious body-check, as 13 stone of truculent Romanian landed on him. The wannabe rustler had clearly decided not to leave the local forces of law and order to their fate, and Ali felt fierce blows land on his jaw and his eye socket and the side of his head. He managed to land a couple of blows back with his elbow, and only got back on parity as he switched grip on the pistol and clubbed the Romanian again and again with the butt. Finally, landing a blow on the temple, he felt his attacker sag and weaken, and he could haul himself unsteadily to his feet.

He found the action was over. Abaya had finally managed to reload, and abandoning shooting at the cab, had poured bullets into the front right tyre of the Transit.

Exploding loudly, the blown tyre threw the van to the right, and at the best part of 30 mph it smashed into the radiator of the lorry in a shower of shattered plastic and twisted metal. The impact sent the sheep into turmoil, bleating in a frenzy at the noise and impact. But Abaya was unhurt, going around to the passenger side to check on the policeman who lay unconscious and bleeding in the footwell of the front seats. In another world and another life she would have been checking his vital signs, doing C.P.R., putting him in the recovery position. In this world and this time, she briefly thought of shooting him dead, but wearily decided to leave him to whatever fate had in store.

Ali dragged the now conscious and struggling Romanian by the scruff of the neck. He could have looked up on GoogleTranslate how to offer the bruised and dazed man a choice between moving the lorry or being shot in the head. It seemed the slightest gesture with the muzzle of the pistol achieved the same goal admirably, and the man mounted up and started up, the lorry ploughing the battered front of the Transit out of the way. With space now made to get through, Ali and Abaya remounted the Cactus and sped past.

The whole incident had taken maybe 3 minutes from start to finish.

Ali wasn't sure they had three minutes to spare.

~~

Joop initially put a cautious two wheels up on the empty pavement to go up the inside of the Friday night traffic on the increasingly busy A6 into Lancaster, but then decided he was being far too conventional and took the whole car off the carriageway. In back Mazz was busy staring down at her phone, but using it while being thrown side to side as Joop dodged litter bins, post boxes, bus shelters, and startled civilians was no easy task.

Now back as near civilisation as Northern Lancashire would achieve, Mazz had decent enough 4G to be looking at Google Maps, and had loaded up satellite imagery of Bay City Motors' quayside premises. It was impossible to see much other than the scale of the place from a birds-eye view, but a main road separated the large forecourt from a seawall, which would supposedly contain the River Lune at high tide. Presumably the forecourt would have been the site of petrol pumps before supermarkets cornered the market. Mazz could see ranks of parked cars flanking the forecourt at each end, and Street View confirmed these were second-hand vehicles arrayed for sale in a double row. Maybe 24 vehicles in all. Mazz thought they might provide some cover to get closer to the main building of the premises. From above it was simply a long rectangular grey flat roof, but street-view, taken clearly during the working day, showed maybe four bays for working on individual vehicles: it was too gloomy on the image to assess if there were pits inside to allow work on the underside of vehicles, or if they were put on ramps and lifted. At the extreme left end of the frontage a single door with frosted glass would allow access inside even if the shutters on the four car bays were closed down; at the other end, a more welcoming double door and glass windows suggested a reception area. A Channel 4 makeover show would doubtless comment on the scruffy concrete forecourt, tired paintwork, and bent venetian blinds, which created a look for the business which was not so much tired as exhausted. Maryam was more interested in what lay behind the structure, and the satellite view suggested a not unexpected combination of a couple of vehicle wrecks, barrels doubtless containing dozens of litres of oil, Swarfega, and other nasties, and boxes of paperwork which had somehow never made it to the tax office. It might suggest a way in covered from view

– but there was no sign of how you might access the back of the garage from there.

Next to her Shona had emerged from her cataplectic state and was animatedly directing Joop. She almost had to pinch herself as they came off the big Roundabout and sped past the Royal Lancaster Infirmary - it was bizarre to think that this was where she and Abaya had first met, where they had talked about Syria, and Trident, and where the doctor had already been hatching her plans. Directing Joop through the one-way system and down to the river, road now lined by heritage street lamps, she leaned forward to speak to Ben.

"What are you going to do?"

Ben didn't turn, scanning the road ahead for any sign of the Syrians.

"If they are not there yet, we set up an ambush and kill them when they arrive. If the Cactus is already there, we go in and kill them inside."

"Shouldn't we give them a chance?" Shona suggested.

"Not on your life," Ben replied.

He checked his own C8, and showed Mazz in the back how to cock the action and release the safety. Fixated on the chase and cramped within the car, they didn't manage to don the body armour sets they have scavenged, but filled pockets with magazines from them.

"How far Shona?" Joop asked.

"Around this left-hand corner, then maybe 100 yards on the left."

"Don't overshoot it Joop," Ben said, the Q8's alarm dinging as he took off his seat belt with the car still moving.

Joop pulled in to the left and stopped in front of a two-story office which shared the same riverside aspect as Bay City Motors. From his position in the front right seat, he could see better ahead than the others. He could make out a

Cactus parked up in front of the double row of vehicles on sale at the far side of the forecourt.

"The good news is, they are here."

"And the bad news?" Shona asked.

"Is also, that they are here."

There would be no easy ambush, peppering the target with bullets as it arrived. They would have to go in and fetch them. And what they had stolen.

~~

True to Kiwi's instructions, C.I.Wood had lit a fire under some of the more important agencies down South, and now had on the secure phone a specialist from the National Nuclear Laboratory at Sellafield.

He had impressed on her one simple truth: if the intent of the Syrians was indeed to set fire to the plutonium pit, the impact would be catastrophic within minutes but with impact into years. In fact, it would be worse than if they had stolen a whole functioning warhead and the means to detonate it: much as with Hiroshima in 1945, the blast might obliterate a community, but not poison half a county. With three kilos or so of Pu239 at their disposal, the potential fatalities could be substantial. While not uniquely toxic, and relatively similar in threat to inhaling vapour from cadmium or mercury, 20mg of plutonium in an optimally sized form of 1 micron particles would kill within a month if inhaled, generally from pulmonary fibrosis or pulmonary oedema. 20mg is not a lot of plutonium – and as Rachel pointed out, "saying something isn't much worse than inhaling cadmium or mercury" is not much of a recommendation. As for the cancer risk, while inhaling a single particle would have nothing like the risk people might fear, every 0.15mg of plutonium inhaled across the local population could be expected to lead to one additional cancer.

Admittedly the particulate weight might lead much of it to fall to earth un-inhaled; and studies had shown that once fallen to the ground it didn't tend to translocate, wind-blow along the floor, and pose a further risk. Nevertheless, if there was a major plutonium fire the City of Lancaster would need evacuation immediately, and would be uninhabitable for a decade: you could shut the M6 for good, and the delays on the West Coast Mainline would be of the order of 7 years instead of 70 minutes. Depending on the success of the attackers in getting the core alight, and the wind, and whether it rained, the contamination might stay to the West Side of the Pennines: but with the prevailing westerly wind forecast to blow at force 4 overnight, you could expect contamination to carry across to Newcastle and the big urban centres of the North East. And that was just the public health and environmental effect. The Mandarins of Whitehall were thinking more of the destruction of agriculture; of the collapse of the economy of the North; wholesale unemployment; the likely loss of cross-party support for Trident and its replacement; a new clamour for Scottish independence.

A lot of contaminated Lancastrians and a marginally inflated death rate for decades seemed small beer in comparison.

Chapter 18

Combustion

Ali knew the workshop area like the back of his hand, but he didn't dare flick the bank of neon lights on, and he found himself stumbling as he crossed the three work bays from the entry door to where the lathe and exhaust fan stood. As his eyes started to adjust, he felt his way along the work benches which lined the rear wall right across the building, stubbing a toe on a jack and banging his knee on a tyre fitting press. Some car repair businesses may have gone all "Vorshprung Durch Technic", polished floors, peopled by white coated technicians who look like they could double up as opticians in a SpecSavers advert. Bay City, conversely, went for the more "authentic" feel, stinking of 40 years-worth of cigarette smoke, unwashed overalls, lubricating oil and festering coffee mugs. Abaya stayed at the door, kneeling on the floor, scanning outside for any pursuit, and Ali was adamant that they had little time. She checked her weapon and willed Ali to hurry up.

And hurry up he did. Reaching the final working bay, he kept going into the reception space beyond and flicked on one single light. Hopefully no one would think someone working past closing in the office space worthy of scrutiny, and helpfully the light washed through the open connecting door to give a sparse illumination to the workshop. Ali placed his Vitaz on the metal worktop to the side of the lathe, where it made a novel neighbour for a can of WD40 and a topless calendar from a local van hire company.

For the first time, he had the chance to get a proper look at the pit. Taking the ovoid lump of grey metal in both hands, he turned it in the wan light to see its lustre. It was hard to imagine the turmoil such a small thing could cause. Opening the cover of the lathe, he opened the three-jaw chuck and guided one end of the pit into it, pushing a button to move the jaws to grip it tightly. Another button turned off the two hoses which would, in normal work, feed milky white coolant fluid into the spot where whatever spinning metal in the chuck was carved by the tungsten carbide "roughing tool", a sharp point which would strip and shape whatever part was being machined. This coolant was not to prevent a fire, as the metal being worked was normally benign and unexotic; but if you fail to keep the tip of the tool cool, it heats and becomes brittle and breaks. An uncooled edge cutting into tough plutonium-gallium alloy would almost certainly break in due course – but by then the die of plutonium, the lathe, and much of the workshop should be well alight, and destined to burn all night.

Finally, there was the string of computer code instructions to load, to ensure that the lathe would sense the size of the plutonium in the chuck, assess its initial shape, and then track its size through the process. On one hand the elongated ball of plutonium would get smaller as its was shaved into ribbon – but at the same time, as it heats, plutonium tends to expand, so adjustment for that would be needed. All of this was well within the capability of the Bay City lathe – as Ali had checked and practiced long before when assessing their much less ambitious plan with the cobalt core.

Nearly all was ready, apart from the barbeque trays to catch and ignite the "swarf": the fragments, ribbon, threads and filament coils of plutonium as they came off the lathe.

Ali had read up enough to know that igniting plutonium involves a web of complex interactions: on the surface of the metal, a plutonium sesquoxide layer tends to form through oxidisation with the environment, and this compound is easy to ignite if the filament or ribbon is thin enough. It will try to burn spontaneously, and get it to 150 degrees Centigrade and it will light nicely. Once the sesquoxide starts burning, it burns so hot that it will easily raise the temperature of the actual plutonium metal itself to 500 degrees, and then the rapidly shedding ribbons of metal will blaze. From that point there should be no stopping it. Once the swarf is alight, the main mass of the pit, still spinning in the chuck, will catch and swiftly reach its melting point of 640 degrees. Easily within five minutes, the bed of the lathe would be a white-hot pool of liquid metal, impossible to put out, and with its heavy particulate smoke being sucked by the ventilator out of the upper window and into the night sky.

Placing the two disposable barbeque trays just so, Ali turned to get the concertina nylon pipe of the ventilator inlet right above where the blaze would burn. But before he could hit the button to run the ventilator up to speed, trouble was brewing. From the deep shadow back the way he had came, he heard a hiss from Abaya.

"Ali! There are soldiers coming."

~~

Pulling up short of the garage, it didn't take long to report that the Cactus was there, and to ascertain from Zero Alpha that while R.T.T. was now airborne, they were still minutes out. When the light flicked on in Bay City's reception, Ben reported that the suspected hostiles were on the premises. And that Clyde 44 was not waiting for anyone.

One essential feature of a take-down is to try to complete the approach unseen. Beyond that knowing as much as possible about the enemy and the internal layout is good; it's best to have specialist breaching equipment; and good to be able to enter through an upper or unguarded access. It was depressingly obvious to Joop and Ben that none of these terms would be satisfied, but Kiwi was insistent.

"If they are keen to burn it, they will have all they need to get it started in there. We have maybe three minutes."

That settled it. They established that Joop would move in plain view across the front of the garage, hogging the wall by the river bank, and looking to draw attention. If he failed to provoke a reaction, he should set up in place 50 yards down the road, opposite the office window, and ready to cover. Meanwhile Ben and Mazz would lead Kiwi through the maze of used cars for sale on the near forecourt, which was gloomy and not easily seen from the workshop. The aim would be to get close, assess what they could see or hear, and then the two soldiers would breach through the single door on the left of the workshop.

"What about me?" None of them had sensed Shona levering herself out of the middle of the three rear seats to join them looking towards their target.

"I think you have done enough harm for one day," said Kiwi.

"I know. But these fuckers have played me for a fool all along. What can I do?"

It was hard for Ben and Mazz to imagine Shona doing much other than tuck into deep fried Mars Bars, sing "Flower of Scotland", or make a lentil bake. And yet. In 60 years of anti-nuclear protest, she had achieved more than most of her contemporaries, until her protest was hijacked by whoever was inside the workshop.

"What do you want to do?" asked Ben.

"Can I go with Joop? If you want a distraction what is more distracting than a fat Scottish lesbian with blue hair trying not to get shot?"

"I think she makes a good point," smiled Joop.

"Can you shoot?" Maryam asked.

"I'm a quick learner," Shona replied.

Mazz reached behind her back where she had once again stowed her Glock 17, the trusty companion from a conflict far away. She didn't have time to think how lost she might feel without it. Re-loading a new magazine, cocking the weapon, and passing it to Shona, she offered an encouraging smile. "Look after Joop." She reached up high to ruffle his blond hair. "He's not very good at this stuff…"

As Joop and Shona peeled off to the right, Ben took Maryam by one elbow and looked into her eyes.

"Mazz? Will you be O.K.?" he asked, doubtfully.

Maryam glared back.

"I will show you. Let's go!"

~~

Abaya gestured out of the door she was guarding towards the river, having alerted Ali to the all too obvious scuttle of Joop across the frontage of the garage.

Ali moved swiftly across the work space, not towards Abaya but to where a corrugated metal shutter sealed the workshops shut when the business was out of hours. The shutter was of a powered roll-up style, with joints and narrow gaps between each 6-inch-high panel of aluminium to allow it to be raised and stored – giving Ali the chance to snatch a view through the cracks and out over the forecourt. At first, he struggled to see the camouflaged shape of their pursuer, but then the shuffling run of a familiar form gave the game away. Shona jogged across the frontage at a speed where she could have been taken over by glaciers and tectonic plates. She went to ground next to a wooden bench on the opposite pavement, and it was at that point that Ali spotted Joop's prone form, underneath the bench facing the shutter.

"And the loud Scottish woman is here too," Ali said. "Come away from the door," he added, and Abaya picked her way across towards him and stole her own view of the outside through the cracks.

"You see them by the bench?" It was barely fifty yards, and the orange wash of sodium street lights lit them well. Abaya nodded.

"Get a decent aim on them. When I fire, you shoot too."

~~

Ben and Mazz had made decent progress creeping through the used car lot, the elongated shadows cast by the vehicles giving plenty of gloom to cover them from view. Noise might have given them away, but the ambient noise of the evening traffic carried well in the wind, and they got within 20 metres of the left entry door to the workshop. Kiwi was right behind them, glad to be done with running, weary and sick. He thought for a moment about having another slug of Oromorph, but decided, on balance, that he might need his wits about him in the next couple of minutes.

Without warning, the night air was rent by the pap-pap-pap of automatic weapons fire, amplified and intensified by the echoing space of the workshop. The noise of the shots was accompanied by a plinking sound, as they saw the aluminium shutter perforated, rows of black dots appearing in uneven stripes in two places across the frontage. Each ran from around waist height up to head height, one row rapidly joined by another and another, as the shooters inside had to control the rising barrel of their Vitaz cabines and reset to shoot again. Joining the cacophony of sound was the "whack" of the over-pressure bullets striking to their right. Some pinged off the camber of the middle of the road, the ricochet disappearing across the river over the far bank. Others took big chunks out of the river bank wall, leaving ugly rents in the concrete; others turned the hardwood of the bench into splinters and pulp; and at least one hit their friend. First they heard a yelp, then a pained gasp, then finally a re-assuring stream of invective.

"Fuck! Fucking fuck! Here are you the size of a fucking barn and it's me that gets hit."

Joop's Dutch political correctness clearly wasn't fully embedded, but if Shona was offended she didn't pause, and Mazz could see her, on her knees, drag the soldier away from the bench and back towards the river bank wall. From the side she could see that while there was no structure to save them from the relentless fire from the workshop, the camber of the road and the canted angle of the pavement meant they were in dead ground, covered from fire so long as they stayed completely prone and moved nowhere. She was about to shout to them to stay put, when Ben grabbed her wrist and held a finger to his lips. He was right. They were still undetected. And if both the gunmen from the ambush were in the workshop space shooting through the shutters, they could not also be guarding the door which stood in front of them.

~~

Abaya squinted as she tried to make out the effects of their gunfire on the two targets beside the bench. There was little now to see, apart from an inch or so of shadow visible beyond the tip of the kerb on the far side of the road. She was still wondering as to whether she could hit so small a target when the door she had been guarding was kicked in.

Spinning around, two silhouetted shapes darted into the door way, one leaning in to hard target the void to the right of the door, the other standing tall and covering the space down the length of the workshop. And it was the latter who opened fire. And opened fire at her.

Instinctively she dropped to the floor, and the first burst of fire went over her head, further peppering the shutters. The only cover was a metre to her right: one of the four stilts of metal which acted as supports for one of the metal platforms used to raise vehicles to head height so they could be worked on from beneath. For most people the slender pillar would have been next to useless as cover, only 10 inches of so wide: but Abaya was slight enough for it to offer decent protection, and she hugged into its cold metal form for a moment. But only a moment. Guessing that the firer would have gone to ground themselves, somewhere in front of the unhelpfully well-lit doorway, she held the Vitaz out to the right side of the cover and sprayed a burst in that direction. Immediately return fire came, but far from the wayward and hopeful fire of the Vitaz, what came back was aimed and on target. There was a rhythmic "bad-dam, bad-dam, bad-dam," of a series of double taps, and each bullet struck the post beside her head, knocking flakes of paint and rust over her face and into her hair. Abaya trembled. And that worsened, as a second set of shots came from a further shooter who had ducked through the door, moved to the right, and was shooting at her parallel to the frontage of the workshop. Her 10 inches of cover was now effectively 8 inches, and she squirmed to huddle into the tiny safe space left available.

It occurred to her to call from help from Ali, but in her heart, she didn't doubt that help would be on the way. Mazz and Ben knew there had to be a second gunman further over towards the office, but there was no-one in view. Their eyes had yet to adjust to the gloom, and all they could make out was the dark shape of the single vehicle which was still in the space from the previous day, sat in Bay 3.

Their adjustment to the dark halted the moment a foot-long muzzle flash spat bullets at them from across the bonnet of the disabled vehicle, and this time the gunman was able to keep his fire aimed and effective. He picked out the shape to the right of the door: Collins, who felt a sledgehammer blow first to his right thigh, and then to his left shoulder, the remaining bullets of the burst smacking into the wall of tools hung on the wall behind him. It felt like he had been hit by a truck, senses jumbled, each wound numbed for a moment, before a deep ache formed and turned into a wall of pain. Immediately more worried by the thigh wound, where a femoral artery could bleed out in seconds, Ben gripped his upper leg as tight as he could, feeling a warm puddle form below him on the cold concrete. Shit. He winced and stage-whispered to Maryam to his right that he was hit, and he saw her head pop up and turn his way.

Instinctively she knew the next best step: it was now 2 v 1, and the odds needed evening up. The shooter down the way was invisible, but she had a clear bead on the nearer one behind the stanchion. For a moment long-lost words from a French general popped into her head from a class at Sandhurst. "*Mon centre cède, ma droite recule, situation excellente, j'attaque.*" "My centre is giving way; my right is retreating. Situation excellent, I shall attack."

Which is just what she did. Even a month earlier, the pain of her injury would have fixed her to the floor; but adrenalin shot her to her feet, and she burst forward the ten metres between her prone position by the door towards Abaya. The Syrian heard the steps, and rolled to her left, Vitaz tucked into her front as she went, before she came right side up again, facing the door.

Abaya had only a fraction of a second to take in the sight of the young Anglo-Iranian soldier coming at her before Mazz opened fire with her C8. The first round struck the floor before cannoning into Abaya's jaw, the second shot took off the top of her head, while the rest of the burst punched holes in her back, buttock, leg, and foot. Maryam's charge carried her to the floor within touching distance of the radiologist, in cover, with the metal pillar now shielding her from any fire from behind the vehicle in repair concealing Ali.

What to do next? There was one remaining target, presumably still holding the plutonium pit from the ambush. Behind her lay Ben, bleeding badly, in shock, and with no immediate chance of help. Apart from a terminally ill New Zealander, somewhere lurking outside. Mazz wondered what Ben would do. She remembered what Woolley *did* do. What was she for? Who did she serve?

Maryam changed magazine, stood, and fired all thirty 5.56mm rounds on full automatic through and over the darkened shape of the vehicle to her front. Then she darted back ten yards, grabbed Ben literally by the scruff of the neck, and pulled him out of the door to safety.

~~

There is a scene in the cult Jean Reno film "Leon" where the eponymous anti-hero is holed up in a building and is shooting S.W.A.T. team officers wholesale. When Gary Oldman's corrupt D.E.A. agent is asked who else should be sent in support, he responds with rabid venom: "EVERYONE!"

And that is what the Octopus was generating at that moment. The specialist advisors on nuclear contamination were on their way from Bristol; Land Forces Command at Wilton, the home of the team which runs Operation Temperer, military support against terrorist attack, had stood up a unit from 22 S.A.S., in case Recapture Tactics Troop needed the help. 5131 Bomb Disposal Squadron at R.A.F. Wittering, the specialists in nuclear E.O.D., were making ready, as were Falcon Squadron of 1 Royal Tank Regiment, whose Fuchs reconnaissance vehicles could augment civil police units in sampling any contaminated zone. Units of Royal Military Police, transport units of the

Royal Logistics Corps, and the R.A.M.C. were being alerted to manage any necessary cordon and evacuation, including the evacuation of the vulnerable sick and elderly from the R.L.I. and care and nursing homes. A major incident alert was active at the Royal Preston Hospital. Fire service units, civilian, military, and nuclear, were moving to a staging post north of the City.

None of this would make a jot of difference. Time was up.

~~

Ali had been about to unleash another burst of fire towards the door when Maryam's spray of covering fire plinked over and through the bodywork of the Vauxhall Corsa he was hiding behind, and he had to throw himself to the floor. By the time he popped up again, all he could see was Ben's legs, as the Marine was dragged roughly through the door. He fired a couple of single shots that way, before standing properly to look down and across to where Abaya lay.

In a peaceful and civilised era, he would doubtless have been shocked, stunned, distraught. But Ali had spent much of his early adulthood learning about how transient and disposable and fragile human life was. He felt an urge to move forward and witness her loss; to connect somehow with her departure. But even in the dim light he could see the top of her head was gone, bone and brain and gore spread in a fan down her back and across the floor. Abaya was dead. Just as his friends had been crushed in Aleppo. Just as Reem had been gassed in Damascus.

Ali turned back to the ventilator and flipped a switch on it to start it up. Right away he felt the familiar draught of air being pulled through the concertina tube above the lathe. He reached up to a spray-painting face mask, hanging on a bent nail on the rear wall, and pulled it on. Next, he pulled a box of matches from the pocket of his blue overalls, struck one, and put it to the corner of the paraffin-soaked brown bag retaining the charcoal of each barbeque tray. Each lit instantly, the bag burning with an oily yellow flame which would soon set light to the impregnated charcoal within. He waited, his gaze flitting between the door which Maryam and Ben had left through, and the growing conflagration to his side. Had all gone as planned, and had they got clean away from the ambush site, he could have set the machine to start work 15 minutes later; by which time they would have been well on the way to the airport, and the charcoal would be red hot and easily able to ignite the ribbon. There would be no "they" leaving now.

Finally, he could wait no longer. It was too soon but he suddenly felt more alone than he could ever remember, bereft of Abaya and Emad, and of the purpose which had driven him for so long. Punching the button to activate the lathe, he heard the whirr of the plutonium pit being spun to high speed; and then the tooth grinding vibration of the roughing tool making contact with the metal, stripping a thin and fragile ribbon of highly reactive metal to fall into the flames. He watched transfixed as a pile of swarf fell into the barbeque trays, where it sat momentarily, then burst into a fire unlike any he had ever seen before: a white/blue flame which distorted the air around it into a shimmering blur of air and light. And as the fire built, so did the smoke: a strange black soot, which seemed to want to hug the floor of the lathe, but which the ventilator sucked away and up. Ali took a final glance across to the door which the soldiers had breached. Then he ducked the opposite way, to the right, and through the door leading to Reception.

~~

Kiwi struggled to bend down to help Mazz, as she emerged grunting with the effort of pulling Ben out of the door, but he slipped one hand under the armpit of Collins' uninjured side and did his best to heave a share of the weight. Even in the gloom he could see a spreading dark stain on the Marine's leg, and a big tear in his multi-cam where the bullet exited, a grim sign of what might lie beneath. At least the blood which ran onto the tarmac seemed to be flowing rather than pumping. But Ben was in big trouble, and Maryam struggled to pull her stable belt through the belt loops of her combats so that she could get a tourniquet set on Ben.

Kneeling next to Collins, she spoke without looking up.

"Kiwi, I shot the woman, but the man is still alive and armed. He is at the far end of the workshop, the other side of the car."

The New Zealander took stock. Both his proteges were shot, and Collins was clearly in big trouble: face turning grey, eyes glassy, unresponsive. Off towards the river was Joop, also down, with little ability to join the fight. For all the time he had spent with the military, he really didn't know one end of a firearm from another. He did, however, have little to lose, and the words of Aelfwin at Maldon in his head:

"Think of ye times when we oft spake at mead,
When we on the benches did raise up our boast,
Now may each one make trial of how bold he be.."

"No worries," he grunted.

Chapter 19

Contamination

Kiwi stepped over Ben's prostrate form and into the doorway from which the two soldiers had emerged. As he crept hunched over into the workshop, and looked along the servicing bays, he was struck first by the strange light. Adding to the meagre illumination from the neon light through in Reception was a yellow flickering shadow, and also an unearthly white glare coming from the far end of the space. With an appalling grinding sound coming from some unknown machinery in the same direction, and the industrial debris of the workshop, it could have passed for an interesting avant-garde performance-art piece, had Kiwi not realised what was going on. The Syrians had got the plutonium pit alight, and Kiwi knew better than anyone the desperate hazard he now faced.

Where was the gunman? No one was in sight, but who was to say he was not still hidden behind the single vehicle in view. Logic told Kiwi otherwise. You would have to be suicidal or retarded to go anywhere near burning plutonium.

"Or from New Zealand…." he thought.

Still keeping a watchful eye for any sign of the gunman, Kiwi advanced, his way lit by the growing conflagration he could see ahead. Inside the open case of an industrial lathe could be seen a growing blaze, strands of plutonium metal from a spinning elongated egg of metal falling and burning as they came to rest. While the pit itself was not yet lit, cloying thick smoke from the fire was being pulled upwards by a flexible concertina ventilation duct. Kiwi was in no shape to race anywhere, but he hustled as best he could, trying to ignore the tendrils of combustion products which had evaded the fan, and which were roiling across towards him. And trying not to think about what he was breathing into his already corrupted lungs.

"Fuck, fuck, fuck, fuck, fuck," might be a mantra more suitable if you have stubbed you toe or burned your finger on the iron, but it held Kiwi's nerve together as he covered the last few yards, smoke spilling eerily either side of him like a dodgy new romantic music video. Surveying the carnage, he knew he had to improvise before the whole thing went up.

First Kiwi reached up and threw the ventilation hose to the side, cutting off the suction which was sending the desperately radioactive combustion products off into the night. This, of course, made his personal situation all the worse, as denied the draught of the fan the thickening black dust could barely get head height. Enough of it did for Kiwi to be able to taste its gritty metallic flavour, but for all his liking for stamp-collecting exotic nuclear experiences, he didn't relish the uniqueness of his situation. Trying to control his breathing, he cast his eyes for something to remove what he now saw to be disposable barbeque trays from the floor of the lathe, their charcoal and metal-mesh now covered with a white hot semi molten pulp of burning plutonium. To get the burning ribbon and fragments away from the pit had to be the first job, and Kiwi got lucky. Finding two pairs of pliers hanging in the rack of tools on the wall, he kept his face as far away from the burning metal as he could, and reached gingerly into the bed of the lathe and lifted. As ever, the incredible density of plutonium messed with his judgment, and he had to pull much harder than expected, and then step backwards and drop in a squat as he lowered the burning metal shreds, leaning back to try to keep his face in cleaner air. When the first foil tray lay at his feet, he repeated the exercise, and sighed with relief when both were on the floor – even if they were both still burning fiercely, smoke spreading in an expanding tide across the workshop.

In a less ramshackle set up, Kiwi's problems would still have been dire. Any proper, modern auto repair business would have the full range of fire extinguishers: water, CO_2, foam, the works. "Health and Safety" and all that. But Bay City's dissolute penny-pinching ownership were not of that mind set; an attribute the Health and Safety Executive would later view in an unprecedentedly generous way. Because the upshot of their atrocious lack of investment was that all Kiwi had was, in fact, exactly what he needed: a bucket of sand and an asbestos fire blanket. Seeing the former over in a corner in the classic old school red metal bucket with "FIRE" in big white letters, Kiwi heaved it awkwardly off the floor. He staggered back to the two burning trays, hauled the bucket up to waist height, slipped the fingers of his right hand under its base, and tipped the sand over the flames.

The fire blanket probably dated back twenty years, tucked into its red cylinder on the back wall, but it slipped out as easily as a cloth rat from a drainpipe at a school fete. Kiwi cast it over the smoking heap like a retiring matador throwing down his cape. The sand offered no free oxygen or chlorine or hydrogen to the fiery plutonium lava, and while it continued to smoke and spit underneath its overcoat, the fire was done.

And so was Kiwi. He had no idea what radiation dose he had got, let alone the chemical toxicity he had inhaled. The space was plunged back into semi-darkness and with the room spinning, it was all he could do to hit a big red power cut-off, and lean against the workbench, as the computer withdrew the roughing tool and the lathe spun down. In a few seconds it had run to a stop, and there sat the plutonium pit, half of its surface shaved shiny by the progressive movement of the cutting blade across its face. Kiwi was not going to let it out of his sight, but conscious of the thermal and kinetic abuse it had undergone, he donned a welder's glove on his right hand and poked it. He could feel the heat from its surface through the material, but it was quite bearable, and after a moment considering the control panel, a push of a button labelled "reset" freed the pit from the three-jaw chuck.

Time to get outside. The shortest route to fresh air appeared to be directly ahead, the door leading to the half-lit reception area. That's where he went.

~~

Ali unlatched the Reception door and emerged cautiously into the open, mindful that the soldier by the bench might still be armed and capable. But no fire came. And no shadow could be seen prone beneath it.

Time to go. A handful of metres away sat the Daihatsu hatchback which should have been the getaway for all three of them. However broken their plan and however pointless were further efforts to get away, what else was there to do other than to continue? And with the plutonium fire underway, and the smoke being fanned out of the workshop to be spread by the wind across the city, this was no place to stay.

Standing in the lee of the Daihatsu and out of sight of the road, he laid the Vitaz on its roof and began shuffling out of his mechanics overalls. And it was then that a familiar figure stepped out of the gloom behind the row of used cars.

"Hello, Ali."

It was Shona. Her body language exuded the contempt that she felt – contempt she affirmed with an automatic pistol pointed right at Ali's head.

But the contempt went both ways.

"Shona don't be pathetic. You are way out of your depth here. Where are your soldiers now?"

"Where is your brother? Where is Abaya? And you are the one facing the gun, not me." Shona could generally give as good as she got. But Ali was right. She was out of her depth, the trembling of the short barrel of the Glock a giveaway, even as her curled finger tensed against the trigger. Ali called her bluff. His arms and torso freed from the coveralls, he slowly picked up his carbine from the roof of the car and brought it up to his shoulder.

"Well? That was the moment to shoot me? What happened? You and your little gang were a joke. It's people like you who are to blame for this country being so spineless. Your talk of peace? It is just weakness. Because your politicians listen to your nonsense, they stand by and let evil stand. They watch while cities are laid waste, while little children are gassed, and while elderly women are murdered."

"And you solve that how? With this nonsense? With all this killing?"

"If that's what it takes, yes. In any case, what's that in your hand? It didn't take you long to join in threatening people with weapons. I cannot say it suits you. Why don't you put it down and go give yourself up? What is it you say in this country? "Time to face the music""

~~

Kiwi emerged from the door of Bay City Reception hoping to see the authorities arrive like the Seventh Cavalry. Instead he found himself five yards from the back of a half undressed Syrian mechanic, who was apparently in a duel with a middle-aged Scottish peace protestor.

Desperate to breathe, and to cough, his airway and lungs tingling and stinging from the poisoned air in the workshop, Kiwi had no idea how long he could stay upright. The dose of alpha radiation emitting isotopes he had sucked into his lungs was impossible to know. The chemical toxicity of the plutonium as an element, regardless of radiation, was going to trash an elderly frame already riven with progressing cancer. Whether Shona or Ali would shoot each other, or which one would get the other, was not something he had time to wait to see. If Shona's gaze were to shift focus from the muzzle of the Vitaz pointing right at her face, and catch his shadow coming out of the dark, her reaction would surely give him away. He had come this far, and done so much, and now was the time for one last effort.

Kiwi took one hesitant step, then another, trying to get close without Ali hearing his foot fall, or Shona seeing him. He succeeded in the former; but in spite of the dark he saw the Scot's eyes widen as he took a final step around the rear of the Daihatsu. He still had a yard and a half to go, and had it been a playground game he might have held a finger to his lips and tried to tip toe across the gap to striking distance. But Ali's head started to turn to the right, torso twisting to see what had startled Shona, gun barrel of his Vitaz leading the way.

Kiwi was slow, too slow, old, grumpy, ill and irradiated. But he was also an angry man holding what was still a 2kg lump of milled plutonium. And somewhere, he found the will to raise it in his gloved hand to shoulder height, and smashed it into the temple of the Syrian, before he saw it coming.

~

There is plenty of documented research on the toxicity of particulate plutonium; but it tends to look at particles around the 1 micron size. The poor outcomes for humans struck in the head with a particle the size of a grapefruit had been unexamined. But Kiwi was pleased to see the initial results. The impact of the heavy metal weight on skull gave a loud crack, and Ali went down in a heap, gun clattering to the floor.

Kiwi took a single step back, surprised at his handiwork. As was Shona, who stood open mouthed the other side of the prostrate body of the gunman.

The New Zealander looked down at Ali's comatose form. And then looked up and smiled at Shona.

"Plutonium poisoning eh Shona? What a fucker."

Chapter 20

Fallout

Plutonium poisoning was, indeed, a fucker. Which made the medics at University College London Hospital pleased they had so few survivors to treat.

But a week after the gun battle at Bay City, Kiwi was up and about. He had expected to be sealed off in a plastic bubble, or surrounded by worried faces in Hazmat suits. It was almost disappointing to be sat in a standard side room, somewhere on an upper floor of a hospital, with a view of what looked like the British Library and the St. Pancras Hotel some way away. And far from being tended by the pick of the hospital's young female nurses, all he had was an earnest and rather troll-like middle-aged medic, all wire-framed glasses and eyebrows. University College London Hospital's radiation toxicology department. In person. Accompanied by a house officer who looked like he was just about old enough to tie his shoelaces unaided.

"Ah, Prof. Barton, you are awake! How are you feeling?" He perched on the bed in which Kiwi was, for the moment, incarcerated.

"Better than I expected to be honest. What have you done to me?"

"Well to be honest we have been making it up as we have gone along a little. As I am sure you know, inhaled plutonium is the real hazard, but as the Merlin got you down here quickly we got started quickly. First a chelating agent. We got you inhaling an aerosol which would bind with plutonium molecules in the blood-stream so they can be eliminated from the body. We injected a dose too, just for luck."

"D.T.P.A.?" Kiwi was referring to Diethylene Triamine Penta Acetic Acid, used to treat plutonium exposures in places such as Sellafield for years.

"Indeed. We used the calcium version. It can reduce the plutonium load by anything between 10% or 90% of the burden. We don't know how effective it was yet because we haven t studied enough of your excrement. But it should have protected the places the plutonium normally goes to, like the liver and bones."

"What about in the operating theatre?" Kiwi had been whisked there within an hour of the helicopter decanting him onto the pad on the U.C.L.H. roof. He had been told it was a phenomenal piece of flying: the pad is only stressed for little air ambulances, not a giant load carrier, and the pilot had to hold inches off the floor in the pitch dark while they got the casualties off the back.

"We got you on bypass and did a bronchial lavage with isotonic fluid to get as much particulate out as we could. It will have worked to some degree. Unfortunately, plutonium oxide particles are going to be down there for good, and doing some bad things. That's the bad news."

"You mean there is good news?"

"Well, maybe grounds for optimism. You will know the story of Albert Stevens?"

Kiwi shook his head.

"Stevens is a cause celebre in nuclear medicine. In the Manhattan project in 1945, scientists concerned at plutonium contamination of the project's workers selected 18 supposedly terminally ill cancer patients from California hospitals. They would be injected, without their consent, with what experimenters called "the product": in Stevens' case. 0.95 micrograms of plutonium. They then intended to assay his urine and excrement for the weeks he had left to live. Except Stevens didn't have weeks to live – because he didn't have cancer. After his injection, his clinicians found he only had a badly inflamed stomach ulcer. But he did now have in his body a dose of radiation 60 times higher than the permitted annual dose for radiation workers – equivalent to standing next to the Chernobyl nuclear core right after it melted down for a leisurely 10 minutes.

Yet he lived till 1966, when he died aged 79. Some of the other experimentees were still alive in 1975. They far exceeded any reasonable expectation."

"You know I don't need to worry about lung cancer?" Kiwi smiled ruefully. "Given I have already got it."

"Indeed. And I think that is much more worth worrying about than plutonium poisoning. On one hand you are worse placed than Stevens because your dose was inhaled – and the plutonium will emit alpha particles as it decays, which in the lung is not great. But because what you inhaled was weapons grade Pu239, you are way better off than he was. Most of his dose was 239, but 0.2 micrograms was Pu238."

Kiwi understood why this mattered. Pu238 has a half-life of only 87 years, compared to 25,000 years for Pu239. And that short half-life comes from it decaying rapidly, shedding Helium nuclei, alpha particles, as it does so. Pu238 is "hotter". So, while your corpse will still retain half its Pu239 contamination 25 millenia after your demise, contamination with it is much less likely to be the thing that actually kills you.

"Of course," continued the troll, "Your other problems remain."

"Indeed," said Kiwi. "Which is why you will understand if I don't take up any more of your time." Feeling a little bereft without his much loved but now heavily radioactive brown pullover, Kiwi donned his feeble blue cagoule. "There is a beer in a Dutch bar in Soho with my name on it."

The troll seemed minded to protest.

"Don't worry doc. I will be back for bedtime. And I promise that if I shit or piss while I am out, I'll save it for you."

~~

Unlike Kiwi, Ben was still very much an in-patient. His thigh was encased in an external scaffold of metalwork, fixing his femur securely while the bone knitted. The break in the neck of his ulna was less of a concern, though it meant his left arm had been immobilised in an old-school sling. Blood loss had been the risk in the immediate aftermath of the shoot out, but once R.T.T. had arrived on site in the Merlin, the troop medic rapidly got two lines of blood expanders running into him. For once, the Velcro blood-type indicators which the forces wear along with their name tag had more value than just making the wearer look hard core. While inevitably contaminated by the sooty smoke of the plutonium fire, Ben had been out on the forecourt by the time Kiwi removed the ventilator hose, and had been upwind for the brief time it was in place. The troll had been upbeat about the limited chance of harm from radiation.

Maryam, unwounded, had been able to leave the hospital, if only to face a lengthy debrief at the MOD. Followed by another "chat" at SO15, where the detectives winding down from the Salisbury poisonings now had another load of crap to deal with. At least, in this case, the perpetrators were in the bag. Literally, in one case. The arguments were still raging as to how the body of Abaya could be disposed of; it had lain in the workshop shrouded in plutonium soot for three days, and was about as contaminated as you could get. Bay City Motors itself was to be completely demolished, parcelled into nuclear waste containers, and shipped off to secure storage in Sellafield. That is, if it hadn't dissolved first: like the rest of the 10 acres unhelpfully labelled "The Hot Zone" by the media, it was sitting under a deluge of water from batteries of fire hoses, drawing water from the nearby River Lune, into which the contaminated run off was flowing. Army JCBs driven by soldiers encased in green nylon N.B.C. suits had broken great gashes in the river wall to allow the water to egress and flow down the couple of miles to Morecombe bay.

Of course, this had generated outrage from the Irish government, the Scottish Assembly, the Fleetwood fishing fleet, and those with a love of estuary bird life. No-one was buying the argument that there are, in fact, 4 tons or more of plutonium spread across the planet from decades of nuclear testing. Nor did they buy the pronouncements of the I.A.E.A. that plutonium washed out to sea was pretty benign. Scaremongering environmental groups were trotting out the figure that shellfish concentrate whatever plutonium is in sea water by a factor of 3000: the I.A.E.A. had countered that plutonium in the sea sits as an insoluble solid, and you would need to eat half a tea spoon of plutonium to kill you because it is hardly absorbed if ingested orally. It gave Nicola Sturgeon plenty to moan about. Her Scottish disciple Shona would probably have been on the same side of the argument; but as she was spending her time in Paddington Green Police Station chatting at length to SO15, it was hard to say. At least she had some company. Down the cell block were a middle-aged Geography lecturer and a couple of his students, wondering how they had ended up there. And, in Duncan's case, wondering if he would ever see his beloved Citroen Cactus again.

Ben shifted his position awkwardly in bed, sorted his table top for the 5th time that day, and braced at the knock on his door for yet another blood test. But instead of the gangly male phlebotomist, it was something altogether better: Mazz. She opened the door with a beaming smile, flowers in one hand,, other hand oddly held out of view behind her back. Collins was too busy taking her in to wonder what she was hiding. Bob of black hair held back in a clip, make up applied with her trademark precision, her simple floral shirt was untucked and had one too many buttons undone to be good for Ben's blood pressure. He noted that the flattened bullet pendant was still in place, but knew that her other talisman, her Afghanistan Glock, was now in a scenes of crime lab somewhere. Ben had become more conscious of legs since he got shot in one, but he would, in any event, have stolen a long look at Maryam's, encased in tight fitting denim, fixed at the waist with a broad brown leather belt which matched her stylish Hobbs boots.

"Can I sit down?"

"Of course. I cannot tell you how good it is to see you. How was the "goon squad"?"

Maryam sat on the bedside chair. She placed the flowers on top of Ben's cabinet, glimpsing as she did so a card she might not have expected to see: sent by the Woolleys, who had maybe found a surrogate son to replace the one they had lost in Katdelay.

"Better than expected. The only awkward moments were when they asked if I had any idea why a pistol that was signed out to me in Kandahar, and was lost in action there, could have turned up on a petrol station forecourt in the hand of a dead Syrian garage mechanic. And how come the Audi that was signed out to me had a load of bullet holes in the windscreen, but there was no glass inside the car from the bullets coming in."

"What did you say?"

"I said it was all very confusing. They didn't seem minded to push the point."

"Have you seen the others?"

"I just passed them on the way out. Joop is taking Kiwi out on the piss."

"And how is our token Dutchman?"

"Well, his collarbone should heal O.K. It gave him a chance to do the old "Will I be able to play the piano" gag with his surgeon, so he hasn't changed his shit sense of humour. He has spent much of the afternoon with the Dutch Ambassador. The knives have been out back in Holland, with lots of people very embarrassed at how one of their Marine officers ended up protecting a nuclear weapons convoy. They seem to have decided in the end to push the "Dutch hero comes to the aid of Royal Marines and damsel in distress" angle."

"And are you a damsel in distress?"

Mazz paused for thought.

"Actually no. In fact, I am better than I have been since I went to Kandahar." She smiled. "I think I am over Katdelay, and with that in mind, I have a present for you."

She finally took her hand from behind her back, and placed on the bed in front of him the Leki ski pole which had served her well for so many weeks. "Only one not very careful owner."

"I don't know what to say," Collins said.

"Then don't say anything," said Maryam, as she leant in to kiss him.

Further reading:

"Command and Control", Eric Schlosser, Allen Lane, 2013
"The Doomsday Machine", Daniel Elsberg, Bloomsbury, 2017
"Ablaze – the story of Chernobyl", Piers Paul Read, Mandarin, 1995
"Periodic Tales – The Curious Lives of the Elements", Hugh Aldersey-Williams, Viking, 2011
"Nuclear Emergencies – Information for the Public", Public Health England, 2015
"Local Authority and Emergency Services Information (L.A.E.S.I.) Edition 11, Ministry of Defence, 2017
"JSP 471 Defence Nuclear Emergency Response", Ministry of Defence, 2013
"A Better Defence Estate", Ministry of Defence, 2016
"Safe Handling and Storage of Plutonium", Safety Report Series no.9, IAEA, 1998
"Nuclear Convoys", House of Commons Briefing Paper 07542, June 2016
Maclennan Commission, National Archives of Australia, **www.naa.gov.au**
Muralinga – the Clean-up of a Nuclear Test Site, www.ippnw.org
www.rafbarnham-nss.weebly.com
www.historicengland.org.uk
www.nukewatch.org.uk
www.eliteforces.info

Glossary

40 Commando

Pronounced "Four-Oh", a standard "Commando 21" format light infantry unit made up of four companies of Marines and a Command Company. Based in Norton Manor Camp, Taunton.

42 Commando

Pronounced "Four-Two", in 2018 re-roled from a standard Lead Commando Group formation to "Maritime Operations Commando". Provides detachments for maritime security, training and mentoring of partner nation forces, downed aircrew recovery. Based at Bickleigh near Plymouth.

43 Commando

Pronounced "Four-Three", comprises O, P, and R Squadrons, as well as HQ Squadron. Styled as "Fleet Protection Group" Royal Marines, provides protection to the UK nuclear deterrent as well as Royal Navy shipping.

45 Commando

Pronounced "Four-Five", a standard "Commando 21" format light infantry unit made up of four companies of Marines and a Command Company. Based at Arbroath in Scotland.

5131 (E.O.D.) Squadron, RAF

Explosive ordnance disposal unit based at R.A.F. Wittering; supports counter C.B.R.N. operations.

Andreev Bay

Site of Soviet Naval Base 569, 35 miles Northwest of Murmansk on the Barents Sea. Site of a nuclear waste storage leak in 1982-3.

Androstenediol

A steroid hormone with potential value in minimising radiation injury by stimulating platelet and white cell production.

Civil Nuclear Constabulary (C.N.C.)
Provide armed security for civil nuclear sites, as well as the ships of Pacific Nuclear Transport Limited. Can, on occasion, be released to support other police forces: 450 armed C.N.C. officers did such duty following the Manchester bombing in May 2017.
Commando Helicopter Force
Based at Yeovilton in Somerset, comprises 845, 846, and 847 Naval Air Squadrons, flying a mixture of Merlin HC3A and Wildcat AH1 helicopters
Coulport
Royal Naval Armaments Depot on the shore of Loch Long near Faslane, Scotland
Cyberknife
Radiotherapy treatment device, combining a lightweight linear accelerator and a robotic head, with the ability to monitor in real time the movement of the patient and tumour and adjust accordingly.
Entolimod
Experimental recombinant protein for radiation injury protection.
Ex-Rad
Experimental treatment for radiation injury which claims to be able to repair damaged D.N.A.
Fizzle
A nuclear detonation which totally fails to reach its expected yield. First seen at the “Buster Able” test in Nevada, October 22, 1951
Kyshtym disaster
The third most serious radiation accident ever recorded, behind only Chernobyl and Fukushima. The result of an explosion in a storage tank holding 80 tons of liquid nuclear waste.

Lake Karachay
Located near the Mayak nuclear plant in the Ural mountains, the most radiologically polluted place on earth, able to deliver a lethal dose to a human in a single hour of exposure.

Lop Nor
Site of Chinese nuclear testing since 1959. Site of the first Chinese nuclear test in 1964.

Muralinga
British nuclear test site in South Australia, 800km North West of Adelaide. Site of seven atomic bomb tests and the "Project Vixen" safety series.

Merlin HC3A
Three engine medium capacity helicopter, with a crew of 3 and a load capacity of 24 seated troops or 3 tonnes of equipment.

Nuclear Accident Response Organisation (N.A.R.O.)
Cell within the MOD combining military and civilian staff to plan nuclear movements and respond to accidents or incidents

Pit
Named after the American term for the stone within fruit such as apricots. The metallic core of an implosion nuclear weapon, nowadays generally made from plutonium. Can be solid, or more latterly, hollow; in the latter case, explosive power can be "boosted" by injection of tritium gas into the pit at the moment of detonation.

Plutonium
A silvery grey metal, element 94 in the periodic table, first produced in 1940 in Berkeley, California. Comes in 6 allotropes (different crystalline structures, much as Carbon can be both diamond and graphite). Pu239 and Pu241 are both fissile, capable of generating a nuclear chain reaction if in critical mass. Weapons grade plutonium is 93% Pu239 or better. The remainder is non-fissile Pu238 and Pu240.

Pu240 is unwanted as it has a high rate of spontaneous fission, which can cause pre-detonation. Pu238 is the isotope which is generally used as a power and heat source in satellites and spacecraft.

Primary

The initial fission part of a warhead – the "A-bomb", composed of a pit of plutonium which is compressed by a focused blast from conventional explosives.

Proton Beam Therapy

An emerging radiological technology used where tumours are seen as potentially responsive to higher radiation dose e.g. ocular or skull base tumours, inoperable sarcomas. Allows highly focused treatment with correspondingly less damage to normal tissue.

Project 56

Series of 4 U.S.A. nuclear safety tests conducted in 1955-56 in Area 11, Nevada, which subsequently acquired the nickname "Plutonium Valley".

R.A.F. Barnham

Air force station 2 miles from Thetford, once home of 94 Maintenance Unit, 3 Group. From 1954 a "Specialist Storage Site" for R.A.F. nuclear weapons

Sarin

Toxic nerve gas, 81 times more lethal than Hydrogen Cyanide, 550 times more lethal than Chlorine, discovered in 1938 in Germany

Secondary

As one might expect, the second, H-bomb component of the warhead, made up of Uranium 235 along with lithium deuteride fuel surrounded by a tamper of U238 and "Fogbank" foam.

Special Escort Group (S.E.G.)

Unit of MOD Police which provides staff for close escort and close protection of nuclear weapons convoy movements. Based at A.W.E. Aldermaston in Berkshire.

Sukhoi Su-34
N.A.T.O. codename "Fullback", a twin-engine fighter bomber with a side-by-side crew of two.
T.C.H.D. – Truck, Cargo, Heavy-Duty
A nuclear warhead carrier. The current version is based on the Mercedes Benz Actros, with a 12 litre V6 engine.
Uranium
A naturally occurring element coming in two principle isotopes, U235 and U238. Naturally 0.7% of Uranium is U235, and this has to be increased by an enrichment process to around 90% for a nuclear weapon. While not capable of sustaining a chain reaction itself, U238 can still be included in nuclear warheads as a "tamper" to reflect neutrons back at the plutonium pit; and if the tamper encases fusion fuel, the H-bomb blast splits the U238 atoms adding to the yield.
Wildcat AH1
Light utility helicopter with crew of two and capacity for a door gunner and four additional troops. Developed by AugustaWestland, with appearance similar to its forebear the Lynx, compared to which it is much more expensive while carrying a smaller load.
Winterborne Gunner
Established in 1917 as part of the Porton Down Research Facility, home of the Defence C.B.R.N. Centre. Sits within a small village 4 miles from Salisbury.
W88
The standard nuclear warhead carried by a Trident nuclear missile on it's Mark 5 re-entry vehicle. Designed in the 1970s, the latest version, the W88 ALT 370, has a yield of 475 kilotons.

ABOUT THE AUTHOR

Paddy Storrie is Deputy Head of a State Secondary School in Hertfordshire, England. This is his first novel.

23688395R00189

Printed in Great Britain
by Amazon